The Precipice
A Novel

by

Elia W. Peattie

Double 9
BOOKS

The precipice
A Novel
by Elia W. Peattie

Copyright © 2024

All Rights reserved.

ISBN: 978-93-64285-72-8

Published by

DOUBLE 9 BOOKS

2/13-B, Ansari Road
Daryaganj, New Delhi – 110002
info@double9books.com
www.double9books.com
Tel. 011-40042856

This book is under public domain

ABOUT THE AUTHOR

Elia W. Peattie (1862–1935) was an American author and journalist. in Aurora, Illinois known for her contributions to literature and social commentary. Her work often reflected her keen observations of society and her interest in exploring the human condition. Peattie was educated in local schools and later attended the University of Chicago. Her early exposure to literature and journalism shaped her future career. Peattie is best known for her short stories and essays, which often explore themes of identity, society, and human experience. Her literary style is characterized by its attention to character development and social observation. Her collection *Painted Windows* (1908) features a series of short stories that delve into the complexities of personal and social identity. Elia W. Peattie is remembered for her contributions to American literature, particularly her insightful short stories and essays that offer a nuanced exploration of human emotions and social dynamics. Her work frequently incorporated **social commentary,** offering insights into societal norms, cultural practices, and social issues. Peattie's writing reflects her observations on the human condition and the intricacies of social interactions. Her work remains a valuable part of the literary canon, reflecting the concerns and perspectives of early 20th-century America. The exploration of **deep emotions** is a hallmark of Peattie's writing. Her stories often delve into the psychological and emotional struggles of her characters.

CONTENTS

CHAPTER I

It was all over. Kate Barrington had her degree and her graduating honors; the banquets and breakfasts, the little intimate farewell gatherings, and the stirring convocation were through with. So now she was going home.

With such reluctance had the Chicago spring drawn to a close that, even in June, the campus looked poorly equipped for summer, and it was a pleasure, as she told her friend Lena Vroom, who had come with her to the station to see her off, to think how much further everything would be advanced "down-state."

"To-morrow morning, the first thing," she declared, "I shall go in the side entry and take down the garden shears and cut the roses to put in the Dresden vases on the marble mantelshelf in the front room."

"Don't try to make me think you're domestic," said Miss Vroom with unwonted raillery.

"Domestic, do you call it?" cried Kate. "It isn't being domestic; it's turning in to make up to lady mother for the four years she's been deprived of my society. You may not believe it, but that's been a hardship for her. I say, Lena, you'll be coming to see me one of these days?"

Miss Vroom shook her head.

"I haven't much feeling for a vacation," she said. "I don't seem to fit in anywhere except here at the University."

"I've no patience with you," cried Kate. "Why you should hang around here doing graduate work year after year passes my understanding. I declare I believe you stay here because it's cheap and passes the time; but really, you know, it's a makeshift."

"It's all very well to talk, Kate, when you have a home waiting for you. You're the kind that always has a place. If it wasn't your father's house it would be some other man's--Ray McCrea's, for example. As for me, I'm lucky to have acquired even a habit--and that's what college *is* with me--since I've no home."

Kate Barrington turned understanding and compassionate eyes upon her friend. She had seen her growing a little thinner and more tense everyday; had seen her putting on spectacles, and fighting anaemia with tonics, and yielding unresistingly to shabbiness. Would she always be speeding breathlessly from one classroom to another, palpitantly yet sadly seeking for the knowledge with which she knew so little what to do?

The train came thundering in--they were waiting for it at one of the suburban stations--and there was only a second in which to say good-bye. Lena, however, failed to say even that much. She pecked at Kate's cheek with her nervous, thin lips, and Kate could only guess how much anguish was concealed beneath this aridity of manner. Some sense of it made Kate fling her arms about the girl and hold her in a warm embrace.

"Oh, Lena," she cried, "I'll never forget you--never!"

Lena did not stop to watch the train pull out. She marched away on her heelless shoes, her eyes downcast, and Kate, straining her eyes after her friend, smiled to think there had been only Lena to speed her drearily on her way. Ray McCrea had, of course, taken it for granted that he would be informed of the hour of her departure, but if she had allowed him to come she might have committed herself in some absurd way--said something she could not have lived up to.

As it was, she felt quite peaceful and more at leisure than she had for months. She was even at liberty to indulge in memories and it suited her mood deliberately to do so. She went back to the day when she had persuaded her father and mother to let her leave the Silvertree Academy for Young Ladies and go up to the University of Chicago. She had been but eighteen then, but if she lived to be a hundred she never could forget the hour she streamed with five thousand others through Hull Gate and on to Cobb Hall to register as a student in that young, aggressive seat of learning.

She had tried to hold herself in; not to be too "heady"; and she hoped the lank girl beside her--it had been Lena Vroom, delegated by the League of the Young Women's Christian Association--did not find her rawly enthusiastic. Lena conducted her from chapel to hall, from office to woman's building, from registrar to dean, till at length Kate stood before the door of Cobb once more, fagged but not fretted, and able to look about her with appraising eyes.

Around her and beneath her were swarms, literally, of fresh-faced, purposeful youths and maidens, an astonishingly large number of whom were meeting after the manner of friends long separated. Later Kate discovered how great a proportion of that enthusiasm took itself out in mere gesture and vociferation; but it all seemed completely genuine to her that first day and she thought with almost ecstatic anticipation of the relationships which soon would be hers. Almost she looked then to see the friend-who-was-to-be coming toward her with miraculous recognition in her eyes.

But she was none the less interested in those who for one reason or another were alien to her--in the Japanese boy, concealing his wistfulness beneath his rigid breeding; in the Armenian girl with the sad, beautiful eyes; in the Yiddish youth with his bashful earnestness. Then there were the women past their first youth, abstracted, and obviously disdainful of their personal appearance; and the girls with heels too high and coiffures too elaborate, who laid themselves open to the suspicion of having come to college for social reasons. But all appealed to Kate. She delighted in their variety--yes, and in all these forms of aspiration. The vital essence of their spirits seemed to materialize into visible ether, rose-red or violet-hued, and to rise about them in evanishing clouds.

She was recalled to the present by a brisk conductor who asked for her ticket. Kate hunted it up in a little flurry. The man had broken into the choicest of her memories, and when he was gone and she returned to her retrospective occupation, she chanced upon the most irritating of her recollections. It concerned an episode of that same first day in Chicago. She had grown weary with the standing and waiting, and when Miss Vroom left her for a moment to speak to a friend, Kate had taken a seat upon a great, unoccupied stone bench which stood near Cobb door. Still under the influence of her high idealization of the scene she lost herself in happy reverie. Then a widening ripple of laughter told her that something amusing was happening. What it was she failed to imagine, but it dawned upon her gradually that people were looking her way. Knots of the older students were watching her; bewildered newcomers were trying, like herself, to discover the cause of mirth. At first she smiled sympathetically; then suddenly, with a thrill of mortification, she perceived that she was the object of derision.

What was it? What had she done?

She knew that she was growing pale and she could feel her heart pounding at her side, but she managed to rise, and, turning, faced a blond young man near at hand, who had protruding teeth and grinned at her like a sardonic rabbit.

"Oh, what is it, please?" she asked.

"That bench isn't for freshmen," he said briefly.

Scarlet submerged the pallor in Kate's face.

"Oh, I didn't know," she gasped. "Excuse me."

She moved away quickly, dropping her handbag and having to stoop for it. Then she saw that she had left her gloves on the bench and she had to turn back for those. At that moment Lena hastened to her.

"I'm so sorry," she cried. "I ought to have warned you about that old senior bench."

Kate, disdaining a reply, strode on unheeding. Her whole body was running fire, and she was furious with herself to think that she could suffer such an agony of embarrassment over a blunder which, after all, was trifling. Struggling valiantly for self-command, she plunged toward another bench and dropped on it with the determination to look her world in the face and give it a fair chance to stare back.

Then she heard Lena give a throaty little squeak.

"Oh, my!" she said.

Something apparently was very wrong this time, and Kate was not to remain in ignorance of what it was. The bench on which she was now sitting had its custodian in the person of a tall youth, who lifted his hat and smiled upon her with commingled amusement and commiseration.

"Pardon," he said, "but--"

Kate already was on her feet and the little gusts of laughter that came from the onlookers hit her like so many stones.

"Isn't this seat for freshmen either?" she broke in, trying not to let her lips quiver and determined to show them all that she was, at any rate, no coward.

The student, still holding his hat, smiled languidly as he shook his head.

"I'm new, you see," she urged, begging him with her smile to be on her side,--"dreadfully new! Must I wait three years before I sit here?"

"I'm afraid you'll not want to do it even then," he said pleasantly. "You understand this bench--the C bench we call it--is for men; any man above a freshman."

Kate gathered the hardihood to ask:--

"But why is it for men, please?"

"I don't know why. We men took it, I suppose." He wasn't inclined to apologize apparently; he seemed to think that if the men wanted it they had a right to it.

"This bench was given to the men, perhaps?" she persisted, not knowing how to move away.

"No," admitted the young man; "I don't believe it was. It was presented to the University by a senior class."

"A class of men?"

"Naturally not. A graduating class is composed of men and women. C bench," he explained, "is the center of activities. It's where the drum is beaten to call a mass meeting, and the boys gather here when they've anything to talk over. There's no law against women sitting here, you know. Only they never do. It isn't--oh, I hardly know how to put it--it isn't just the thing--"

"Can't you break away, McCrea?" some one called.

The youth threw a withering glance in the direction of the speaker.

"I can conduct my own affairs," he said coldly.

But Kate had at last found a way to bring the interview to an end.

"I said I was new," she concluded, flinging a barbed shaft. "I thought it was share and share alike here--that no difference was made between men and women. You see--I didn't understand."

The C bench came to be a sort of symbol to her from then on. It was the seat of privilege if not of honor, and the women were not to sit on it.

Not that she fretted about it. There was no time for that. She settled in Foster Hall, which was devoted to the women, and where she expected to make many friends. But she had been rather unfortunate in that. The women were not as coöperative as she had expected them to be. At table, for example, the conversation dragged heavily. She had expected to find it liberal, spirited, even gay, but the girls had a way of holding back. Kate had to confess that she didn't think men would be like that. They would--most of them--have understood that the chief reason a man went to a university was to learn to get along with his fellow men and to hold his own in the world. The girls labored under the idea that one went to a university for the exclusive purpose of making high marks in their studies. They put in stolid hours of study and were quietly glad at their high averages; but it actually seemed as if many of them used college as a sort of shelter rather than an opportunity for the exercise of personality.

However, there were plenty of the other sort--gallant, excursive spirits, and as soon as Kate became acquainted she had pleasure in picking and choosing. She nibbled at this person and that like a cautious and discriminating mouse, venturing on a full taste if she liked the flavor, scampering if she didn't.

Of course she had her furores. Now it was for settlement work, now for dramatics, now for dancing. Subconsciously she was always looking about for some one who "needed" her, but there were few such. Patronage would have been resented hotly, and Kate learned by a series of discountenancing experiences that friendship would not come--any more than love--at beck and call.

Love!

That gave her pause. Love had not come her way. Of course there was Ray McCrea. But he was only a possibility. She wondered if she would turn to him in trouble. Of that she was not yet certain. It was pleasant to be with him, but even for a gala occasion she was not sure but that she was happier with Honora Daley than with him. Honora Daley was Honora Fulham now--married to a "dark man" as the gypsy fortune-tellers would have called him. He seemed very dark to Kate, menacing even; but Honora found it worth her while to shed her brightness on his tenebrosity, so that was, of course, Honora's affair.

Kate smiled to think of how her mother would be questioning her about her "admirers," as she would phrase it in her mid-Victorian parlance. There was really only Ray to report upon. He would be the beau ideal "young gentleman,"--to recur again to her mother's phraseology,--the son of a member of a great State Street dry-goods firm, an excellently mannered, ingratiating, traveled person with the most desirable social connections.

Kate would be able to tell of the two mansions, one on the Lake Shore Drive, the other at Lake Forest, where Ray lived with his parents. He had not gone to an Eastern college because his father wished him to understand the city and the people among whom his life was to be spent. Indeed, his father, Richard McCrea, had made something of a concession to custom in giving his son four years of academic life. Ray was now to be trained in every department of that vast departmental concern, the Store, and was soon to go abroad as the promising cadet of a famous commercial establishment, to make the acquaintance of the foreign importers and agents of the house. Oh, her mother would quite like all that, though she would be disappointed to learn that there had thus far been no rejected suitors. In her mother's day every fair damsel carried scalps at her belt, figuratively speaking--and after marriage, became herself a trophy of victory. Dear "mummy" was that, Kate thought tenderly--a willing and reverential parasite, "ladylike" at all costs, contented to have her husband provide for her, her pastor think for her, and Martha Underwood, the domineering "help" in the house at Silvertree, do the rest. Kate knew "mummy's" mind very well--knew how she looked on herself as sacred because she had been the mother to one child and a good wife to one husband. She was all swathed around in the chiffon-sentiment of good Victoria's day. She didn't worry about being a "consumer" merely. None of the disturbing problems that were shaking femininity disturbed her calm. She was "a lady," the "wife of a professional man." It was proper that she should "be well cared for." She moved by her well-chosen phrases; they were like rules set in a copybook for her guidance.

Kate seemed to see a moving-picture show of her mother's days. Now she was pouring the coffee from the urn, seasoning it scrupulously to suit her lord and master, now arranging the flowers, now feeding the goldfish; now polishing the glass with tissue paper. Then she answered the telephone for her husband, the doctor,--answered the door, too, sometimes. She received calls and paid them, read the ladies' magazines, and knew all about what was "fitting for a lady." Of course, she had her prejudices. She couldn't endure Oriental rugs, and didn't believe that smuggling was wrong; at least, not when done by the people one knew and when the things smuggled were pretty.

Kate, who had the spirit of the liberal comedian, smiled many times remembering these things. Then she sighed, for she realized that her ability to see these whimsicalities meant that she and her mother were, after all, creatures of diverse training and thought.

CHAPTER II

What! Silver tree? She hadn't realized how the time had been flying. But there was the sawmill. She could hear the whir and buzz! And there was the old livery-stable, and the place where farm implements were sold, and the little harness shop jammed in between;--and there, to convince her no mistake had been made, was the lozenge of grass with "Silvertree" on it in white stones. Then, in a second, the station appeared with the busses backed up against it, and beyond them the familiar surrey with a woman in it with yearning eyes.

Kate, the specialized student of psychology, the graduate with honors, who had learned to note contrasts and weigh values, forgot everything (even her umbrella) and leaped from the train while it was still in motion. Forgotten the honors and degrees; the majors were mere minor affairs; and there remained only the things which were from the beginning.

She and her mother sat very close together as they drove through the familiar village streets. When they did speak, it was incoherently. There was an odor of brier roses in the air and the sun was setting in a "bed of daffodil sky." Kate felt waves of beauty and tenderness breaking over her and wanted to cry. Her mother wanted to and did. Neither trusted herself to speak, but when they were in the house Mrs. Barrington pulled the pins out of Kate's hat and then Kate took the faded, gentle woman in her strong arms and crushed her to her.

"Your father was afraid he wouldn't be home in time to meet you," said Mrs. Barrington when they were in the parlor, where the Dresden vases stood on the marble mantel and the rose-jar decorated the three-sided table in the corner. "It was just his luck to be called into the country. If it had been a really sick person who wanted him, I wouldn't have minded, but it was only Venie Sampson."

"Still having fits?" asked Kate cheerfully, as one glad to recognize even the chronic ailments of a familiar community.

"Well, she thinks she has them," said Mrs. Barrington in an easy, gossiping tone; "but my opinion is that she wouldn't be troubled with them if only there were some other way in which she could call attention to herself. You see, Venie was a very pretty girl."

"Has that made her an invalid, mummy?"

"Well, it's had something to do with it. When she was young she received no end of attention, but some way she went through the woods and didn't even pick up a crooked stick. But she got so used to being the center of interest that when she found herself growing old and plain, she couldn't think of any way to keep attention fixed on her except by having these collapses. You know you mustn't call the attacks 'fits.' Venie's far too refined for that."

Kate smiled broadly at her mother's distinctive brand of humor. She loved it all--Miss Sampson's fits, her mother's jokes; even the fact that when they went out to supper she sat where she used in the old days when she had worn a bib beneath her chin.

"Oh, the plates, the cups, the everything!" cried Kate, ridiculously lifting a piece of the "best china" to her lips and kissing it.

"Absurdity!" reproved her mother, but she adored the girl's extravagances just the same.

"Everything's glorious," Kate insisted. "Cream cheese and parsley! Did you make it, mummy? Currant rolls--oh, the wonders! Martha Underwood, don't dare to die without showing me how to make those currant rolls. Veal loaf--now, what do you think of that? Why, at Foster we went hungry sometimes--not for lack of quantity, of course, but because of the quality. I used to be dreadfully ashamed of the fact that there we were, dozens of us women in that fine hall, and not one of us with enough domestic initiative to secure a really good table. I tried to head an insurrection and to have now one girl and now another supervise the table, but the girls said they hadn't come to college to keep house."

"Yes, yes," chimed in her mother excitedly; "that's where the whole trouble with college for women comes in. They not only don't go to college to keep house, but most of them mean not to keep it when they come out. We allowed you to go merely because you overbore us. You used to be a terrible little tyrant, Katie,--almost as bad as--"

She brought herself up suddenly.

"As bad as whom, mummy?"

There was a step on the front porch and Mrs. Barrington was spared the need for answering.

"There's your father," she said, signaling Kate to meet him.

Dr. Barrington was tall, spare, and grizzled. The torpor of the little town had taken the light from his eyes and reduced the tempo of his movements, but, in spite of all, he had preserved certain vivid features of his personality. He had the long, educated hands of the surgeon and the tyrannical aspect of the physician who has struggled all his life with disobedience and perversity. He returned Kate's ardent little storm of kisses with some embarrassment, but he was unfeignedly pleased at her appearance, and as the three of them sat about the table in their old juxtaposition, his face relaxed. However, Kate had seen her mother look up wistfully as her husband passed her, as if she longed for some affectionate recognition of the occasion, but the man missed his opportunity and let it sink into the limbo of unimproved moments.

"Well, father, we have our girl home again," Mrs. Barrington said with pardonable sentiment.

"Well, we've been expecting her, haven't we?" Dr. Barrington replied, not ill-naturedly but with a marked determination to make the episode matter-of-fact.

"Indeed we have," smiled Mrs. Barrington. "But of course it couldn't mean to you, Frederick, what it does to me. A mother's--"

Dr. Barrington raised his hand.

"Never mind about a mother's love," he said decisively. "If you had seen it fail as often as I have, you'd think the less said on the subject the better. Women are mammal, I admit; maternal they are not, save in a proportion of cases. Did you have a pleasant journey down, Kate?"

He had the effect of shutting his wife out of the conversation; of definitely snubbing and discountenancing her. Kate knew it had always been like that, though when she had been young and more passionately determined to believe her home the best and dearest in the world, as children will, she had overlooked the fact--had pretended that what was a habit was only a mood, and that if "father was cross" to-day, he would be pleasant to-morrow. Now he began questioning Kate about college, her instructors and her friends. There was conversation enough, but the man's wife sat silent, and she knew that Kate knew that he expected her to do so.

Custard was brought on and Mrs. Barrington diffidently served it. Her husband gave one glance at it.

"Curdled!" he said succinctly, pushing his plate from him. "It's a pity it couldn't have been right Kate's first night home."

Kate thought there had been so much that was not right her first night home, that a spoiled confection was hardly worth comment.

"I'm dreadfully sorry," Mrs. Barrington said. "I suppose I should have made it myself, but I went down to the train--"

"That didn't take all the afternoon, did it?" the doctor asked.

"I was doing things around the house--"

"Putting flowers in my room, I know, mummy," broke in Kate, "and polishing up the silver toilet bottles, the beauties. You're one of those women who pet a home, and it shows, I can tell you. You don't see many homes like this, do you, dad,--so ladylike and brier-rosy?"

She leaned smilingly across the table as she addressed her father, offering him not the ingratiating and seductive smile which he was accustomed to see women--his wife among the rest--employ when they wished to placate him. Kate's was the bright smile of a comradely fellow creature who asked him to play a straight game. It made him take fresh stock of his girl. He noted her high oval brow around which the dark hair clustered engagingly; her flexible, rather large mouth, with lips well but not seductively arched, and her clear skin with its uniform tinting. Such beauty as she had, and it was far from negligible, would endure. She was quite five feet ten inches, he estimated, with a good chest development and capable shoulders. Her gestures were free and suggestive of strength, and her long body had the grace of flexibility and perfect unconsciousness. All of this was good; but what of the spirit that looked out of her eyes? It was a glance to which the man was not accustomed--feminine yet unafraid, beautiful but not related to sex. The physician was not able to analyze it, though where women were concerned he was a merciless analyst. Gratified, yet unaccountably disturbed, he turned to his wife.

"Martha has forgotten to light up the parlor," he said testily. "Can't you impress on her that she's to have the room ready for us when we've finished inhere?"

"She's so excited over Kate's coming home," said Mrs. Barrington with a placatory smile. "Perhaps you'll light up to-night, Frederick."

"No, I won't. I began work at five this morning and I've been going all day. It's up to you and Martha to run the house."

"The truth is," said Mrs. Barrington, "neither Martha nor I can reach the gasolier."

Dr. Barrington had the effect of pouncing on this statement.

"That's what's the matter, then," he said. "You forgot to get the tapers. I heard Martha telling you last night that they were out."

A flush spread over Mrs. Barrington's delicate face as she cast about her for the usual subterfuge and failed to find it. In that moment Kate realized that it had been a long programme of subterfuges with her mother--subterfuges designed to protect her from the onslaughts of the irritable man who dominated her.

"I'll light the gas, mummy," she said gently. "Let that be one of my fixed duties from now on."

"You'll spoil your mother, Kate," said the doctor with a whimsical intonation.

His jesting about what had so marred the hour of reunion brought a surge of anger to Kate's brain.

"That's precisely what I came home to do, sir," she said significantly. "What other reason could I have for coming back to Silvertree? The town certainly isn't enticing. You've been doctoring here for forty years, but you havn't been able to cure the local sleeping-sickness yet."

It stung and she had meant it to. To insult Silvertree was to hurt the doctor in his most tender vanity. It was one of his most fervid beliefs that he had selected a growing town, conspicuous for its enterprise. In his young manhood he had meant to do fine things. He was public-spirited, charitable, a death-fighter of courage and persistence. Though not a religious man, he had one holy passion, that of the physician. He respected himself and loved his wife, but he had from boyhood confused the ideas of masculinity and tyranny. He believed that women needed discipline, and he had little by little destroyed the integrity of the woman he would have most wished to venerate. That she could, in spite of her manifest cowardice and moral circumventions, still pray nightly and read the book that had been the light to countless faltering feet, furnished him with food for acrid sarcasm. He saw in this only the essential furtiveness, inconsistency, and superstition of the female.

The evening dragged. The neighbors who would have liked to visit them refrained from doing so because they thought the reunited family would prefer to be alone that first evening. Kate did her best to preserve some tattered fragments of the amenities. She told college stories, talked of Lena Vroom and of beautiful Honora Fulham,--hinted even at Ray McCrea,--and by dint of much ingenuity wore the evening away.

"In the morning," she said to her father as she bade him good-night, "we'll both be rested." She had meant it for an apology, not for herself any more than for him, but he assumed no share in it.

Up in her room her mother saw her bedded, and in kissing her whispered,--

"Don't oppose your father, Kate. You'll only make me unhappy. Anything for peace, that's what I say."

CHAPTER III

It was sweet to awaken in the old room. Through the open window she could see the fork in the linden tree and the squirrels making free in the branches. The birds were at their opera, and now and then the shape of one outlined itself against the holland shade. Kate had been commanded to take her breakfast in bed and she was more than willing to do so. The after-college lassitude was upon her and her thoughts moved drowsily through her weary brain.

Her mother, by an unwonted exercise of self-control, kept from the room that morning, stopping only now and then at the door for a question or a look. That was sweet, too. Kate loved to have her hovering about like that, and yet the sight of her, so fragile, so fluttering, added to the sense of sadness that was creeping over her. After a time it began to rain softly, the drops slipping down into the shrubbery and falling like silver beads from the window-hood. At that Kate began to weep, too, just as quietly, and then she slept again. Her mother coming in on tiptoe saw tears on the girl's cheek, but she did not marvel. Though her experience had been narrow she was blessed with certain perceptions. She knew that even women who called themselves happy sometimes had need to weep.

The little pensive pause was soon over. There was no use, as all the sturdier part of Kate knew, in holding back from the future. That very afternoon the new life began forcing itself on her. The neighbors called, eager to meet this adventurous one who had turned her back on the pleasant conventions and had refused to content herself with the Silvertree Seminary for Young Ladies. They wanted to see what the new brand of young woman was like. Moreover, there was no one who was not under obligations to be kind to her mother's daughter. So, presently the whole social life of Silvertree, aroused from its midsummer torpor by this exciting event, was in full swing.

Kate wrote to Honora a fortnight later:--

> I am trying to be the perfect young lady according to dear mummy's definition. You should see me running baby ribbon in my *lingerie* and combing out the fringe on tea-

napkins. Every afternoon we are 'entertained' or give an entertainment. Of course we meet the same people over and over, but truly I like the cordiality. Even the inquisitiveness has an affectionate quality to it. I'm determined to enjoy my village and I do appreciate the homely niceties of the life here. Of course I have to 'pretend' rather hard at times--pretend, for example, that I care about certain things which are really of no moment to me whatever. To illustrate, mother and I have some recipes which nobody else has and it's our rôle to be secretive about them! And we have invented a new sort of 'ribbon sandwich.' Did you ever hear of a ribbon sandwich? If not, you must be told that it consists of layers and layers of thin slices of bread all pressed down together, with ground nuts or dressed lettuce in between. Each entertainer astonishes her guests with a new variety. That furnishes conversation for several minutes.

"How long can I stand it, Honora, my dear old defender of freedom? The classrooms are mine no more; the campus is a departed glory; I shall no longer sing the 'Alma Mater' with you when the chimes ring at ten. The whole challenge of the city is missing. Nothing opposes me, there is no task for me to do. I must be supine, acquiescent, smiling, non-essential. I am like a runner who has trained for a race, and, ready for the speeding, finds that no race is on. But I've no business to be surprised. I knew it would be like this, didn't I? the one thing is to make and keep mummy happy. She needs me *so* much. And I am happy to be with her. Write me often--write me everything. Gods, how I'd like a walk and talk with you!"

Mrs. Barrington did not attempt to conceal her interest in the letters which Ray McCrea wrote her daughter. She was one of those women who thrill at a masculine superscription on a letter. Perhaps she got more satisfaction out of these not too frequent missives than Kate did herself. While the writer didn't precisely say that he counted on Kate to supply the woof of the fabric of life, that expectation made itself evident between the lines to Mrs. Barrington's sentimental perspicacity.

Kate answered his letters, for it was pleasant to have a masculine correspondent. It provided a needed stimulation. Moreover, in the back of her mind she knew that he presented an avenue of escape if Silvertree and home became unendurable. It seemed piteous enough that her life with her parents should so soon have become a mere matter of duty and endurance, but there was a feeling of perpetually treading on eggs in the Barrington house. Kate could have screamed with exasperation as one eventless day after another dawned and the blight of caution and apprehension was never lifted from her mother and Martha. She writhed with shame at the sight of her mother's cajolery of the tyrant she served--and loved. To have spoken out once, recklessly, to have entered a wordy combat without rancor and for the mere zest of tournament, to have let the winnowing winds of satire blow through the house with its stale sentimentalities and mental attitudes, would have reconciled her to any amount of difference in the point of view. But the hushed voice and covertly held position afflicted her like shame.

Were all women who became good wives asked to falsify themselves? Was furtive diplomacy, or, at least, spiritual compromise, the miserable duty of woman? Was it her business to placate her mate, and, by exercising the cunning of the weak, to keep out from under his heel?

There was no one in all Silvertree whom the discriminating would so quickly have mentioned as the ideal wife as Mrs. Barrington. She herself, no doubt, so Kate concluded with her merciless young psychology, regarded herself as noble. But the people in Silvertree had a passion for thinking of themselves as noble. They had, Kate said to herself bitterly, so few charms that they had to fall back on their virtues. In the face of all this it became increasingly difficult to think of marriage as a goal for herself, and her letters to McCrea were further and further apart as the slow weeks passed. She had once read the expression, "the authentic voice of happiness," and it had lived hauntingly in her memory. Could Ray speak that? Would she, reading his summons from across half the world, hasten to him, choose him from the millions, face any future with him? She knew she would not. No, no; union with the man of average congeniality was not her goal. There must be something more shining than that for her to speed toward it.

However, one day she caught, opportunely, a hint of the further meanings of a woman's life. Honora provided a great piece of news, and illuminated with a new understanding, Kate wrote:--

"MY DEAR, DEAR GIRL:--

"You write me that something beautiful is going to happen to you. I can guess what it is and I agree that it is glorious, though it does take my breath, away. Now there are two of you--and by and by there will be three, and the third will be part you and part David and all a miracle. I can see how it makes life worth living, Honora, as nothing else could--nothing else!

"Mummy wouldn't like me to write like this. She doesn't approve of women whose understanding jumps ahead of their experiences. But what is the use of pretending that I don't encompass your miracle? I knew all about it from the beginning of the earth.

"This will mean that you will have to give up your laboratory work with David, I suppose. Will that be a hardship? Or are you glad of the old womanly excuse for passing by the outside things, and will you now settle down to be as fine a mother as you were a chemist? Will you go further, my dear, and make a fuss about your house and go all delicately bedizened after the manner of the professors' nice little wives--go in, I mean, for all the departments of the feminine profession?

"I do hope you'll have a little son, Honora, not so much on your account as on his. During childhood a girl's feet are as light as a boy's bounding over the earth; but when once childhood is over, a man's life seems so much more coherent than a woman's, though it is not really so important. But it takes precisely the experience you are going through to give it its great significance, doesn't it?

"What other career is there for real women, I wonder? What, for example, am I to do, Honora?, There at the University I prepared myself for fine work, but I'm trapped here in this silly Silvertree cage. If I had a talent I could make out very well, but I am talentless, and all I do now is to answer the telephone for father and help mummy embroider the towels. They won't let me do anything else. Some one asked me the other day what colors I intended wearing this autumn. I wanted to tell them smoke-of-disappointment, ashes-of-dreams, and dull-as-wash-Monday. But I only said ashes-of-roses.

"'Not all of your frocks, surely, Kate,' one of the girls cried. 'All,' I declared; 'street frocks, evening gowns, all.' 'But you mustn't be odd,' my little friend warned. 'Especially as people are a little suspicious that you will be because of your going to a co-educational college.'

"I thought it would be so restful here, but it doesn't offer peace so much as shrinkage. Silvertree isn't pastoral--it's merely small town. Of course it is possible to imagine a small town that would be ideal--a community of quiet souls leading the simple life. But we aren't great or quiet souls here, and are just as far from simple as our purses and experience will let us be.

"I dare say that you'll be advising me, as a student of psychology, to stop criticizing and to try to do something for the neighbors here--go in search of their submerged selves. But, honestly, it would require too much paraphernalia in the way of diving-bells and air-pumps.

"I have, however, a reasonable cause of worry. Dear little mummy isn't well. At first we thought her indisposition of little account, but she seems run down. She has been flurried and nervous ever since I came home; indeed, I may say she has been so for years. Now she seems suddenly to have broken down. But I'm going to do everything I can for her, and I know father will, too; for he can't endure to have any one sick. It arouses his great virtue, his physicianship."

A week later Kate mailed this:--

"I am turning to you in my terrible fear. Mummy won't answer our questions and seems lost in a world of thought. Father has called in other physicians to help him. I can't tell you how like a frightened child I feel. Oh, my poor little bewildered mummy! What do you suppose she is thinking about?"

Then, a week afterward, this--on black-bordered paper:--

"SISTER HONORA:--

"She's been gone three days. To the last we couldn't tell why she fell ill. We only knew she made no effort to get well. I am tormented by the fear that I had something to do with her breaking like that. She was appalled--shattered--at the idea of any friction between father and me. When I stood up for my own ideas against his, it was to her as sacrilegious as if I had lifted my hand against a king. I might have capitulated--ought, I suppose, to have foregone everything!

"There is one thing, however, that gives me strange comfort. At the last she had such dignity! Her silence seemed fine and brave. She looked at us from a deep still peace as if, after all her losing of the way, she had at last found it and Herself. The search has carried her beyond our sight.

"Oh, we are so lonely, father and I. We silently accuse each other. He thinks my reckless truth-telling destroyed her timid spirit; I think his twenty-five years of tyranny did it. We both know how she hated our rasping, and we hate it ourselves. Yet, even at that hour when we stood beside her bed and knew the end was coming, he and I were at sword's points. What a hackneyed expression, but how terrible! Yes, the hateful swords of our spirits, my point toward his breast and his toward mine, gleamed there almost visibly above that little tired creature. He wanted her for himself even to the last: I wanted her for Truth--wanted her to walk up to God dressed in her own soul-garments, not decked out in the rags and tags of those father had tossed to her.

"She spoke only once. She had been dreaming, I suppose, and a wonderful illuminated smile broke over her face. In the midst of what seemed a sort of ecstasy, she looked up and saw father watching her. She shivered away from him with one of those apologetic gestures she so often used. 'It wasn't a heavenly vision,' she said--she knew he wouldn't have believed in that--'it was only that I thought my little brown baby was in my arms.' She meant me, Honora,--think of it. She had gone back to those tender days when I had been dependent on her for all my well-being. My mummy! I gathered her close and held her till she was gone, my little, strange, frightened love.

"Now father and I hide our thoughts from each other. He wanted to know if I was going to keep house for him. I said I'd try, for six months. He flew in one of his rages because I admitted that it would be an experiment. He wanted to know what kind of a daughter I was, and I told him the kind he had made me. Isn't that hideous?

"I've no right to trouble you, but I must confide in some one or my heart will break. There's no one here I can talk to, though many are kind. And Ray--perhaps you think I should have written all this to him. But I wasn't moved to do so, Honora. Try to forgive me for telling you these troubles now in the last few days before your baby comes. I suppose I turn to you because you are one of the blessed corporation of mothers--part and parcel of the mother-fact. It's like being a part of the good rolling earth, just as familiar and comforting. Thinking of you mysteriously makes me good. I'm going to forget myself, the way you do, and 'make a home' for father.

"Your own

KATE."

In September she sent Honora a letter of congratulation.

"So it's twins! Girls! Were you transported or amused? Patience and Patricia--very pretty. You'll stay at home with the treasures, won't you? You see, there's something about you I can't quite understand, if you'll forgive me for saying it. You were an exuberant girl, but after marriage you grew austere--put your lips together in a line that discouraged kissing. So I'm not sure of you even now that the babies have come. Some day you'll have to explain yourself to me.

"I'm one who needs explanations all along the road. Why? Why? Why? That is what my soul keeps demanding. Why couldn't I go back to Chicago with Ray McCrea? He was down here the other day, but I wouldn't let him say the things he obviously had come to say, and now he's on his way abroad and very likely we shall not meet again. I feel so numb since mummy died that I can't care about Ray. I keep crying 'Why?' about Death among other things. And about that horrid gulf between father and me. If we try to get across we only fall in. He has me here ready to his need. He neither knows nor cares what my thoughts are. So long as I answer the telephone faithfully, sterilize the drinking-water, and see that he gets his favorite dishes, he is content. I have no liberty to leave the house and my restlessness is torture. The neighbors no longer flutter in as they used when mummy was here. They have given me over to my year of mourning--which means vacuity.

"Partly for lack of something better to do I have cleaned the old house from attic to cellar, and have been glad to creep to bed lame and sore from work, because then I could sleep. Father won't let me read at night--watches for signs of the light under my door and calls out to me if it shows. It is golden weather without, dear friend, and within is order and system. But what good? I am stagnating, perishing. I can see no release--cannot even imagine in what form I would like it to come. In your great happiness remember my sorrow. And with your wonderful sweetness forgive my bitter egotism. But truly, Honora, I die daily."

The first letter Honora Fulham wrote after she was able to sit at her desk was to Kate. No answer came. In November Mrs. Fulham telephoned to Lena Vroom to ask if she had heard, but Lena had received no word.

"Go down to Silvertree, Lena, there's a dear," begged her old schoolmate. But Lena was working for her doctor's degree and could not spare the time. The holidays came on, and Mrs. Fulham tried to imagine her friend as being at last broken to her galling harness. Surely there must be compensations for any father and daughter who can dwell together. Her own Christmas was a very happy one, and she was annoyed with herself that her thoughts so continually turned to Kate. She had an uneasy sense of apprehension in spite of all her verbal assurances to Lena that Kate could master any situation.

What really happened in Silvertree that day changed, as it happened, the course of Kate's life. Sorrow came to her afterward, disappointment, struggle, but never so heavy and dragging a pain as she knew that Christmas Day.

She had been trying in many unsuspected ways to relieve her father's grim misery,--a misery of which his gaunt face told the tale,--and although he had said that he wished for "no flubdub about Christmas," she really could not resist making some recognition of a day which found all other homes happy. When the doctor came in for his midday meal, Kate had a fire leaping in the old grate with the marble mantel and a turkey smoking on a table which was set forth with her choicest china and silver. She had even gone so far as to bring out a dish distinctly reminiscent of her mother,--the delicious preserved peaches, which had awaked unavailing envy in the breasts of good cooks in the village. There was pudding, too, and brandy sauce, and holly for decorations. It represented a very mild excursion into the land of festival, but it was too much for Dr. Barrington.

He had come in cold, tired, hungry, and, no doubt, bitterly sorrowful at the bottom of his perverse heart. He discerned Kate in white--it was the first time she had laid off her mourning--and with a chain of her mother's about her neck. Beyond, he saw the little Christmas feast and the old silver vase on the table, red with berries.

"You didn't choose to obey my orders," he said coldly, turning his unhappy blue eyes on her.

"Your orders?" she faltered.

"There was to be no fuss and feathers of any sort," he said. "Christmas doesn't represent anything recognized in my philosophy, and you know it. We've had enough of pretense in this house. I've been working to get things on a sane basis and I believed you were sensible enough to help me. But you're just like the rest of them--you're like all of your sex. You've got to have your silly play-time. I may as well tell you now that you don't give me any treat when you give me turkey, for I don't like it."

"Oh, dad!" cried Kate; "you do! I've seen you eat it many times! Come, really it's a fine dinner. I helped to get it. Let's have a good time for once."

"I have plenty of good times, but I have them in my own way."

"They don't include me!" cried Kate, her lips quivering. "You're too hard on me, dad,--much too hard. I can't stand it, really."

He sat down to the table and ran his finger over the edge of the carving-knife.

"It wouldn't cut butter," he declared. "Martha, bring me the steel!"

"I sharpened it, sir," protested Martha.

"Sharpened it, did you? I never saw a woman yet who could sharpen a knife."

He began flashing the bright steel, and the women, their day already in ashes, watched him fascinatedly. He was waiting to pounce on them. They knew that well enough. The spirit of perversity had him by the throat and held him, writhing. He carved and served, and then turned again to his daughter.

"So I'm too hard on you, am I?" he said, looking at her with a cold glint in his eye. "I provide you with a first-class education, I house you, clothe you, keep you in idleness, and I'm too hard on you. What do you expect?"

"Why, I want you to like me," cried Kate, her face flushing. "I simply want to be your daughter. I want you to take me out with you, to give me things. I wanted you to give me a Christmas present. I want other things, too,--things that are not favors."

She paused and he looked at her with a tightening of the lips.

"Go on," he said.

"I am not being kept in idleness, as I think you know very well. My time and energies are given to helping you. I look after your office and your house. My time is not my own. I devote it to you. I want some recognition of my services--I want some money."

She leaned back in her chair, answering his exasperated frown with a straight look, which was, though he did not see it, only a different sort of anger from his own.

"Well, you won't get it," he said. "You won't get it. When you need things you can tell me and I'll get them for you. But there's been altogether too much money spent in this house in years gone by for trumpery. You know that well enough. What's in that chest out there in the hall? Trumpery! What's in those bureau drawers upstairs? Truck! Hundreds of dollars, that might have been put out where it would be earning something, gone into mere flubdub."

He paused to note the effect of his words and saw that he had scored. Poor Mrs. Barrington, struggling vaguely and darkly in her own feminine way for some form of self-expression, had spent her household allowance many a time on futile odds and ends. She had haunted the bargain counter, and had found herself unable to get over the idea that a thing cheaply purchased was an economic triumph. So in drawers and chests and boxes she had packed her pathetic loot--odds and ends of embroidery, of dress goods, of passementerie, of chair coverings; dozens of spools of thread and crochet cotton; odd dishes; jars of cold cream; flotsam and jetsam of the shops, a mere wreckage of material. Kate remembered it with vicarious shame and the blood that flowed to her face swept on into her brain. She flamed with loyalty to that little dead, bewildered woman, whose feet had walked so falteringly in her search for the roses of life. And she said--

But what matter what she said?

Her father and herself were at the antipodes, and they were separated no less by their similarities than by their differences. Their wistful and inexpressive love for each other was as much of a blight upon them as their inherent antagonism. The sun went down that bleak Christmas night on a house divided openly against itself.

The next day Kate told her father he might look for some one else to run his house for him. He said he had already done so. He made no inquiry where she was going. He would not offer her money, though he secretly wanted her to ask for it. But it was past that with her. The miserable, bitter drama--the tawdry tragedy, whose most desperate accent was its shameful approach to farce--wore itself to an end.

Kate took her mother's jewelry, which had been left to her, and sold it at the local jeweler's. All Silvertree knew that Kate Barrington had left her home in anger and that her father had shown her the back of his hand.

CHAPTER IV

Honora Fulham, sitting in her upper room and jealously guarding the slumbers of Patience and Patricia, her tiny but already remarkable twin daughters, heard a familiar voice in the lower hallway. She dropped her book, "The Psychological Significance of the Family Group," and ran to the chamber door. A second later she was hanging over the banisters.

"Kate!" she called with a penetrating whisper. "You!"

"Yes, Honora, it's bad Kate. She's come to you--a penny nobody else wanted."

Honora Fulham sailed down the stairs with the generous bearing of a ship answering a signal of distress. The women fell into each other's arms, and in that moment of communion dismissed all those little alien half-feelings which grow up between friends when their enlarging experience has driven them along different roads. Honora led the way to her austere drawing-room, from which, with a rigorous desire to economize labor, she had excluded all that was superfluous, and there, in the bare, orderly room, the two women--their girlhood definitely behind them--faced each other. Kate noted a curious retraction in Honora, an indescribable retrenchment of her old-time self, as if her florescence had been clipped by trained hands, so that the bloom should not be too exuberant; and Honora swiftly appraised Kate's suggestion of freedom and force.

"Kate," she announced, "you look like a kind eagle."

"A wounded one, then, Honora."

"You've a story for me, I see. Sit down and tell it."

So Kate told it, compelling the history of her humiliating failure to stand out before the calm, adjudging mind of her friend.

"But oughtn't we to forgive everything to the old?" cried Honora at the conclusion of the recital.

"Oh, is father old?" responded Kate in anguish. "He doesn't seem old--only formidable. If I'd thought I'd been wrong I never would have come up here to ask you to sustain me in my obstinacy. Truly, Honora, it isn't a question of age. He's hardly beyond his prime, and he has been using all of his will, which has grown strong with having his own way, to break me down the way most of the men in Silvertree have broken their women down. I was getting to be just like the others, and to start when I heard him coming in at the door, and to hide things from him so that he wouldn't rage. I'd have been lying next."

"Kate!"

"Oh, you think it isn't decent for me to speak that way of my father! You can't think how it seems to me--how--how irreligious! But let me save my soul, Honora! Let me do that!"

The girl's pallid face, sharpened and intensified, bore the imprint of genuine misery. Honora Fulham, strong of nerve and quick of understanding, embraced her with a full sisterly glance.

"I always liked and trusted you, Kate," she said. "I was sorry when our ways parted, and I'd be happy to have them joined again. I see it's to be a hazard of new fortune for you, and David and I will stand by. I don't know, of course, precisely what that may mean, but we're yours to command."

A key turned in the front door.

"There's David now," said his wife, her voice vibrating, and she summoned him.

David Fulham entered with something almost like violence, although the violence did not lie in his gestures. It was rather in the manner in which his personality assailed those within the room. Dark, with an attractive ugliness, arrogant, with restive and fathomless eyes, he seemed to unite the East and the West in his being. Had his mother been a Jewess of pride and intellect, and his father an adventurous American of the superman type? Kate, looking at him with fresh interest, found her thoughts leaping to the surmise. She knew that he was, in a way, a great man--a man with a growing greatness. He had promulgated ideas so daring that his brother scientists were embarrassed to know where to place him. There were those who thought of him as a brilliant charlatan; but the convincing intelligence and self-control of his glance repudiated that idea. The Faust-like aspect of the man might lay him open to the suspicion of having too experimental and inquisitive a mind. But he had, it would seem, no need for charlatanism.

He came forward swiftly and grasped Kate's hand.

"I remember you quite well," he said in his deep, vibratory tones. "Are you here for graduate work?"

"No," said Kate; "I'm not so humble."

"Not so humble?" He showed his magnificent teeth in a flashing but somewhat satiric smile.

"I'm here for Life--not for study."

"Not 'in for life,' but 'out' for it," he supplemented. "That's interesting. What is Honora suggesting to you? She's sure to have a theory of what will be best. Honora knows what will be best for almost everybody, but she sometimes has trouble in making others see it the same way."

Honora seemed not to mind his chaffing.

"Yes," she agreed, "I've already thought, but I haven't had time to tell Kate. Do you remember that Mrs. Goodrich said last night at dinner that her friend Miss Addams was looking about for some one to take the place of a young woman who was married the other day? She was an officer of the Children's Protective League, you remember."

"Oh, that--" broke in Fulham. He turned toward Kate and looked her over from head to foot, till the girl felt a hot wave of indignation sweep over her. But his glance was impersonal, apparently. He paid no attention to her embarrassment. He seemed merely to be getting at her qualities by the swiftest method. "Well," he said finally, "I dare say you're right. But--" he hesitated.

"Well?" prompted his wife.

"But won't it be rather a--a waste?" he asked. And again he smiled, this time with some hidden meaning.

"Of course it won't be a waste," declared Honora. "Aren't women to serve their city as well as men? It's a practical form of patriotism, according to my mind."

Kate broke into a nervous laugh.

"I hope I'm to be of some use," she said. "Work can't come a moment too soon for me. I was beginning to think--"

She paused.

"Well?" supplied Fulham, still with that watchful regard of her.

"Oh, that I had made a mistake about myself--that I wasn't going to be anything in particular, after all."

They were interrupted. A man sprang up the outside steps and rang the doorbell imperatively.

"It's Karl Wander," announced Fulham, who had glanced through the window. "It's your cousin, Honora."

He went to the door, and Kate heard an emphatic and hearty voice making hurried greetings.

"Stopped between trains," it was saying. "Can stay ten minutes precisely--not a second longer. Came to see the babies."

Honora had arisen with a little cry and gone to the door. Now she returned, hanging on to the arm of a weather-tanned man.

"Miss Barrington," she said, "my cousin, Mr. Wander. Oh, Karl, you're not serious? You don't really mean that you can't stay--not even over night?"

The man turned his warm brown eyes on Kate and she looked at him expectantly, because he was Honora's cousin. For the time it takes to draw a breath, they gazed at each other. Oddly enough, Kate thought of Ray McCrea, who was across the water, and whose absence she had not regretted. She could not tell why her thoughts turned to him. This man was totally unlike Ray. He was, indeed, unlike any one she ever had known. There was that about him which held her. It was not quite assertion; perhaps it was competence. But it was competence that seemed to go without tyranny, and that was something new in her experience of men. He looked at her on a level, spiritually, querying as to who she might be.

The magical moment passed. Honora and David were talking. They ran away up the stairs with their guest, inviting Kate to follow.

"I'll only be in the way now," she called. "By and by I'll have the babies all to myself."

Yet after she had said this, she followed, and looked into the nursery, which was at the rear of the house. Honora had thrust the two children into her cousin's big arms and she and David stood laughing at him. Another man might have appeared ridiculous in this position; but it did not, apparently, occur to Karl Wander to be self-conscious. He was wrapped in contemplation of the babies, and when he peered over their heads at Kate, he was quite grave and at ease.

Then, before it could be realized, he was off again. He had kissed Honora and congratulated her, and he and Kate had again clasped hands.

"Sorry," he said, in his explosive way, "that we part so soon." He held her hand a second longer, gave it a sudden pressure, and was gone.

Honora shut the door behind him reluctantly.

"So like Karl!" she laughed. "It's the second time he's been in my house since I was married."

"You'd think we had the plague, the way he runs from us," said David.

"Oh," responded Honora, not at all disturbed, "Karl is forever on important business. He's probably been to New York to some directors' meeting. Now he's on his way to Denver, he says--'men waiting.' That's Karl's way. To think of his dashing up here between trains to see my babies!" The tears came to her eyes. "Don't you think he's fine, Kate?"

The truth was, there seemed to be a sort of vacuum in the air since he had left--as if he had taken the vitality of it with him.

"But where does he live?" she asked Honora.

"Address him beyond the Second Divide, and he'll be reached. Everybody knows him there. His post-office bears his own name--Wander."

"He's a miner?"

"How did you know?"

"Oh, by process of elimination. What else could he be?"

"Nothing else in all the world," agreed David Fulham. "I tell Honora he's a bit mad."

"No, no," Honora laughed; "he's not mad; he's merely Western. How startled you look, Kate--as if you had seen an apparition."

It was decided that Kate was to stay there at the Fulhams', and to use one of their several unoccupied rooms. Kate chose one that looked over the Midway, and her young strength made nothing of the two flights of stairs which she had to climb to get to it. At first the severity of the apartment repelled her, but she had no money with which to make it more to her taste, and after a few hours its very barrenness made an appeal to her. It seemed to be like her own life, in need of decoration, and she was content to let things take their course. It seemed probable that roses would bloom in their time.

No one, it transpired, ate in the house.

"I found out," explained Honora, "that I couldn't be elaborately domestic and have a career, too, so I went, with some others of similar convictions and circumstances, into a coöperative dining-room scheme."

Kate gave an involuntary shrug of her shoulders.

"You think that sounds desolate? Wait till you see us all together. This talk about 'home' is all very well, but I happen to know--and I fancy you do, too--that home can be a particularly stultifying place. When people work as hard as we do, a little contact with outsiders is stimulating. But you'll see for yourself. Mrs. Dennison, a very fine woman, a widow, looks after things for us. Dr. von Shierbrand, one of our number, got to calling the place 'The Caravansary,' and now we've all fallen into the way of it."

The Caravansary was but a few doors from the Fulhams'; an old-fashioned, hospitable affair, with high ceilings, white marble mantels, and narrow windows. Mrs. Dennison, the house-mother, suited the place well. Her widow's cap and bands seemed to go with the grave pretentiousness of the rooms, to which she had succeeded in giving almost a personal atmosphere. There was room for her goldfish and her half-dozen canary cages as well as for her "coöperators"--no one there would permit himself to be called a boarder.

Kate, sensitive from her isolation and sore from her sorrows, had imagined that she would resent the familiarities of those she would be forced to meet on table terms. But what was the use in trying, to resent Marna Cartan, the young Irish girl who meant to make a great singer of herself, and who evidently looked upon the world as a place of rare and radiant entertainment? As for Mrs. Barsaloux, Marna's patron and benefactor, with her world-weary eyes and benevolent smile, who could turn a cold shoulder to her solicitudes? Then there were Wickersham and Von Shierbrand, members, like Fulham, of the faculty of the University. The Applegates and the Goodriches were pleasant folk, rather settled in their aspect, and all of literary leanings. The Applegates were identified--both husband and wife--with a magazine of literary criticism; Mr. Goodrich ran a denominational paper with an academic flavor; Mrs. Goodrich was president of an orphan asylum and spent her days in good works. Then, intermittently, the company was joined by George Fitzgerald, a preoccupied young physician, the nephew of Mrs. Dennison.

They all greeted Kate with potential friendship in their faces, and she could not keep back her feeling of involuntary surprise at the absence of anything like suspicion. Down in Silvertree if a new woman had come into a boarding-house, they would have wondered why. Here they seemed tacitly to say, "Why not?"

Mrs. Dennison seated Kate between Dr. von Shierbrand and Marna Cartan. Opposite to her sat Mrs. Goodrich with her quiet smile. Everyone had something pleasant to say; when Kate spoke, all were inclined to listen. The atmosphere was quiet, urbane, gracious. Even David Fulham's exotic personality seemed to soften under the regard of Mrs. Dennison's gray eyes.

"Really," Kate concluded, "I believe I can be happy here. All I need is a chance to earn my bread and butter."

And what with the intervention of the Goodriches and the recommendation of the Fulhams, that opportunity soon came.

CHAPTER V

A fortnight later she was established as an officer of the Children's Protective Association, an organization with a self-explanatory name, instituted by women, and chiefly supported by them. She was given an inexhaustible task, police powers, headquarters at Hull House, and a vocation demanding enough to satisfy even her desire for spiritual adventure.

It was her business to adjust the lives of children--which meant that she adjusted their parents' lives also. She arranged the disarranged; played the providential part, exercising the powers of intervention which in past times belonged to the priest, but which, in the days of commercial feudalism, devolve upon the social workers.

Her work carried her into the lowest strata of society, and her compassion, her efficiency, and her courage were daily called upon. Perhaps she might have found herself lacking in the required measure of these qualities, being so young and inexperienced, had it not been that she was in a position to concentrate completely upon her task. She knew how to listen and to learn; she knew how to read and apply. She went into her new work with a humble spirit, and this humility offset whatever was aggressive and militant in her. The death of her mother and the aloofness of her father had turned all her ardors back upon herself. They found vent now in her new work, and she was not long in perceiving that she needed those whom she was called upon to serve quite as much as they needed her.

Mrs. Barsaloux and Marna Carton, who had been shopping, met Kate one day crossing the city with a baby in her arms and two miserable little children clinging to her skirts. Hunger and neglect had given these poor small derelicts that indescribable appearance of depletion and shame which, once seen, is never to be confused with anything else.

"My goodness!" cried Mrs. Barsaloux, glowering at Kate through her veil; "what sort of work is this you are doing, Miss Barrington? Aren't you afraid of becoming infected with some dreadful disease? Wherever do you find the fortitude to be seen in the company of such wretched little creatures? I would like to help them myself, but I'd never be willing to carry such filthy little bags of misery around with me."

Kate smiled cheerfully.

"We've just put their mother in the Bridewell," she said, "and their father is in the police station awaiting trial. The poor dears are going to be clean for once in their lives and have a good supper in the bargain. Maybe they'll be taken into good homes eventually. They're lovely children, really. You haven't looked at them closely enough, Mrs. Barsaloux."

"I'm just as close to them as I want to be, thank you," said the lady, drawing back involuntarily. But she reached for her purse and gave Kate a bill.

"Would this help toward getting them something?" she asked.

Marna laughed delightedly.

"I'm sure they're treasures," she said. "Mayn't I help Miss Barrington take them to wherever they're going, *tante*? I shan't catch a thing, and I love to know what becomes of homeless children."

Kate saw a look of acute distress on Mrs. Barsaloux's face.

"This isn't your game just now, Miss Cartan," Kate said in her downright manner. "It's mine. I'm moving my pawns here and there, trying to find the best places for them. It's quite exhilarating."

Her arms were aching and she moved the heavy baby from one shoulder to the other.

"A game, is it?" asked the Irish girl. "And who wins?"

"The children, I hope. I'm on the side of the children first and last."

"Oh, so am I. I think it's just magnificent of you to help them."

Kate disclaimed the magnificence.

"You mustn't forget that I'm doing it for money," she said. "It's my job. I hope I'll do it well enough to win the reputation of being honest, but you mustn't think there's anything saintly about me, because there isn't. Goodbye. Hold on tight, children!"

She nodded cheerfully and moved on, fresh, strong, determined, along the crowded thoroughfare, the people making way for her smilingly. She saw nothing of the attention paid her. She was wondering if her arms would hold out or if, in some unguarded moment, the baby would slip from them. Perhaps the baby was fearful, too, for it reached up its little clawlike hands and clasped her tight about the neck. Kate liked the feeling of those little hands, and was sorry when they relaxed and the weary little one fell asleep.

Each day brought new problems. If she could have decided these by mere rule of common sense, her new vocation might not have puzzled her as much as it did. But it was uncommon, superfine, intuitive sense that was required. She discovered, for example, that not only was sin a virtue in disguise, but that a virtue might be degraded into a sin.

She put this case to Honora and David one evening as the three of them sat in Honora's drawing-room.

"It's the case of Peggy Dunn," she explained. "Peggy likes life. She has brighter eyes than she knows what to do with and more smiles than she has a chance to distribute. She has finished her course at the parochial school and she's clerking in a downtown store. That is slow going for Peggy, so she evens things up by attending the Saturday night dances. When she's whirling around the hall on the tips of her toes, she really feels like herself. She gets home about two in the morning on these occasions and finds her mother waiting up for her and kneeling before a little statue of the Virgin that stands in the corner of the sitting-room. As soon as the mother sees Peggy, she pounces on her and weeps on her shoulder, and after Peggy's in bed and dead with the tire in her legs, her mother gets down beside the bed and prays some more. 'What would you do, please,' says Peggy to me, 'if you had a mother that kept crying and praying every time you had a bit of fun? Wouldn't you run away from home and get where they took things aisier?'"

David threw back his head and roared in sympathetic commendation of Peggy's point of view.

"Poor little mother," sighed Honora. "I suppose she'll send her girl straight on the road to perdition and never know what did it."

"Not if I can help it," said Kate. "I don't believe in letting her go to perdition at all. I went around to see the mother and I put the responsibility on her. 'Every time you make Peggy laugh,' I said, 'you can count it for glory. Every time you make her swear,--for she does swear,--you can know you've blundered. Why don't you give her some parties if you don't want her to be going out to them?'"

"How did she take that?" asked Honora.

"It bothered her a good deal at first, but when I went down to meet Peggy the other day as she came out of the store, she told me her mother had had the little bisque Virgin moved into her own bedroom and that she had put a talking-machine in the place where it had stood. I told Peggy the talking-machine was just a new kind of prayer, meant to make her happy, and that it wouldn't do for her to let her mother's prayers go unanswered. 'Any one with eyes like yours,' I said to her, 'is bound to have beaux in plenty, but you've only one mother and you'd better hang on to her.'"

"Then what did she say?" demanded the interested Honora.

"She's an impudent little piece. She said, 'You've some eyes yourself, Miss Barrington, but I suppose you know how to make them behave."

"Better marry that girl as soon as you can, Miss Barrington," counseled David; "that is, if any hymeneal authority is vested in you."

"That's what Peggy wanted to know," admitted Kate. "She said to me the other day: 'Ain't you Cupid, Miss Barrington? I heard about a match you made up, and it was all right--the real thing, sure enough.' 'Have you a job for me--supposing I was Cupid?' I asked. That set her off in a gale. So I suppose there's something up Peggy's very short sleeves."

The Fulhams liked to hear her stories, particularly as she kept the amusing or the merely pathetic ones for them, refraining from telling them of the unspeakable, obscene tragedies which daily came to her notice. It might have been supposed that scenes such as these would so have revolted her that she could not endure to deal with them; but this was far from being the case. The greater the need for her help, the more determined was she to meet the demand. She had plenty of superiors whom she could consult, and she suffered less from disgust or timidity than any one could have supposed possible.

The truth was, she was grateful for whatever absorbed her and kept her from dwelling upon that dehumanized house at Silvertree. Her busy days enabled her to fight her sorrow very well, but in the night, like a wailing child, her longing for her mother awoke, and she nursed it, treasuring it as those freshly bereaved often do. The memory of that little frustrated soul made her tender of all women, and too prone, perhaps, to lay to some man the blame of their shortcomings. She had no realization that she had set herself in this subtle and subconscious way against men. But whether she admitted it or not, the fact remained that she stood with her sisters, whatever their estate, leagued secretly against the other sex.

By way of emphasizing her devotion to her work, she ceased answering Ray McCrea's letters. She studiously avoided the attentions of the men she met at the Settlement House and at Mrs. Dennison's Caravansary.

Sometimes, without her realizing it, her thoughts took on an almost morbid hue, so that, looking at Honora with her chaste, kind, uplifted face, she resented her close association with her husband. It seemed offensive that he, with his curious, half-restrained excesses of temperament, should have domination over her friend who stood so obviously for abnegation. David manifestly was averse to bounds and limits. All that was wild and desirous of adventure, in Kate informed her of like qualities in this man. But she held--and meant always to hold--the restless falcons of her spirit in leash. Would David Fulham do as much? She could not be quite sure, and instinctively she avoided anything approaching intimacy with him.

He was her friend's husband. "Friend's husband" was a sort of limbo into which men were dropped by scrupulous ladies; so Kate decided, with a frown at herself for having even thought that David could wish to emerge from that nondescript place of spiritual residence. Anyway, she did not completely like him, though she thought him extraordinary and stimulating, and when Honora told her something of the great discovery which the two of them appeared to be upon the verge of making concerning the germination of life without parental interposition, she had little doubt that David was wizard enough to carry it through. He would have the daring, and Honora the industry, and--she reflected--if renown came, that would be David's beyond all peradventure.

No question about it, Kate's thoughts were satiric these days. She was still bleeding from the wound which her father had inflicted, and she did not suspect that it was wounded affection rather than hurt self-respect which was tormenting her. She only knew that she shrank from men, and that at times she liked to imagine what sort of a world it would be if there were no men in it at all.

Meantime she met men every day, and whether she was willing to admit it or not, the facts were that they helped her on her way with brotherly good will, and as they saw her going about her singular and heavy tasks, they gave her their silent good wishes, and hoped that the world of pain and shame would not too soon destroy what was gallant and trustful in her.

But here has been much anticipation. To go back to the beginning, at the end of her first week in the city she had a friend. It was Marna Cartan. They had fallen into the way of talking together a few minutes before or after dinner, and Kate would hasten her modest dinner toilet in order to have these few marginal moments with this palpitating young creature who moved to unheard rhythms, and whose laughter was the sweetest thing she had yet heard in a city of infinite dissonances.

"You don't know how to account for me very well, do you?" taunted Marna daringly, when they had indulged their inclination for each other's society for a few days. "You wonder about me because I'm so streaked. I suppose you see vestiges of the farm girl peeping through the operatic student. Wouldn't you like me to explain myself?"

She had an iridescent personality, made up of sudden shynesses, of bright flashes of bravado, of tenderness and hauteur, and she contrived to be fascinating in all of them. She held Kate as the Ancient Mariner held the wedding-guest.

"Of course I'd love to know all about you," answered Kate. "Inquisitiveness is the most marked of my characteristics. But I don't want you to tell me any more than I deserve to hear."

"You deserve everything," cried Marna, seizing Kate's firm hand in her own soft one, "because you understand friendship. Why, I always said it could be as swift and surprising as love, and just as mysterious. You take it that way, too, so you deserve a great deal. Well, to begin with, I'm Irish."

Kate's laugh could be heard as far as the kitchen, where Mrs. Dennison was wishing the people would come so that she could dish up the soup. Marna laughed, too.

"You guessed it?" she cried. She didn't seem to think it so obvious as Kate's laugh indicated.

"You don't leave a thing to the imagination in that direction," Kate cried. "Irish? As Irish as the shamrock! Go on."

"Dear me, I want to begin so far back! You see, I don't merely belong to modern Ireland. I'm--well, I'm traditional. At least, Great-Grandfather Cartan, who came over to Wisconsin with a company of immigrants, could tell you things about our ancestors that would make you feel as if we came up out of the Irish hills. And great-grandfather, he actually looked legendary himself. Why, do you know, he came over with these people to be their story-teller!"

"Their story-teller?"

"Yes, just that--their minstrel, you understand. And that's what my people were, 'way back, minstrels. All the way over on the ship, when the people were weeping for homesickness, or sitting dreaming about the new land, or falling sick, or getting wild and vicious, it was great-granddaddy's place to bring them to themselves with his stories. Then when they all went on to Wisconsin and took up their land, they selected a small beautiful piece for great-grandfather, and built him a log house, and helped him with his crops. He, for his part, went over the countryside and was welcomed everywhere, and carried all the friendly news and gossip he could gather, and sat about the fire nights, telling tales of the old times, and keeping the ancient stories and the ancient tongue alive for them."

"You mean he used the Gaelic?"

"What else would he be using, and himself the descendant of minstrels? But after a time he learned the English, too, and he used that in his latter years because the understanding of the Gaelic began to die out."

"How wonderful he must have been!"

"Wonderful? For eighty years he held sway over the hearts of them, and was known as the best story-teller of them all. This was the more interesting, you see, because every year they gathered at a certain place to have a story-telling contest; and great-grandfather was voted the master of them until--"

Marna hesitated, and a flush spread over her face.

"Until--" urged Kate.

"Until a young man came along. Finnegan, his name was. He was no more than a commercial traveler who heard of the gathering and came up there, and he capped stories with great-grandfather, and it went on till all the people were thick about them like bees around a flower-pot. Four days it lasted, and away into the night; and in the end they took the prize from great-grandfather and gave it to Gerlie Finnegan. And that broke great-granddad's heart."

"He died?"

"Yes, he died. A hundred and ten he was, and for eighty years had been the king of them. When he was gone, it left me without anybody at all, you see. So that was how I happened to go down to Baraboo to earn my living."

"What were you doing?"

Marna looked at the tip of her slipper for a moment, reflectively. Then she glanced up at Kate, throwing a supplicating glance from the blue eyes which looked as if they were snared behind their long dark lashes.

"I wouldn't be telling everybody that asked me," she said. "But I was singing at the moving-picture show, and Mrs. Barsaloux came in there and heard me. Then she asked me to live with her and go to Europe, and I did, and she paid for the best music lessons for me everywhere, and now--"

She hesitated, drawing in a long breath; then she arose and stood before Kate, breathing deep, and looking like a shining butterfly free of its chrysalis and ready to spread its emblazoned wings.

"Yes, bright one!" cried Kate, glowing with admiration. "What now?"

"Why, now, you know, I'm to go in opera. The manager of the Chicago Opera Company has been Mrs. Barsaloux's friend these many years, and she has had him try out my voice. And he likes it. He says he doesn't care if I haven't had the usual amount of training, because I'm really born to sing, you see. Perhaps that's my inheritance from the old minstrels--for they chanted their ballads and epics, didn't they? Anyway, I really can sing. And I'm to make my debut this winter in 'Madame Butterfly.' Just think of that! Oh, I love Puccini! I can understand a musician like that--a man who makes music move like thoughts, flurrying this way and blowing that. It's to be very soon--my debut. And then I can make up to Mrs. Barsaloux for all she's done for me. Oh, there come all the people! You mustn't let Mrs. Fulham know how I've chattered. I wouldn't dare talk about myself like that before her. This is just for you--I *knew* you wanted to know about me. I want to know all about you, too."

"Oh," said Kate, "you mustn't expect me to tell my story. I'm different from you. I'm not born for anything in particular--I've no talents to point out my destiny. I keep being surprised and frustrated. It looks to me as if I were bound to make mistakes. There's something wrong with me. Sometimes I think that I'm not womanly enough--that there's too much of the man in my disposition, and that the two parts of me are always going to struggle and clash."

Chairs were being drawn up to the table.

"Come!" called Dr. von Shierbrand. "Can't you young ladies take time enough off to eat?"

He looked ready for conversation, and Kate went smilingly to sit beside him. She knew he expected women to be amusing, and she found it agreeable to divert him. She understood the classroom fag from which he was suffering; and, moreover, after all those austere meals with her father, it really was an excitement and a pleasure to talk with an amiable and complimentary man.

CHAPTER VI

"We're to have a new member in the family, Kate," Honora said one morning, as she and Kate made their way together to the Caravansary. "It's my cousin, Mary Morrison. She's a Californian, and very charming, I understand."

"She's to attend the University?"

"I don't quite know as to that," admitted Honora, frowning slightly. "Her father and mother have been dead for several years, and she has been living with her brother in Santa Barbara. But he is to go to the Philippines on some legal work, and he's taking his family with him. Mary begs to stay here with me during his absence."

"Is she the sort of a person who will need a chaperon? Because I don't seem to see you in that capacity, Honora."

"No, I don't know that I should care to sit against the wall smiling complacently while other people were up and doing. I've always felt I wouldn't mind being a chaperon if they'd let me set up some sort of a workshop in the ballroom, or even if I could take my mending, or a book to read. But slow, long hours of vacuous smiling certainly would wear me out. However, I don't imagine that Mary will call upon me for any such service."

"But if your cousin isn't going to college, and doesn't intend to go into society, how will she amuse herself?"

"I haven't an idea--not an idea. But I couldn't say no to her, could I? I've so few people belonging to me in this world that I can't, for merely selfish reasons, bear to turn one of my blood away. Mary's mother and my mother were sisters, and I think we should be fond of each other. Of course she is younger than I, but that is immaterial."

"And David--does he like the idea? She may be rather a fixture, mayn't she? Haven't you to think about that?"

"Oh, David probably won't notice her particularly. People come and go and it's all the same to him. He sees only his great problems." Honora choked a sigh.

"Who wants him to do anything else!" defended Kate quickly. "Not you, surely! Why, you're so proud of him that you're positively offensive! And to think that you are working beside him every day, and helping him--you know it's all just the way you would have it, Honora."

"Yes, it is," agreed Honora contritely, "and you should see him in the laboratory when we two are alone there, Kate! He's a changed man. It almost seems as if he grew in stature. When he bends over those tanks where he is making his great experiments, all of my scientific training fails to keep me from seeing him as one with supernatural powers. And that wonderful idea of his, the finding out of the secret of life, the prying into this last hidden place of Nature, almost overwhelms me. I can work at it with a matter-of-fact countenance, but when we begin to approach the results, I almost shudder away from it. But you must never let David know I said so. That's only my foolish, feminine, reverent mind. All the trained and scientific part of me repudiates such nonsense."

They turned in at the door of the Caravansary.

"I don't want to see you repudiating any part of yourself," cried Kate with sudden ardor. "It's so sweet of you, Honora, to be a mere woman in spite of all your learning and your power."

Honora stopped and grasped Kate's wrist in her strong hand.

"But am I that?" she queried, searching her friend's face with her intense gaze. "You see, I've tried--I've tried--"

She choked on the words.

"I've tried not to be a woman!" she declared, drawing her breath sharply between her teeth. "It's a strange, strange story, Kate."

"I don't understand at all," Kate declared.

"I've tried not to be a woman because David is so completely and triumphantly a man."

"Still I don't understand."

"No, I suppose not. It's a hidden history. Sometimes I can't believe it myself. But let me ask you, am I the woman you thought I would be?"

Kate smiled slowly, as her vision of Honora as she first saw her came back to her.

"How soft and rosy you were!" she cried. "I believe I actually began my acquaintance with you by hugging you. At any rate, I wanted to. No, no; I

never should have thought of you in a scientific career, wearing Moshier gowns and having curtain-less windows. Never!"

Honora stood a moment there in the dim hall, thinking. In her eyes brooded a curiously patient light.

"Do you remember all the trumpery I used to have on my toilet-table?" she demanded. "I sent it to Mary Morrison. They say she looks like me."

She put her hand on the dining-room door and they entered. The others were there before them. There were growing primroses on the table, and the sunlight streamed in at the window. A fire crackled on the hearth; and Mrs. Dennison, in her old-fashioned widow's cap, sat smiling at the head of her table.

Kate knew it was not really home, but she had to admit that these busy undomestic moderns had found a good substitute for it: or, at least, that, taking their domesticity through the mediumship of Mrs. Dennison, they contrived to absorb enough of it to keep them going. But, no, it was not really home. Kate could not feel that she, personally, ever had been "home." She thought of that song of songs, "The Wanderer."

"Where art thou? Where art thou, O home so dear?"

She was thinking of this still as, her salutation over, she seated herself in the chair Dr. von Shierbrand placed for her.

"Busy thinking this morning, Miss Barrington?" Mrs. Dennison asked gently. "That tells me you're meaning to do some good thing to-day. I can't say how splendid you social workers seem to us common folks."

"Oh, my dear Mrs. Dennison!" Kate protested. "You and your kind are the true social workers. If only women--all women--understood how to make true homes, there wouldn't be any need for people like us. We're only well-intentioned fools who go around putting plasters over the sores. We don't even reach down as far as the disease--though I suppose we think we do when we get a lot of statistics together. But the men and women who go about their business, doing their work well all of the time, are the preventers of social trouble. Isn't that so, Dr. von Shierbrand?"

That amiable German readjusted his glasses upon his handsome nose and began to talk about the Second Part of "Faust." The provocation, though slight, had seemed to him sufficient.

"My husband has already eaten and gone!" observed Honora with some chagrin. "Can't you use your influence, Mrs. Dennison, to make him spend a proper amount of time at the table?"

"Oh, he doesn't need to eat except once in a great while. He has the ways of genius, Mrs. Fulham. Geniuses like to eat at odd times, and my own feeling is that they should be allowed to do as they please. It is very bad for geniuses to make them follow a set plan," said Mrs. Dennison earnestly.

"That woman," observed Dr. von Shierbrand under his breath to Kate, "has the true feminine wisdom. She should have been the wife of a great man. It was such qualities which Goethe meant to indicate in his Marguerite."

Honora, who had overheard, lifted her pensive gray eyes and interchanged a long look with Dr. von Shierbrand. Each seemed to be upon the verge of some remark.

"Well," said Kate briskly, "if you want to speak, why don't you? Are your thoughts too deep for words?"

Von Shierbrand achieved a laugh, but Honora was silent. She seemed to want to say that there was more than one variety of feminine wisdom; while Von Shierbrand, Kate felt quite sure, would have maintained that there was but one--the instinctive sort which "Marguerite knew."

The day that Mary Morrison was to arrive conflicted with the visit of a very great Frenchman to Professor Fulham's laboratory.

"I really don't see how I'm to meet the child, Kate," Honora said anxiously to her friend. "Do you think you could manage to get down to the station?"

Kate could and did go. This girl, like herself, was very much on her own resources, she imagined. She was coming, as Kate had come only the other day, to a new and forbidding city, and Kate's heart warmed to her. It seemed rather a tragedy, at best, to leave the bland Californian skies and to readjust life amid the iron compulsion of Chicago. Kate pictured her as a little thing, depressed, weary with her long journey, and already homesick.

The reality was therefore somewhat of a surprise. As Kate stood waiting by the iron gate watching the outflowing stream of people with anxious eyes, she saw a little furore centered about the person of an opulent young woman who had, it appeared, many elaborate farewells to make to her fellow-passengers. Two porters accompanied her, carrying her smart bags, and, even with so much assistance, she was draped with extra garments, which hung from her arms in varying and seductive shades of green. She herself was in green of a subtle olive shade, and her plumes and boa, her chains and chatelaine, her hand-bags and camera, marked her as the traveler triumphant and expectant. Like an Arabian princess, borne across the desert to the home of her future lord, she came panoplied with splendor. The consciousness of being a personage, by the mere right conferred by regal womanhood-in-flower, emanated from her. And the world accepted her smilingly at her own estimate. She wished to play at being queen. What more simple? Let her have her game. On every hand she found those who were--or who delightedly pretended to be--her subjects.

Once beyond the gateway, this exuberant creature paused. "And now," she said to a gentleman more assiduous than the rest, who waited upon her and who was laden with her paraphernalia, "you must help me to identify my cousin. That will be easy enough, too, for they say we resemble each other."

That gave Kate her cue. She went forward with outstretched hand.

"I am your cousin's emissary, Miss Morrison," she said. "I am Kate Barrington, and I came to greet you because your cousin was unable to get here, and is very, very sorry about it."

Miss Morrison revealed two deep dimples when she smiled, and held out so much of a hand as she could disengage from her draperies. She presented her fellow-traveler; she sent a porter for a taxi. All was exhilaratingly in commotion about her; and Kate found herself apportioning the camera and some of the other things to herself.

They had quite a royal setting-forth. Every one helped who could find any excuse for doing so; others looked on. Miss Morrison nodded and smiled; the chauffeur wheeled his machine splendidly, making dramatic gestures which had the effect of causing commerce to pause till the princess was under way.

"Be sure," warned Miss Morrison, "to drive through the pleasantest streets."

Then she turned to Kate with a deliciously reproachful expression on her face.

"Why didn't you order blue skies for me?" she demanded.

Kate never forgot the expression of Miss Morrison's face when she was ushered into Honora's "sanitary drawing-room," as Dr. von Shierbrand had dubbed it. True, the towers of Harper Memorial Library showed across the Plaisance through the undraped windows, mitigating the gravity of the outlook, and the innumerable lights of the Midway already began to render less austere the January twilight. But the brown walls, the brown rug, the Mission furniture in weathered oak, the corner clock,--an excellent time-piece,--the fireplace with its bronze vases, the etchings of foreign architecture, and the bookcase with Ruskin, Eliot, Dickens, and all the Mid-Victorian celebrities in sets, produced but a grave and unillumined interior.

"Oh!" cried Miss Morrison with ill-concealed dismay. And then, after a silence: "But where do you sit when you're sociable?"

"Here," said Kate. She wasn't going to apologize for Honora to a pair of exclamatory dimples!

"But you can be intimate here?" Miss Morrison inquired.

"We're not intimate," flashed Kate. "We're too busy--and we respect each other too much."

Miss Morrison sank into a chair and revealed the tint of her lettuce-green petticoat beneath her olive-green frock.

"I'm making you cross with me," she said regretfully. "Please don't dislike me at the outset. You see, out in California we're not so up and down as you are here. If you were used to spending your days in the shade of yellow walls, with your choice of hammocks, and with nothing to do but feed the parrot and play the piano, why, I guess you'd--"

She broke off and stared about her.

"Why, there isn't any piano!" she cried. "Do you mean Honora has no piano?"

"What would be the use? She doesn't play."

"I must order one in the morning, then. Honora wouldn't care, would she? Oh, when do you suppose she'll be home? Does she like to stay over in that queer place you told me of, fussing around with those frogs?"

Kate had been rash enough to endeavor to explain something of the Fulhams' theories regarding the mechanistic conception of life. There was nothing to do but accord Miss Morrison the laugh which she appeared to think was coming to her.

"I can see that I shouldn't have told you about anything like that," Kate said. "I see how mussy you would think any scientific experiment to be. And, really, matters of greater importance engage your attention."

She was quite serious. She had swiftly made up her mind that Mary Morrison, with her conscious seductions, was a much more important factor in the race than austere Honora Fulham. But Miss Morrison was suspicious of satire.

"Oh, I think science important!" she protested.

"No, you don't," declared Kate; "you only wish you did. Come, we'll go to your room."

It was the rear room on the second floor, and it presented a stern parallelogram occupied by the bare necessaries of a sleeping-apartment. The walls and rug were gray, the furniture of mahogany. Mary Morrison looked at it a moment with a slow smile. Then she tossed her green coat and her hat with its sweeping veil upon the bed. She flung her camera and her magazines upon the table. She opened her traveling-bag, and, with hands that almost quivered with impatience, placed upon the toilet-table the silver implements that Honora had sent her and scattered broadcast among them her necklaces and bracelets.

"I'll have some flowering plants to-morrow," she told Kate. "And when my trunks and boxes come, I'll make the wilderness blossom like a rose. How have you decorated your room?"

"I haven't much money," said Kate bluntly; "but I've--well, I've ventured on my own interpretations of what a bed-sitting-room should be."

Miss Morrison threw her a bright glance.

"I'll warrant you have," she said. "I should think you'd contrive a very original sort of a place. Thank you so much for looking after me. I brought along a gown for dinner. Naturally, I didn't want to make a dull impression at the outset. Haven't I heard that you dine out at some sort of a place where geniuses congregate?"

Years afterward, Kate used to think about the moment when Honora and her cousin met. Honora had come home, breathless from the laboratory. It had been a stirring afternoon for her. She had heard words of significant appreciation spoken to David by the men whom, out of all the world, she would have chosen to have praise him. She looked at Miss Morrison, who had come trailing down in a cerise evening gown as if she were a bright creature of another species, somewhat, Kate could not help whimsically thinking, as a philosophic beaver might have looked at a bird of paradise. Then Honora had kissed her cousin.

"Dear blue-eyed Mary!" she had cried. "Welcome to a dull and busy home."

"How good of you to take me in," sighed Miss Morrison. "I hated to bother you, Honora, but I thought you might keep me out of mischief."

"Have you been getting into mischief?" Honora asked, still laughing.

"Not quite," answered her cousin, blushing bewitchingly. "But I'm always on the verge of it. It's the Californian climate, I think."

"So exuberant!" cried Honora.

"That's it!" agreed "Blue-eyed Mary." "I thought you'd understand. Here, I'm sure, you're all busy and good."

"Some of us are," agreed Honora. "There's my Kate, for example. She's one of the most useful persons in town, and she's just as interesting as she is useful."

Miss Morrison turned her smiling regard on Kate. "But, Honora, she's been quite abrupt with me. She doesn't approve of me. I suppose she discovered at once that I *wasn't* useful."

"I didn't," protested Kate. "I think decorative things are of the utmost use."

"There!" cried Miss Morrison; "you can see for yourself that she doesn't like me!"

"Nonsense," said Kate, really irritated. "I shall like you if Honora does. Let me help you dress, Honora dear. Are you tired or happy that your cheeks are so flushed?"

"I'm both tired and happy, Kate. Excuse me, Mary, won't you? If David comes in you'll know him by instinct. Believe me, you are very welcome."

Up in Honora's bedroom, Kate asked, as she helped her friend into the tidy neutral silk she wore to dinner: "Is the blue-eyed one going to be a drain on you, girl? You oughtn't to carry any more burdens. Are you disturbed? Is she more of a proposition than you counted on?"

Honora turned her kind but troubled eyes on Kate.

"I can't explain," she said in *so* low a voice that Kate could hardly catch the words. "She's like me, isn't she? I seemed to see--"

"What?"

"Ghosts--bright ghosts. Never mind."

"You're not thinking that you are old, are you?" cried Kate. "Because that's absurd. You're wonderful--wonderful."

Laughter arose to them--the mingled voices of David Fulham and his newfound cousin by marriage.

"Good!" cried Honora with evident relief. "They seem to be taking to each other. I didn't know how David would like her."

He liked her very well, it transpired, and when the introductions had been made at the Caravansary, it appeared that every one was delighted with her. If their reception of her differed from that they had given to Kate, it was nevertheless kindly--almost gay. They leaped to the conclusion that Miss Morrison was designed to enliven them. And so it proved. She threw even the blithe Marna Cartan temporarily into the shade; and Dr. von Shierbrand, who was accustomed to talking with Kate upon such matters as the national trait of incompetence, or the reprehensible modern tendency of coddling the unfit, turned his attention to Miss Morrison and to lighter subjects.

Two days later a piano stood in Honora's drawing-room, and Miss Morrison sat before it in what may be termed occult draperies, making lovely music. Technically, perhaps, the music left something to be desired. Mrs. Barsaloux and Marna Cartan thought so, at any rate. But the habitués of Mrs. Dennison's near-home soon fell into the way of trailing over to the Fulhams' in Mary Morrison's wake, and as they grouped themselves about on the ugly Mission furniture, in a soft light produced by many candles, and an atmosphere drugged with highly scented flowers, they fell under the spell of many woven melodies.

When Mary Morrison's tapering fingers touched the keys they brought forth a liquid and caressing sound like falling water in a fountain, and when she leaned over them as if to solicit them to yield their kind responses, her attitude, her subtle garments, the swift interrogative turns of her head, brought visions to those who watched and listened. Kate dreamed of Italian gardens--the gardens she never had seen; Von Shierbrand thought of dark German forests; Honora, of a moonlit glade. These three confessed so much. The others did not tell their visions, but obviously they had them. Blue-eyed Mary was one of those women who inspire others. She was the quintessence of femininity, and she distilled upon the air something delicately intoxicating, like the odor of lotus-blossoms.

It was significant that the Fulhams' was no longer a house of suburban habits. Ten o'clock and lights out had ceased to be the rule. After music there frequently was a little supper, and every one was pressed into service in the preparation of it. Something a trifle fagged and hectic began to show in the faces of Mrs. Dennison's family, and that good woman ventured to offer some reproof.

"You all are hard workers," she said, "and you ought to be hard resters, too. You're not acting sensibly. Any one would think you were the idle rich."

"Well, we're entitled to all the pleasure we can get," Mary Morrison had retorted. "There are people who think that pleasure isn't for them. But I am just the other way--I take it for granted that pleasure is my right. I always take everything in the way of happiness that I can get my hands on."

"You mean, of course, my dear child," said the gentle Mrs. Goodrich, "all that you can get which does not belong to some one else."

Blue-eyed Mary laughed throatily.

"Fortunately," she said, "there's pleasure enough to go around. It's like air, every one can breathe it in."

.

CHAPTER VII

But though Miss Morrison had made herself so brightly, so almost universally at home, there was one place into which she did not venture to intrude. This was Kate's room. Mary had felt from the first a lack of encouragement there, and although she liked to talk to Kate, and received answers in which there appeared to be no lack of zest and response, yet it seemed to be agreed that when Miss Barrington came tramping home from her hard day's work, she was to enjoy the solitude of her chamber.

Mary used to wonder what went on there. Miss Barrington could be very still. The hours would pass and not a sound would issue from that high upper room which looked across the Midway and included the satisfactory sight of the Harper Memorial and the massed University buildings. Kate would, indeed, have had difficulty in explaining that she was engaged in the mere operation of living. Her life, though lonely, and to an extent undirected, seemed abundant. Restless she undoubtedly was, but it was a restlessness which she succeeded in holding in restraint. At first when she came up to the city the daze of sorrow was upon her. But this was passing. A keen awareness of life suffused her now and made her observant of everything about her. She felt the tremendous incongruities of city life, and back of these incongruities, the great, hidden, passionate purpose which, ultimately, meant a city of immeasurable power. She rejoiced, as the young and gallant dare to do, that she was laboring in behalf of that city. Not one bewildered, wavering, piteous life was adjusted through her efforts that she did not feel that her personal sum of happiness had received an addition. That deep and burning need for religion, or for love, or for some splendid and irresistible impetus, was satisfied in part by her present work.

To start out each morning to answer the cry of distress, to understand the intricate yet effective machinery of benevolent organizations, so that she could call for aid here and there, and have instant and intelligent coöperation, to see broken lives mended, the friendless befriended, the tempted lifted up, the evil-doer set on safe paths, warmed and sustained her. That inquisitive nature of hers was now so occupied with the answering of practical and immediate questions that it had ceased to beat upon the hollow doors of the Unknown with unavailing inquiries.

So far as her own life was concerned, she seemed to have found, not a haven, but a broad sea upon which she could triumphantly sail. That shame at being merely a woman, with no task, no utility, no independence, had been lifted from her. So, in gratitude, everywhere, at all times, she essayed to help other women to a similar independence. She did not go so far as to say that it was the panacea for all ills, but she was convinced that more than half of the incoherent pain of women's lives could be avoided by the mere fact of financial independence. It became a religion with her to help the women with whom she came in contact, to find some unguessed ability or applicability which would enable them to put money in their purses. With liberty to leave a miserable condition, one often summoned courage to remain and face it. She pointed that out to her wistful constituents, the poor little wives who had found in marriage only a state of supine drudgery, and of unexpectant, monotonous days. She was trying to give them some game to play. That was the way she put it to them. If one had a game to play, there was use in living. If one had only to run after the balls of the players, there was not zest enough to carry one along.

She began talking now and then at women's clubs and at meetings of welfare workers. Her abrupt, picturesque way of saying things "carried," as an actor would put it. Her sweet, clear contralto held the ear; her aquiline comeliness pleased the eye without enticing it; her capable, fit-looking clothes were so happily secondary to her personality that even the women could not tell how she was dressed. She was the least seductive person imaginable; and she looked so self-sufficient that it seldom occurred to any one to offer her help. Yet she was in no sense bold or aggressive. No one ever thought of accusing her of being any of those things. Many loved her--loved her wholesomely, with a love in which trust was a large element. Children loved her, and the sick, and the bad. They looked to her to help them out of their helplessness. She was very young, but, after all, she was maternal. A psychologist would have said that there was much of the man about her, and her love of the fair chance, her appetite for freedom, her passion for using her own capabilities might, indeed, have seemed to be of the masculine variety of qualities; but all this was more than offset by this inherent impulse for maternity. She was born, apparently, to care for others, but she had to serve them freely. She had to be the dispenser of good. She was unconsciously on the outlook against those innumerable forms of slavishness which affection or religion gilded and made to seem like noble service.

Among those who loved her was August von Shierbrand. He loved her apparently in spite of himself. She did not in the least accord with his romantic ideas of what a woman should be. He was something of a poet, and a specialized judge of poetry, and he liked women of the sort who inspired a man to write lyrics. He had tried unavailingly to write lyrics about Kate, but they never would "go." He confessed his fiascoes to her.

"Nothing short of martial measures seems to suit you," he said laughingly.

"But why write about me at all, Dr. von Shierbrand?" she inquired. "I don't want any one writing about me. What I want to do is to learn how to write myself--not because I feel impelled to be an author, but because I come across things almost every day which ought to be explained."

"You are completely absorbed in this extraordinary life of yours!" he complained.

"Why not!" demanded Kate. "Aren't you completely absorbed in your life?"

"Of course I am. But teaching is my chosen profession."

"Well, life is my chosen profession. I want to see, feel, know, breathe, Life. I thought I'd never be able to get at it. I used to feel like a person walking in a mist. But it's different now. Everything has taken on a clear reality to me. I'm even beginning to understand that I myself am a reality and that my thoughts as well as my acts are entities. I'm getting so that I can define my own opinions. I don't believe there's anybody in the city who would so violently object to dying as I would, Dr. von Shierbrand."

The sabre cut on Von Shierbrand's face gleamed.

"You certainly seem at the antipodes of death, Miss Barrington," he said with a certain thickness in his utterance. "And I, personally, can think of nothing more exhilarating than in living beside you. I meant to wait--to wait a long time before asking you. But what is the use of waiting? I want you to marry me. I feel as if it must be--as if I couldn't get along without you to help me enjoy things."

Kate looked at him wonderingly. It was before the afternoon concert and they were sitting in Honora's rejuvenated drawing-room while they waited for the others to come downstairs.

"But, Dr. von Shierbrand!" she cried, "I don't like a city without suburbs!"

"I beg your pardon!"

"I like to see signs of my City of Happiness as I approach--outlying villas, and gardens, and then straggling, pleasant neighborhoods, and finally Town."

"Oh, I see. You mean I've been too unexpected. Can't you overlook that? You're an abrupt person yourself, you know. I'm persuaded that we could be happy together."

"But I'm not in love, Dr. von Shierbrand. I'm sorry. Frankly, I'd like to be."

"And have you never been? Aren't you nursing a dream of--"

"No, no; I haven't had a hopeless love if that's what you mean. I'm all lucid and clear and comfortable nowadays--partly because I've stopped thinking about some of the things to which I couldn't find answers, and partly because Life is answering some of my questions."

"How to be happy without being in love, perhaps."

"Well, I am happy--temperately so. Perhaps that's the only degree of happiness I shall ever know. Of course, when I was younger I thought I should get to some sort of a place where I could stand in swimming glory and rejoice forever, but I see now how stupid I was to think anything of the sort. I hoped to escape the commonplace by reaching some beatitude, but now I have found that nothing really is commonplace. It only seems so when you aren't understanding enough to get at the essential truth of things."

"Oh, that's true! That's true!" cried Von Shierbrand.

"Oh, Kate, I do love you. You seem to complete me. When I'm with you I understand myself. Please try to love me, dear. We'll get a little home and have a garden and a library--think how restful it will be. I can't tell you how I want a place I can call home."

"There they come," warned Kate as she heard footsteps on the stairs. "You must take 'no' for your answer, dear man. I feel just like a mother to you."

Dr. von Shierbrand arose, obviously offended, and he allied himself with Mary Morrison on the way to the concert. Kate walked with Honora and David until they met with Professor Wickersham, who was also bound for Mandel Hall and the somewhat tempered classicism which the Theodore Thomas Orchestra offered to "the University crowd."

"Please walk with me, Miss Barrington," said Wickersham. "I want you to explain the universe to me."

"I can do that nicely," retorted Kate, "because Dr. von Shierbrand has already explained it to me."

Blue-eyed Mary was pouting. She never liked any variety of amusement, conversational or otherwise, in which she was not the center.

So Kate's life sped along. It was not very significant, perhaps, or it would not have seemed so to the casual onlooker, but life is measured by its inward rather than its outward processes, and Kate felt herself being enriched by her experiences.

She enjoyed being brought into contact with the people she met in her work--not alone the beneficiaries of her ministrations, but the policemen and the police matrons and the judges of the police court. She joined a society of "welfare workers," and attended their suppers and meetings, and tried to learn by their experience and to keep her own ideas in abeyance.

She could not help noticing that she differed in some particulars from most of these laborers in behalf of the unfortunate. They brought practical, unimaginative, and direct minds to bear upon the problems before them, while she never could escape her theories or deny herself the pleasure of looking beyond the events to the causes which underlay them. This led her to jot down her impressions in a notebook, and to venture on comments concerning her experiences.

Moreover, not only was she deeply moved by the disarrangement and bewilderment which she saw around her, but she began to awaken to certain great events and developing powers in the world. She read the sardonic commentators upon modern life--Ibsen, Strindberg, and many others; and if she sometimes passionately repudiated them, at other times she listened as if she were finding the answers to her own inquiries. It moved her to discover that men, more often than women, had been the interpreters of women's hidden meanings, and that they had been the setters-forth of new visions of sacredness and fresh definitions of liberty.

It was these men--these aloof and unsentimental ones--who had pointed out that the sin of sins committed by women had been the indifference to their own personalities. They had been echoers, conformers, imitators;

even, in their own way, cowards. They had feared the conventions, and had been held in thrall by their own carefully nursed ideals of themselves. They had lacked the ability to utilize their powers of efficiency; had paid but feeble respect to their own ideals; had altogether measured themselves by too limited a standard. Failing wifely joy, they had too often regarded themselves as unsuccessful, and had apologized tacitly to the world for using their abilities in any direction save one. They had not permitted themselves that strong, clean, robust joy of developing their own powers for mere delight in the exercise of power.

But now, so Kate believed,--so her great instructors informed her,--they were awakening to their privileges. An intenser awareness of life, of the right to expression, and of satisfaction in constructive performances was stirring in them. If they desired enfranchisement, they wanted it chiefly for spiritual reasons. This was a fact which the opponents of the advancing movement did not generally recognize. Kate shrank from those fruitless arguments at the Caravansary with the excellent men who gravely and kindly rejected suffrage for women upon the ground that they were protecting them by doing so. They did not seem to understand that women desired the ballot because it was a symbol as well as because it was an instrument and an argument. If it was to benefit the working woman in the same way in which it benefited the working man, by making individuality a thing to be considered; if it was to give the woman taxpayer certain rights which would put her on a par with the man taxpayer, a thousand times more it was to benefit all women by removing them from the class of the unconsidered, the superfluous, and the negligible.

Yes, women were wanting the ballot because it included potentiality, and in potentiality is happiness. No field seems fair if there is no gateway to it--no farther field toward which the steps may be turned. Kate was getting hold of certain significant similes. She saw that it was past the time of walls and limits. Walled cities were no longer endurable, and walled and limited possibilities were equally obsolete. If the departure of the "captains and the kings" was at hand, if the new forces of democracy had routed them, if liberty for all men was now an ethic need of civilization, so political recognition was necessary for women. Women required the ballot because the need was upon them to perform great labors. Their unutilized benevolence, their disregarded powers of organization, their instinctive sense of economy, their maternal-oversoul, all demanded exercise. Women were the possessors of certain qualities so abundant, so ever-renewing, that the ordinary requirements of life did not give them adequate employment.

With a divine instinct of high selfishness, of compassion, of realization, they were seeking the opportunity to exercise these powers.

"The restlessness of women," "the unquiet sex," were terms which were becoming glorious in Kate's ears. She saw no reason why women as well as men should not be allowed to "dance upon the floor of chance." All about her were women working for the advancement of their city, their country, and their race. They gave of their fortunes, of their time, of all the powers of their spirit. They warred with political machines, with base politicians, with public contumely, with custom. What would have crushed women of equally gentle birth a generation before, seemed now of little account to these workers. They looked beyond and above the irritation of the moment, holding to the realization that their labors were of vital worth. Under their administration communities passed from shameless misery to self-respect; as the result of their generosity, courts were sustained in which little children could make their plea and wretched wives could have justice. Servants, wantons, outcasts, the insane, the morally ill, all were given consideration in this new religion of compassion. It was amazing to Kate to see light come to dull eyes--eyes which had hitherto been lit only with the fires of hate. As she walked the gray streets in the performance of her tasks, weary and bewildered though she often was, she was sustained by the new discovery of that ancient truth that nothing human can be foreign to the person of good will. Neither dirt nor hate, distrust, fear, nor deceit should be permitted to blind her to the essential similarity of all who were "bound together in the bundle of life."

It was not surprising that at this time she should begin writing short articles for the women's magazines on the subjects which presented themselves to her in her daily work. Her brief, spontaneous, friendly articles, full of meat and free from the taint of bookishness, won favor from the first. She soon found her evenings occupied with her somewhat matter-of-fact literary labors. But this work was of such a different character from that which occupied her in the daytime that so far from fatiguing her it gave an added zest to her days.

She was not fond of idle evenings. Sitting alone meant thinking, and thought meant an unconquerable homesickness for that lonely man back in Silvertree from whom she had parted peremptorily, and toward whom she dared not make any overtures. Sometimes she sent him an article clipped from the magazines or newspapers dealing with some scientific subject, and once she mailed him a number of little photographs which she had taken with her own camera and which might reveal to him, if he were inclined to follow their suggestions, something of the life in which she was engaged. But no recognition of these wordless messages came from him. He had been unable to forgive her, and she beat down the question that would arise as to whether she also had been at fault. She was under the necessity of justifying herself if she would be happy. It was only after many months had passed that she learned how a heavy burden may become light by the confession of a fault.

Meantime, she was up early each morning; she breakfasted with the most alert residents of the Caravansary; then she took the street-car to South Chicago and reported at a dismal office. Here the telephone served to put her into communication with her superior at Settlement House. She reported what she had done the day before (though, to be sure, a written report was already on its way), she asked advice, she talked over ways and means. Then she started upon her daily rounds. These might carry her to any one of half a dozen suburbs or to the Court of Domestic Relations, or over on the West Side of the city to the Juvenile Court. She appeared almost daily before some police magistrate, and not long after her position was assumed, she was called upon to give evidence before the grand jury.

"However do you manage it all?" Honora asked one evening when Kate had been telling a tale of psychically sinister import. "How can you bring yourself to talk over such terrible and revolting subjects as you have to, before strange men in open court?"

"A nice old man asked me that very question to-day as I was coming out of the courtroom," said Kate. "He said he didn't like to see young women doing such work as I was doing. 'Who will do it, then?' I asked. 'The men,' said he. 'Do you think we can leave it to them?' I asked. 'Perhaps not,' he admitted. 'But at least it could be left to older women.' 'They haven't the strength for it,' I told him, and then I gave him a notion of the number of miles I had ridden the day before in the street-car-it was nearly sixty, I believe. 'Are you sure it's worth it?' he asked. He had been listening to the complaint I was making against a young man who has, to my knowledge, completely destroyed the self-respect of five girls--and I've known him but a short time. You can make an estimate of the probable number of crimes of his if it amuses you. 'Don't you think it's worth while if that man is shut up where he can't do any more mischief?' I asked him. Of course he thought it was; but he was still shaking his head over me when I left him. He still thought I ought to be at home making tidies. I can't imagine that it ever occurred to him that I was a disinterested economist in trying to save myself from waste."

She laughed lightly in spite of her serious words.

"Anyway," she said, "I find this kind of life too amusing to resign. One of the settlement workers was complaining to me this morning about the inherent lack of morals among some of our children. It appears that the Harrigans--there are seven of them--commandeered some old clothes that had been sent in for charitable distribution. They poked around in the trunks when no one was watching and helped themselves to what they wanted. The next day they came to a party at the Settlement House togged up in their plunder. My friend reproved them, but they seemed to be impervious to her moral comments, so she went to the mother. 'Faith,' said Mrs. Harrigan, 'I tould them not to be bringing home trash like that. "It ain't worth carryin' away," says I to them.'"

About this time Kate was invited to become a resident of Hull House. She was touched and complimented, but, with a loyalty for which there was, perhaps, no demand, she remained faithful to her friends at the Caravansary. She was loath to take up her residence with a group which would have too much community of interest. The ladies at Mrs. Dennison's offered variety. Life was dramatizing itself for her there. In Honora and Marna and Mrs. Barsaloux and those quiet yet intelligent gentlewomen, Mrs. Goodrich and Mrs. Applegate, in the very servants whose pert individualism distressed the mid-Victorian Mrs. Dennison, Kate saw working those mysterious world forces concerning which she was so curious. The frequent futility of Nature's effort to throw to the top this hitherto unutilized feminine force was no less absorbing than the success which sometimes attended the impulsion. To the general and widespread convulsion, the observer could no more be oblivious than to an earthquake or a tidal wave.

CHAPTER VIII

Kate had not seen Lena Vroom for a long time, and she had indefinitely missed her without realizing it until one afternoon, as she was searching for something in her trunk, she came across a package of Lena's letters written to her while she was at Silvertree. That night at the table she asked if any one had seen Lena recently.

"Seen her?" echoed David Fulham. "I've seen the shadow of her blowing across the campus. She's working for her doctor's degree, like a lot of other silly women. She's living by herself somewhere, on crackers and cheese, no doubt."

"Would she really be so foolish?" cried Kate. "I know she's devoted to her work, but surely she has some sense of moderation."

"Not a bit of it," protested the scientist. "A person of mediocre attainments who gets the Ph.D. bee in her bonnet has no sense of any sort. I see them daily, men and women,--but women particularly,--stalking about the grounds and in and out of classes, like grotesque ghosts. They're staggering under a mental load too heavy for them, and actually it might be a physical load from its effects. They get lop-sided, I swear they do, and they acquire all sorts of miserable little personal habits that make them both pitiable and ridiculous. For my part, I believe the day will come when no woman will be permitted to try for the higher degrees till her brain has been scientifically tested and found to be adequate for the work."

"But as for Lena," said Kate, "I thought she was quite a wonder at her lessons."

"Up to a certain point," admitted Fulham, "I've no doubt she does very well. But she hasn't the capacity for higher work, and she'll be the last one to realize it. My advice to you, Miss Barrington, is to look up your friend and see what she is doing with herself. You haven't any of you an idea of the tragedies of the classroom, and I'll not tell them to you. But they're serious enough, take my word for it."

"Yes, do look her up, Kate," urged Honora.

"It's hard to manage anything extra during the day," said Kate. "I must go some evening."

"Perhaps Cousin Mary could go with you," suggested Honora. Honora threw a glance of affectionate admiration at her young cousin, who had blossomed out in a bewitching little frock of baby blue, and whose eyes reflected the color.

She was, indeed, an entrancing thing, was "Blue-eyed Mary." The tenderness of her lips, the softness of her complexion, the glamour of her glance increased day by day, and without apparent reason. She seemed to be more eloquent, with the sheer eloquence of womanly emotion. Everything that made her winning was intensified, as if Love, the Master, had touched to vividness what hitherto had been no more than a mere promise.

What was the secret of this exotic florescence? She went out only to University affairs with Honora or Kate, or to the city with Marna Cartan. Her interests appeared to be few; and she was neither a writer nor a receiver of letters. Altogether, the sources of that hidden joy which threw its enchantment over her were not to be guessed.

But what did it all matter? She was an exhilarating companion--and what a contrast to poor Lena! That night, lying in bed, Kate reproached herself for her neglect of her once so faithful friend. Lena might be going through some severe experience, alone and unaided. Kate determined to find out the truth, and as she had a half-holiday on Saturday, she started on her quest.

Lena, it transpired, had moved twice during the term and had neglected to register her latest address. So she was found only after much searching, and twilight was already gathering when Kate reached the dingy apartment in which Lena had secreted herself. It was a rear room up three flights of stairs, approached by a long, narrow corridor which the economical proprietor had left in darkness. Kate rapped softly at first; then, as no one answered, most sharply. She was on the point of going away when the door was opened a bare crack and the white, pinched face of Lena Vroom peered out.

"It's only Kate, Lena!" Then, as there was no response: "Aren't you going to let me in?"

Still Lena did not fling wide the door.

"Oh, Kate!" she said vaguely, in a voice that seemed to drift from a Maeterlinckian mist. "How are you?"

"Pretty sulky, thank you. Why don't you open the door, girl?"

At that Lena drew back; but she was obviously annoyed. Kate stepped into the bare, unkempt room. Remnants of a miserable makeshift meal were to be seen on a rickety cutting-table; the bed was unmade; and on the desk, in the center of the room, a drop-lamp with a leaking tube polluted the air. There was a formidable litter of papers on a great table, and before it stood a swivel chair where Lena Vroom had been sitting preparing for her degree.

Kate deliberately took this all in and then turned her gaze on her friend.

"What's the use, girl?" she demanded with more than her usual abruptness. "What are you doing it all for?"

Lena threw a haggard glance at her.

"We won't talk about that," she said in that remote, sunken voice. "I haven't the strength to discuss it. To be perfectly frank, Kate, you mustn't visit me now. You see, I'm studying night and day for the inquisition."

"The--"

"Yes, inquisition. You see, it isn't enough that my thesis should be finished. I can't get my degree without a last, terrible ordeal. Oh, Kate, you can't imagine what it is like! Girls who have been through it have told me. You are asked into a room where the most important members of the faculty are gathered. They sit about you in a semicircle and for hours they hurl questions at you, not necessarily questions relating to anything you have studied, but inquiries to test your general intelligence. It's a fearful experience."

She sank on her unmade cot, drawing a ragged sweater about her shoulders, and looked up at Kate with an almost furtive gaze. She always had been a small, meagre creature, but now she seemed positively shriveled. The pride and plenitude of womanhood were as far from her realization as they could be from a daughter of Eve. Sexless, stranded, broken before an undertaking too great for her, she sat there in the throes of a sudden, nervous chill. Then, after a moment or two, she began to weep and was rent and torn with long, shuddering sobs.

"I'm so afraid," she moaned. "Oh, Kate, I'm so terribly, terribly afraid! I know I'll fail."

Kate strangled down, "The best thing that could happen to you"; and said instead, "You aren't going about the thing in the best way to succeed."

"I've done all I could," moaned her friend. "I've only allowed myself four hours a night for sleep; and have hardly taken out time for meals. I've concentrated as it seems to me no one ever concentrated before."

"Oh, Lena, Lena!" Kate cried compassionately. "Can it really be that you have so little sense, after all? Oh, you poor little drowned rat, you." She bent over her, pulled the worn slippers from her feet, and thrust her beneath the covers.

"No, no!" protested Lena. "You mustn't, Kate! I've got to get at my books."

"Say another word and I'll throw them out of the window," cried Kate, really aroused. "Lie down there."

Lena began again to sob, but this time with helpless anger, for Kate looked like a grenadier as she towered there in the small room and it was easy to see that she meant to be obeyed. She explored Lena's cupboard for supplies, and found, after some searching, a can of soup and the inevitable crackers. She heated the soup, toasted the crackers, and forced Lena to eat. Then she extinguished the lamp, with its poisonous odor, and, wrapping herself in her cloak threw open the window and sat in the gloom, softly chatting about this and that. Lena made no coherent answers. She lay in sullen torment, casting tearful glances at her benevolent oppressor.

But Kate had set her will to conquer that of her friend and Lena's hysteric opposition was no match for it. Little by little the tense form beneath the blankets relaxed. Her stormily drawn breath became more even. At last she slept, which gave Kate an opportunity to slip out to buy a new tube for the lamp and adjust it properly. She felt quite safe in lighting it, for Lena lay in complete exhaustion, and she took the liberty of looking over the clothes which were bundled into an improvised closet on the back of the door. Everything was in wretched condition. Buttons and hooks were lacking; a heap of darning lay untouched; Lena's veil, with which she attempted to hide the ruin of her hat, was crumpled into the semblance of a rain-soaked cobweb; and her shoes had gone long without the reassurance of a good blacking.

Kate put some irons over the stove which served Lena as a cooking-range, and proceeded on a campaign of reconstruction. It was midnight when she finished, and she was weary and heartsick. The little, strained face on the pillow seemed to belong to one whom the furies were pursuing. Yet nothing was pursuing her save her own fanatical desire for a thing which, once obtained, would avail her nothing. She had not personality enough to meet life on terms which would allow her one iota of leadership. She was discountenanced by her inherent drabness: beaten by the limits of her capacity. When Kate had ordered the room,--scrupulously refraining from touching any of Lena's papers,--she opened the window and, putting the catch on the door, closed it softly behind her.

Kate's frequent visits to Lena, though brief, were none too welcome. Even the food she brought with her might better, in Lena's estimation, be dispensed with than that the all-absorbing reading and research should be interrupted. Finally Kate called one night to find Lena gone. She had taken her trunk and oil-stove and the overworked gas-lamp and had stolen away. To ferret her out would have been inexcusable.

"It shows how changed she is," Kate said to Honora. "Fancy the old-time Lena hiding from me!"

"You must think of her as having a run of fever, Kate. Whatever she does must be regarded as simply symptomatic," said Honora, understandingly. "She's really half-mad. David says the graduates are often like that--the feminine ones."

Kate tried to look at it in a philosophic way, but her heart yearned and ached over the poor, infatuated fugitive. The February convocation was drawing near, and with it Lena's dreaded day of examination. The night before its occurrence, the conversation at the Caravansary turned to the candidates for the honors.

"There are some who meet the quiz gallantly enough," David Fulham remarked. "But the majority certainly come like galley slaves scourged to their dungeon. Some of them would move a heart of stone with their sufferings. Honora, why don't you and Miss Barrington look up your friend Miss Vroom once more? She's probably needing you pretty badly."

"I don't mind being a special officer, Mr. Fulham," said Kate, "and it's my pride and pleasure to make child-beaters tremble and to arrest brawny fathers,--I make rather a specialty of six-foot ones,--but really I'm timid about going to Lena's again. She has given me to understand that she doesn't want me around, and I'm not enough of a pachyderm to get in the way of her arrows again."

But David Fulham couldn't take that view of it.

"She's not sane," he declared. "Couldn't be after such a course as she's been putting herself through. She needs help."

However, neither Kate nor Honora ventured to offer it. They spent the evening together in Honora's drawing-room. The hours passed more rapidly than they realized, and at midnight David came stamping in. His face was white.

"You haven't been to the laboratory, David?" reproached his wife. "Really, you mustn't. I thought it was agreed between us that we'd act like civilized householders in the evening." She was regarding him with an expression of affectionate reproof.

"I've been doing laboratory work," he said shortly, "but it wasn't in the chemical laboratory. Wickersham and I hunted up your friend--and we found her in a state of collapse."

"No!" cried Kate, starting to her feet.

"I told you, didn't I?" returned David. "Don't I know them, the geese? We had to break in her door, and there she was sitting at her study-table, staring at her books and seeing nothing. She couldn't talk to us--had a temporary attack of severe aphasia, I suppose. Wickersham said he'd been anxious about her for weeks--she's been specializing with him, you know."

"What did you do with her?" demanded Honora.

"Bundled her up in her outside garments and dragged her out of doors between us and made her walk. She could hardly stand at first. We had to hold her up. But we kept right on hustling her along, and after a time when the fresh air and exercise had got in their work, she could find the right word when she tried to speak to us. Then we took her to a restaurant and ordered a beefsteak and some other things. She wanted to go back to her room--said she had more studying to do; but we made it clear to her at last that it wasn't any use,--that she'd have to stand or fall on what she had. She promised us she wouldn't look at a book, but would go to bed and sleep, and anybody who has the hardihood to wish that she wins her degree may pray for a good night for her."

Honora was looking at her husband with a wide, shining gaze.

"How did you come to go to her, David?" she asked admiringly. "She wasn't in any of your classes."

"Now, don't try to make out that I'm benevolent, Honora," Fulham said petulantly. "I went because I happened to meet Wickersham on the Midway. She's been hiding, but he had searched her out and appealed to me to go with him. What I did was at his request."

"But she'll be refreshed in the morning," said Honora. "She'll come out all right, won't she?"

"How do I know?" demanded Fulham. "I suppose she'll feel like a man going to execution when she enters that council-room. Maybe she'll stand up to it and maybe she'll not. She'll spend as much nervous energy on the experience as would carry her through months of sane, reasonable living in the place she ought to be in--that is to say, in a millinery store or some plain man's kitchen."

"Oh, David!" said Honora with gentle wifely reproach.

But Fulham was making no apologies.

"If we men ill-treated women as they ill-treat themselves," he said, "we'd be called brutes of the worst sort."

"Of course!" cried Kate. "A person may have some right to ill-treat himself, but he never has any right to ill-treat another."

"If we hitched her up to a plough," went on Fulham, not heeding, "we shouldn't be overtaxing her physical strength any more than she overtaxes her mental strength when she tries--the ordinary woman, I mean, like Miss Vroom--to keep up to the pace set by men of first-rate caliber."

He went up to bed on this, still disturbed, and Honora and Kate, much depressed, talked the matter over. But they reached no conclusion. They wanted to go around the next morning and help Lena,--get her breakfast and see that she was properly dressed,--but they knew they would be unwelcome. Later they heard that she had come through the ordeal after a fashion. She had given indications of tremendous research. But her eyes, Wickersham told Kate privately, looked like diseased oysters, and it was easy to see that she was on the point of collapse.

Kate saw nothing of her until the day of convocation, though she tried several times to get into communication with her. There must have been quite two hundred figures in the line that wound before the President and the other dignitaries to receive their diplomas; and the great hall was thronged with interested spectators. Kate could have thrilled with pride of her *alma mater* had not her heart been torn with sympathy for her friend whose emaciated figure looked more pathetic than ever before. Now and then a spasmodic movement shook her, causing her head to quiver like one with the palsy and her hands to make futile gestures. And although she was the most touching and the least joyous of those who went forward to victory, she was not, after all, so very exceptional.

Kate could not help noticing how jaded and how spent were many of the candidates for the higher degrees. They seemed to move in a tense dream, their eyes turning neither to right nor left, and the whole of them bent on the one idea of their dear achievement. Although there were some stirring figures among them,--men and women who seemed to have come into the noble heritage which had been awaiting them,--there were more who looked depleted and unfit. It grew on Kate, how superfluous scholarship was when superimposed on a feeble personality. The colleges could not make a man, try as they might. They could add to the capacity of an endowed and adventurous individual, but for the inept, the diffident, their learning availed nothing. They could cram bewildered heads with facts and theories, but they could not hold the mediocre back from their inevitable anticlimax.

"A learned derelict is no better than any other kind," mused Kate compassionately. She resolved that now, at last, she would command Lena's obedience. She would compel her to take a vacation,--would find out what kind of a future she had planned. She would surround her with small, friendly offices; would help her to fit herself out in new garments, and would talk over ways and means with her.

She went the next day to the room where Lena's compassionate professors had found her that night of dread and terror before her examination. But she had disappeared again, and the landlady could give no information concerning her.

CHAPTER IX

The day was set. Marna was to sing. It seemed to the little group of friends as if the whole city palpitated with the fact. At any rate, the Caravansary did so. They talked of little else, and Mary Morrison wept for envy. Not that it was mean envy. Her weeping was a sort of tribute, and Marna felt it to be so.

"You're going to be wonderful," Mary sobbed. "The rest of us are merely young, or just women, or men. We can't be anything more no matter how hard we try, though we keep feeling as if we were something more. But you're going to SING! Oh, Marna!"

Time wore on, and Marna grew hectic with anticipation. Her lips were too red, her breath came too quickly; she intensified herself; and she practiced her quivering, fitful, passionate songs with religious devotion. So many things centered around the girl that it was no wonder that she began to feel a disproportionate sense of responsibility. All of her friends were taking it for granted that she would make a success.

Mrs. Barsaloux was giving a supper at the Blackstone after the performance. The opera people were coming and a number of other distinguished ones; and Marna was having a frock made of the color of a gold-of-Ophir rose satin which was to clothe her like sunshine. Honora brought out a necklace of yellow opals whimsically fashioned.

"I no longer use such things, child," she said with a touch of emotion. "And I want you to wear them with your yellow dress."

"Why, they're like drops of water with the sun in them!" cried Marna. "How good you all are to me! I can't imagine why."

When the great night came, the audience left something to be desired, both as to numbers and fashion. Although Marna's appearance had been well advertised, it was evident that the public preferred to listen to the great stars. But the house was full enough and enthusiastic enough to awaken in the little Irish girl's breast that form of elation which masks as self-obliteration, and which is the fuel that feeds the fires of art.

Kate had gone with the Fulhams and they, with Blue-eyed Mary and Dr. von Shierbrand, sat together in the box which Mrs. Barsaloux had given them, and where, from time to time, she joined them. But chiefly she hovered around Marna in that dim vast world back of the curtain.

They said of Marna afterward that she was like a spirit. She seemed less and more than a woman, an evanescent essence of feminine delight. Her laughter, her tears, her swift emotions were all as something held for a moment before the eye and snatched away, to leave but the wavering eidolon of their loveliness. She sang with a young Italian who responded exquisitely to the swift, bright, unsubstantial beauty of her acting, and whom she seemed fairly to bathe in the amber loveliness of her voice.

Kate, quivering for her, seeming indefinably to be a part of her, suffering at the hesitancies of the audience and shaken with their approval, was glad when it was all over. She hastened out to be with the crowd and to hear what they were saying. They were warm in their praise, but Kate was dissatisfied. She longed for something more emphatic--some excess of acclaim. She wondered if they were waiting for more authoritative audiences to set the stamp of approval on Marna. It did not occur to her that they had found the performance too opalescent and elusive.

Kate wondered if the girl would feel that anything had been missing, but Marna seemed to be basking in the happiness of the hour. The great German prima donna had kissed her with tears in her eyes; the French baritone had spoken his compliments with convincing ardor; dozens had crowded about her with congratulations; and now, at the head of the glittering table in an opulent room, the little descendant of minstrels sat and smiled upon her friends. A gilded crown of laurel leaves rested on her dark hair; her white neck arose delicately from the yellowed lace and the shining silk; the sunny opals rested upon her shoulders.

"I drink," cried the French baritone, "to a voice of honey and an ivory throat."

"To a great career," supplemented David Fulham.

"And happiness," Kate broke in, standing with the others and forgetting to be abashed by the presence of so many. Then she called to Marna:--

"I was afraid they would leave out happiness."

Kate might have been the belated fairy godmother who brought this gift in the nick of time. Those at the table smiled at her indulgently,--she was so eager, so young, so almost fierce. She had dressed herself in white without frill or decoration, and the clinging folds of her gown draped her like a slender, chaste statue. She wore no jewels,--she had none, indeed,-- and her dark coiled hair in no way disguised the shape of her fine head.

The elaborate Polish contralto across from her, splendid as a mediaeval queen, threw Kate's simplicity into sharp contrast. Marna turned adoring eyes upon her; Mrs. Barsaloux, that inveterate encourager of genius, grieved that the girl had no specialty for her to foster; the foreigners paid her frank tribute, and there was no question but that the appraisement upon her that night was high.

As for Mama's happiness, for which Kate had put in her stipulation, it was coming post-haste, though by a circuitous road.

Mrs. Dennison, who had received tickets from Marna, and who had begged her nephew, George Fitzgerald, to act as her escort, was, in her fashion, too, wondering about the question of happiness for the girl. She was an old-fashioned creature, mid-Victorian in her sincerity. She had kissed one man and one only, and him had she married, and sorrowing over her childless estate she had become, when she laid her husband in his grave, "a widow indeed." Her abundant affection, disused by this accident of fate, had spent itself in warm friendships, and in her devotion to her dead sister's child. She had worked for him till the silver came into her hair; had sent him through his classical course and through the medical college, and the day when she saw him win his title of doctor of medicine was the richest one of her middle life.

He sat beside her now, strangely pale and disturbed. The opera, she was sorry to note, had not interested him as she had expected it would. He had, oddly enough, been reluctant to accompany her, and, as she was accustomed to his quick devotion, this distressed her not a little. Was he growing tired of her? Was he ashamed to be seen at the opera with a quiet woman in widow's dress, a touch shabby? Was her much-tired heart to have a last cruel blow dealt it? Accustomed to rather somber pathways of thought, she could not escape this one; yet she loyally endeavored to turn from it, and from time to time she stole a look at the stern, pale face beside her to discover, if she could, what had robbed him of his good cheer.

For he had been a happy boy. His high spirits had constituted a large part of his attraction for her. When he had come to her orphaned, it had been with warm gratitude in his heart, and with the expectation of being loved. As he grew older, that policy of life had become accentuated. He was expectant in all that he did. His temperamental friendliness had carried him through college, winning for him a warm group of friends and the genuine regard of his professors. It was helping him to make his way in the place he had chosen for his field of action. He had not gone into the more fashionable part of town, but far over on the West Side, where the slovenliness of the central part of the city shambles into a community of parks and boulevards, crude among their young trees surrounded by neat, self-respecting apartment houses. Such communities are to be found in all American cities; communities which set little store by fashion, which prize education (always providing it does not prove exotic and breed genius or any form of disturbing beauty), live within their incomes and cultivate the manifest virtues. The environment suited George Fitzgerald. He had an honest soul without a bohemian impulse in him. He recognized himself as being middle-class, and he was proud and glad of it. He liked to be among people who kept their feet on the earth--people whose yea was yea and whose nay was nay. What was Celtic in him could do no more for him than lend a touch of almost flaring optimism to the Puritan integrity of his character.

Sundays, as a matter of habit, and occasionally on other days, he was his aunt's guest at the Caravansary. The intellectual coöperatives there liked him, as indeed everybody did, everywhere. Invariably Mrs. Dennison was told after his departure that she was a fortunate woman to have such an adopted son. Yet Fitzgerald knew very well that he was unable to be completely himself among his aunt's patrons. Their conversation was too glancing; they too often said what they did not mean, for mere conversation's sake; they played with ideas, tossing them about like juggler's balls; and they attached importance to matters which seemed to him of little account.

Of late he had been going to his aunt's but seldom, and he had stayed away because he wanted, above all things in the world, to go. It had become an agony to go--an anguish to absent himself. Which being interpreted, means that he was in love. And whom should he love but Marna? Why should any man trouble himself to love another woman when this glancing, flashing, singing bird was winging it through the blue? Were any other lips so tender, so tremulous, so arched, so sweet? The breath that came between them was perfumed with health; the little rows of gleaming teeth were indescribably provocative. Actually, the little red tongue itself seemed to fold itself upward, at the edges, like a tender leaf. As for her nostrils, they were delicately flaring like those of some wood creature, and fashioned for the enjoyment of odorous banquets undreamed of by duller beings. Her eyes, like pools in shade, breathing mystery and dreams, got between him and his sleep and held him intoxicated in his bed.

Yes, that was Marna as she looked to the eye of love. She was made for one man's love and nothing else, yet she was about to become the well-loved of the great world! She was not for him--was not made for a man of his mould. She had flashed from obscurity to something rich and plenteous, obviously the child of Destiny--a little princess waiting for her crown. He had not even talked to her many times, and she had no notion that when she entered the room he trembled; and that when she spoke to him and turned the swimming loveliness of her eyes upon him, he had trouble to keep his own from filling with tears.

And this was the night of her dedication to the world; the world was seating her upon her throne, acclaiming her coronation. There was nothing for him but to go on through an interminably long life, bearing a brave front and hiding his wound.

He loathed the incoherent music; detested the conductor; despised the orchestra; felt murderous toward the Italian tenor; and could have slain the man who wrote the opera, since it made his bright girl a target for praise and blame. He feared his aunt's scrutiny, for she had sharp perceptions, and he could have endured anything better than that she should spy upon his sacred pain. So he sat by her side, passionately solitary amid a crowd and longing to hide himself from the society of all men.

But he must be distrait, indeed, if he could forget the claim his good aunt had upon him. He knew how she loved gayety; and her daily life offered her little save labor and monotony.

"Supper next," he said with forced cheerfulness as they came out of the opera-house together. "I'll do the ordering. You'll enjoy a meal for once which is served independently of you."

He tried to talk about this and that as they made their way on to a glaring below-stairs restaurant, where after-theater folk gathered. The showy company jarred hideously on Fitzgerald, yet gave him a chance to save his face by pretending to watch it. He could tell his aunt who some of the people were, and she would transfer her curiosity from him to them.

"They'll be having a glorious time at Miss Cartan's supper," mused Mrs. Dennison. "How she shines, doesn't she, George? And when you think of her beginnings there on that Wisconsin farm, isn't it astonishing?"

"Those weren't her beginnings, I fancy," George said, venturing to taste of discussion concerning her as a brandy-lover may smell a glass he swears he will not drink. "Her beginnings were very long ago. She's a Celt, and she has the witchery of the Celts. How I'd love to hear her recite some of the new Irish poems!"

"She'd do it beautifully, George. She does everything beautifully. If I'd had a daughter like that, boy, what a different thing my life would be! Or if you were to give me--"

George clicked his ice sharply in his glass. "See," he said, "there's Hackett coming in--Hackett the actor. Handsome devil, isn't he?"

"Don't use that tone, George," said his aunt reprovingly. "Handsome devil, indeed! He's a good-looking man. Can't you say that in a proper way? I don't want you to be sporty in your talk, George. I always tried when you were a little boy to keep you from talking foolishly."

"Oh, there's no danger of my being foolish," he said. "I'm as staid and dull as ever you could wish me to be!"

For the first time in her life she found him bitter, but she had the sense at last to keep silent. His eyes were full of pain, and as he looked about the crowded room with its suggestions of indulgent living, she saw something in his face leap to meet it--something that seemed to repudiate the ideals she had passed on to him. Involuntarily, Anne Dennison reached out her firm warm hand and laid it on the quivering one of her boy.

"A new thought has just come to you!" she said softly. "Before you were through with your boast, lad, your temptation came. I saw it. Are you lonely, George? Are you wanting something that Aunt Anne can give you? Won't you speak out to me?"

He drew his hand away from hers.

"No one in the world can give me what I want," he said painfully. "Forgive me, auntie; and let's talk of other things."

He had pushed her back into that lonely place where the old often must stand, and she shivered a little as if a cold wind blew over her. He saw it and bent toward her contritely.

"You must help me," he said. "I am very unhappy. I suppose almost everybody has been unhappy like this sometime. Just bear with me, Aunt Anne, dear, and help me to forget for an hour or two."

Anne Dennison regarded him understandingly.

"Here comes our lobster," she said, "and while we eat it, I'll tell you the story of the first time I ever ate at a restaurant."

He nodded gratefully. After all, while she lived, he could not be utterly bereft.

CHAPTER X

He had taken her home and was leaving, when a carriage passed him. He could hear the voices of the occupants--the brisk accents of Mrs. Barsaloux, and the slow, honey-rich tones of Marna. He had never dreamed that he could do such a thing, but he ran forward with an almost frantic desire to rest his eyes upon the girl's face, and he was beside the curb when the carriage drew up at the door of the house where Mrs. Barsaloux and Marna lodged. He flung open the door in spite of the protests of the driver, who was not sure of his right to offer such a service, and held out his hand to Mrs. Barsaloux. That lady accepted his politeness graciously, and, weary and abstracted, moved at once toward the house-steps, searching meantime for her key. Fitzgerald had fifteen seconds alone with Marna. She stood half-poised upon the carriage-steps, her hand in his, their eyes almost on a level. Then he said an impossible and insane thing. It was wrung out of his misery, out of his knowledge of her loveliness.

"I've lost you!" he whispered. "Do you know that to-night ended my happiness?"

Mama's lips parted delicately; her eyes widened; her swift Celtic spirit encompassed his grief.

"Oh!" she breathed. "Don't speak so! Don't spoil my beautiful time!"

"Not I," he retorted sharply, speaking aloud this time. "Far be it from me! Good-bye."

Mrs. Barsaloux heard him vaguely above the jangling of coins and keys and the rushing of a distant train.

"You're not going to leave town, are you, Dr. Fitzgerald?" she inquired casually. "I thought your good-bye had a final accent to it."

She was laughing in her easy way, quite unconscious of what was taking place. She had made an art of laughing, and it carried her and others over many difficult places. But for once it was powerless to lessen the emotional strain. Mysteriously, Fitzgerald and Marna were experiencing a sweet torment in their parting. It was not that she loved him or had thought of him in that way at all. She had seen him often and had liked his hearty ways, his gay spirits, and his fine upstanding figure, but he had been as one who passed by with salutations. Now, suddenly, she was conscious that he was a man to be desired. She saw his wistful eyes, his avid lips, his great shoulders. The woman in her awoke to a knowledge of her needs. Upon such a shoulder might a woman weep, from such eyes might a woman gather dreams; to allay such torment as his might a woman give all she had to give. It was incoherent, mad, but not unmeaning. It had, indeed, the ultimate meaning.

He said nothing more; she spoke no word. Each knew they would meet on the morrow.

The next night, Kate Barrington, making her way swiftly down the Midway in a misty gloom, saw the little figure of Marna Cartan fluttering before her. It was too early for dinner, and Kate guessed that Marna was on her way to pay her a visit--a not rare occurrence these last few weeks. She called to her, and Marna waited, turning her face for a moment to the mist-bearing wind.

"I was going to you," she said breathlessly.

"So I imagined, bright one."

"Are you tired, Kate, mavourneen?"

"A little. It's been a hard day. I don't see why my heart isn't broken, considering the things I see and hear, Marna! I don't so much mind about the grown-ups. If they succeed in making a mess of things, why, they can take the consequences. But the kiddies--they're the ones that torment me. Try as I can to harden myself, and to say that after I've done my utmost my responsibility ends, I can't get them off my mind. But what's on *your* mind, bright one?"

"Oh, Kate, so much! But wait till we get to the house. It's not a thing to shriek out here on the street."

The wind swept around the corner, buffeting them, and Kate drew Marna's arm in her own and fairly bore the little creature along with her. They entered the silent house, groped through the darkened hall and up the stairs to Kate's own room.

"Honora isn't home, I fancy," she said, in apology for the pervading desolation. "She stays late at the laboratory these nights. She says she's on the verge of a wonderful discovery. It's something she and David have been working out together, but she's been making some experiments in secret, with which she means to surprise David. Of course she'll give all the credit to him--that's her policy. She's his helpmate, she says, nothing more."

"But the babies?" asked Marna with that naïveté characteristic of her. "Where are they?"

"Up in the nursery at the top of the house. It will be light and warm there, I think. Honora had a fireplace put in so that it would be cheerful. I always feel sure it's pleasant up there, however forbidding the rest of the house may look."

"Mary has made a great difference with it since she came, hasn't she? Of course Honora couldn't do the wonderful things she's doing and be fussing around the house all the time. Still, she might train her servants, mightn't she?"

"Well, there aren't really any to train," said Kate. "There's Mrs. Hays, the nurse, a very good woman, but as we take our meals out, and are all so independent, there's no one else required, except occasionally. Honora wouldn't think of such an extravagance as a parlor maid. We're a community of working folk, you see."

Marna had been lighting the candles which Kate usually kept for company; and, moreover, since there was kindling at hand, she laid a fire and touched a match to it.

"I must have it look homey, Kate--for reasons."

"Do whatever it suits you to do, child."

"But can I tell you what it suits me to do, Kate?"

"How do I know? Are you referring to visible things or talking in parables? There's something very eerie about you to-night, Marna. Your eyes look phosphorescent. What's been happening to you? Is it the glory of last night that's over you yet?"

"No, not that. It's--it's a new glory, Kate."

"A new glory, is it? Since last night? Tell me, then."

Kate flung her long body into a Morris chair and prepared to listen. Marna looked about her as if seeking a chair to satisfy her whim, and, finding none, sank upon the floor before the blaze. She leaned back, resting on one slight arm, and turned her dream-haunted face glowing amid its dark maze of hair, till her eyes could hold those of her friend.

"Oh, Kate!" she breathed, and made her great confession in those two words.

"A man!" cried Kate, alarmed. "Now!"

"Now! Last night. And to-day. It was like lightning out of a clear sky. I've seen him often, and now I remember it always warmed me to see him, and made me feel that I wasn't alone. For a long time, I believe, I've been counting him in, and being happier because he was near. But I didn't realize it at all--till last night."

"You saw him after the opera?"

"Only for half a minute, at the door of my house. We only said a word or two. He whispered he had lost me--that I had killed him. Oh, I don't remember what he said. But we looked straight at each other. I didn't sleep all night, and when I lay awake I tried to think of the wonderful fact that I had made my debut, and that it wasn't a failure, at any rate. But I couldn't think about that, or about my career. I couldn't hold to anything but the look in his eyes and the fact that I was to see him to-day. Not that he said so. But we both knew. Why, we couldn't have lived if we hadn't seen each other to-day."

"And you did?"

"Oh, we did. He called me up on the telephone about two o'clock, and said he had waited as long as he could, and that he'd been walking the floor, not daring to ring till he was sure that I'd rested enough after last night. So I told him to come, and he must have been just around the corner, for he was there in a minute. I wanted him to come in and sit down, but he said he didn't believe a house could hold such audacity as his. So we went out on the street. It was cold and bleak. The Midway was a long, gray blankness. I felt afraid of it, actually. All the world looked forbidding to me--except just the little place where I walked with him. It was as if there were a little warm beautiful radius in which we could keep together, and live for each other, and comfort each other, and keep harm away."

"Oh, Marna! And you, with a career before you! What do you mean to do?"

"I don't know what to do. We don't either of us know what to do. He says he'll go mad with me on the stage, wearing myself out, the object of the jealousy of other women and of love-making from the men. He--says it's a profanation. I tried to tell him it couldn't be a profanation to serve art; but,

Kate, he didn't seem to know what I meant. He has such different standards. He wanted to know what I was going to do when I was old. He said I'd have no real home, and no haven of love; and that I'd better be the queen of his home as long as I lived than to rule it a little while there on the stage and then--be forgotten. Oh, it isn't what he said that counts. All that sounds flat enough as I repeat it. It's the wonder of being with some one that loves you like that and of feeling that there are two of you who belong--"

"How do you know you belong?" asked Kate with sharp good sense. "Why, bright one, you've been swept off your feet by mere--forgive me--by mere sex."

That glint of the eyes which Kate called Celtic flashed from Marna.

"Mere sex!" she repeated. "Mere sex! You're not trying to belittle that, are you? Why, Kate, that's the beginning and the end of things. What I've always liked about you is that you look big facts in the face and aren't afraid of truth. Sex! Why, that's home and happiness and all a woman really cares for, isn't it?"

"No, it isn't all she cares for," declared Kate valiantly. "She cares for a great many other things. And when I said mere sex I was trying to put it politely. Is it really home and lifelong devotion that you two are thinking about, or are you just drunk with youth and--well, with infatuation?"

Marna turned from her to the fire.

"Kate," she said, "I don't know what you call it, but when I looked in his eyes I felt as if I had just seen the world for the first time. I have liked to live, of course, and to study, and it was tremendously stirring, singing there before all those people. But, honestly, I can see it would lead nowhere. A few years of faint celebrity, an empty heart, a homeless life--then weariness. Oh, I know it. I have a trick of seeing things. Oh, he's the man for me, Kate. I realized it the moment he pointed it out. We could not be mistaken. I shall love him forever and he'll love me just as I love him."

"By the way," said Kate, "who is he? Someone from the opera company?"

"Who is he? Why, he's George Fitzgerald, of course."

"Mrs. Dennison's nephew?"

"Certainly. Who else should it be?"

"Why, he's a pleasant enough young man--very cheerful and quite intelligent--but, Marna--"

Marna leaped to her feet.

"You're not in a position to pass judgment upon him, Kate. How can you know what a wonderful soul he has? Why, there's no one so brave, or so humble, or so sweet, or with such a worship for women--"

"For you, you mean."

"Of course I mean for me. You don't suppose I'd endure it to have him worshiping anybody else, do you? Oh, it's no use protesting. I only hope that Mrs. Barsaloux won't."

"Yes, doesn't that give you pause? Think of all Mrs. Barsaloux has done for you; and she did it with the understanding that you were to go on the stage. She was going to get her reward in the contribution you made to art."

Marna burst into rippling laughter.

"I'll give her something better than art, Kate Crosspatch. I'll give her a home--and I'll name my first girl after her."

"Marna!" gasped Kate. "You do go pretty fast for a little thing."

"Oh, I'm Irish," laughed Marna. "We Irish are a very old people. We always knew that if you loved a man, you had to have him or die, and that if you had him, you'd love to see the look of him coming out in your sons and daughters."

Suddenly the look of almost infantile blitheness left her face. The sadness which is inherent in the Irish countenance spread over it, like sudden mist over a landscape. The ancient brooding aspect of the Celts was upon her.

"Yes," she repeated, "we Irish are very old, and there is nothing about life--or death--that we do not know."

Kate was not quite sure what she meant, but with a sudden impulse she held out her arms to the girl, who, with a low cry, fled to them. Then her bright bravery melted in a torrent of tears.

CHAPTER XI

They had met like flame and wind. It was irrational and wonderful and conclusive. But after all, it might not have come to quite so swift a climax if Marna, following Kate's advice, had not confided the whole thing to Mrs. Barsaloux.

Now, Mrs. Barsaloux was a kind woman, and one with plenty of sentiment in her composition. But she believed that there were times when Love should not be given the lead. Naturally, it seemed to her that this was one of them. She had spent much money upon the education of this girl whom she had "assumed," as Marna sometimes playfully put it. Nothing but her large, active, and perhaps interfering benevolence and Mama's winning and inexplicable charm held the two together, and the very slightness of their relationship placed them under peculiar obligations to each other.

"It's ungrateful of you," Mrs. Barsaloux explained, "manifestly ungrateful! It's your rôle to love nothing but your career." She was not stern, merely argumentative.

"But didn't you expect me ever to love any one?" queried Marna.

Mrs. Barsaloux contemplated a face and figure made for love from the beginning, and delicately ripened for it, like a peach in the sun.

"But you could have waited, my dear girl. There's time for both the love and the career."

Marna shook her head slowly.

"George says there isn't," she answered with an irritating sweetness. "He says I'm not to go on the stage at all. He says--"

"Don't 'he says' me like that, Marna," cried her friend. "It sounds too unutterably silly. Here you are with a beautiful talent--every one agrees about that--and a chance to develop it. I've made many sacrifices to give you that chance. Very well; you've had your trial before the public. You've made good. You could repay yourself and me for all that has been involved in your development, and you meet a man and come smiling to me and say that we're to throw the whole thing over because 'he says' to."

Marna made no answer at all, but Mrs. Barsaloux saw her settle down in the deep chair in which she was sitting as if to huddle away from the storm about to break over her.

"She isn't going to offer any resistance," thought the distressed patron with dismay. "Her mind is completely made up and she's just crouching down to wait till I'm through with my private little hurricane."

So, indeed, it proved. Mrs. Barsaloux felt she had the right to say much, and she said it. Marna may or may not have listened. She sat shivering and smiling in her chair, and when it was fit for her to excuse herself, she did, and walked out bravely; but Mrs. Barsaloux noticed that she tottered a little as she reached the door. She did not go to her aid, however.

"It's an infatuation," she concluded. "I must treat her as if she had a violent disease and take care of her. When people are delirious they must be protected against themselves. It's a delirium with her, and the best thing I can do is to run off to New York with her. She can make her next appearance when the opera company gets there. I'll arrange it this afternoon."

She refrained from telling Marna of her plans, but she went straight to the city and talked over the situation with her friend the impresario. He seemed anything but depressed. On the contrary, he was excited--even exalted.

"Spirit her away, madam," he advised. "Of course she will miss her lover horribly, and that will be the best thing that can happen to her. Why did not the public rise to her the other night? Not because she could not sing: far from it. If a nightingale sings, then Miss Cartan does. But she left her audience a little cold. Let us face the facts. You saw it. We all saw it. And why? Because she was too happy, madam; too complaisant; too uninstructed in the emotions. Now it will be different. We will take her away; we will be patient with her while she suffers; afterward she will bless us, for she will have discovered the secret of the artist, and then when she opens her little silver throat we shall have SONG."

Mrs. Barsaloux, with many compunctions, and with some pangs of pure motherly sympathy, nevertheless agreed.

"If only he had been a man above the average," she said, as she tearfully parted from the great man, "perhaps it would not have mattered so much."

The impresario lifted his eyebrows and his mustaches at the same time and assumed the aspect of a benevolent Mephistopheles.

"The variety of man, madam," he said sententiously, "makes no manner of difference. It is the tumult in Miss Marna's soul which I hope we shall be able to utilize"--he interrupted himself with a smile and a bow as he opened the door for his departing friend--"for the purposes of art."

Mrs. Barsaloux sat in the middle of her taxi seat all the way home, and saw neither street, edifice, nor human being. She was looking back into her own busy, confused, and frustrated life, and was remembering certain things which she had believed were buried deep. Her heart misgave her horribly. Yet to hand over this bright singing bird, so exquisite, so rare, so fitted for purposes of exposition, to the keeping of a mere male being of unfortunate contiguity, to permit him to carry her into the seclusion of an ordinary home to wait on him and regulate her life according to his whim, was really too fantastic for consideration. So she put her memories and her tendernesses out of sight and walked up the stairs with purpose in her tread.

She meant to "have it out" with the girl, who was, she believed, reasonable enough after all.

"She's been without her mother for so long," she mused, "that it's no wonder she's lacking in self-control. I must have the firmness that a mother would have toward her. It would be the height of cruelty to let her have her own way in this."

If the two could have met at that moment, it would have changed the course of both their lives. But a trifle had intervened. Marna Cartan had gone walking; and she never came back. Only, the next day, radiantly beautiful, with fresh flowers in her hands, Marna Fitzgerald came running in begging to be forgiven. She tried to carry the situation with her impetuosity. She was laughing, crying, pleading. She got close to her old friend as if she would enwrap her in her influence. She had the veritable aspect of the bride. Whatever others might think regarding her lost career, it was evident that she believed the great hour had just struck for her. Her husband was with her.

"Haven't you any apology to make, sir?" poor Mrs. Barsaloux cried to him. He looked matter-of-fact, she thought, and as if he ought to be able to take a reasonable view of things. But she had misjudged. Perhaps it was his plain, everyday, commercial garments which deceived her and made her think him open to week-day arguments; for at that moment he was really a knight of romance, and at Mrs. Barsaloux's question his eyes gleamed with unsuspected fires.

"Who could be so foolish as to apologize for happiness like ours?" he demanded.

"Aren't you going to forgive us, dear?" pleaded Marna.

But Mrs. Barsaloux couldn't quite stand that.

"You sound like an old English comedy, Marna," she said impatiently. "You're of age; I'm no relation to you; you've a perfect right to be married. Better take advantage of being here to pack your things. You'll need them."

"You mean that I'm not expected to come here again, *tante*?"

"I shall sail for France in a week," said Mrs. Barsaloux wearily.

"For France, *tante*? When did you decide?"

"This minute," said the lady, and gave the married lovers to understand that the interview was at an end.

Marna went weeping down the street, holding on to her George's arm.

"If she'd been Irish, she'd have cursed me," she sobbed, "and then I'd have had something to go on, so to speak. Perhaps I could have got her to take it off me in time. But what are you going to do with a snubbing like that?"

"Oh, leave it for the Arctic explorers to explain. They're used to being in below-zero temperature," George said with a troubled laugh. "I'm sure I can't waste any time thinking about a woman who could stand out against you, Marna, the way you are this day, and the way you're looking."

"But, George, she thinks I'm a monster."

"Then there's something wrong with her zoology. You're an--"

"Don't call me an angel, dear, whatever you do! There are some things I hate to be called--they're so insipid. If any one called me an angel I'd know he didn't appreciate me. Come, let's go to Kate's. She's my court of last appeal. If Kate can't forgive me, I'll know I've done wrong."

Kate was never to forget that night. She had come in from a day of difficult and sordid work. For once, the purpose back of all her toil among the people there in the great mill town was lost sight of in the sheer repulsiveness of the tasks she had had to perform. The pathos of their temptations, the terrific disadvantages under which they labored, their gray tragedies, had some way lost their import. She was merely a dreadfully fagged woman, disgusted with evil, with dirt and poverty. She was at outs with her world and impatient with the suffering involved in the mere living of life.

Moreover, when she had come into the house, she had found it dark as usual. The furnace was down, and her own room was cold. But she had set her teeth together, determined not to give way to depression, and had made her rather severe toilet for dinner when word was brought to her by the children's nurse that Dr. and Mrs. Fitzgerald desired to see her. For a moment she could not comprehend what that might mean; then the truth assailed her, took her by the hand, and ran her down the stairs into Mama's arms.

"But it's outrageous," she cried, hugging Marna to her. "How could you be so willful?"

"It's glorious," retorted Marna. "And if I ever was going to be willful, now's the time."

"Right you are," broke in George. "What does Stevenson say about that? 'Youth is the time to be up and doing.' You're not going to be severe with us, Miss Barrington? We've been counting on you."

"Have you?" inquired Kate, putting Marna aside and taking her husband by the hand. "Well, you are your own justification, you two. But haven't you been ungrateful?"

Marna startled her by a bit of Dionysian philosophy.

"Is it ungrateful to be happy?" she demanded. "Would anybody have been in the right who asked us to be unhappy? Why don't you call us brave? Do you imagine it isn't difficult to have people we love disapproving of us? But you know yourself, Kate, if we'd waited forty-eight hours, I'd have been dragged off to live with my career."

She laughed brightly, sinking back in her chair and throwing wide her coat. Kate looked at her appraisingly, and warmed in the doing of it.

"You don't look as if you were devoted to a career, she admitted.

"Oh," sighed Fitzgerald, "I only just barely got her in time!"

"And now what do you propose doing?"

"Why, to-morrow we shall look for a place to live--for a home."

"Do you mean a flat?" asked Kate with a flick of satire.

"A flat, or anything. It doesn't matter much what."

"Or where?"

"It will be on the West Side," said the matter-of-fact Fitzgerald.

"And who'll keep house for you? Must you find servants?"

"Why, Kate, we're dreadfully poor," cried Marna excitedly, as if poverty were a mere adventure. "Didn't you know that? I shall do my own work."

"Oh, we've both got to work," added Fitzgerald.

He didn't say he was sorry Marna had to slave with her little white hands, or that he realized that he was doing a bold--perhaps an impious--thing in snatching a woman from her service to art to go into service for him. Evidently he didn't think that way. Neither minded any sacrifice apparently. The whole of it was, they were together. Suddenly, they seemed to forget Kate. They stood gazing at each other as if their sense of possession overwhelmed them. Kate felt something like angry resentment stir in her. How dared they, when she was so alone, so weary, so homeless?

"Will you stay to dinner with me?" she asked with something like asperity.

"To dinner?" they murmured in vague chorus. "No, thanks."

"But where do you intend to have dinner?"

"We--we haven't thought," confessed Marna.

"Oh, anywhere," declared Fitzgerald.

Marna rose and her husband buttoned her coat about her.

They smiled at Kate seraphically, and she saw that they wanted to be alone, and that it made little difference to them whether they were sitting in a warm room or walking the windy streets. She kissed them both, with tears, and said:--

"God bless you."

That seemed to be what they wanted. They longed to be blessed.

"That's what Aunt Dennison said," smiled Fitzgerald.

Then Kate realized that now the exotic Marna would be calling the completely domesticated Mrs. Dennison "aunt." But Marna looked as if she liked that, too. It was their hour for liking everything. As Kate opened the outer door for them, the blast struck through her, but the lovers, laughing, ran down the stairs together. They were, in their way, outcasts; they were poor; the future might hold bitter disillusion. But now, borne by the sharp wind, their laughter drifted back like a song.

Kate wrapped her old coat about her and made her solitary way to Mrs. Dennison's depressed Caravansary.

CHAPTER XII

There was no question about it. Life was supplying Kate Barrington with a valuable amount of "data." On every hand the emergent or the reactionary woman offered herself for observation, although to say that Kate was able to take a detached and objective view of it would be going altogether too far. The truth was, she threw herself into every friend's trouble, and she counted as friends all who turned to her, or all whom she was called upon to serve.

A fortnight after Mama's marriage, an interesting episode came Kate's way. Mrs. Barsaloux had introduced to the Caravansary a Mrs. Leger whom she had once met on the steamer on her way to Brindisi, and she had invited her to join her during a stay in Chicago. Mrs. Barsaloux, however, having gone off to France in a hot fit of indignation, Mrs. Leger presented herself with a letter from Mrs. Barsaloux to Mrs. Dennison. That hospitable woman consented to take in the somewhat enigmatic stranger.

That she was enigmatic all were quick to perceive. She was beautiful, with a delicate, high-bred grace, and she had the manner of a woman who had been courted and flattered. As consciously beautiful as Mary Morrison, she bore herself with more discretion. Taste governed all that she said and did. Her gowns, her jewels, her speech were distinguished. She seemed by all tokens an accomplished worldling; yet it was not long before Kate discovered that it was anything but worldly matters which were consuming her attention.

She had come to Chicago for the purpose of adjusting her fortune,--a large one, it appeared,--and of concluding her relations with the world. She had decided to go into a convent, and had chosen one of those numerous sisterhoods which pass their devotional days upon the bright hill-slopes without Naples. She refrained from designating the particular sisterhood, and she permitted no discussion of her motives. She only said that she had not been born a Catholic, but had turned to Mother Church when the other details of life ceased to interest her. She was a widow, but she seemed to regard her estate with quiet regret merely. If tragedy had entered her life, it must have been subsequent to widowhood. She had a son, but it appeared that he had no great need of her. He was in the care of his paternal grandparents, who were giving him an education. He was soon to enter Oxford, and she felt confident that his life would be happy. She was leaving him an abundance; she had halved her fortune and was giving her share to the convent.

If she had not been so exquisite, so skilled in the nuances of life, so swift and elusive in conversation, so well fitted for the finest forms of enjoyment, her renunciation of liberty would not have proved so exasperating to Kate. A youthful enthusiasm for religion might have made her step understandable. But enthusiasm and she seemed far apart. Intelligent as she unquestionably was, she nevertheless seemed to have given herself over supinely to a current of emotions which was sweeping her along. She looked both pious and piteous, for all of her sophisticated manner and her accomplishments and graces, and Kate felt like throwing a rope to her. But Mrs. Leger was not in a mood to seize the rope. She had her curiously gentle mind quite made up. Though she was still young,--not quite eighteen years older than her son,--she appeared to have no further concern for life. To the last, she was indulging in her delicate vanities--wore her pearls, walked in charming foot-gear, trailed after her the fascinating gowns of the initiate, and viewed with delight the portfolios of etchings which Dr. von Shierbrand chanced to be purchasing.

She was glad, she said, to be at the Caravansary, quite on a different side of the city from her friends. She made no attempt to renew old acquaintances or to say farewell to her former associates. Her extravagant home on the Lake Shore Drive was passed over to a self-congratulatory purchaser; the furnishings were sold at auction; and her other properties were disposed of in such a manner as to make the transfer of her wealth convenient for the recipients.

She asked Kate to go to the station with her.

"I've given you my one last friendship," she said. "I shall speak with no one on the steamer. My journey must be spent in preparation for my great change. But it seems human and warm to have you see me off."

"It seems inhuman to me, Mrs. Leger," Kate cried explosively. "Something terrible has happened to you, I suppose, and you're hiding away from it. You think you're going to drug yourself with prayer. But can you? It doesn't seem at all probable to me. Dear Mrs. Leger, be brave and stay out in the world with the other living people."

"You are talking of something which you do not understand," said Mrs. Leger gently. "There is a secret manna for the soul of which the chosen may eat."

"Oh!" cried Kate, almost angrily. "Are these your own words? I cannot understand a prepossession like this on your part. It doesn't seem to set well on you. Isn't there some hideous mistake? Aren't you under the influence of some emotional episode? Might it not be that you were ill without realizing it? Perhaps you are suffering from some hidden melancholy, and it is impelling you to do something out of keeping with the time and with your own disposition."

"I can see how it might appear that way to you, Miss Barrington. But I am not ill, except in my soul, which I expect to be healed in the place to which I am going. Try to understand that among the many kinds of human beings in this world there are the mystics. They have a right to their being and to their belief. Their joys and sorrows are different from those of others, but they are just as existent. Please do not worry about me."

"But you understand so well how to handle the material things in the world," protested Kate. "You seem so appreciative and so competent. If you have learned so much, what is the sense of shutting it all up in a cell?"

"Did you never read of Purun Bhagat," asked Mrs. Leger smilingly, "who was rich with the riches of a king; who was wise with the learning of Calcutta and of Oxford; who could have held as high an office as any that the Government of England could have given him in India, and who took his beggar's bowl and sat upon a cavern's rim and contemplated the secret soul of things? You know your Kipling. I have not such riches or such wisdom, but I have the longing upon me to go into silence."

The lips from which these words fell were both tender and ardent; the little gesticulating hands were clad in modish, mouse-colored suede; orris root mixed with some faint, haunting odor, barely caressed the air with perfume. Kate looked at her companion in despair.

"I must be an outer barbarian!" she cried. "I can imagine religious ecstasy, but you are not ecstatic. I can imagine turning to a convent as a place of hiding from shame or despair. But you are not going into it that way. As for wishing to worship, I understand that perfectly. Prayer is a sort of instinct with me, and all the reasoning in the world couldn't make me cast myself out of communion with the unknown something roundabout me that seems to answer me. But what you are doing seems, as I said, so obsolete."

"I am looking forward to it," said Mrs. Leger, "as eagerly as a girl looks forward to her marriage. It is a beautiful romance to me. It is the completely beautiful thing that is going to make up to me for all the ugliness I have encountered in life."

For the first time a look of passion disturbed the serenity of the high-bred, conventional face.

Kate threw out her hands with a repudiating gesture.

"Well," she said, "in the midst of my freedom I shall think of you often and wonder if you have found something that I have missed. You are leaving the world, and books, and friends, and your son for some pale white idea. It seems to me you are going to the embrace of a wraith."

Mrs. Leger smiled slowly, and it was as if a lamp showed for a moment in a darkened house and then mysteriously vanished.

"Believe me," she reiterated, "you do not understand."

Kate helped her on the train, and left her surrounded by her fashionable bags, her flowers, fruit, and literature. She took these things as a matter of course. She had looked at her smart little boots as she adjusted them on a hassock and had smiled at Kate almost teasingly.

"In a month," she said, "I shall be walking with bared feet, or, if the weather demands, in sandals. I shall wear a rope about my waist over my brown robe. My hair will be cut, my head coiffed. When you are thinking of me, think of me as I really shall be."

"So many things are going to happen that you will not see!" cried Kate. "Why, maybe in a little while we shall all be going up in flying-machines! You wouldn't like to miss that, would you? Or your son will be growing into a fine man and you'll not see him--nor the woman he marries--nor his children." She stopped, breathing hard.

"It is like the sound of the surf on a distant shore," smiled Mrs. Leger. "Good-bye, Miss Barrington. Don't grieve about me. I shall be happier than you can know or dream."

The conductor swung Kate off the train after it was in motion.

So, among other things, she had that to think of. She could explain it all merely upon the hypothesis that the sound of the awakening trumpets-

-the trumpets which were arousing woman from her long torpor--had not reached the place where this wistful woman dwelt, with her tender remorses, her delicate aversions, her hunger for the indefinite consolations of religion.

Moreover, she was beginning to understand that not all women were maternal. She had, indeed, come across many incidents in her work which emphasized this. Good mothers were quite as rare as good fathers; and it was her growing belief that more than half of the parents in the world were undeserving of the children born to them. Also, she realized that a child might be born of the body and not of the spirit, and a mother might minister well to a child's corporeal part without once ministering to its soul. It was within the possible that there never had been any bond save a physical one between Mrs. Leger and her son. Perhaps they looked at each other with strange, uncomprehending eyes. That, she could imagine, would be a tantalization from which a sensitive woman might well wish to escape. It was within the realm of possibility that he was happier with his grandmother than with his mother. There might be temperamental as well as physical "throwbacks."

Kate remembered a scene she once had witnessed at a railway station. Two meagre, hard-faced, work-worn women were superintending the removal of a pine-covered coffin from one train to another, and as the grim box was wheeled the length of a long platform, a little boy, wild-eyed, gold-haired, and set apart from all the throng by a tragic misery, ran after the truck calling in anguish:--

"Grandmother! Grandmother! Don't leave me! I'm so lonesome, grandmother! I'm so afraid!"

"Stop your noise," commanded the woman who must have been his mother. "Don't you know she can't hear you?"

"Oh, maybe she can! Maybe she can," sobbed the boy. "Oh, grandmother, don't you hear me calling? There's nobody left for me now."

The woman caught him sharply by the arm.

"I'm left, Jimmy. What makes you say such a thing as that? Stay with mother, that's a good boy."

They were lifting the box into the baggage-car. The boy saw it. He straightened himself in the manner of one who tries to endure a mortal wound.

"She's gone," he said. He looked at his mother once, as if measuring her value to him. Then he turned away. There was no comfort for him there.

Often, since, Kate had wondered concerning the child. She had imagined his grim home, his barren days; the plain food; the compulsory task; the kind, yet heavy-handed, coarse-voiced mother. She was convinced that the grandmother had been different. In the corner where she had sat, there must have been warmth and welcome for the child. Perhaps there were mellow old tales, sweet old songs, soft strokings of the head, smuggled sweets--all the beautiful grandmotherly delights.

CHAPTER XIII

Since Kate had begun to write, a hundred--a thousand--half-forgotten experiences had come back to her. As they returned to her memory, they acquired significance. They related themselves with other incidents or with opinions. They illustrated life, and however negligible in themselves, they attained a value because of their relation to the whole.

It was seldom that she felt lonely now. Her newly acquired power of self-expression seemed to extend and supplement her personality. August von Shierbrand had said that he wished to marry her because she completed him. It had occurred to her at the time--though she suppressed her inclination to say so--that she was born for other purposes than completing him, or indeed anybody. She wished to think of herself as an individual, not as an addendum. But, after all, she had sympathized with the man. She was beginning to understand that that "solitude of the soul," which one of her acquaintances, a sculptor, had put into passionate marble, was caused from that sense of incompletion. It was not alone that others failed one--it was self-failure, secret shame, all the inevitable reticences, which contributed most to that.

She fell into the way of examining the men and women about her and of asking:--

"Is he satisfied? Is she companioned? Has this one realized himself? Is that one really living?"

She remembered one person--one only--who had given her the impression of abounding physical, mental, and spiritual life. True, she had seen him but a moment--one swift, absurd, curiously haunting moment. That was Karl Wander, Honora's cousin, and the cousin of Mary Morrison. They were the children of three sisters, and from what Kate knew of their descendants' natures, she felt these sisters must have been palpitating creatures.

Yes, Karl Wander had seemed complete--a happy man, seething with plans, a wise man who took life as it came; a man of local qualities yet of cosmopolitan spirit--one who would not have fretted at his environment or counted it of much consequence, whatever it might have been.

If she could have known him--

But Honora seldom spoke of him. Only sometimes she read a brief note from him, and added:--

"He wishes to be remembered to you, Kate."

She did not hint: "He saw you only a second." Honora was not one of those persons who take pleasure in pricking bubbles. She perceived the beauty of iridescence. If her odd friend and her inexplicable cousin had any satisfaction in remembering a passing encounter, they could have their pleasure of it.

Kate, for her part, would not have confessed that she thought of him. But, curiously, she sometimes dreamed of him.

At last Ray McCrea was coming home. His frequent letters, full of good comment, announced the fact.

"I've been winning my spurs, commercially speaking," he wrote. "The old department heads, whom my father taught me to respect, seem pleased with what I have done. I believe that when I come back they will have ceased to look on me as a cadet. And if they think I'm fit for responsibilities, perhaps you will think so, too, Kate. At any rate, I know you'll let me say that I am horribly homesick. This being in a foreign land is all very well, but give me the good old American ways, crude though they may be. I want a straightforward confab with some one of my own sort; I want the feeling that I can move around without treading on somebody's toes. I want, above all, to have a comfortable entertaining evening with a nice American girl--a girl that takes herself and me for granted, and isn't shying off all the time as if I were a sort of bandit. What a relief to think that you'll not be accompanied by a chaperon! I shall get back my self-respect once I'm home again with you nice, self-confident young American women."

"It will be good to see him, I believe," mused Kate. "After all, he always looked after me. I can't seem to remember just how much pleasure I had in his society. At any rate, we'll have plenty of things to talk about. He'll tell me about Europe, and I'll tell him about my work. That ought to carry us along quite a while."

She set about making preparations for him. She induced Honora to let her have an extra room, and she made her fine front chamber into a sitting-room, with a knocker on the door, and some cheerful brasses and old prints within. She came across oddities of this sort in her Russian and Italian neighborhoods, but until now she had not taken very much interest in what she was inclined to term "sublimated junk."

Mary Morrison took an almost vicious amusement in Kate's sudden efforts at aesthetic domestication, and Marna Fitzgerald--who was delighted--considered it as a frank confession of sentiment. Kate let them think what they pleased. She presented to their inspection--even Mary was invited up for the occasion--a cheerful room with a cream paper, a tawny-colored rug, some comfortable wicker chairs, an interesting plaster cast or two, and the previously mentioned "loot." Mary, in a fit of friendliness, contributed a Japanese wall-basket dripping with vines; Honora proffered a lamp with a soft shade; and Marna took pride in bestowing some delicately embroidered cushions, white, and beautiful with the beauty of Belfast linen.

It did not appear to occur to Kate, however, that personal adornment would be desirable, and it took the united efforts of Marna and Mary to persuade her that a new frock or two might be needed. Kate had a way of avoiding shabbiness, but of late her interest in decoration had been anything but keen. However, she ventured now on a rather beguiling dress for evening--a Japanese crêpe which a returned missionary sold her for something more than a song. Dr. von Shierbrand said it was the color of rust, but Marna affirmed that it had the hue of copper--copper that was not too bright. It was embroidered gloriously with chrysanthemums, and she had great pleasure in it. Mary Morrison drew from her rainbow collection a scarf which accentuated the charm of the frock, and when Kate had contrived a monk's cape of brown, she was ready for possible entertainments--panoplied for sentiment. She would make no further concessions. Her practical street clothes and her home-made frocks of white linen, with which she made herself dainty for dinner at Mrs. Dennison's, had to serve her.

"I'm so poor," she said to Marna, "that I feel like apologizing for my inefficiency. I'm getting something now for my talks at the clubs, and I'm paid for my writing, too. Now that it's begun to be published, I ought to be opulent presently."

"You're no poorer than we," Marna said. "But of course there are two of us to be poor together; and that makes it more interesting."

"Love doesn't seem to be flying out of your window," smiled Kate.

"We've bars on the windows," laughed Marna. "Some former occupant of the flat put them on to keep the babies from dashing their brains out on the pavement below, and we haven't taken them off." She blushed. "No," responded Kate with a *moue*; "what was the use?"

Unfortunately McCrea, the much-expected, had not made it quite plain when he was to land in New York. To be sure, Kate might have consulted the steamer arrivals, but she forgot to do that. So it happened that when a wire came from Ray saying that he would be in Chicago on a certain Saturday night in mid-May, Kate found herself under compulsion to march in a suffrage procession.

David Fulham thought the circumstance uproariously funny, and he told them about it at the Caravansary. They made rather an annoying jest of it, but Kate held to her promise.

"It's an historic event to my mind," she said with all the dignity she could summon. "I wouldn't excuse myself if I could. And I can't. I've promised to march at the head of a division. We hope there'll be twenty thousand of us."

Perhaps there were. Nobody knew. But all the city did know that down the broad boulevard, in the mild, damp air of the May night, regiment upon regiment of women marched to bear witness to their conviction and their hope. Bands played, choruses sang, transparencies proclaimed watchwords, and every woman in the seemingly endless procession swung a yellow lantern. The onlookers crowded the sidewalks and hung from the towering office buildings, to watch that string of glowing amber beads reaching away to north and to south. College girls, working-girls, home-women, fine ladies, efficient business women, vague, non-producing, half-awakened women,--all sorts, all conditions, black, white, Latin, Slav, Germanic, English, American, American, American,--they came marching on. They were proud and they were diffident; they were sad and they were merry; they were faltering and they were enthusiastic. Some were there freely, splendidly, exultantly; more were there because some force greater than themselves impelled them. Through bewilderment and hesitancy and doubt, they saw the lights of the future shining, and they fixed their eyes upon the amber lanterns as upon the visible symbols of their faith; they marched and marched. They were the members of a new revolution, and, as always, only a portion of the revolutionists knew completely what they desired.

At the Caravansary there had been sharp disapproval of the whole thing. The men had brought forth arguments to show Kate her folly. Mrs. Dennison, Mrs. Goodrich, and Mrs. Applegate had spoken gentle words of warning; Honora had vaguely suggested that the matter was immaterial; Mary Morrison had smiled as one who avoided ugliness; and Kate had laughingly defied them.

"I march!" she had declared. "And I'm not ashamed of my company."

It was, indeed, a company of which she was proud. It included the names of the most distinguished, the most useful, the most talented, the most exclusive, and the most triumphantly inclusive women in the city.

"Poor McCrea," put in Fulham. "Aren't you making him ridiculous? He'll come dashing up here the moment he gets off the train. As a matter of fact, he'll be half expecting you to meet him. You're making a mistake, Miss Barrington, if you'll let a well-meaning fellow-being say so. You're leaving the substance for the shadow."

"I've misled you about Ray, I'm afraid," Kate said with unexpected patience. "He hasn't really any right to expect me to be waiting, and I don't believe he will. Come to think of it, I don't know that I want to be found waiting."

"Oh, well, of course--" said Fulham with a shrug, leaving his sentence unfinished.

"Anyway," said Kate flushing, "I march!"

They told her afterward how McCrea had come toof-toofing up to the door in a taxi, and how he had taken the steps two at a time.

"He wrung my hand," said Honora, "and got through the preliminary amenities with a dispatch I never have seen excelled. Then he demanded you. 'Is she upstairs?' he asked. 'May I go right up? She wrote me she had a parlor of her own.' 'She has a parlor,' I said, 'but she isn't in it.' He balanced on the end of a toe. 'Where is she?' I thought he was going to fly. 'She's out with the suffragists,' I said. I didn't try to excuse you. I thought you deserved something pretty bad. But I did tell him you'd promised to go and that you hadn't known he was coming that day. 'She's in that mess?' he cried. 'I saw the Amazon march as I came along. You don't mean Kate's tramping the streets with those women!' 'Yes, she is,' I said, 'and she's proud to do it. But she was sorry not to be here to welcome you.' 'Sorry!' he said; 'why, Mrs. Fulham, I've been dreaming of this meeting for months.' Honestly, Kate, I was ashamed for you. I asked him in. I told him you'd be home before long. But he would not come in. 'Tell her I--I came,' he said. Then he went."

It was late at night, and Kate was both worn and exhilarated with her marching. Honora's words let her down considerably. She sat with tears in her eyes staring at her friend.

"But couldn't he see," she pleaded, "that I had to keep my word? Didn't he understand how important it was? I can see him to-morrow just as well."

"Then you'll have to send for him," said Honora decisively. "He'll not come without urging."

She went up to bed with a stern aspect, and left Kate sitting staring before her by the light of one of Mary's foolish candles.

"They seem to think I'm a very unnatural woman," said Kate to herself. "But can't they see how much more important it was that the demonstration should be a success than that two lovers should meet at a certain hour?"

The word "lovers" had slipped inadvertently into her mind; and no sooner had she really recognized it, looked at it, so to speak, fairly in the face, than she rejected it with scorn.

"We're just friends," she protested. "One has many friends."

But her little drawing-room, all gay and fresh, accused her of deceiving herself; and a glimpse of the embroidered frock reminded her that she was contemptibly shirking the truth. One did not make such preparations for a mere "friend." She sat down and wrote a note, put stamps on it to insure its immediate delivery, and ran out to the corner to mail it. Then she fell asleep arguing with herself that she had been right, and that he ought to understand what it meant to give one's word, and that it could make no difference that they were to meet a few hours later instead of at the impetuous moment of his arrival.

She spent the next day at the Juvenile Court, and came home with the conviction that there ought to be no more children until all those now wandering the hard ways of the world were cared for. She was in no mood for sweethearting, yet she looked with some covert anxiety at the mail-box. There was an envelope addressed to her, but the superscription was not in Ray's handwriting. The Colorado stamp gave her a hint of whom it might have come from, and ridiculously she felt her heart quickening. Yet why should Karl Wander write to her? She made herself walk slowly up the stairs, and insisted that her hat and gloves and jacket should be put scrupulously in their places before she opened her letter. It proved not to be a letter, after all, but only a number of photographs, taken evidently by the sender, who gave no word of himself. He let the snow-capped solitary peaks utter his meanings for him. The pictures were beautiful and, in some indescribable way, sad--cold and isolate. Kate ran her fingers into the envelope again and again, but she could discover no note there. Neither was there any name, save her own on the cover.

"At least," said Kate testily, "I might have been told whom to thank."

But she knew whom to thank--and she knew with equal positiveness that she would send no thanks. For the gift had been a challenge. It seemed to say: "I dare you to open communication with me. I dare you to break the conscious silence between us!"

Kate did not lift the glove that had been thrown down. She hid the photographs in her clock and told no one about them.

At the close of the third day a note came from Ray. Her line, he said, had followed him to Lake Forest and he had only then found time to answer it. He was seeing old friends and was very much occupied with business and with pleasure, but he hoped to see her before long. Kate laughed aloud at the rebuff. It was, she thought, a sort of Silvertree method of putting her in her place. But she was sorry, too,--sorry for his hurt; sorry, indefinitely and indescribably, for something missed. If it had been Karl Wander whom she had treated like that he would have waited on her doorstep till she came, and if he had felt himself entitled to a quarrel, he would have "had it out" before men and the high gods.

At least, so she imagined he would have done; but upon consideration there were few persons in the world about whom she knew less than about Karl Wander. It seemed as if Honora were actually perverse in the way she avoided his name.

CHAPTER XIV

The spring was coming. Signs of it showed at the park edges, where the high willow hedges began to give forth shoots of yellowish-green; at times the lake was opalescent and the sky had moments of tenderness and warmth. Even through the pavement one seemed to scent the earth; and the flower shops set up their out-of-door booths and solicited the passer-by with blossoms.

When Kate could spare the money, she bought flowers for Marna—for it was flower-time with Marna, and she had seen the Angel of the Annunciation. All that was Celtic in her was coming uppermost. She dreamed and brooded and heard voices. Kate liked to sit in the little West-Side flat and be comforted of the happiness there. She was feeling very absurd herself, and she was ashamed of her excursion into the realms of feminine folly. That was the way she put her defection from "common sense," and her little flare of sentiment for Ray, and all her breathless, ridiculous preparation for him. She had never worn the chrysanthemum dress, and she so loathed the sight of it that she boxed it and put it in the bottom of her trunk.

No word came from Ray. "Sometime" had not materialized and he had failed to call. His name was much in the papers as "best man" or cotillion leader or host at club dinners. He moved in a world of which Kate saw nothing—a rather competitive world, where money counted and where there was a brisk exchange of social amenities. Kate's festivities consisted of settlement dinners and tea here and there, at odd, interesting places with fellow "welfare workers"; and now and then she went with Honora to some University affair. A great many ladies sent her cards to their "afternoons"—ladies whom she met at the home of the President of the University, or with whom she came in contact at Hull House or some of the other settlements. But such diversions she was obliged to deny herself. They would have taken time from her too-busy hours; and she had not the strength to do her work according to her conscience, and then to drag herself halfway across town, merely for the amiability of making her bow and eating an ice in a charming house. Not but that she enjoyed the atmosphere of luxury—the elusive sense of opulence given her by the flowers, the distant music, the smiling, luxurious, complimentary women, the contrast between the glow within and the chill of twilight without--twilight sparkling with the lights of the waiting motors, and the glittering procession on the Drive. But, after all, while others rode, she walked, and sometimes she was very weary. To be sure, she was too gallant, too much at ease in her entertaining world, too expectant of the future, to fret even for a moment about the fact that she was walking while others rode. She hardly gave it a thought. But her disadvantages made her unable to cope with other women socially. She was, as she often said, fond of playing a game; but the social game pushed the point of achievement a trifle too far.

Moreover, there was the mere bother of "dressing the part." Her handsome heavy shoes, her strong, fashionable street gloves, her well-cared-for street frock, and becoming, practical hat she could obtain and maintain in freshness. She was "well-groomed" and made a sort of point of looking competent, as if she felt mistress of herself and her circumstances; she could even make herself dainty for a little dinner, but the silks and furs, the prodigality of yard-long gloves, the fetching boots and whimsical jewels of the ladies who made a fine art of feminine entertainments, were quite beyond her. So, sensibly, she counted it all out.

That Ray was at home in such surroundings, and that, had she been willing to give him the welcome he expected, she might have had a welcome at these as yet unopened doors through which he passed with conscious suavity, sometimes occurred to her. She was but human--and but woman--and she could not be completely oblivious to such things. But they did not, after all, wear a very alluring aspect.

When she dreamed of being happy, as she often did, it was not amid such scenes. Sometimes, when she was half-sleeping, and vague visions of joy haunted the farther chambers of her brain, she saw herself walking among mountains. The setting sun glittered on distant, splendid snows; the torrent rushed by her, filling the world with its clamor; beneath lay the valley, and through the gathering gloom she could see the light of homes. Then, as sleep drew nearer and the actual world slipped farther away, she seemed to be treading the path--homeward--with some companion. Which of those lights spelled home for her she did not know, and whenever she tried to see the face of her companion, the shadows grew deeper,--as deep as oblivion,--and she slept.

She was lonely. She felt she had missed much in missing Ray. She knew her friends disapproved of her; and she was profoundly ashamed that they should have seen her in that light, expectant hour in which she awaited this lover who appeared to be no lover, after all. But she deserved her humiliation. She had conducted herself like the expectant bride, and she had no right to any such attitude because her feelings were not those of a bride.

The thing that she did desperately care about just now was the fitting-up of a home for mothers and babes in the Wisconsin woods. It was to be a place where the young Polish mothers of a part of her district could go and forget the belching horror of the steel mills, and the sultry nights in the crowded, vermin-haunted homes. She hoped for much from it--much more than the physical recuperation, though that was not to be belittled. There was some hitch, at the last, about the endowment. A benevolent spinster had promised to remember the prospective home in her will and neglected to do so and now there were several thousands to be collected from some unknown source. Kate was absorbed with that when she was not engaged with her regular work. Moreover, she made a point of being absorbed. She could not endure the thought that she might be going about with a love-lorn, he-cometh-not expression.

Life has a way of ambling withal for a certain time, and then of breaking into a headlong gallop--bolting free--plunging to catastrophe or liberty. Kate went her busy ways for a fortnight, somewhat chastened in spirit, secretly a little ashamed, and altogether very determined to make such a useful person of herself that she could forget her apparent lack of attractions (for she told herself mercilessly that if she had been very much desired by Ray he would not have been able to leave her upon so slight a provocation). Then, one day,--it was the last day of May and the world had rejuvenated itself,--she came across him.

A more unlikely place hardly could have been chosen for their meeting than an "isle of safety" in mid-street, with motors hissing and toof-toofing round about, policemen gesticulating, and the crowd ceaselessly surging. The two were marooned with twenty others, and met face to face, squarely, like foes who set themselves to combat. At first he tried not to see her, and she, noting his impulse, thought it would be the part of propriety not to see him. Then that struck her as so futile, so childish, so altogether a libel on the good-fellowship which they had enjoyed in the old days, that she held out her hand.

He swept his hat from his head and grasped the extended hand in a violent yet tremulous clutch.

"We seem to be going in opposite directions," she said. There was just a hint of a rising inflection in the accent.

He laughed with nervous delight.

"We are going the same way," he declared. "That's a well-established fact."

An irritable policeman broke in on them with:--

"Do you people want to get across the street or not?"

"Personally," said McCrea, smiling at him, "I'm not particular."

The policeman was Irish and he liked lovers. He thought he was looking at a pair of them.

"Well, it's not the place I'd be choosing for conversation, sir," he said.

"Right you are," agreed Ray. "I suppose you'd prefer a lane in Ballamacree?"

"Yes, sir. Good luck to you, sir."

"Same to you," called back Ray.

He and Kate swung into the procession on the boulevard. Kate was smiling happily.

"You haven't changed a bit!" she cried. "You keep right on enjoying yourself, don't you?"

"Not a bit of it," retorted Ray indignantly. "I've been miserable! You know I have. The only satisfaction I got at all was in hoping I was making you miserable, too. Was I?"

"I wouldn't own to it if you had," said Kate. "Shall we forgive each other?"

"Do you want it to be as easy as that--after all we've been through? Wouldn't it be more satisfactory to quarrel?"

"You can if you want, of course," Kate laughed. "But hadn't it better be with some other person? Really, I wanted to see you dreadfully--or, at least, I wanted to see you pleasantly. I had made preparations. You didn't let me know when to expect you, and I had an engagement when you did come. Weren't you foolish to get in a rage?"

"But I was so frightfully disappointed. I expected so much and I had expected it so long."

"Ray!" Her voice was almost stern, and he turned to look at her half with amusement, half with apprehension. "Expect nothing. Enjoy yourself to-day."

"But how can I enjoy myself to-day unless I am made to understand that there is something I may expect from you? Circumstances have kept us playing fast and loose long enough. Can't we come to an understanding, Kate?"

Kate stopped to look in a florist's window and fixed her eyes upon a vast bouquet of pale pink roses.

"Do say something," he said after a time. "Shall I speak from the heart?"

"Oh, yes, please." He drew his breath in sharply between his teeth.

"Well, then, I'm not ready to give up my free life, Ray. I can't seem to see my way to relinquishing any part of my liberty. I think you know why. I've told you everything in my letters. I feel too experimental to settle down."

"You don't love me!"

"Did I ever say I did?"

"You gave me to understand that you might."

"You wanted me to try."

"But you haven't succeeded? Then, for heaven's sake, let me go and make out some other programme for myself. I've come back to you because I couldn't be satisfied away from you. I've seen women, if it comes to that,-- cities of women. But there's no one like you, Kate, to my mind; no one who so makes me enjoy the hour, or so plan for the future. Ever since that day when you stood up by the C Bench and fought for the right of women to sit on it,--that silly old C Bench,--I've liked your warring spirit. And I come back, by Jove, to find you marching with the militant women! Well, I didn't know whether to laugh or swear! Anyway, you do beat the world."

"A pretty sweetheart I'd make," cried Kate, disgusted with herself. "I'm only good to provide you with amusement, it seems."

"You provide me with the breath of life! Heavens, what a spring you have when you walk! And you 're as straight as a grenadier. I'm so sick of seeing slouching, die-away women! It's only you American women who know how to carry yourselves. Oh, Kate, if you can't answer me, don't, but let me see you once in a while. I'm a weak character, and I've got to enjoy your society a little longer."

"You can enjoy as much of it as you please, only you mustn't be holding me up to some tremendous responsibility, and blaming me by and by for things I can't help."

"I give you my word I'll not. Oh, Kate, is this a busy day with you? Can't you come out into the country somewhere? We could take the electric and in an hour we'd be out where we could see orchards in bloom."

"I *could* go," mused Kate. "I've a half-holiday coming to me, and really, if I were to take it to-day, no one would care."

"The ayes have it! Let us go to the station-I'll buy plenty of tickets and we can get off at any place where the climate seems mild and the natives kind."

It proved to be a day of encounters.

They had traveled well beyond the city, past the straggling suburbs and the comfortable, friendly old villages, some of which antedated the city of which they were now the fringe, and had reached the wider sweeps of the prairie, with the fine country homes of those who sought privacy. At length they came to a junction of the road.

"All out here for--"

They could not catch the name.

"Isn't that where we're going?" laughed Kate.

"Of course it is," Ray responded.

They hastened out and looked about them for the train they had supposed would be in waiting. It was not yet in, however, but was showing its dark nose a mile or two down the track.

"I must see about our tickets," said Ray. "Perhaps we'll have to buy others."

Kate had been standing with her back to the ticket station window, but now she turned, and through the ticker-seller's window envisaged the pale, bitterly sullen face of Lena Vroom. It looked sunken and curiously alien, as if its possessor felt herself unfriended of all the world.

"Lena!" cried Kate, too startled to use tact or to wait for Lena to give the first sign of recognition.

Lena nodded coolly.

"Oh, is this where you are?" cried Kate. "We've looked everywhere for you."

"If I'd wanted to be found, I could have been, you know." The tone was muffled and pitifully insolent.

"You are living out here?"

"I live a few miles from here."

"And you like the work? Is it--is it well with you, Lena?"

"It will never be well with me, and you know it. I broke down, that's all. I can't stand anything now that takes thought. This just suits me--a little mechanical work like this. I'm not fit to talk, Kate. You'll have to excuse me. It upsets me. I'm ordered to keep very quiet. If I get upset, I'll not be fit even for this."

"I'll go," said Kate contritely. "And I'll tell no one." She battled to keep the tears from her eyes. "Only tell me, need you work at all? I thought you had enough to get along on, Lena. You often told me so--forgive me, but we've *been* close friends, you know, even if we aren't now."

"My money's gone," said Lena in a dead voice. "I used up my principal. It wasn't much. I'm in debt, too, and I've got to get that paid off. But I've a comfortable place to live, Kate, with a good motherly German woman. I tell you for your peace of mind, because I know you--you always think you have to be affectionate and to care about what people are doing. But you'll serve me best by leaving me alone. Understand?"

"Oh, Lena, yes! I'll not come near you, but I can't help thinking about you. And I beg and pray you to write me if you need me at any time."

"I can't talk about anything any more. It tires me. There's your train."

Ray bought his tickets to nowhere in particular. The little train came on like a shuttle through the blue loom of the air; they got on, and were shot forward through bright green fields, past expectant groves and flowering orchards, cheered by the elate singing of innumerable birds.

Ray had recognized Lena, but Kate refused to discuss her.

"Life has hurt her," she said, "and she's in hiding like a wounded animal. I couldn't talk about her. I--I love her. It's like that with me. Once I've loved a person, I can't get it out of my system."

She was staring from the window, trying to get back her happiness. Ray snatched her hand and held it in a crushing grip.

"For God's sake, Kate, try to love me, then!" he whispered.

It was spring all about them,--"the pretty ring-time,"--and she had just seen what it was to be a defeated and unloved woman. She felt a thrill go through her, and she turned an indiscreetly bright face upon her companion.

"Don't expect too much," she whispered back, "but I *will* try."

They went on, almost with the feeling that they were in Arcadia, and drew up at a platform in the midst of woods, through which they could see a crooked trail winding.

"Here's our place!" cried Ray. "Don't you recognize it? Not that you've ever seen it before."

They dashed, laughing, from the train, and found themselves a minute later in a bird-haunted solitude, among flowers, at the beginning of the woodland walk. There seemed to be no need to comment upon the beauty of things. It was quite enough that the bland, caressing air beat upon their cheeks in playful gusts, that the robins gave no heed to them, and that "the little gray leaves were kind" to them.

Never was there a more capricious trail than the one they set themselves to follow. It skirted the edge of a little morass where the young flags were coming up; it followed the windings of a brook where the wild forget-me-not threw up its little azure buds; it crossed the stream a dozen times by means of shaking bridges, or fallen trees; it had magnificent gateways between twin oaks--gateways to yet pleasanter reaches of leaving woodland.

"Whatever can it lead to?" wondered Kate.

"To some new kind of Paradise, perhaps," answered Ray. "And see, some one has been before us! Hush--"

He drew her back into the bushes at the side, beneath a low-hanging willow. A man and a woman were coming toward them. The woman was walking first, treading proudly, her head thrown back, her body in splendid motion, like that of an advancing Victory. The man, taller than she, was resting one hand upon her shoulder. He, too, looked like one who had mastered the elements and who felt the pangs of translation into some more ethereal and liberating world. As they came on, proud as Adam and Eve in the first days of their existence, Kate had a blinding recognition of them. They were David Fulham and Mary Morrison.

She looked once, saw their faces shining with pagan joy, and, turning her gaze from them, sank on the earth behind the screen of bushes. Ray perceived her desire to remain unseen, and stepped behind the wide-girthed oak. The two passed them, still treading that proud step. When they were gone, Kate arose and led the way on along the path. She wished to turn back, but she dared not, fearing to meet the others on the station platform. Ray had recognized Fulham, but he did not know his companion, and Kate would not tell him.

"What a fool!" he said. "I thought he loved his wife. She's a fine woman."

"He loves his wife," affirmed Kate stalwartly. "But there's a hedonistic fervor in him. He's--"

"He's a fool!" reaffirmed Ray. "Shall we talk of something else?"

"By all means," agreed Kate.

They tried, but the glory of the day was slain. They had seen the serpent in their Eden--and where there is one reptile there may always be another.

When they thought it discreet, they went back to the junction. Lena Vroom was still there. She was nibbling at some dry-looking sandwiches. Her glance forbade them to say anything personal to her, and Kate, with a clutch at the heart, passed her by as if she had been any ticket-seller.

She wondered if any one, seeing that gray-faced, heavy-eyed woman, would dream of her so dearly won Ph.D. or of the Phi Beta Kappa key which she had won but not claimed! She had not even dared to converse, lest Lena's fragile self-possession should break. She evidently was in the clutches of nervous fatigue and was fighting it with her last remnant of courage. Even the veriest layman could guess as much.

Kate hastened home, and as she opened the door she heard the voice of Honora mingled with the happy cries of the twins. They were down in the drawing-room, and Honora had bought some colored balloons for them, and was running to and fro with them in her hand, while Patience and Patricia shrieked with delight.

"What a lovely day it's been, hasn't it?" Honora queried, pausing in her play. "I've so longed to be in the country, but matters had reached such a critical point at the laboratory that I couldn't get away. Do you know, Kate, the great experiment that David and I are making is much further along than he surmises! I'm going to have a glorious surprise for him one of these days. Business took him over to the Academy of Science to-day and I was so glad of it. It gave me the laboratory quite to myself. But really, I've got to get out into the country. I'm going to ask David if he won't take me next Sunday."

Kate felt herself growing giddy. She dared not venture to reply. She kissed the babies and sped up to her room. But Honora's happy laughter followed her even there. Then suddenly there was a scurrying. Kate guessed that David was coming. The babies were being carried up to the nursery lest they should annoy him.

Kate beat the wall with her fists.

"Fool! Fool!" she cried. "Why didn't she let him see her laughing and dancing like that? Why didn't she? She'll come down all prim and staid for him and he'll never dream what she really is like. Oh, how can she be so blind? I don't know how to stand it! And I don't know what to do! Why isn't there some one to tell me what I ought to do?"

Mary Morrison was late to dinner. She said she had run across an old Californian friend and they had been having tea together and seeing the shops. She had no appetite for dinner, which seemed to carry out her story. Her eyes were as brilliant as stars, and a magnetic atmosphere seemed to emanate from her. The men all talked to her. They seemed disturbed--not themselves. There was something in her glowing lips, in her swimming glance, in the slow beauty of her motions, that called to them like the pipes o' Pan. She was as pagan and as beautiful as the spring, and she brought to them thoughts of elemental joys. It was as if, sailing a gray sea, they had come upon a palm-shaded isle, and glimpsed Calypso lying on the sun-dappled grass.

CHAPTER XV

That night Kate said she would warn Honora; but in the morning she found herself doubtful of the wisdom of such a course. Or perhaps she really lacked the courage for it. At any rate, she put it off. She contemplated talking to Mary Morrison, and of appealing to her honor, or her compassion, and of advising her to go away. But Mary was much from home nowadays, and Kate, who had discouraged an intimacy, did not know how to cultivate it at this late hour. Several days went by with Kate in a tumult of indecision. Sometimes she decided that the romance between Mary and David was a mere spring madness, which would wear itself out and do little damage. At other moments she felt it was laid upon her to speak and avert a catastrophe.

Then, in the midst of her indecision, she was commanded to go to Washington to attend a national convention of social workers. She was to represent the Children's Protective Agency, and to give an account of the method of its support and of its system of operation. She was surprised and gratified at this invitation, for she had had no idea that her club and settlement-house addresses had attracted attention to that extent. She made so little effort when she spoke that she could not feel much respect for her achievement. It was as if she were talking to a friend, and the size of her audience in no way affected her neighborly accent.

She did not see that it was precisely this thing which was winning favor for her. Her lack of self-consciousness, her way of telling people precisely what they wished to know about the subject in hand, her sense of values, which enabled her to see that a human fact is the most interesting thing in the world, were what counted for her. If she had been "better trained," and more skilled in the dreary and often meaningless science of statistics, or had become addicted to the benevolent jargon talked by many welfare workers, her array of facts would have fallen on more or less indifferent ears. But she offered not vital statistics, but vital documents. She talked in personalities--in personalities so full of meaning that, concrete as they were, they took on general significance--they had the effect of symbols. She furnished watchwords for her listeners, and she did it unconsciously. She would have been indignant if she had been told how large a part her education in Silvertree played in her present aptitude. She had grown up in a town which feasted on dramatic gossip, and which thrived upon the specific personal episode. To the vast and terrific city, and to her portion of the huge task of mitigating the woe of its unfit, Kate brought the quality which, undeveloped, would have made of her no more than an entertaining village gossip.

What stories there were to tell! What stories of bravery in defeat, of faith in the midst of disaster, of family devotion in spite of squalor and subterfuges and all imaginable shiftlessness and shiftiness.

Kate had got hold of the idea of the universality of life--the universality of joy and pain and hope. She was finding it easy now to forgive "the little brothers" for all possible perversity, all defects, all ingratitude. Wayward children they might be,--children uninstructed in the cult of goodness, happiness, serenity,--but outside the pale of human consideration they could not be. The greater their fault the greater their need. Kate was learning, in spite of her native impatience and impulsiveness, to be very patient. She was becoming the defender of those who stumbled, the explainer of those who themselves lacked explanations or who were too defiant to give them.

So she was going to Washington. She was to talk on a proposed school for the instruction of mothers. She often had heard her father say that a good mother was an exception. She had not believed him--had taken it for granted that this idea of his was a part of his habitual pessimism. But since she had come up to the city and become an officer of the Children's Protective Association, she had changed her mind, and a number of times she had been on the point of writing to her father to tell him that she was beginning to understand his point of view.

This idea of a school for mothers had been her own, originally, and a development of the little summer home for Polish mothers which she had helped to establish. She had proposed it, half in earnest, merely, at Hull House on a certain occasion when there were a number of influential persons present. It had appealed to them, however, as a practical means of remedying certain difficulties daily encountered.

Just how large a part Jane Addams had played in the enlightenment of Kate's mind and the dissolution of her inherent exclusiveness, Kate could not say. Sometimes she gave the whole credit to her. For here was a woman with a genius for inclusiveness. She was the sister of all men. If a youth sinned, she asked herself if she could have played any part in the prevention of that sin had she had more awareness, more solicitude. It was she who had, more than others,--though there was a great army of men and women of good will to sustain her,--promulgated this idea of responsibility. A city, she maintained, was a great home. She demanded, then, to know if the house was made attractive, instructive, protective. Was it so conducted that the wayward sons and daughters, as well as the obedient ones, could find safety and happiness within it? Were the privileges only for the rich, the effective, and the out-reaching? Or were they for those who lacked the courage to put out their hands for joy and knowledge? Were they for those who had not yet learned the tongue of the family into which they had newly entered? Were they for those who fought the rules and shirked the cares and dug for themselves a pit of sorrow? She believed they were for all. She could not countenance disinheritance. Yes, always, in high places and low, among friends and enemies, this sad, kind, patient, quiet woman, Jane Addams, of Hull House, had preached the indissolubility of the civic family. Kate had listened and learned. Nay, more, she had added her own interpretations. She was young, strong, brave, untaught by rebuff, and she had the happy and beautiful insolence of those who have not known defeat. She said things Jane Addams would have hesitated to say. She lacked the fine courtesy of the elder woman; but she made, for that very reason, a more dramatic propaganda.

Kate had known what it was to tramp the streets in rain and wind; she had known what it was to face infection and drunken rage; she had looked on sights both piteous and obscene; but she had now begun--and much, much sooner than was usual with workers in her field--to reap some of the rewards of toil.

Soon or late things in this life resolve themselves into a question of personality. History and art, success and splendor, plenitude and power, righteousness and immortal martyrdom, are all, in the last resolve, personality and nothing more. Kate was having her swift rewards because of that same indescribable, incontestable thing. The friendship of remarkable women and men--women, particularly--was coming to her. Fine things were being expected of her. She had a vitality which indicated genius--that is, if genius is intensity, as some hold. At any rate, she was vividly alert, naturally eloquent, physically capable of impressing her personality upon others.

She thought little of this, however. She merely enjoyed the rewards as they came, and she was unfeignedly surprised when, on her way to

Washington, whither she traveled with many others, her society was sought by those whom she had long regarded with something akin to awe. She did not guess how her enthusiasm and fresh originality stimulated persons of lower vitality and more timid imagination.

At Washington she had a signal triumph. The day of her speech found the hall in which the convention was held crowded with a company including many distinguished persons--among them, the President of the United States. Kate had expected to suffer rather badly from stage fright, but a sense of her opportunity gave her courage. She talked, in her direct "Silvertree method," as Marna called it, of the ignorance of mothers, the waste of children, the vast economic blunder which for one reason and another even the most progressive of States had been so slow to perceive. She said that if the commercial and agricultural interests of the country were fostered and protected, why should not the most valuable product of all interests, human creatures, be given at least an equal amount of consideration. In her own way, which by a happy instinct never included what was hackneyed, she drew a picture of the potentialities of the child considered merely from an economic point of view, and in impulsive words she made plain the need for a bureau, which she suggested should be virtually a part of the governmental structure, in which should be vested authority for the care of children,--the Bureau of Children, she denominated it,--a scientific extension of motherhood!

It seemed a part of the whole stirring experience that she should be asked with several others to lunch at the White House with the President and his wife. The President, it appeared, was profoundly interested. A quiet man, with a judicial mind, he perceived the essential truth of Kate's propaganda. He had, indeed, thought of something similar himself, though he had not formulated it. He went so far as to express a desire that this useful institution might attain realization while he was yet in the presidential chair.

"I would like to ask you unofficially, Miss Barrington," he said at parting, "if you are one to whom responsibility is agreeable?"

"Oh," cried Kate, taken aback, "how do I know? I am so young, Mr. President, and so inexperienced!"

"We must all be that at some time or other," smiled the President. "But it is in youth that the ideas come; and enthusiasm has a value which is often as great as experience."

"Ideas are accidents, Mr. President," answered Kate. "It doesn't follow that one can carry out a plan because she has seen a vision."

"No," admitted the President, shaking hands with her. "But you don't look to me like a woman who would let a vision go to waste. You will follow it up with all the power that is in you."

It happened that Kate's propaganda appealed to the popular imagination. The papers took it up; they made much of the President's interest in it; they wrote articles concerning the country girl who had come up to town, and who, with a simple faith and courage, had worked among the unfortunate and the delinquent, and whose native eloquence had made her a favorite with critical audiences. They printed her picture and idealized her in the interests of news.

A lonely, gruff old man in Silvertree read of it, and when the drawn curtains had shut him away from the scrutiny of his neighbors, he walked the floor, back and forth, following the worn track in the dingy carpet, thinking.

They talked of it at the Caravansary, and were proud; and many men and women who had met her by chance, or had watched her with interest, openly rejoiced.

"They're coming on, the Addams breed of citizens," said they. "Here's a new one with the trick--whatever it is--of making us think and care and listen. She's getting at the roots of our disease, and it's partly because she's a woman. She sees that it has to be right with the children if it's to be right with the family. Long live the Addams breed!"

Friends wired their congratulations, and their comments were none the less acceptable because they were premature. Many wrote her; Ray McCrea, alone, of her intimate associates, was silent. Kate guessed why, but she lacked time to worry. She only knew that her great scheme was afoot--that it went. But she would have been less than mortal if she had not felt a thrill of commingled apprehension and satisfaction at the fact that Kate Barrington, late of Silvertree and its gossiping, hectoring, wistful circles, was in the foreground. She had had an Idea which could be utilized in the high service of the world, and the most utilitarian and idealistic public in the world had seized upon it.

So, naturally enough, the affairs of Honora Fulham became somewhat blurred to Kate's perception. Besides, she was unable to decide what to do. She had heard that one should never interfere between husband and wife. Moreover, she was very young, and she believed in her friends. Others might do wrong, but not one's chosen. People of her own sort had temptations, doubtless, but they overcame them. That was their business--that was their obligation. She might proclaim herself a democrat, but she was a moral aristocrat, at any rate. She depended upon those in her class to do right.

She was a trifle chilled when she returned to find how little time Honora had to give to her unfolding of the great new scheme. Honora had her own excitement. Her wonderful experiment was drawing to a culmination. Honora could talk of nothing else. If Kate wanted to promulgate a scheme for the caring for the Born, very well. Honora had a tremendous business with the Unborn. So she talked Kate down.

CHAPTER XVI

Then came the day of Honora's victory!

It had been long expected, yet when it came it had the effect of a miracle. It was, however, a miracle which she realized. She was burningly aware that her great moment had come.

She left the lights flaring in the laboratory, and, merely stopping to put the catch on the door, ran down the steps, fastening her linen coat over her working dress as she went. David would be at home. He would be resting, perhaps,--she hoped so. For days he had been feverish and strange, and she had wondered if he were tormented by that sense of world-stress which was forever driving him. Was there no achievement that would satisfy him, she wondered. Yes, yes, he must be satisfied now! Moreover, he should have all the credit. To have found the origin of life, though only in a voiceless creature,--a reptile,--was not that an unheard-of victory? She would claim no credit; for without him and his daring to inspire her she would not have dreamed of such an experiment.

Of course, she might have telephoned to him, but it never so much as occurred to her to do that. She wanted to cry the words into his ear:--

"We have it! The secret is ours! There *is* a hidden door into the house of life--and we've opened it!"

Oh, what treasured, ancient ideas fell with the development of this new fact! She did not want to think of that, because of those who, in the rearrangement of understanding, must suffer. But as for her, she would be bold to face it, as the mate and helper of a great scientist should be. She would set her face toward the sun and be unafraid of any glory. Her thoughts spun in her head, her pulses throbbed. She did not know that she was thinking it, but really she was feeling that in a moment more she would be in David's arms. Only some such gesture would serve to mark the climax of this great moment. Though they so seldom caressed, though they had indulged so little in emotion, surely now, after their long and heavy task, they could have the sweet human comforts. They could be lovers because they were happy.

Perhaps, after all, she would only cry out to him:--"It will be yours, David--the Norden prize!" That would tell the whole thing.

People looked after her as she sped down the street. At first they thought she was in distress, but a glance at her shining face, its nobility accentuated by her elation, made that idea untenable. She was obviously the bearer of good tidings.

Dr. von Shierbrand, passing on the other side of the street, called out:--

"Carrying the good news from Ghent to Aix?"

An old German woman, with a laden basket on her arm nodded cheerfully.

"It's a baby," she said aloud to whoever might care to corroborate.

But Honora carried happiness greater than any dreamed,--a secret of the ages,--and the prize was her man's fame.

She reached her own door, and with sure, swift hands, fitted the key in the lock. The house wore a welcoming aspect. The drawing-room was filled with blossoming plants, and the diaphanous curtains which Blue-eyed Mary had hung at the windows blew softly in the breeze. The piano, with its suggestive litter of music, stood open, and across the bench trailed one of Mary's flowered chiffon scarfs.

"David!" called Honora. "David!"

Two blithe baby voices answered her from the rear porch. The little ones were there with Mrs. Hays, and they excitedly welcomed this variation in their day's programme.

"In a minute, babies," called Honora. "Mamma will come in a minute."

Yes, she and David would go together to the babies, and they would "tell them," the way people "told the bees."

"David!" she kept calling. "David!"

She looked in the doors of the rooms she passed, and presently reached her own. As she entered, a large envelope addressed in David's writing, conspicuously placed before the face of her desk-clock, caught her eye. She imagined that it contained some bills or memoranda, and did not stop for it, but ran on.

"Oh, he's gone to town," she cried with exasperation, "and I haven't an idea where to reach him!"

Closing her ears to the calls of the little girls, she returned to her own room and shut herself in. She was completely exasperated with the need for patience. Never had she so wanted David, and he was not there--he was not there to hear that the moment of triumph had come for both of them and that they were justified before their world.

Petulantly she snatched the envelope from the desk and opened it. It was neither bills nor memoranda which fell out, but a letter. Surprised, she unfolded it.

Her eyes swept it, not gathering its meaning. It might have been written in some foreign language, so incomprehensible did it seem. But something deep down in her being trembled as if at approaching dissolution and sent up its wild messages of alarm. Vaguely, afar off, like the shouts of a distant enemy on the hills, the import besieged her spirit.

"I must read it again," she said simply.

She went over it slowly, like one deciphering an ancient hieroglyph.

"My DEAR HONORA:--" (it ran.)

"I am off and away with Mary Morrison. Will this come to you as a complete surprise? I hardly think so. You have been my good comrade and assistant; but Mary Morrison is my woman. I once thought you were, but there was a mistake somewhere. Either I misjudged, or you changed. I hope you'll come across happiness, too, sometime. I never knew the meaning of the word till I met Mary. You and I haven't been able to make each other out. You thought I was bound up heart and soul in the laboratory. I may as well tell you that only a fractional part of my nature was concerned with it. Mary is an unlearned person compared with you, but she knew that, and it is the great fact for both of us.

"It is too bad about the babies. We ought never to have had them. See that they have a good education and count on me to help you. You'll find an account at the bank in your name. There'll be more there for you when that is gone.

"DAVID."

The old German woman was returning, her basket emptied of its load, when Honora came down the steps and crossed the Plaisance.

"My God," said the old woman in her own tongue, "the child did not live!"

Honora walked as somnambulists walk, seeing nothing. But she found her way to the door of the laboratory. The white glare of the chemical lights was over everything--over all the significant, familiar litter of the place. The workmanlike room was alive and palpitating with the personality which had gone out from it--the flaming personality of David Fulham.

The woman who had sold her birthright of charm and seduction for his sake sat down to eat her mess of pottage. Not that she thought even as far as that. Thought appeared to be suspended. As a typhoon has its calm center, so the mad tumult of her spirit held a false peace. She rested there in it, torpid as to emotion, in a curious coma.

Yet she retained her powers of observation. She took her seat before the tanks in which she had demonstrated the correctness of David's amazing scientific assumption. Yet now the creatures that he had burgeoned by his skill, usurping, as it might seem to a timid mind, the very function of the Creator, looked absurd and futile--hateful even. For these things, bearing, as it was possible, after all, no relation to actual life, had she spent her days in desperate service. Then, suddenly, it swept over her, like a blasting wave of ignited gas, that she never had had the pure scientific flame! She had not worked for Truth, but that David might reap great rewards. With her as with the cave woman, the man's favor was the thing! If the cave woman won his approval with base service, she, the aspiring creature of modern times, was no less the slave of her own subservient instincts! And she had failed as the cave woman failed--as all women seemed eventually to fail. The ever repeated tragedy of woman had merely been enacted once more, with herself for the sorry heroine.

Yet none of these thoughts was distinct. They passed from her mind like the spume puffed from the wave's crest. She knew nothing of time. Around her blazed and sputtered the terrible white lights. The day waned; the darkness fell; and when night had long passed its dark meridian and the anticipatory cocks began to scent the dawn and to make their discovery known, there came a sharp knocking at the door.

It shattered Honora's horrible reverie as if it had been an explosion. The chambers of her ears quaked with the reverberations. She sprang to her feet with a scream which rang through the silent building.

"Let me in! Let me in!" called a voice. "It's only Kate. Let me in, Honora, or I'll call some one to break down the door."

Kate had mercy on that distorted face which confronted her. It was not the part of loyalty or friendship to look at it. She turned out the spluttering, glaring lights, and quiet and shadow stole over the room.

"Well, Honora, I found the note and I know the whole of your trouble. Remember," she said quietly, "it's your great hour. You have a chance to show what you're made of now."

"What I'm made of!" said Honora brokenly. "I'm like all the women. I'm dying of jealousy, Kate,--dying of it."

"Jealousy--you?" cried Kate. "Why, Honora--"

"You thought I couldn't feel it, I suppose,--thought I was above it? I'm not above anything--not anything--" Her voice straggled off into a curious, shameless sob with a sound in it like the bleating of a lamb.

"Stop that!" said Kate, sharply. "Pull yourself together, woman. Don't be a fool."

"Go away," sobbed Honora. "Don't stay here to watch me. My heart is broken, that's all. Can't you let me alone?"

"No, I can't--I won't. Stand up and fight, woman. You can be magnificent, if you want to. It can't be that you'd grovel, Honora."

"You know very little of what you're talking about," cried Honora, whipped into wholesome anger at last. "I've been a fool from the beginning. The whole thing's my fault."

"I don't see how."

Kate was getting her to talk; was pulling her up out of the pit of shame and anguish into which she had fallen. She sat down in a deal chair which stood by the window, and Honora, without realizing it, dropped into a chair, too. The neutral morning sky was beginning to flush and the rosiness reached across the lead-gray lake, illuminated the windows of the sleeping houses, and tinted even the haggard monochrome of the laboratory with a promise of day.

"Why, it's my fault because I wouldn't take what was coming to me. I wouldn't even be what I was born to be!"

"I know," said Kate, "that you underwent some sort of a transformation. What was it?"

She hardly expected an answer, but Honora developed a perfervid lucidity.

"Oh, Kate, you've said yourself that I was a very different girl when you knew me first. I was a student then, and an ambitious one, too; but there wasn't a girl in this city more ready for a woman's rôle than I. I longed to be loved--I lived in the idea of it. No matter how hard I tried to devote myself to the notion of a career, I really was dreaming of the happiness that was going to come to me when--when Life had done its duty by me."

She spoke the words with a dramatic clearness. The terrific excitement she had undergone, and which she now held in hand, sharpened her faculties. The powers of memory and of expression were intensified. She fairly burned upon Kate there in the beautiful, disguising light of the morning. Her weary face was flushed; her eyes were luminous. Her terrific sorrow put on the mask of joy.

"You see, I loved David almost from the first--I mean from the beginning of my University work. The first time I saw him crossing the campus he held my attention. There was no one else in the least like him, so vivid, so exotic, so almost fierce. When I found out who he was, I confess that I directed my studies so that I should work with him. Not that I really expected to know him personally, but I wanted to be near him and have him enlarge life for me. I felt that it would take on new meanings if I could only hear his interpretations of it."

Kate shivered with sympathy at the woman's passion, and something like envy stirred in her. Here was a world of delight and torment of which she knew nothing, and beside it her own existence, restless and eager though it had been, seemed a meager affair.

"Well, the idea burned in me for months and years. But I hid it. No one guessed anything about it. Certainly David knew nothing of it. Then, when I was beginning on my graduate work, I was with him daily. But he never seemed to see me--he saw only my work, and he seldom praised that. He expected it to be well done. As for me, I was satisfied. The mere fact that we were comrades, forced to think of the same matters several hours of each day, contented me. I couldn't imagine what life would be away from him; and I was afraid to think of him in relation to myself."

"Afraid?"

"Afraid--I mean just that. I knew others thought him a genius in relation to his work. But I knew he was a genius in regard to life. I felt sure that, if he turned that intensity of his upon life instead of upon science, he would be a destructive force--a high explosive. This idea of mine was confirmed in time. It happened one evening when a number of us were over in the Scammon Garden listening to the out-of-door players. I grew tired of sitting and slipped from my seat to wander about a little in the darkness. I had reached the very outer edge of seats and was standing there enjoying the garden, when I overheard two persons talking together. A man said: 'Fulham will go far if he doesn't meet a woman.' 'Nonsense,' the woman said; 'he's an anchorite.' 'An inflammatory one,' the man returned. 'Mind, I don't say he knows it. Probably he thinks he's cast for the scientific rôle to the end of his days, but I know the fellow better than he does himself. I tell you, if a woman of power gets hold of him, he'll be as drunk as Abélard with the madness of it. Over in Europe they allow for that sort of thing. They let a man make an art of loving. Here they insist that it shall be incidental. But Fulham won't care about conventionalities if the idea ever grips him. He's born for love, and it's a lucky thing for the University that he hasn't found it out.' 'We ought to plan a sane and reasonable marriage for him,' said the woman. 'Wouldn't that be a good compromise?' 'It would be his salvation,' the man said."

Honora poured the words out with such rapidity that Kate hardly could follow her.

"How you remember it all!" broke in Kate.

"If I remember anything, wouldn't it be that? As I say, it confirmed me in what I already had guessed. I felt fierce to protect him. My jealousy was awake in me. I watched him more closely than ever. His daring in the laboratory grew daily. He talked openly about matters that other men were hardly daring to dream of, and his brain seemed to expand every day like some strange plant under calcium rays. I thought what a frightful loss to science it would be if the wilder qualities of his nature got the upper hand, and I wondered how I could endure it if--"

She drew herself up with a horror of realization. The thing that so long ago she had thought she could not endure was at last upon her! Her teeth began to chatter again, and her hands, which had been clasped, to twist themselves with the writhing motion of the mentally distraught.

"Go on!" commanded Kate. "What happened next?"

"I let him love me!"

"I thought you said he hadn't noticed you."

"He hadn't; and I didn't talk with him more than usual or coquette with him. But I let down the barriers in my mind. I never had been ashamed of loving him, but now I willed my love to stream out toward him like--like banners of light. If I had called him aloud, he couldn't have answered more quickly. He turned toward me, and I saw all his being set my way. Oh, it was like a transfiguration! Then, as soon as ever I saw that, I began holding him steady. I let him feel that we were to keep on working side by side, quietly using and increasing our knowledge. I made him scourge his love back; I made him keep his mind uppermost; I saved him from himself."

"Oh, Honora! And then you were married?"

"And then we were married. You remember how sudden it was, and how wonderful; but not wonderful in the way it might have been. I kept guard over myself. I wouldn't wear becoming dresses; I wouldn't even let him dream what I really was like--wouldn't let him see me with my hair down because I knew it was beautiful. I combed it plainly and dressed like a nurse or a nun, and every day I went to the laboratory with him and kept him at his work. He had got hold of this dazzling idea of the extraneous development of life, and he set himself to prove it. I worked early and late to help him. I let him go out and meet people and reap honors, and I stayed and did the drudgery. But don't imagine I was a martyr. I liked it. I belonged to him. It was my honor and delight to work for him. I wanted him to have all of the credit. The more important the result, the more satisfaction I should have in proclaiming him the victor. I was really at the old business of woman, subordinating myself to a man I loved. But I was doing it in a new way, do you see? I was setting aside the privilege of my womanhood for him, refraining from making any merely feminine appeal. You remember hearing Dr. von Shierbrand say there was but one way woman should serve man--the way in which Marguerite served Faust? It made me laugh. I knew a harder road than that to walk--a road of more complete abnegation."

"But the babies came."

"Yes, the babies came. I was afraid even to let him be as happy in them as he wanted to be. I held him away. I wouldn't let him dwell on the thought of me as the mother of those darlings. I dared not even be as happy myself as I wished, but I had secret joys that I told him nothing about, because I was saving him for himself and his work. But at what a cost, Kate!"

"Honora, it was sacrilegious!"

Honora leaped to her feet again.

"Yes, yes," she cried, "it was. And now all has happened according to prophecy, and he's gone with this woman! He thinks she's his mate, but, I--I was his mate. And I defrauded him. So now he's taken her because she was kind, because she loved him, because--she was beautiful!"

"She looks like you."

"Don't I know it? It's my beauty that he's gone away with--the beauty I wouldn't let him see. Of course, he doesn't realize it. He only knows life cheated him, and now he's trying to make up to himself for what he's lost."

"Oh, can you excuse him like that?"

The daylight was hardening, and it threw Honora's drawn face into repellent relief.

"I don't excuse him at all!" she said. "I condemn him! I condemn him! With all his intellect, to be such a fool! And to be so cruel--so hideously cruel!"

But she checked herself sharply. She looked around her with eyes that seemed to take in things visible and invisible--all that had been enacted in that curious room, all the paraphernalia, all the significance of those uncompleted, important experiments. Then suddenly her face paled and yet burned with light.

"But I know a great revenge," she said. "I know a revenge that will break his heart!"

"Don't say things like that," begged Kate. "I don't recognize you when you're like that."

"When you hear what the revenge is, you will," said Honora proudly.

"We're going now," Kate told her with maternal decision. "Here's your coat."

"Home?" She began trembling again and the haunted look crept back into her eyes.

Kate paid no heed. She marched Honora swiftly along the awakened streets and into the bereaved house, past the desecrated chamber where David's bed stood beside his wife's, up to Kate's quiet chamber. Honora stretched herself out with an almost moribund gesture. Then the weight of her sorrow covered her like a blanket. She slept the strange deep sleep of those who dare not face the waking truth.

CHAPTER XVII

Kate, who *was* facing it, telegraphed to Karl Wander. It was all she could think of to do.

"Can you come?" she asked. "David Fulham has gone away with Mary Morrison. Honora needs you. You are the cousin of both women. Thought I had better turn to you." She was brutally frank, but it never occurred to her to mince matters there. However, where the public was concerned, her policy was one of secrecy. She called, for example, on the President of the University, who already knew the whole story.

"Can't we keep it from being blazoned abroad?" she appealed to him. "Mrs. Fulham will suffer more if he has to undergo public shame than she possibly could suffer from her own desertion. She's tragically angry, but that wouldn't keep her from wanting to protect him. We must try to prevent public exposure. It will save her the worst of torments." She brooded sadly over the idea, her aspect broken and pathetic.

The President looked at her kindly.

"Did she say so?"

"Oh, she didn't need to say so!" cried Kate. "Any one would know that."

"You mean, any good woman would know that. Of course, I can give it out that Fulham has been called abroad suddenly, but it places me in a bad position. I don't feel very much like lying for him, and I shan't be thought any too well of if I'm found out. I should like to place myself on record as befriending Mrs. Fulham, not her husband."

"But don't you see that you are befriending her when you shield him?"

"Woman's logic," said the President. "It has too many turnings for my feeble masculine intellect. But I've great confidence in you, Miss Barrington. You seem to be rather a specialist in domestic relations. If you say Mrs. Fulham will be happier for having me bathe neck-deep in lies, I suppose I shall have to oblige you. Shall it be the lie circumstantial? Do you wish to specify the laboratory to which he has gone?"

Kate blushed with sudden contrition.

"Oh, I'll not ask you to do it!" she cried. "Truth is best, of course. I'm not naturally a trimmer and a compromiser--but, poor Honora! I pity her so!"

Her lips quivered like a child's and the tears stood in her eyes. She had arisen to go and the President shook hands with her without making any promise. However the next day a paragraph appeared in the University Daily to the effect that Professor Fulham had been called to France upon important laboratory matters.

At the Caravansary they had scented tragedy, and Kate faced them with the paragraph. She laid a marked copy of the paper at each place, and when all were assembled, she called attention to it. They looked at her with questioning eyes.

"Of course," said Dr. von Shierbrand, flicking his mustache, "this isn't true, Miss Barrington."

"No," said Kate, and faced them with her chin tilted high.

"But you wish us to pretend to believe it?"

"If you please, dear friends," Kate pleaded.

"We shall say that Fulham is in France! And what are we to say about Miss Morrison?"

"Who will inquire? If any one should, say that a friend desired her as a traveling companion."

"Nothing," said Von Shierbrand, "is easier for me than truth."

"Please don't be witty," cried Kate testily, "and don't sneer. Remember that nothing is so terrible as temptation. I'm sure I see proof of that every day among my poor people. After all, doesn't the real surprise lie in the number that resist it?"

"I beg your pardon," said the young German gently. "I shall not sneer. I shall not even be witty. I'm on your side,--that is to say, on Mrs. Fulham's side,--and I'll say anything you want me to say."

"I beg you all," replied Kate, sweeping the table with an imploring glance, "to say as little as possible. Be matter-of-fact if any one questions you. And, whatever you do, shield Honora."

They gave their affirmation solemnly, and the next day Honora appeared among them, pallid and courageous. They were simple folk for all of their learning. Sorrow was sorrow to them. Honora was widowed by an accident more terrible than death. No mockery, no affected solicitude detracted from the efficacy of their sympathy. If they saw torments of jealousy in this betrayed woman's eyes, they averted their gaze; if they saw shame, they gave it other interpretations. Moreover, Kate was constantly beside her, eagle-keen for slight or neglect. Her fierce fealty guarded the stricken woman on every side. She had the imposing piano which Mary had rented carted back to the warehouse to lie in deserved silence with Mary's seductive harmonies choked in its recording fibre; she stripped from their poles the curtains Mary had hung at the drawing-room windows and burned them in the furnace; the miniatures, the plaster casts, all the artistic rubbish which Mary's exuberance had impelled her to collect, were tossed out for the waste wagons to cart away. The coquetry of the room gave way to its old-time austerity; once more Honora's room possessed itself.

A wire came from Karl Wander addressed to Kate.

"Fractured leg. Can't go to you. Honora and the children must come here at once. Have written."

That seemed to give Honora a certain repose--it was at least a spar to which to cling. With Kate's help she got over to the laboratory and put the finishing touches on things there. The President detailed two of Fulham's most devoted disciples to make a record of their professor's experiments.

"Fulham shall have full credit," the President assured Honora, calling on her and comforting her in the way in which he perceived she needed comfort. "He shall have credit for everything."

"He should have the Norden prize," Honora cried, her hot eyes blazing above her hectic cheeks. "I want him to have the prize, and I want to be the means of getting it for him. I told Miss Barrington I meant to have my revenge, and that's it. How can he stand it to know he ruined my life and that I got the prize for him? A generous man would find that torture! You understand, I'm willing to torture him--in that way. He's subtle enough to feel the sting of it."

The President looked at her compassionately.

"It's a noble revenge--and a poignant one," he agreed.

"It's not noble," repudiated Honora. "It's terrible. For he'll remember who did the work."

But shame overtook her and she sobbed deeply and rendingly. And the President, who had thought of himself as a mild man, left the house regretting that duels were out of fashion.

Then the letter came from the West. Kate carried it up to Honora, who was in her room crouched before the window, peering out at the early summer cityscape with eyes which tried in vain to observe the passing motors, and the people hastening along the Plaisance, but which registered little.

"Your cousin's letter, woman, dear," announced Kate.

Honora looked up quickly, her vagueness momentarily dissipated. Kate always had noticed that Wander's name had power to claim Honora's interest. He could make folk listen, even though he spoke by letter. She felt, herself, that whatever he said, she would listen to.

Honora tore open the envelope with untidy eagerness, and after she had read the letter she handed it silently to Kate. It ran thus:--

"COUSIN HONORA, MY DEAR AND PRIZED:--

"Rather a knock-out blow, eh? I shan't waste my time in telling you how I feel about it. If you want me to follow David and kill him, I will--as soon as this damned leg gets well. Not that the job appeals to me. I'm sensitive about family honor, but killing D. won't mend things. As I spell the matter out, there was a blunder somewhere. *Perhaps you know where it was.*

"Of course you feel as if you'd gone into bankruptcy. Women invest in happiness as men do in property, and to 'go broke' the way you have is disconcerting. It would overwhelm some women; but it won't you--not if you're the same Honora I played with when I was a boy. You had pluck for two of us trousered animals--were the best of the lot. I want you to come here and stake out a new claim. You may get to be a millionaire yet--in good luck and happiness, I mean.

"I'm taking it for granted that you and the babies will soon be on your way to me, and I'm putting everything in readiness. The fire is laid, the cupboard stored, the latchstring is hanging where you'll see it as you cross the state line.

"You understand I'm being selfish in this. I not only want, but I need, you. You always seemed more like a sister than a cousin to me, and to have you come here and make a home out of my house seems too good to be true.

"There are a lot of things to be learned out here, but I'll not give them a name. All I can say is, living with these mountains makes you different. They're like men and women, I take it. (The mountains, I mean.) The more they are ravaged by internal fires and scoured by snow-slides, the more interesting they become.

"Then it's so still it gives you a chance to think, and by the time you've had a good bout of it, you find out what is really important and what isn't. You'll understand after you've been here awhile.

"I mean what I say, Honora. I want you and the babies. Come ahead. Don't think. Work--pack--and get out here where Time can have a chance at your wounds.

"Am I making you understand how I feel for you? I guess you know your old playmate and coz,

"KARL WANDER.

"P.S. My dried-up old bach heart jumps at the thought of having the kiddies in the house. I'll bet they're wonders."

There was an inclosure for Kate. It read:--

"MY DEAR MISS BARRINGTON:--

"I see that you're one of the folk who can be counted on. You help Honora out of this and then tell me what I can do for you. I'd get to her some way even with this miserable plaster-of-Paris leg of mine if you weren't there. But I know you'll play the cards right. Can't you come with her and stay with her awhile till she's more used to the change? You'd be as welcome as sunlight. But I don't even need to say that. I saw you only a moment, yet I think you know that I'd count it a rich day if I could see you again. You are one of those who understand a thing without having it bellowed by megaphone.

"Don't mind my emphatic English. I'm upset. I feel like murdering a man, and the sensation isn't pleasant. Using language is too common out here to attract attention--even on the part of the man who uses it. Oh, my poor Honora! Look after her, Miss Barrington, and add all my pity and love to your own. It will make quite a sum. Yours faithfully,

"KARL WANDER."

"He wrote to you, too?" inquired Honora when Kate had perused her note.

"Yes, begging me to hasten you on your way."

"Shall I go?"

"What else offers?"

"Nothing," said Honora in her dead voice. "If I kept a diary, I would be like that sad king of France who recorded '*Rien*' each day."

Kate made a practical answer.

"We must pack," she said.

"But the house--"

"Let it stand empty if the owner can't find a tenant. Pay your rent till he does, if that's in the contract. What difference does all that make? Get out where you'll have a chance to recuperate."

"Oh, Kate, do you think I ever shall? How does a person recuperate from shame?"

"There isn't really any shame to you in what others do," Kate said.

"But you--you'll have to go somewhere."

"So I shall. Don't worry about me. I shall take good care of myself."

Honora looked about her with the face of a spent runner.

"I don't see how I'm going to go through with it all," she said, shuddering.

So Kate found packers and movers and the breaking-up of the home was begun. It was an ordeal--even a greater ordeal than they had thought it would be. Every one who knew Honora had supposed that she cared more for the laboratory than for her home, but when the packers came and tore the pictures from the walls, it might have been her heart-strings that were severed.

Just before the last things were taken out, Kate found her in an agony of weeping on David's bed, which stood with an appalling emptiness beside Honora's. Honora always had wakened first in the morning, Kate knew, and now she guessed at the memories that wrung that great, self-obliterating creature, writhing there under her torment. How often she must have raised herself on her arm and looked over at her man, so handsome, so strong, so completely, as she supposed, her own, and called to him, summoning him to another day's work at the great task they had undertaken for themselves. She had planned to be a wife upon an heroic model, and he had wanted mere blitheness, mere feminine allure. Then, after all, as it turned out, here at hand were all the little qualities, he had desired, like violets hidden beneath their foliage.

Kate thought she never had seen anything more feminine than Honora, shivering over the breaking-tip of the linen-closet, where her housewifely stores were kept.

"I don't suppose you can understand, dear," she moaned to Kate. "But it's a sort of symbol--a linen-closet is. See, I hemmed all these things with my own hands before I was married, and embroidered the initials!"

How could any one have imagined that the masculine traits in her were getting the upper hand! She grew more feminine every hour. There was an increasing rhythm in her movements--a certain rich solemnity like that of Niobe or Hermione. Her red-brown hair tumbled about her face and festooned her statuesque shoulders. The severity of her usual attire gave place to a negligence which enhanced her picturesqueness, and the heaving of her troubled bosom, the lifting of her wistful eyes gave her a tenderer beauty than she ever had had before. She was passionate enough now to have suited even that avid man who had proved himself so delinquent.

"If only David could have seen her like this!" mused Kate. "His 'Blue-eyed One' would have seemed tepid in comparison. To think she submerged her splendor to so little purpose!"

She wondered if Honora knew how right Karl Wander had been in saying that some one had blundered, and if she had gained so much enlightenment that she could see that it was herself who had done so. She had renounced the mistress qualities which the successful wife requires to supplement her wifely character, and she had learned too late that love must have other elements than the rigidly sensible ones.

Honora was turning to the little girls now with a fierce sense of maternal possession. She performed personal services for them. She held them in her arms at twilight and breathed in their personality as if it were the one anaesthetic that could make her oblivious to her pain.

Kate hardly could keep from crying out:--

"Too late! Too late!"

There was a bleak, attic-like room at the Caravansary, airy enough, and glimpsing the lake from its eastern window, which Kate took temporarily for her abiding-place. She had her things moved over there and camped amid the chaos till Honora should be gone.

The day came when the two women, with the little girls, stood on the porch of the house which had proved so ineffective a home. Kate turned the key.

"I hope never to come back to Chicago, Kate," Honora said, lifting her ravaged face toward the staring blankness of the windows. "I'm not brave enough."

"Not foolish enough, you mean," corrected Kate. "Hold tight to the girlies, Honora, and you'll come out all right."

Honora refrained from answering. Her woe was epic, and she let her sunken eyes and haggard countenance speak for her.

Kate saw David Fulham's deserted family off on the train. Mrs. Hays, the children's nurse, accompanied them. Honora moved with a slow hauteur in her black gown, looking like a disenthroned queen, and as she walked down the train aisle Kate thought of Marie Antoinette. There were plenty of friends, as both women knew, who would have been glad to give any encouragement their presence could have contributed, but it was generally understood that the truth of the situation was not to be recognized.

When Kate got back on the platform, Honora became just Honora again, thinking of and planning for others. She thrust her head from the window.

"Oh, Kate," she said, "I do hope you'll get well settled somewhere and feel at home. Don't stay in that attic, dear. It would make me feel as if I had put you into it."

"Trust me!" Kate reassured her. She waved her hand with specious gayety. "Give my love to Mr. Wander," she laughed.

CHAPTER XVIII

Kate was alone at last. She had time to think. There were still three days left of the vacation for which she had begged when she perceived Honora's need of her, and these she spent in settling her room. It would not accommodate all of the furniture she had accumulated during those days of enthusiasm over Ray McCrea's return, so she sold the superfluous things. Truth to tell, however, she kept the more decorative ones. Honora's fate had taught her an indelible lesson. She saw clearly that happiness for women did not lie along the road of austerity.

Was it humiliating to have to acknowledge that women were desired for their beauty, their charm, for the air of opulence which they gave to an otherwise barren world? Her mind cast back over the ages--over the innumerable forms of seduction and subserviency which the instinct of women had induced them to assume, and she reddened to flame sitting alone in the twilight. Yet, an hour later, still thinking of the subject, she realized that it was for men rather than for women that she had to blush. Woman was what man had made her, she concluded.

Yet man was often better than woman--more generous, more just, more high-minded, possessed of a deeper faith.

Well, well, it was at best a confusing world! She seemed to be like a ship without a chart or a port of destination. But at least she could accept things as they were--even the fact that she herself was not "in commission," and was, philosophically speaking, a derelict.

"Other women seem to do things by instinct," she mused, "but I have, apparently, to do them from conviction. It must be the masculine traits in me. They say all women have masculine traits, that if they were purely feminine, they would be monstrous; and that all civilized men have much of the feminine in them or they would not be civilized. I suppose there's rather more of the masculine in me than in the majority of women."

Now Mary Morrison, she concluded, was almost pure feminine--she was the triumphant exposition of the feminine principle.

Some lines of Arthur Symons came to her notice--lines which she tried in vain not to memorize.

> "'I am the torch,' she saith; 'and what to me
>   If the moth die of me? I am the flame
> Of Beauty, and I burn that all may see
>   Beauty, and I have neither joy nor shame,
> But live with that clear light of perfect fire
> Which is to men the death of their desire.
>
> "'I am Yseult and Helen, I have seen
>   Troy burn, and the most loving knight lies dead.
> The world has been my mirror, time has been
>   My breath upon the glass; and men have said,
> Age after age, in rapture and despair,
> Love's few poor words before my mirror there.
>
> "'I live and am immortal; in my eyes
>   The sorrow of the world, and on my lips
> The joy of life, mingle to make me wise!'"...

Was it wisdom, then, that Mary Morrison possessed--the immemorial wisdom of women?

Oh, the shame of it! The shame of being a woman!

Kate denied herself to McCrea when he called. She plunged into the development of her scheme for an extension of motherhood. State motherhood it would be. Should the movement become national, as she hoped, perhaps it had best be called the Bureau of Children.

It was midsummer by now and there was some surcease of activity even in "welfare" circles. Many of the social workers, having grubbed in unspeakable slums all winter, were now abroad among palaces and cathedrals, drinking their fill of beauty. Many were in the country near at hand. For the most part, neophytes were in charge at the settlement houses. Kate was again urged to domesticate herself with Jane Addams's corps of workers, but she had an aversion to being shut between walls. She had been trapped once,--back at the place she called home,--and she had not liked it. There was something free and adventurous in going from house to house, authoritatively rearranging the affairs of the disarranged. It suited her to be "a traveling bishop." Moreover, it left her time for the development of her great Idea. In a neighborhood house privacy and leisure were the two unattainable luxuries.

She was still writing at odd times'; and now her articles were appearing. They were keen, simple, full of meat, and the public liked them. As Kate read them over, she smiled to find them so emphatic. She was far from *feeling* emphatic, but she seemed to have a trick of expressing herself in that way. She was still in need of great economy. Her growing influence brought little to her in the way of monetary rewards, and it was hard for her to live within her income because she had a scattering hand. She liked to dispense good things and she liked to have them. A liberal programme suited her best--whatever gave free play to life. She was a wild creature in that she hated bars. Of all the prison houses of life, poverty seemed one of the most hectoring.

But poverty, to be completely itself, must exclude opportunity. Kate had the key to opportunity, and she realized it. In the letters she received and wrote bringing her into association with men and women of force and aspiration, she had a privilege to which, for all of her youth, she could not be indifferent. She liked the way these purposeful persons put things, and felt a distinct pleasure in matching their ideas with her own. As the summer wore on, she was asked to country homes of charm and taste--homes where wealth, though great, was subordinated to more essential things. There she met those who could further her purposes--who could lend their influence to aid her Idea, now shaping itself excellently. At the suggestion of Miss Addams, she prepared an article in which her plan unfolded itself in all its benevolent length and breadth--an article which it was suggested might yet form a portion of a speech made before a congressional committee. There was even talk of having Kate deliver this address, but she had not yet reached the point where she could contemplate such an adventure with calmness.

However, she was having training in her suffrage work, which was now assuming greater importance in her eyes. She addressed women audiences in various parts of the city, and had even gone on a few flying motor excursions with leading suffragists, speaking to the people in villages and at country schoolhouses.

There was an ever-increasing conviction in this department of her work. She had learned to count the ballot as the best bulwark of liberty, and she could find no logic to inform her why, if it was a protection for man,--for the least and most insignificant of men,--it was not equally a weapon which women, searching now as never before for defined and enduring forms of liberty, should be permitted to use. She not only desired it for other women,--women who were supposed to "need it" more,--but she wished it for herself. She felt it to be merely consistent that she, in whom service to her community was becoming a necessity, should have this privilege. It never would be possible for her to exercise murderous powers of destruction in behalf of her country. She would not be allowed to shoot down innocent men whose opinions were opposed to her own, or to make widows and orphans. She would be forbidden to stand behind cannon or to sink submarine torpedoes. But it was within her reach to add to the sum total of peace and happiness. She would, if she could get her Bureau of Children established, exercise a constructive influence completely in accord with the spirit of the time. This being the case, she thought she ought to have the ballot. It would make her stand up straighter, spiritually speaking. It would give her the authority which would point her arguments; put a cap on the sheaf of her endeavors. She wanted it precisely as a writer wants a period to complete a sentence. It had a structural value, to use the term of an architect. Without it her sentence was foolish, her building insecure.

"Why is it," she demanded of the women of Lake Geneva when, in company with a veteran suffragist, she addressed them there, "that you grow weary in working for your town? It is because you cannot demonstrate your meaning nor secure the continuation of your works by the ballot. Your efforts are like pieces of metal which you cannot weld into useful form. You toil for deserted children, indigent mothers, for hospitals and asylums, starting movements which, when perfected, are absorbed by the city. What happens then to these benevolent enterprises? They are placed in the hands of politicians and perfunctorily administered. Your disinterested services are lost sight of; the politicians smile at the manner in which you have toiled and they have reaped. You see sink into uselessness, institutions, which, in the compassionate hands of women, would be the promoters of good through the generations. The people you would benefit are treated with that insolent arrogance which only a cheap man in office can assume. Causes you have labored to establish, and which no one denies are benefits, are capriciously overthrown. And there is one remedy and one only: for you to cast your vote--for you to have your say as you sit in your city council, on your county board, or in your state legislature and national congress.

"You may shrink from it; you may dread these new responsibilities; but strength and courage will come with your need. You dare not turn aside from the road which opens before you, for to tread it is now the test of integrity."

"Ought you to have said that?" inquired the older suffragist, afterward looking at Kate with earnest and burning eyes from her white spiritual face. "I dare say I care much more about suffrage than you. I have been interested in it since I was a child, and I am now no longer a young woman. Yet I feel that integrity is not allied to this or that opinion. It is a question of sincerity--of steadfastness of purpose."

"There, there," said Kate, "don't expect me to be too moderate. How can I care about anything just now if I have to be moderate? I love suffrage because it gives me something to care about and to work for. The last generation has destroyed pretty much all of the theology, hasn't it? Service of man is all there is left--particularly that branch of it known as the service of woman. Isn't that what all of the poets and playwrights and novelists are writing about? Isn't that the most interesting thing in the world at present? You've all urged me to go into it, haven't you? Very well, I have. But I can't stay in it if I'm to be tepid. You mustn't expect me to modify my utterance and cut down my climaxes. I've got to make a hot propaganda of the thing. I want the exhilaration of martyrdom--though I'm not keen for the discomforts of it. In other words, dear lady, because you are judicious, don't expect me to be. I don't want to be judicious--yet. I want to be fervid."

"You are a dear girl," said the elder woman, "but you are an egotist, as of course you know."

"If I had been a modest violet by a mossy stone," laughed Kate, "should I have taken up this work?"

"I'm free to confess that you would not," said the other, checking a sigh as if she despaired of bringing this excited girl down to the earth. "Yet I am bound to say--" She hesitated and Kate took up the word.

"I *do* know--I really understand," she cried contritely. "You are not an egotist at all, dear lady. Though you have held many positions of honor, you have never thought of yourself. Your sacrifices have been *bona fide*. You who are so delicate and tender have done things which men might have shrunk from. I know what you mean by sincerity, and I am aware that you have it completely and steadily, whereas I have more enthusiasm than is good either for myself or the cause. But you wouldn't want me to form myself on you, would you now? Temperament is just as much a fact as physique. I've got to dramatize woman's disadvantages if I am to preach on the subject.

Though I really think there are tragedies of womanhood which none could exaggerate."

"Oh, there are, there are, Miss Barrington."

"How shall I make you understand that I am to be trusted!" Kate cried. "I know I'm avid. I want both pain and joy. I want to suffer with the others and enjoy with the others. I want my cup of life full and running over with a brew of a thousand flavors, and I actually believe I want to taste of the cup each neighbor holds. I have to know how others feel and it's my nature to feel for them and with them. When I see this great wave of aspiration sweeping over women,--Chinese and Persian women as well as English and American,--I feel magnificent. I, too, am standing where the stream of influence blows over me. It thrills me magnificently, and I am meaning it when I say that I think the women who do not feel it are torpid or cowardly."

The elder woman smiled patiently. After all, who was she that she should check her flaming disciple?

CHAPTER XIX

Whenever Kate had a free Sunday, she and Mrs. Dennison, the mistress of the Caravansary, would go together to the West Side to visit George and Marna Fitzgerald. It amused and enchanted Kate to think that in the midst of so much that was commonplace, with dull apartment buildings stretching around for miles, such an Arcadia should have located itself. It opened her eyes to the fact that there might be innumerable Arcadians concealed in those monotonous rows of three-and four-story flat buildings, if only one had the wisdom and wit to find them. Marna seemed to know of some. She had become acquainted with a number of these happy unknown little folk, to whom it never had occurred that celebrity was an essential of joy, and she liked them mightily. Marna, indeed, liked high and low--always providing she didn't dislike them. If they were Irish, her inclination toward them was accelerated. There were certain wonders of Marna's ardent soul which were for "Irish faces only"--Irish eyes were the eyes she liked best to have upon her. But she forgave Kate her Anglo-Saxon ancestry because of her talent for appreciating the Irish character.

Time was passing beautifully with Marna, and her Bird of Hope was fluttering nearer. She told Kate that now she could see some sense in being a woman.

"If you'd ask me," she said with childish audacity, "if such a foolish little thing as I could actually have a wonderful, dear little baby, I'd have said 'no' right at the start. I'm as flattered as I can be. And what pleases me so is that I don't have to be at all different from what I naturally am. I don't have to be learned or tremendously good; it isn't a question of deserts. It has just come to me--who never did deserve any such good!"

Next door to Marna there was a young Irishwoman of whom the Fitzgeralds saw a good deal, the mother of five little children, with not more than sixteen months between the ages of any of them. Mary Finn had been beautiful--so much was evident at a glance. But she already wore a dragged expression; and work, far beyond her powers to accomplish, was making a sloven of her. She was petulant with the children, though she adored them--at least, sporadically. But her burden tired her patience out. Timothy Finn's income had not increased in proportion to his family. He was now in his young manhood, at the height of his earning capacity, and early middle-age might see him suffering a reduction.

Mrs. Finn dropped in Sunday afternoon to share the cup of tea which Marna was offering her guests, and as she looked wistfully out of her tangle of dark hair,--in which lines of silver already were beginning to appear,-- she impressed herself upon Kate's mind as one of the innumerable army of martyrs to the fetish of fecundity which had borne down men and women through the centuries.

She had her youngest child with her.

"It was a terrible time before I could get up from the last one," she said, "me that was around as smart as could be with the first. I'm in living terror all the time for fear of what's coming to me. A mother has no business to die, that's what I tell Tim. Who'd look to the ones I have, with me taken? I'm sharp with them at times, but God knows I'd die for 'em. Blessed be, they understand my scolding, the dears. It's a cuff and a kiss with me, and I declare I don't know which they like best. They may howl when I hurt them, but they know it's their own mother doing the cuffing, and in their hearts they don't care. It's that way with cubs, ye see. Mother bear knows how hard to box the ears of 'em. But it's truth I'm saying, Mrs. Fitzgerald; there's little peace for women. They don't seem to belong to themselves at all, once they're married. It's very happy you are, looking forward to your first, and you have my good wishes. More than that, I'll be proud to be of any service to you I can when your time comes--it's myself has had experience enough! But, I tell you, the joy runs out when you're slaving from morning to night, and then never getting the half done that you ought; and when you don't know what it is to have two hours straight sleep at night; and maybe your husband scolding at the noise the young ones make. Love 'em? Of course, you love 'em. But you can stand only so much. After that, you're done for. And the agony of passing and leaving the children motherless is something I don't like to think about."

She bared her thin breast to her nursing babe, rocking slowly, her blue eyes straining into the future with its menace.

"But," said Marna, blushing with embarrassment, "need there be such--such a burden? Don't you think it right to--to--"

"Neither God nor man seems to have any mercy on me," cried the little woman passionately. "I say I'm in a trap--that's the truth of it. If I was a selfish, bad mother, I could get out of it; if I was a mean wife, I could, too,

I suppose. I've tried to do what was right,--what other people told me was right,--and I pray it won't kill me--for I ought to live for the children's sake."

The child was whining because of lack of nourishment, and Mrs. Finn put it to the other breast, but it fared little better there. Mrs. Dennison was looking on with her mild, benevolent aspect.

"My dear," she said at last with an air of gentle authority, "I'm going out to get a bottle and good reliable infant food for that child. You haven't strength enough to more than keep yourself going, not to say anything about the baby."

She took the child out of the woman's arms and gave it to Kate.

"But I don't think I ought to wean it when it's so young," cried Mrs. Finn, breaking down and wringing her thin hands with an immemorial Hibernian gesture. "Tim wouldn't like it, and his mother would rage at me."

"They'll like it when they see the baby getting some flesh on its bones," insisted Mrs. Dennison. "There's more than one kind of a fight a mother has to put up for her children. They used to think it fine for a woman to kill herself for her children, but I don't think it's so much the fashion now. As you say, a mother has no business to die; it's the part of intelligence to live. So you just have a set-to with your old-fashioned mother-in-law if it's necessary."

"Yes," put in Kate, "the new generation always has to fight the old in the interests of progress."

Marna broke into a rippling laugh.

"That's her best platform manner," she cried. "Just think, Mrs. Finn, my friend talks on suffrage."

"Oh!" gasped the little Irishwoman, involuntarily putting out her hands as if she would snatch her infant from such a contaminating hold.

But Kate drew back smilingly.

"Yes," she said significantly, "I believe in woman's rights."

She held on to the baby, and Mrs. Dennison, putting on her hat and coat, went in search of a nursing-bottle.

On the way home, Mrs. Dennison, who was of the last generation, and Kate, who was of the present one, talked the matter over.

"She didn't seem to understand that she had been talking 'woman's rights,'" mused Kate, referring to Mrs. Finn. "The word frightened the poor dear. She didn't see that fatal last word of her 'love, honor, and obey' had her where she might even have to give her life in keeping her word."

"Well, for my part," said Mrs. Dennison, in her mellow, flowing tones, "I always found it a pleasure to obey my husband. But, then, to be sure, I don't know that he ever asked anything inconsiderate of me."

"You were a well-shielded woman, weren't you?" asked Kate.

"I didn't need to lift my hand unless I wished," said Mrs. Dennison in reminiscence.

"And you had no children--"

"But that was a great sorrow."

"Yes, but it wasn't a living vexation and drain. It didn't use up your vitality and suck up your brain power and make a slattern and a drudge of you as having five children in seven years has of little Mrs. Finn. It's all very well to talk of obeying when you aren't asked to obey--or, at least, when you aren't required to do anything difficult. But good Tim Finn, I'll warrant, tells his Mary when she may go and where, and he'd be in a fury if she went somewhere against his desire. Oh, she's playing the old medieval game, you can see that!"

"Dear Kate," sighed Mrs. Dennison, "sometimes your expressions seem to me quite out of taste. I do hope you won't mind my saying so. You're so very emphatic."

"I don't mind a bit, Mrs. Dennison. I dare say I am getting to be rather violent and careless in my way of talking. It's a reaction from the vagueness and prettiness of speech I used to hear down in Silvertree, where they begin their remarks with an 'I'm not sure, but I think,' et cetera. But, really, you must overlook my vehemence. If I could spend my time with sweet souls like you, I'd be a different sort of woman."

"I can't help looking forward, Kate, to the time when you'll be in your own home. You think you're all bound up in this public work, but I can tell by the looks of you that you're just the one to make a good wife for some fine man. I hope you don't think it impertinent of me, but I can't make out why you haven't taken one or the other of the men who want you."

"You think some one wants me?" asked Kate provokingly.

"Oh, we all know that Dr. von Shierbrand would rather be taking you home to see his old German mother than to be made President of the

University of Chicago; and that nice Mr. McCrea is nearly crazy over the way you treat him."

"But it would seem so stale--life in a home with either of them! Should I just have to sit at the window and watch for them to come home?"

"You know you wouldn't," said Mrs. Dennison, almost crossly. "Why do you tease me? What's good enough for other women ought to be good enough for you."

"Oh, what a bad one I am!" cried Kate. "Of course what is good enough for better women than I ought to be good enough for me. But yet--shall I tell the truth about myself?"

"Do," said Mrs. Dennison, placated. "I want you to confide in me, Kate."

"Well, you see, dear lady, suppose that I marry one of the gentlemen of whom you have spoken. Suppose I make a pleasant home for my husband, have two or three nice children, and live a happy and--well, a good life. Then I die and there's the end."

"Well, of course I don't think that's the end," broke in Mrs. Dennison.

Kate evaded the point.

"I mean, there's an end of my earthly existence. Now, on the other hand, suppose I get this Bureau for Children through. Suppose it becomes a fact. Let us play that I am asked to become the head of it, or, if not that, at least to assist in carrying on its work. Then, suppose that, as a result of my work, the unprotected children have protection; the education of all the children in the country is assured--even of the half-witted, and the blind and the deaf and the vicious. Suppose that the care and development of children becomes a great and generally comprehended science, like sanitation, so that the men and women of future generations are more fitted to live than those we now see about us. Don't you think that will be better worth while than my individual happiness? They think a woman heroic when she sacrifices herself for her children, but shouldn't I be much more heroic if I worked all my life for other people's children? For children yet to be born? I ask you that calmly. I don't wish you to answer me to-day. I'm in earnest now, dear Mrs. Dennison, and I'd like you to give me a true answer."

There was a little pause. Mrs. Dennison was trifling nervously with the frogs on her black silk jacket. When she spoke, it was rather diffidently.

"I could answer you so much better, my dear Kate," she said at length, "if I only knew how much or how little vanity you have."

"Oh!" gasped Kate.

"Or whether you are really an egotist--as some think."

"Oh!" breathed Kate again.

"As for me, I always say that a person can't get anywhere without egotism. The word never did scare me. Egotism is a kind of yeast that makes the human bread rise. I don't see how we could get along without it. As you say, I'd better wait before answering you. You've asked me an important question, and I'd like to give it thought. I can see that you'd be a good and useful woman whichever thing you did. But the question is, would you be a happy one in a home? You've got the idea of a public life in your head, and very likely that influences you without your realizing it."

"I don't say I'm not ambitious," cried Kate, really stirred. "But that ought to be a credit to me! It's ridiculous using the word 'ambitious' as a credit to a man, and making it seem like a shame to a woman. Ambition is personal force. Why shouldn't I have force?"

"There are things I can't put into words," said Mrs. Dennison, taking a folded handkerchief from her bead bag and delicately wiping her face, "and one of them is what I think about women. I'm a woman myself, and it doesn't seem becoming to me to say that I think they're sacred."

"No more sacred than men!" interrupted Kate hotly. "Life is sacred--if it's good. I can't say I think it sacred when it's deleterious. It's that pale, twilight sort of a theory which has kept women from doing the things they were capable of doing. Men kept thinking of them as sacred, and then they were miserably disappointed when they found they weren't. They talk about women's dreams, but I think men dream just as much as women, or more, and that they moon around with ideas about angel wives, and then are horribly shocked when they find they've married limited, commonplace, selfish creatures like themselves. I say let us train them both, make them comrades, give them a chance to share the burdens and the rewards, and see if we can't reduce the number of broken hearts in the world."

"There are some burdens," put in Mrs. Dennison, "which men and women cannot share. The burden of child-bearing, which is the most important one there is, has to be borne by women alone. You yourself were talking about that only a little while ago. It's such a strange sort of a thing,--so sweet and so terrible,--and it so often takes a woman to the verge of the grave, or over it, that I suppose it is that which gives a sacredness to women. Then, too, they'll work all their lives long for some one they love with no thought of any return except love. That makes them sacred, too.

Most of them believe in God, even when they're bad, and they believe in those they love even when they ought not. Maybe they're right in this and maybe they're not. Perhaps you'll say that shows their lack of sense. But I say it helps the world on, just the same. It may not be sensible--but it makes them sacred."

Mrs. Dennison's face was shining. She had pulled the gloves from her warm hands, and Kate, looking down at them, saw how work-worn they now were, though they were softly rounded and delicate. She knew this woman might have married a second time; but she was toiling that she might keep faith with the man she had laid in his grave. She was expecting a reunion with him. Her hope warmed her and kept her redolent of youth. She was still a bride, though she was a widow. She was of those who understood the things of the spirit. The essence of womanhood was in her--the elusive poetry of womanhood. To such implications of mystic beauty there was no retort. Kate saw in that moment that when women got as far as emancipation they were going to lose something infinitely precious. The real question was, should not these beautiful, these evanishing joys be permitted to depart in the interests of progress? Would not new, more robust satisfactions come to take the place of them?

They rode on in silence, and Kate's mind darted here and there--darted to Lena Vroom, that piteous little sister of Icarus, with her scorched wings; darted to Honora Fulham with her shattered faith; to Mary Morrison with her wanton's wisdom; to Mary Finn, whose womanhood was her undoing; to Marna, who had given fame for love and found the bargain good; to Mrs. Leger, who had turned to God; to her mother, the cringing wife, who could not keep faith with herself and her vows of obedience, and who had perished of the conflict; to Mrs. Dennison, happy in her mid-Victorian creed. Then from these, whom she knew, her mind swept on to the others--to all the restless, disturbed, questioning women the world over, who, clinging to beautiful old myths, yet reached out diffident hands to grasp new guidance. The violence and nurtured hatred of some of them offended her deeply; the egregious selfishness of others seemed to her as a flaming sin. Militant, unrestrained, avid of coarse and obvious things, they presented a shameful contrast to this little, gentle, dreaming keeper of a boarding-house who sat beside her, her dove's eyes filled with the mist of memories.

And yet--and yet--

CHAPTER XX

The next day, as it happened, she was invited to Lake Forest to attend a "suffrage tea." A distinguished English suffragette was to be present, and the more fashionable group of Chicago suffragists were gathering to pay her honor.

It was a torrid day with a promise of storm, and Kate would have preferred to go to the Settlement House to do her usual work, which chanced just now to be chiefly clerical. But she was urged to meet the Englishwoman and to discuss with her the matter of the Children's Bureau, in which the Settlement House people were now taking the keenest interest. Kate went, gowned in fresh linen, and well pleased, after all, to be with a holiday crowd riding through the summer woods. Tea was being served on the lawn. It overlooked the lake, and here were gathered both men and women. It was a company of rather notable persons, as Kate saw at a glance. Almost every one there was distinguished for some social achievement, or as the advocate of some reform or theory, or perhaps as an opulent and fashionable patron. It was at once interesting and amusing.

Kate greeted her hostess, and looked about her for the guest of honor. It transpired that the affair was quite informal, after all. The Englishwoman was sitting in a tea-tent discoursing with a number of gentlemen who hung over her with polite attentions. They were well-known bachelors of advanced ideas--men with honorary titles and personal ambitions. The great suffragist was very much at home with them. Her deep, musical voice resounded like a bell as she uttered her dicta and her witticisms. She--like the men--was smoking a cigarette, a feat which she performed without coquetry or consciousness. She was smoking because she liked to smoke. It took no more than a glance to reveal the fact that she was further along in her pregnancy than Marna--Marna who started back from the door when a stranger appeared at it lest she should seem immodest. But the suffragette, having acquired an applauding and excellent husband, saw no reason why she should apologize to the world for the processes of nature. Quite as unconscious of her condition as of her unconventionality in smoking, she discoursed with these diverted men, her transparent frock revealing the full beauties of her neck and bust, her handsome arms well displayed--frankly and insistently feminine, yet possessing herself without hesitation of what may be termed the masculine attitude toward life.

For some reason which Kate did not attempt to define, she refrained from discussing the Bureau of Children with the celebrated suffragette, although she did not doubt that the Englishwoman would have been capable of keen and valuable criticism. Instead, she returned to the city, sent a box of violets to Marna, and then went on to her attic room.

A letter was awaiting her from the West. It read:

"MY DEAR MISS BARRINGTON:--

"Honora and the kiddies are here. I have given my cousin a room where she can see the mountains on two sides, and I hope it will help. I've known the hills to help, even with pretty rough customers. It won't take a creature like Honora long to get hold of the secret, will it? You know what I mean, I guess.

"I wish you had come. I watched the turn in the drive to see if you wouldn't be in the station wagon. There were two women's heads. I recognized Honora's, and I tried to think the second one was yours, but I really knew it wasn't. It was a low head--one of that patient sort of heads--and a flat, lid-like hat. The nurse's, of course! I suppose you wear helmet-shaped hats with wings on them--something like Mercury's or Diana's. Or don't they sell that kind of millinery nowadays?

"Honora tells me you're trying to run the world and that you make up to all kinds of people--hold-up men as well as preachers. Do you know, I'm something like that myself? I can't help it, but I do seem to enjoy folks. One of the pleasantest nights I ever spent was with a lot of bandits in a cave. I was their prisoner, too, which complicated matters. But we had such a bully time that they asked me to join them. I told them I'd like the life in some respects. I could see it was a sort of game not unlike some I'd played when I was a boy. But it would have made me nervous, so I had to refuse them.

"Well, I'm talking nonsense. What if you should think I counted it sense! That would be bad for me. I only thought you'd be having so may pious and proper letters that I'd have to give you a jog if I got you to answer this. And I do wish you would answer it. I'm a lonely man, though a busy one. Of course it's going to be a tremendous comfort having Honora here when once she gets to be herself. She's wild with pain now, and nothing she says means anything. We play chess a good deal, after a fashion. Honora thinks she's amusing me, but as I like 'the rigor of the game,' I can't say that I'm amused at her plays. The first time she thinks before she moves I'll know she's over the worst of her trouble. She seems very weak, but I'm feeding her on cream and eggs. The kiddies are dears--just as cute as young owls. They're not afraid of me even when I pretend I'm a coyote and howl.

"Do write to me, Miss Barrington. I'm as crude as a cabbage, but when I say I'd rather have you write me than have any piece of good fortune befall me which your wildest imagination could depict, I mean it. Perhaps that will scare you off. Anyway, you can't say I didn't play fair.

"I'm worn out sitting around with this fractured leg of mine in its miserable cast. (I know stronger words than 'miserable,' but I use it because I'm determined to behave myself.) Honora says she thinks it would be all right for you to correspond with me. I asked her.

"Yours faithfully,

"KARL WANDER."

"What a ridiculous boy," said Kate to herself. She laughed aloud with a rippling merriment; and then, after a little silence, she laughed again.

"The man certainly is naïf," she said. "Can he really expect me to answer a letter like that?"

She awoke several times that night, and each time she gave a fleeting thought to the letter. She seemed to see it before her eyes--a purple eidolon, a parallelogram in shape. It flickered up and down like an electric sign. When morning came she was quite surprised to find the letter was existent and stationary. She read it again, and she wished tremendously that she might answer it. It occurred to her that in a way she never had had any fun. She had been persistently earnest, passionately honest, absurdly grim. Now to answer that letter would come under the head of mere frolic! Yet would it? Was not this curious, outspoken man--this gigantic, good-hearted, absurd boy--giving her notice that he was ready to turn into her lover at the slightest gesture of acquiescence on her part? No, the frolic would soon end. It would be another of those appalling games-for-life, those woman-trap affairs. And she liked freedom better than anything.

She went off to her work in a defiant frame of mind, carrying, however, the letter with her in her handbag.

What she did write--after several days' delay--was this:--

"MY DEAR MR. WANDER:--

"I can see that Honora is in the best place in the world for her. You must let me know when she has checkmated you. I quite agree that that will show the beginning of her recovery. She has had a terrible misfortune, and it was the outcome of a disease from which all of us 'advanced' women are suffering. Her convictions and her instincts were at war. I can't imagine what is going to happen to us. We all feel very unsettled, and Honora's tragedy is only one of several sorts which may come to any of us. But an instinct deeper than instinct, a conviction beyond conviction, tells me that we are right--that we must go on, studying, working, developing. We may have to pay a fearful price for our advancement, but I do not suppose we could turn back now if we would.

"You ask if I will correspond with you. Well, do you suppose we really have anything to say? What, for example, have you to tell me about? Honora says you own a mine, or two or three; that you have a city of workmen; that you are a father to them. Are they Italians? I think she said so. They're grateful folk, the Italians. I hope they like you. They are so sweet when they do, and so--sudden--when they don't.

"I have had something to do with them, and they are very dear to me. They ask me to their christenings and to other festivals. I like their gayety because it contrasts with my own disposition, which is gloomy.

"Upon reflection, I think we'd better not write to each other. You were too explicit in your letter--too precautionary.

You'd make me have a conscience about it, and I'd be watching myself. That's too much trouble. My business is to watch others, not myself. But I do thank you for giving such a welcome to Honora and the babies. I hope you will soon be about again. I find it so much easier to imagine you riding over a mountain pass than sitting in the house with a leg in plaster.

"Yours sincerely,

"KATE BARRINGTON."

He wrote back:--

"MY DEAR MISS BARRINGTON:--

"I admire your idea of gloom! Not the spirit of gloom but of adventure moves you. I saw it in your eye. When I buy a horse, I always look at his eye. It's not so much viciousness that I'm afraid of as stupidity. I like a horse that is always pressing forward to see what is around the next turn. Now, we humans are a good deal like horses. Women are, anyway. And I saw your eye. My own opinion is that you are having the finest time of anybody I know. You're shaping your own life, at least,--and that's the best fun there is,--the best kind of good fortune. Of course you'll get tired of it after a while. I don't say that because you are a woman, but I've seen it happen over and over again both with men and women. After a little while they get tired of roving and come home.

"You may not believe it, but, after all, that's the great moment in their lives--you just take it from me who have seen more than you might think and who have had a good deal of time to think things out. I do wish you had seen your way to come out here. There are any number of matters I would like to talk over with you.

"You mustn't think me impudent for writing in this familiar way. I write frankly because I'm sure you'll understand, and the conventionalities have been cast aside because in this case they seem so immaterial. I can assure you that I'm not impudent--not where women are concerned, at any rate. I'm a born lover of women, though I have been no woman's lover. I haven't seen much of them. Sometimes I've gone a

year without seeing one, not even a squaw. But I judge them by my mother, who made every one happy who came near her, and by some others I have known; I judge them by you, though I saw you only a minute. I suppose you will think me crazy or insincere in saying that. I'm both sane and honest-
-ask Honora.

"You speak of my Italians. They are making me trouble. We have been good friends and they have been happy here. I gave them lots to build on if they would put up homes; and I advanced the capital for the cottages and let them pay me four per cent--the lowest possible interest. I got a school for their children and good teachers, and I interested the church down in Denver to send a priest out here and establish a mission. I thought we understood each other, and that they comprehended that their prosperity and mine were bound up together. But an agitator came here the other day,--sent by the unions, of course,--and there's discontent. They have lost the friendly look from their eyes, and the men turn out of their way to avoid speaking to me. Since I've been laid up here, things have been going badly. There have been meetings and a good deal of hard talk. I suppose I'm in for a fight, and I tell you it hurts. I feel like a man at war with his children. As I feel just now, I'd throw up the whole thing rather than row with them, but the money of other men is invested in these mines and I'm the custodian of it. So I've no choice in the matter. Perhaps, too, it's for their own good that they should be made to see reason. What do you say?

"Faithfully,

"WANDER."

Honora wrote the same day and to her quiet report of improved nights and endurable days she added:--

"I hope you will answer my cousin's letter. I can't tell you what a good man he is, and so boyish, in spite of his being strong and perfectly brave--oh, brave to the death! He's very lonely. He always has been. You'll have to make allowances for his being so Western and going right to the point in such a reckless way. He hasn't told me what he's written you, but I know if he wants to be friends with you he'll say so without any preliminaries. He's very eager to have me talk of you, so I do. I'm eager to talk, too. I always loved you, Kate, but now I put you and Karl in a class by yourselves as the completely dependable ones.

"The babies send kisses. Don't worry about me. I'm beginning to see that it's not extraordinary for trouble to have come to me. Why not to me as well as to another? I'm one of the great company of sad ones now. But I'm not going to be melancholy. I know how disappointed you'd be if I were. I'm beginning to sleep better, and for all of this still, dark cavern in my heart, so filled with voices of the past and with the horrible chill of the present, I am able to laugh a little at passing things. I find myself doing it involuntarily. So at least I've got where I can hear what the people about me are saying, and can make a fitting reply. Yes, do write Karl. For my sake."

CHAPTER XXI

Meantime, Ray McCrea had neglected to take his summer vacation. He was staying in the city, and twice a week he called on Kate. Kate liked him neither more nor less than at the beginning. He was clever and he was kind, and it was his delight to make her happy. But it was with the surface of her understanding that she listened to him and the skimmings of her thoughts that she passed to him. He had that light, acrid accent of well-to-do American men. Reasonably contented himself, he failed to see why every one else should not be so, too. He was not religious for the same reason that he was not irreligious--because it seemed to him useless to think about such matters. Public affairs and politics failed to interest him because he believed that the country was in the hands of a mob and that the "grafters would run things anyway." He called eloquence spell-binding, and sentiment slush,--sentiment, that is, in books and on the stage,--and he was indulgently inclined to suspect that there was something "in it" for whoever appeared to be essaying a benevolent enterprise. Respectable, liberal-handed, habitually amused, slightly caustic, he looked out for the good of himself and those related to him and considered that he was justified in closing his corporate regards at that point. He had no cant and no hypocrisy, no pose and no fads. A sane, aggressive, self-centered, rational materialist of the American brand, it was not only his friends who thought him a fine fellow. He himself would have admitted so much and have been perfectly justified in so doing.

Kate received flowers, books, and sweets from him, and now and then he asked her why he had lost ground with her. Sometimes he would say:--

"I can see a conservative policy is the one for me, Kate, where you're concerned. I'm going to lie low so as not to give you a chance to send me whistling."

Once, when he grew picturesquely melancholy, she refused to receive his offerings. She told him he was making a villainess out of her, and that she'd end their meetings. But at that he promised so ardently not to be ardent that she forgave him and continued to read the novels and to tend the flowers he brought her. They went for walks together; sometimes she lunched with him in the city, and on pleasant evenings they attended open-air concerts. He tried to be discreet, but in August, with the full moon, he had a relapse. Kate gave him warning; he persisted,--the moon really was quite wonderful that August,--and then, to his chagrin, he received a postcard from Silvertree. Kate had gone to see her father.

She would not have gone but for a chance word in one of Wander's letters.

"I hear your father is still living," he wrote. "That is so good! I have no parents now, but I like to remember how happy I was when I had them. I was young when my mother died, but father lived to a good age, and as long as he was alive I had some one to do things for. He always liked to hear of my exploits. I was a hero to him, if I never was to any one else. It kept my heart warmed up, and when he went he left me very lonely, indeed."

Kate reddened with shame when she read these words. Had Honora told him how she had deserted her father--how she had run from him and his tyranny to live her own life, and was he, Wander, meaning this for a rebuke? But she knew that could not be. Honora would have kept her counsel; she was not a tattler. Karl was merely congratulating her on a piece of good fortune, apparently. It threw a new light on the declaration of independence that had seemed to her to be so fine. Was old-time sentiment right, after all? The ancient law, "Honor thy father and thy mother," did not put in the proviso, "if they are according to thy notion of what they should be."

So Kate was again at Silvertree and in the old, familiar and now lifeless house. It was not now a caressed and pampered home; there was no longer any one there to trick it out in foolish affectionate adornments. In the first half-hour, while Kate roamed from room to room, she could hardly endure the appalling blankness of the place. No stranger could have felt so unwelcomed as she did--so alien, so inconsolably homeless.

She was waiting for her father when he came home, and she hoped to warm him a little by the surprise of her arrival. But it was his cue to be deeply offended with her.

"Hullo, Kate," he said, nodding and holding out his hand with a deliberately indifferent gesture.

"Oh, see here, dad, you know you've got to kiss me!" she cried.

So he did, rather shamefacedly, and they sat together on the dusty veranda and talked. He had been well, he said, but he was far from looking so. His face was gray and drawn, his lips were pale, and his long skillful surgeon's hands looked inert and weary. When he walked, he had the effect of dragging his feet after him.

"Aren't you going to take a vacation, dad?" Kate demanded. "If ever a man appeared to be in need of it, you do."

"What would I do with a vacation? And where could I go? I'd look fine at a summer resort, wouldn't I, sitting around with idle fools? If I could only go somewhere to get rid of this damned neurasthenia that all the fool women think they've got, I'd go; but I don't suppose there's such a place this side of the Arctic Circle."

Kate regarded him for a moment without answering. She saw he was almost at the end of his strength and a victim of the very malady against which he was railing. The constant wear and tear of country practice, year in and year out, had depleted him of a magnificent stock of energy and endurance. Perhaps, too, she had had her share of responsibility in his decline, for she had been severe with him; had defied him when she might have comforted him. She forgot his insolence, his meanness, his conscienceless hectoring, as she saw how his temples seemed fallen in and how his gray hair straggled over his brow. It was she who assumed the voice of authority now.

"There's going to be a vacation," she announced, "and it will be quite a long one. Put your practice in the hands of some one else, let your housekeeper take a rest, and then you come away with me. I'll give you three days to get ready."

He cast at her the old sharp, lance-like look of opposition, but she stood before him so strong, so kind, so daughterly (so motherly, too), that, for one of the few times in his life of senseless domination and obstinacy, he yielded. The tears came to his eyes.

"All right, Kate," he said with an accent of capitulation. He really was a broken old man.

She passed a happy evening with him looking over advertisements of forest inns and fishing resorts, and though no decision was reached, both of them went to bed in a state of pleasant anticipation. The following day she took his affairs in hand. The housekeeper was delighted at her release; a young physician was pleased to take charge of Dr. Barrington's patients.

Kate made him buy new clothes,--he had been wearing winter ones,-- and she set him out in picturesque gear suiting his lank length and old-time manner. Then she induced him to select a place far north in the Wisconsin woods, and the third day they were journeying there together.

It seemed quite incredible that the dependent and affectionate man opposite her was the one who had filled her with fear and resentment such a short time ago. She found herself actually laughing aloud once at the absurdity of it all. Had her dread of him been fortuitous, his tyranny a mere sham? Had he really liked her all the time, and had she been a sensitive fool? She would have thought so, indeed, but for the memory of the perplexed and distracted face of her mother, the cringing and broken spirit of her who missed truth through an obsession of love. No, no, a tyrant he had been, one of a countless army of them!

But now he leaned back on his seat very sad of eye, inert of gesture, without curiosity or much expectancy. He let her do everything for him. She felt her heart warming as she served him. She could hardly keep herself from stooping to kiss his great brow; the hollows of his eyes when he was sleeping moved her to a passion of pity. After all, he was her own; and now she had him again. The bitterness of years began to die, and with it much of that secret, instinctive aversion to men--that terror of being trapped and held to some uninspiring association or dragging task.

For now, when her father awoke from one of his many naps, he would turn to her with: "Have I slept long, Kate?" or "We'll be going in to lunch soon, I suppose, daughter?" or "Will it be very long now before we reach our destination?"

It was reached at dawn of an early autumn day, and they drove ten miles into the pine woods. The scented silence took them. They were at "God's green caravansarie," and the rancor that had poisoned their hearts was gone. They turned toward each other in common trust, father and daughter, forgiving, if not all forgetting, the hurt and angry years.

"It really was your cousin who brought it about," Kate wrote Honora. "He reminded me that I was fortunate to have a father. You see, I hadn't realized it! Oh, Honora, what a queer girl I am--always having to think things out! Always making myself miserable in trying to be happy! Always going wrong in striving to be right! I should think the gods would make Olympus ring laughing at me! I once wrote your cousin that women of my sort were worn out with their struggle to reconcile their convictions and their instincts. And that's true. That's what is making them so restless and so strange and tumultuous. But of course I can't think it their fault--merely their destiny. Something is happening to them, but neither they nor any one else can quite tell what it is."

Dr. Barrington was broken, no question about that. Even the stimulation of the incomparable air of those Northern woods could not charge him with vitality. He lay wrapped in blankets, on the bed improvised for him beneath the trees, or before the leaping fire in the inn, with the odors of the burning pine about him, and he let time slip by as it would.

The people at the inn thought they never had seen a more devoted daughter than his. She sat beside him while he slept; she read or talked to him softly when he awakened; she was at hand with some light but sustaining refreshment whenever he seemed depressed or too relaxed. But there were certain things which the inn people could not make out. The sick man had the air of having forgiven this fine girl for something. He received her service like one who had the right to expect it. He was tender and he was happy, but he was, after all, the dominator. Nor could they quite make out the girl, who smiled at his demands,--which were sometimes incessant,--and who obeyed with the perfect patience of the strong. They did not know that if he had once been an active tyrant, he was now a supine one. As he had been unable, for all of his intelligence, to perceive the meaning of justice from the old angle, so he was equally unable to get it from his present point of view. He had been harsh with his daughter in the old days; so much he would have admitted. That he would have frustrated her completely, absorbed and wasted her power, he could not perceive. He did not surmise that he was now doing in an amiable fashion what he hitherto had tried to do in a masterful and insolent one. He did not realize that the tyranny of the weak is a more destructive thing when levelled at the generous than the tyranny of the strong.

Had he been interrupted in mid-career--in those days when his surgery was sure and bold--to care for a feeble and complaining wife, he would have thought himself egregiously abused. That Kate, whose mail each day exceeded by many times that which he had received in his most influential years, whose correspondence was with persons with whom he could not at any time have held communication, should be taken from her active duties appeared to him as nothing. He was a sick father. His daughter attended him in love and dutifulness. He was at peace--and he knew she was doing her duty. It really did not occur to him that she or any one else could have looked at the matter in a different light, or that any loving expression of regret was due her. Such sacrifices were expected of women. They were not expected of men, although men sometimes magnificently performed them.

To tell the truth, no such idea occurred to Kate either. She was as happy as her father. At last, in circumstances sad enough, she had reached a degree of understanding with him. She had no thought for the inconvenience under which she worked. She was more than willing to sit till past the middle of the night answering her letters, postponing her engagements, sustaining her humbler and more unhappy friends--those who were under practical parole to her--with her encouragement, and always, day by day, extending the idea of the Bureau of Children. For daily it took shape; daily the system of organization became more apparent to her. She wrote to Ray McCrea about it; she wrote to Karl Wander on the same subject. It seemed to suffice or almost to suffice her. It kept her from anticipating the details of the melancholy drama which was now being enacted before her eyes.

For her father was passing. His weakness increased, and his attitude toward life became one of gentle indifference. He was homesick for his wife, too. Though he had seemed to take so little satisfaction in her society, and had not scrupled when she was alive to show the contempt he felt for her opinions, now he liked to talk of her. He had made a great outcry against sentiment all of his life, but in his weakness he found his chief consolation in it. He had been a materialist, denying immortality for the soul, but now he reverted to the phrases of pious men of the past generation.

"I shall be seeing your mother soon, Kate," he would say wistfully, holding his daughter's hand. Kate was involuntarily touched by such words, but she was ashamed for him, too. Where was all his hard-won, bravely flaunted infidelity? Where his scientific outlook?

It was only slowly, and as the result of her daily and nightly association with him, that she began to see how his acquired convictions were slipping away from him, leaving the sentiments and predilections which had been his when he was a boy. Had he never been a strong man, really, and had his violence of opinion and his arrogance of demeanor been the defences erected by a man of spiritual timidity and restless, excitable brain? Had his assertiveness, like his compliance, been part and parcel of a mind not at peace, not grounded in a definite faith? Perhaps he had been afraid of the domination of his gentle wife with her soft insistence, and had girded at her throughout the years because of mere fanatic self-esteem. But now that she had so long been beyond the reach of his whimsical commands, he turned to the thought of her like a yearning child to its mother.

"If you hadn't come when you did, Kate," he would say, weeping with self-pity, "I should have died alone. I wouldn't own to any one how sick I was. Why, one night I was so weak, after being out thirty-six hours with a sick woman, that I had to creep upstairs on my hands and knees." He sobbed for a moment piteously, his nerves too tattered to permit him to retain any semblance of self-control. Kate tried in vain to soothe him. "What would your mother have thought if you had let me die alone?" he demanded of her.

It was useless for her to say that he had not told her he was ill. He was in no condition to face the truth. He was completely shattered--the victim of a country physician's practice and of an unrestrained irritability. Her commiseration had been all that was needed to have him yield himself unreservedly to her care.

It had been her intention to stay in the woods with him for a fortnight, but the end of that time found his lassitude increasing and his need for her greater than ever. She was obliged to ask for indefinite leave of absence. A physician came from Milwaukee once a week to see him; and meantime quiet and comfort were his best medicines.

The autumn began to deepen. The pines accentuated their solemnity, and out on the roadways the hazel bushes and the sumac changed to canary, to russet, and to crimson. For days together the sky would be cloudless, and even in the dead of night the vault seemed to retain its splendor. There are curious cloths woven on Persian and on Turkish looms which appear to the casual eye to be merely black, but which held in sunlight show green and blue, purple and bronze, like the shifting colors on a duck's back. Kate, pacing back and forth in the night after hours of concentrated labor,--labor which could be performed only when her father was resting,--noted such mysterious and evasive hues in her Northern sky. Never had she seen heavens so triumphant. True, the stars shone with a remote glory, but she was more inspired by their enduring, their impersonal magnificence, than she could have been by anything relative to herself.

A year ago, had she been so isolated, she might have found herself lonely, but it was quite different now. She possessed links with the active world. There were many who wanted her--some for small and some for great things. She felt herself in the stream of life; it poured about her, an invisible thing, but strong and deep. Sympathy, understanding, encouragement, reached her even there in her solitude and heartened her. Weary as she often was physically, drained as she could not but be mentally, her heart was warm and full.

October came and went bringing little change in Dr. Barrington's condition. It did not seem advisable to move him. Rest and care were the things required; and the constant ministrations of a physician would have been of little benefit. Kate prayed for a change; and it came, but not as she had hoped. One morning she went to her father to find him terribly altered. It was as if some blight had fallen upon him in the night. His face was gray in hue, his pulse barely fluttering, though his eyes were keener than they had been, as if a sudden danger had brought back his old force and comprehension. Even the tone in which he addressed her had more of its old-time quality. It was the accent of command, the voice he had used as a physician in the sick-room, though it was faint.

"Send for Hudson," he said. "We'll be needing him, Kate. The fight's on. Don't feel badly if we fail. You've done your best."

It was six hours before the physician arrived from Milwaukee.

"I couldn't have looked for anything like this," he said to Kate. "I thought he was safe--that six months' rest would see him getting about again."

They had a week's conflict with the last dread enemy of man, and they lost. Dr. Barrington was quite as much aware of the significance of his steady decline as any one. He had practical, quiet, encouraging talks with his daughter. He sent for an attorney and secured his property to her. Once more, as in his brighter days, he talked of important matters, though no longer with his old arrogance. He seemed to comprehend at last, fully and proudly, that she was the inheritor of the best part of him. Her excursive spirit, her inquisitive mind, were, after all, in spite of all differences, his gift to her. He gave her his good wishes and begged her to follow whatever forces had been leading her. It was as if, in his weakness, he had sunk for a period into something resembling childhood and had emerged from it into a newer, finer manhood.

"I kept abreast of things in my profession," he said, "but in other matters I was obstinate. I liked the old way--a man at the helm, and the crew answering his commands. No matter how big a fool the man was, I still wanted him at the helm." He smiled at her brightly. There was, indeed, a sort of terrible brilliancy about him, the result, perhaps, of heroic artificial stimulation. But these false fires soon burned themselves out. One beautiful Sunday morning they found him sinking. He himself informed his physician that it was his day of transition.

"I've only an hour or two more, Hudson," he whispered cheerfully. "Feel that pulse!"

"Oh, we may manage to keep you with us some time yet, Dr. Barrington," said the other with a professional attempt at optimism.

But the older man shook his head.

"Let's not bother with the stock phrases," he said. "Ask my daughter to come. I'd like to look at her till the last."

So Kate sat where he could see her, and they coaxed the fluttering heart to yet a little further effort. Dr. Barrington supervised everything; counted his own pulse; noted its decline with his accustomed accuracy.

The sunlight streamed into the room through the tall shafts of trees; outside the sighing of the pines was heard, rising now and then to a noble requiem. It lifted Kate's soul on its deep harmonies, and she was able to bear herself with fortitude.

"It's been so sweet to be with you, dear," she murmured in the ears which were growing dull to earthly sounds. "Say that I've made up to you a little for my willfulness. I've always loved you--always."

"I know," he whispered. "I understand--everything--now!"

In fact, his glance answered hers with full comprehension.

"The beat is getting very low now, Doctor," he murmured, the fingers of his right hand on his left wrist; "very infrequent--fifteen minutes more--"

Dr. Hudson tried to restrain him from his grim task of noting his own sinking vitality, but the old physician waved him off.

"It's very interesting," he said. It seemed so, indeed. Suddenly he said quite clearly and in a louder voice than he had used that day: "It has stopped. It is the end!"

Kate sprang to her feet incredulously. There was a moment of waiting so tense that the very trees seemed to cease their moaning to listen. In all the room there was no sound. The struggling breath had ceased. The old physician had been correct--he had achieved the thing he had set himself to do. He had announced his own demise.

CHAPTER XXII

Kate had him buried beside the wife for whom he had so inconsistently longed. She sold the old house, selected a few keepsakes from it, disposed of all else, and came, late in November, back to the city. Marna's baby had been born--a little bright boy, named for his father. Mrs. Barsaloux, relenting, had sent a layette of French workmanship, and Marna was radiantly happy.

"If only *tante* will come over for Christmas," Marna lilted to Kate, "I shall be almost too happy to live. How good she was to me, and how ungrateful I seemed to her! Write her to come, Kate, mavourneen. Tell her the baby won't seem quite complete till she's kissed it."

So Kate wrote Mrs. Barsaloux, adding her solicitation to Marna's. Human love and sympathy were coming to seem to her of more value than anything else in the world. To be loved--to be companioned--to have the vast loneliness of life mitigated by fealty and laughter and tenderness--what was there to take the place of it?

Her heart swelled with a desire to lessen the pain of the world. All her egotism, her self-assertion, her formless ambitions had got up, or down, to that,--to comfort the comfortless, to keep evil away from little children, to let those who were in any sort of a prison go free. Yet she knew very well that all of this would lack its perfect meaning unless there was some one to say to her--to her and to none other: "I understand."

Mrs. Barsaloux did not come to America at Christmas time. Karl Wander did not--as he had thought he might--visit Chicago. The holiday season seemed to bring little to Kate except a press of duties. She aspired to go to bed Christmas night with the conviction that not a child in her large territory had spent a neglected Christmas. This meant a skilled coöperation with other societies, with the benevolently inclined newspapers, and with generous patrons. The correspondence involved was necessarily large, and the amount of detail to be attended to more than she should have undertaken, unaided, but she was spurred on by an almost consuming passion of pity and sisterliness. That sensible detachment which had marked her work at the outset had gradually and perhaps regrettably disappeared. So far from having outgrown emotional struggle, she seemed now, because of something that was taking place in her inner life, to be increasingly susceptible to it.

Her father's death had taken from her the last vestige of a home. She had now no place which she could call her own, or to which she would instinctively turn at Christmas time. To be sure, there were many who bade her to their firesides, and some of these invitations she accepted with gratitude and joy. But she could, of course, only pause at the hearthstones of others. Her thoughts winged on to other things--to the little poor homes where her wistful children dwelt, to the great scheme for their care and oversight which daily came nearer to realization.

A number of benevolent women--rich in purse and in a passion for public service--desired her to lecture. She was to explain the meaning of the Bureau of Children at the state federations of women's clubs, in lyceum courses, and wherever receptive audiences could be found. They advised, among other things, her attendance at the biennial meeting of the General Federation of Women's Clubs which was meeting that coming spring in Southern California.

The time had been not so far distant when she would have had difficulty in seeing herself in the rôle of a public lecturer, but now that she had something imperative to say, she did not see herself in any "rôle" at all. She ceased to think about herself save as the carrier of a message.

Her Christmas letter from Wander was at once a disappointment and a shock.

> "I've made a mess of things," he wrote, "and do not intend to intrude on you until I have shown myself more worthy of consideration. I try to tell myself that my present fiasco is not my fault, but I've more than a suspicion that I'm playing the coward's part when I think that. You can be disappointed in me if you like. *I'm* outrageously disappointed. I thought I was made of better stuff.
>
> "I don't know when I'll have time for writing again, for I shall be very busy. I suppose I'll think about you more than is good for me. But maybe not. Maybe the thoughts of you will be crowded out. I'm rather curious to see. It would be better for me if they would, for I've come to a bad turn in the road, and when I get around it, maybe all of the old familiar scenes--the window out of which your face looked, for

example--will be lost to me. I send my good wishes to you all the same. I shall do that as long as I have a brain and a heart.

"Faithfully,

"WANDER."

"That means trouble," reflected Kate, and had a wild desire to rush to his aid.

That she did not was owing partly--only partly--to another letter which, bearing an English postmark, indicated that Ray McCrea, who had been abroad for a month on business, was turning his face toward home. What he had to say was this:--

"DEAREST KATE:--

"I'm sending you a warning. In a few days I'll be tossing on that black sea of which I have, in the last few days, caught some discouraging glimpses. It doesn't look as if it meant to let me see the Statue of Liberty again, but as surely as I do, I'm going to go into council with you.

"I imagine you know mighty well what I'm going to say. For years you've kept me at your call--or, rather, for years I have kept myself there. You've discouraged me often, in a tolerant fashion, as if you thought me too young to be dangerous, or yourself too high up to be called to account. I've been patient, chiefly because I found your society, as a mere recipient of my awkward attentions, too satisfactory to be able to run the risk of foregoing it. But if I were to sit in the outer court any longer I would be pusillanimous. I'm coming home to force you to make up that strange mind of yours, which seems to be forever occupying itself with the thing far-off and to-be-hoped-for, rather than with what is near at hand.

"You'll have time to think it over. You can't say I've been precipitate.

"Yours--always,

"RAY."

At that she flashed a letter to Colorado.

"What is your cousin's trouble?" she asked Honora. "Is it at the mines?"

"It's at the mines," Honora replied. "Karl's life has been and is in danger. Friends have warned me of that again and again. There's no holding these people--these several hundred Italians that poor Karl insisted upon regarding as his wards, his 'adopted children.' They're preparing to leave their half-paid-for homes and their steady work, and to go threshing off across the country in the wave of a hard-drinking, hysterical labor leader. He has them inflamed to the explosive point. When they've done their worst, Karl may be a poor man. Not that he worries about that; but he's likely to carry down with him friends and business associates. Of course this is not final. He may win out, but such a catastrophe threatens him.

"But understand, all this is not what is tormenting him and turning him gaunt and haggard. No, as usual, the last twist of the knife is given by a woman. In this case it is an Italian girl, Elena Cimiotti, the daughter of one of the strikers and of the woman who does our washing for us. She's a beautiful, wild creature, something as you might suppose the daughter of Jorio to be. She has come for the washing and has brought it home again for months past, and Karl, who is thoughtful of everybody, has assisted her with her burden when she was lifting it from her burro's back or packing it on the little beast. Sometimes he would fetch her a glass of water, or give her a cup of tea, or put some fruit in her saddle-bags. You know what a way he has with all women! I suppose it would turn any foolish creature's head. And he has such an impressive way of saying things! What would be a casual speech on the tongue of another becomes significant, when he has given one of his original twists to it. I think, too, that in utter disregard of Italian etiquette he has sometimes walked on the street with this girl for a few steps. He is like a child in some ways,--as trusting and unconventional,--and he wants to be friends with everybody. I can't tell whether it is because he is such an aristocrat that it doesn't occur to him that any one can suspect him of losing caste, or because he is such a democrat that he doesn't know it exists.

"However that may be, the girl is in love with him. These Italian girls are modest and well-behaved ordinarily, but when once their imagination is aroused they are like flaming meteors. They have no shame because they can't see why any one should be ashamed of love (and, to tell the truth, I can't either). But this girl believes Karl has encouraged her. I suppose she honestly believed that he was sweethearting. He is astounded and dismayed. At first both he and I thought she would get over it, but she has twice been barely prevented from killing herself. Of course her countrymen think her desperately ill-treated. She is the handsomest girl in the settlement, and she has a number of ardent admirers. To the hatred which they have come to bear Karl as members of a strike directed against him, they now add the element of personal jealousy.

"So you see what kind of a Christmas we are having! I have had Mrs. Hays take the babies to Colorado Springs, and if anything happens to us here, I'll trust to you to see to them. You, who mean to look after little children, look after mine above all others, for their mother gave you, long since, her loving friendship. I would rather have you mother my babies, maiden though you are, than any woman I know, for I feel a great force in you, Kate, and believe you are going on until you get an answer to some of the questions which the rest of us have found unanswerable.

"Karl wants me to leave, for there is danger that the ranch house may be blown up almost any time. These men play with dynamite as if it were wood, anyway, and they make fiery enemies. Every act of ours is spied upon. Our servants have left us, and Karl and I, obstinate as mules and as proud as sheiks, after the fashion of our family, hold the fort. He wants me to go, but I tell him I am more interested in life than I ever dared hope I would be again. I have been bayoneted into a fighting mood, and I find it magnificent to really feel alive again, after crawling in the dust so long, with the taste of it in my mouth. So don't pity me. As for Karl--he looks wild and strange, like the Flying Dutchman with his spectral hand on the helm. But I don't know that I want you to pity him either. He is a curious man, with a passionate soul, and if he flares out like a torch in the wind, it will be fitting enough. No, don't pity us. Congratulate us rather."

"Now what," said Kate aloud, "may that mean?"

"Congratulate us!"

The letter had a note of reckless gayety. Had Honora and Karl, though cousins, been finding a shining compensation there in the midst of many troubles? It sounded so, indeed. Elena Cimiotti might swing down the mountain roads wearing mountain flowers in her hair if she pleased, and Kate would not have thought her dangerous to the peace of Karl Wander. If the wind were wild and the leaves driving, he might have kissed her in some mad mood. So much might be granted--and none, not even Elena, be the worse for it. But to live side by side with Honora Fulham, to face danger with her, to have the exhilaration of conflict, they two together, the mountains above them, the treacherous foe below, a fortune lost or gained in a day, all the elements of Colorado's gambling chances of life and fortune at hand, might mean--anything.

Well, she would congratulate them! If Honora could forget a shattered heart so soon, if Wander could take it on such easy terms, they were entitled to congratulations of a sort. And if they were killed some frantic night,--were blown to pieces with their ruined home, and so reached together whatever lies beyond this life,--why, then, they were to be congratulated, indeed! Or if they evaded their enemies and swung their endangered craft into the smooth stream of life, still congratulations were to be theirs.

She confessed to herself that she would rather be in that lonely beleaguered house facing death with Karl Wander than be the recipient of the greatest honor or the participant in the utmost gayety that life could offer.

That the fact was fantastic made it none the less a fact.

Should she write to Honora: "I congratulate you?"

Or should she wire Karl?

She got out his letters, and his words were as a fresh wind blowing over her spirit. She realized afresh how this man, seen but once, known only through the medium of infrequent letters, had invigorated her. What had he not taught her of compassion, of "the glory of the commonplace," of duty eagerly fulfilled, of the abounding joy of life--even in life shadowed by care or sickness or poverty?

No, she would write them nothing. They were her friends in fullness of sympathy. They, like herself, were of those to whom each day and night is a privilege, to whom sorrow is an enrichment, delight an unfoldment, opposition a spur. They were of the company of those who dared to speak the truth, who breathed deep, who partook of the banquet of life without fear.

She had seen Honora in the worst hour of tribulation that can come to a good woman, and she knew she had arisen from her overthrow, stronger for the trial; now Karl was battling, and he had cried out to her in his pain--his shame of defeat. But it would not be his extinction. She was sure of that. They might, among them, slay his body, but she could not read his letters, so full of valiant contrasts, and doubt that his spirit must withstand all adversaries.

No, sardonic with these two she could never be. Like that poor Elena, she might have mistaken Wander's meanings. He was a man of too elaborate gestures; something grandiose, inherently his, made him enact the drama of life with too much fervor. It was easy, Honora had insinuated, for a woman to mistake him!

Kate gripped her two strong hands together and clasped them about her head in the first attitude of despair in which she ever had indulged in her life. She was ashamed! Honora had said there was nothing to be ashamed of in love. But Kate would not call this meeting of her spirit with Karl's by that name. She had no idea whether it was love or not. On the whole, she preferred to think that it was not. But when they faced each other, their glances had met. When they had parted, their thoughts had bridged the space. When she dreamed, she fancied that she was mounting great solitary peaks with him to look at sunsets that blazed like the end of the world; or that he and she were strong-winged birds seeking the crags of the Andes. What girl's folly! The time had come to put such vagrant dreams from her and to become a woman, indeed.

Ray telephoned that he was home.

"Come up this evening, then," commanded Kate.

Then, not being as courageous as her word, she wept brokenly for her mother--the mother who could, at best, have given her but such indeterminate advice.

CHAPTER XXIII

As she heard Ray coming up the stairs, she tossed some more wood on the fire and lighted the candles in her Russian candlesticks.

"It's what any silly girl would do!" she admitted to herself disgustedly.

Well, there was his rap on the foolish imitation Warwick knocker. Kate flung wide the door. He stood in the dim light of the hall, hesitating, it would seem, to enter upon the evening's drama. Tall, graceful as always, with a magnetic force behind his languor, he impressed Kate as a man whom few women would be able to resist; whom, indeed, it was a sort of folly, perhaps even an impiety, to cast out of one's life.

"Kate!" he said, "Kate!" The whole challenge of love was in the accent.

But she held him off with the first method of opposition she could devise.

"My name!" she admitted gayly. "I used to think I didn't like it, but I do."

He came in and swung to the door behind him, flinging his coat and hat upon a chair.

"Do you mean you like to hear me say it?" he demanded. He stood by the fire which had begun to leap and crackle, drawing off his gloves with a decisive gesture.

She saw that she was not going to be able to put him off. The hour had struck. So she faced him bravely.

"Sit down, Ray," she said.

He looked at her a moment as if measuring the value of this courtesy.

"Thank you," he said, almost resentfully, as he sank into the chair she placed for him.

So they sat together before the fire gravely, like old married people, as Kate could not help noticing. Yet they were combatants; not as a married couple might have been, furtively and miserably, but with a frank, almost an exhilarating, sense of equally matched strength, and of their chance to conduct their struggle in the open.

"It's come to this, Kate," he said at length. "Either I must have your promise or I stay away entirely."

"I don't believe you need to do either," she retorted with the exasperating manner of an elder sister. "It's an obsession with you, that's all."

"What man thinks he needs, he does need," Ray responded sententiously. "It appears to me that without you I shall be a lost man. I mean precisely what I say. You wouldn't like me to give out that fact in an hysterical manner, and I don't see that I need to. I make the statement as I would make any other, and I expect to be believed, because I'm a truth-telling person. The fairest scene in the world or the most interesting circumstance becomes meaningless to me if you are not included in it. It isn't alone that you are my sweetheart--the lady of my dreams. It's much more than that. Sometimes when I'm with you I feel like a boy with his mother, safe from all the dreadful things that might happen to a child. Sometimes you seem like a sister, so really kind and so outwardly provoking. Often you are my comrade, and we are completely congenial, neuter entities. The thing is we have a satisfaction when we are together that we never could apart. There it is, Kate, the fact we can't get around. We're happier together than we are apart!"

He seemed to hold the theory up in the air as if it were a shining jewel, and to expect her to look at it till it dazzled her. But her voice was dull as she said: "I know, Ray. I know--now--but shall we stay so?"

"Why shouldn't we, woman? There's every reason to suppose that we'd grow happier. We want each other. More than that, we need each other. With me, it's such a deep need that it reaches to the very roots of my being. It's my groundwork, my foundation stone. I don't know how to put it to make you realize--"

He caught a quizzical smile on her face, and after a moment of bewilderment he leaped from his chair and came toward her.

"God!" he half breathed, "why do I waste time talking?"

He had done what her look challenged him to do,--had substituted action for words,--yet now, as he stretched out his arms to her, she held him off, fearful that she would find herself weeping on his breast. It would be sweet to do it--like getting home after a long voyage. But dizzily, with a stark clinging to a rock of integrity in herself, she fought him off, more with her militant spirit than with her outspread, protesting hands.

"No, no," she cried. "Don't hypnotize me, Ray! Leave me my judgment, leave me my reason. If it's a partnership we're to enter into, I ought to know the terms."

"The terms, Kate? Why, I'll love you as long as I live; I'll treasure you as the most precious thing in all the world."

"And the winds of heaven shall not be allowed to visit my cheek too roughly," she managed to say tantalizingly.

He paused, perplexed.

"I know I bewilder you, dear man," she said. "But this is the point: I don't want to be protected. I mean I don't want to be made dependent; I don't want my interpretations of life at second-hand. I object to having life filter through anybody else to me; I want it, you see, on my own account."

"Why, Kate!" It wasn't precisely a protest. He seemed rather to reproach her for hindering the onward sweep of their happiness--for opposing him with her ideas when they might together have attained a beautiful emotional climax.

"I couldn't stand it," she went on, lifting her eyes to his, "to be given permission to do this, that, or the other thing; or to be put on an allowance; or made to ask a favor--"

He sank down in his chair and folded across his breast the arms whose embrace she had not claimed.

"You seem to mean," he said, "that you don't want to be a wife. You prefer your independence to love."

"I want both," Kate declared, rising and standing before him. "I want the most glorious and abounding love woman ever had. I want so much of it that it never could be computed or measured--so much it will lift me up above anything that I now am or that I know, and make me stronger and freer and braver."

"Well, that's what your love would do for me," broke in McCrea. "That's what the love of a good woman is expected to do for a man."

"Of course," cried Kate; "but is that what the love of a good man is expected to do for a woman? Or is it expected to reconcile her to obscurity, to the dimming of her personality, and to the endless petty sacrifices that ought to shame her--and don't--those immoral sacrifices about which she has contrived to throw so many deceiving, iridescent mists of religion? Oh, yes, we are hypnotized into our foolish state of dependence easily enough! I know that. The mating instinct drugs us. I suppose the unborn generations reach out their shadowy multitudinous hands and drag us to our destiny!"

"What a woman you are! How you put things!" He tried but failed to keep the offended look from his face, and Kate knew perfectly well how hard he was striving not to think her indelicate. But she went on regardlessly.

"You think that's the very thing I ought to want to be my destiny? Well, perhaps I do. I want children--of course, I want them."

She stopped for a moment because she saw him flushing with embarrassment. Yet she couldn't apologize, and, anyway, an apology would avail nothing. If he thought her unwomanly because she talked about her woman's life,--the very life to which he was inviting her,--nothing she could say would change his mind. It wasn't a case for argument. She walked over to the fire and warmed her nervous hands at it.

"I'm sorry, Ray," she said finally.

"Sorry?"

"Sorry that I'm not the tender, trusting, maiden-creature who could fall trembling in your arms and love you forever, no matter what you did, and lie to you and for you the way good wives do. But I'm not--and, oh, I wish I were--or else--"

"Yes, Kate--what?"

"Or else that you were the kind of a man I need, the mate I'm looking for!"

"But, Kate, I protest that I am. I love you. Isn't that enough? I'm not worthy of you, maybe. Yet if trying to earn you by being loyal makes me worthy, then I am. Don't say no to me, Kate. It will shatter me--like an earthquake. And I believe you'll regret it, too. We can make each other happy. I feel it! I'd stake my life on it. Wait--"

He arose and paced the floor back and forth.

"Do you remember the lines from Tennyson's 'Princess' where the Prince pleads with Ida? I thought I could repeat them, but I'm afraid I'll mar them. I don't want to do that; they're too applicable to my case."

He knew where she kept her Tennyson, and he found the volume and the page, and when he had handed the book to her, he snatched his coat and hat.

"I'm coming for my answer a week from to-night," he said. "For God's sake, girl, don't make a mistake. Life's so short that it ought to be happy. At best I'll only be able to live with you a few decades, and I'd like it to be centuries."

He had not meant to do it, she could see, but suddenly he came to her, and leaning above her burned his kisses upon her eyes. Then he flung himself out of the room, and by the light of her guttering candles she read:--

"Come down, O maid, from yonder mountain height.
What pleasure lives in height (the shepherd sang).
In height and cold, the splendor of the hills?
But cease to move so near the Heavens, and cease
To glide a sunbeam by the blasted pine,
To sit a star upon the sparkling spire;
And come, for Love is of the valley, come thou down
And find him; by the happy threshold, he
Or hand in hand with Plenty in the maize,
Or red with spirted purple of the vats,
Or foxlike in the vine; nor cares to walk
With Death and Morning on the Silver Horns,
Nor wilt thou snare him in the white ravine,
Nor find him dropped upon the firths of ice,
That huddling slant in furrow-cloven falls
To roll the torrent out of dusky doors;
But follow; let the torrent dance thee down
To find him in the valley; let the wild
Lean-headed eagles yelp alone, and leave
The monstrous ledges there to slope, and spill
Their thousand wreaths of dangling water-smoke,
That like a broken purpose waste in air;
So waste not thou; but come; for all the vales
Await thee; azure pillars of the hearth
Arise to thee; the children call, and I
Thy shepherd pipe, and sweet is every sound,
Sweeter thy voice, but every sound is sweet;
Myriads of rivulets hurrying thro' the lawn,

The moan of doves in immemorial elms,
And murmuring of innumerable bees."

She read it twice, soothed by its vague loveliness. She could hear, however, only the sound of the suburban trains crashing by in the distance, and the honking of the machines in the Plaisance. None of those spirit sounds of which Ray had dreamed penetrated through her vigorous materialism. But still, she knew that she was lonely; she knew Ray's going left a gray vacancy.

"I can't think it out," she said at last. "I'll go to sleep. Perhaps there--"

But neither voices nor visions came to her in sleep. She awoke the next morning as unillumined as when she went to her bed. And as she dressed and thought of the full day before her, she was indefinably glad that she was under no obligations to consult any one about her programme, either of work or play.

CHAPTER XXIV

Kate had dreaded the expected solitude of the next night, and it was a relief to her when Marna Fitzgerald telephoned that she had been sent opera-tickets by one of her old friends in the opera company, and that she wanted Kate to go with her.

"George offers to stay home with the baby," she said. "So come over, dear, and have dinner with us; that will give you a chance to see George. Then you and I will go to the opera by our two independent selves. I know you don't mind going home alone. 'Butterfly' is on, you know--Farrar sings."

She said it without faltering, Kate noticed, as she gave her enthusiastic acceptance, and when she had put down the telephone, she actually clapped her hands at the fortitude of the little woman she had once thought such a hummingbird--and a hummingbird with that one last added glory, a voice. Marna had been able to put her dreams behind her; why should not her example be cheerfully followed?

When Kate reached the little apartment looking on Garfield Park, she entered an atmosphere in which, as she had long since proved, there appeared to be no room for regret. Marna had, of course, prepared the dinner with her own hands.

"I whipped up some mayonnaise," she said. "You remember how Schumann-Heink used to like my mayonnaise? And she knows good cooking when she tastes it, doesn't she? I've trifle for desert, too."

"But it must have taken you all day, dear, to get up a dinner like that," protested Kate, kissing the flushed face of her friend.

"It took up the intervals," smiled Marna. "You see, my days are made up of taking care of baby, *and* of intervals. How fetching that black velvet bodice is, Kate. I didn't know you had a low one."

"Low *and* high," said Kate. "That's the way we fool 'em--make 'em think we have a wardrobe. Me--I'm glad I'm going to the opera. How good of you to think of me! So few do--at least in the way I want them to."

Marna threw her a quick glance.

"Ray?" she asked with a world of insinuation.

To Kate's disgust, her eyes flushed with hot tears.

"He's waiting to know," she answered. "But I--I don't think I'm going to be able--"

"Oh, Kate!" cried Marna in despair. "How can you feel that way? Just think--just think--" she didn't finish her sentence.

Instead, she seized little George and began undressing him, her hands lingering over the firm roundness of his body. He seemed to be anything but sleepy, and when his mother passed him over to her guest, Kate let him clutch her fingers with those tenacious little hands which looked like rose-leaves and clung like briers. Marna went out of the room to prepare his bedtime bottle, and Kate took advantage of being alone with him to experiment in those joys which his mother had with difficulty refrained from descanting upon. She kissed him in the back of the neck, and again where his golden curls met his brow--a brow the color of a rose crystal. A delicious, indescribable baby odor came up from him, composed of perfumed breath, of clean flannels, and of general adorability. Suddenly, not knowing she was going to do it, Kate snatched him to her breast, and held him strained to her while he nestled there, eager and completely happy, and over the woman who could not make up her mind about life and her part in it, there swept, in wave after wave, like the south wind blowing over the bleak hills, billows of warm emotion. Her very finger-tips tingled; soft, wistful, delightful tears flooded her eyes. Her bosom seemed to lift as the tide lifts to the moon. She found herself murmuring inarticulate, melodious nothings. It was a moment of realization. She was learning what joys could be hers if only--

Marna came back into the room and took the baby from Kate's trembling hands.

"Why, dear, you're not afraid of him, are you?" his mother asked reproachfully.

Kate made no answer, but, dropping a farewell kiss in the crinkly palm of one dimpled hand, she went out to the kitchen, found an apron, and began drawing the water for dinner and dropping Marna's mayonnaise on the salad. She must, however, have been sitting for several minutes in the baby's high chair, staring unseeingly at the wall, when the buzzing of the indicator brought her to her feet.

"It's George!" cried Marna; and tossing baby and bottle into the cradle, she ran to the door.

Kate hit the kitchen table sharply with a clenched hand. What was there in the return of a perfectly ordinary man to his home that should cause such excitement in a creature of flame and dew like Marna?

> "Marna with the trees' life
>   In her veins a-stir!
> Marna of the aspen heart--"

George came into the kitchen with both hands outstretched.

"Well, it's good to see you here," he declared. "Why don't you come oftener? You make Marna so happy."

That proved her worthy; she made Marna happy! Of what greater use could any person be in this world? George retired to prepare for dinner, and Marna to settle the baby for the night, and Kate went on with the preparations for the meal, while her thoughts revolved like a Catherine wheel.

There were the chops yet to cook, for George liked them blazing from the broiler, and there was the black coffee to set over. This latter was to fortify George at his post, for it was agreed that he was not to sleep lest he should fail to awaken at the need and demand of the beloved potentate in the cradle; and Marna now needed a little stimulant if she was to keep comfortably awake during a long evening--she who used to light the little lamps in the windows of her mind sometime after midnight.

They had one of those exclamatory dinners where every one talked about the incomparable quality of the cooking. The potatoes were after a new recipe,--something Spanish,--and they tasted deliciously and smelled as if assailing an Andalusian heaven. The salad was *piquante*; the trifle vivacious; Kate's bonbons were regarded as unique, and as for the coffee, it provoked Marna to quote the appreciative Talleyrand:--

> "Noir comme le diable,
> Chaud comme l'enfer,
> Pur comme un ange,
> Doux comme l'amour."

Other folk might think that Marna had "dropped out," but Kate could see it written across the heavens in letters of fire that neither George nor Marna thought so. They regarded their table as witty, as blessed in such a guest as Kate, as abounding in desirable food, as being, indeed, all that a dinner-table should be. They had the effect of shutting out a world which clamored to participate in their pleasures, and looked on themselves as being not forgotten, but too selfish in keeping to themselves. It kept little streams of mirth purling through Kate's soul, and at each jest or supposed brilliancy she laughed twice--once with them and once at them. But they were unsuspicious--her friends. They were secretly sorry for her, that was all.

After dinner there was Marna to dress.

"Naturally I haven't thought much about evening clothes since I was married," she said to Kate. "I don't see what I'm to put on unless it's my immemorial gold-of-ophir satin." She looked rather dubious, and Kate couldn't help wondering why she hadn't made a decision before this. Marna caught the expression in her eyes.

"Oh, yes, I know I ought to have seen to things, but you don't know what it is, mavourneen, to do all your own work and care for a baby. It makes everything you do so staccato! And, oh, Kate, I do get so tired! My feet ache as if they'd come off, and sometimes my back aches so I just lie on the floor and roll and groan. Of course, George doesn't know. He'd insist on our having a servant, and we can't begin to afford that. It isn't the wages alone; it's the waste and breakage and all."

She said this solemnly, and Kate could not conceal a smile at her "daughter of the air" using these time-worn domestic plaints.

"You ought to lie down and sleep every day, Marna. Wouldn't that help?"

"That's what George is always saying. He thinks I ought to sleep while the baby is taking his nap. But, mercy me, I just look forward to that time to get my work done."

She turned her eager, weary face toward Kate, and her friend marked the delicacy in it which comes with maternity. It was pallid and rather pinched; the lips hung a trifle too loosely; the veins at the temples showed blue and full. Kate couldn't beat down the vision that would rise before her eyes of the Marna she had known in the old days, who had arisen at noon, coming forth from her chamber like Deirdre, fresh with the freshness of pagan delight. She remembered the crowd that had followed in her train, the manner in which people had looked after her on the street, and the little furore she had invariably awakened when she entered a shop or tea-room. As Marna shook out the gold-of-ophir satin, dimmed now and definitely out of date, there surged up in her friend a rebellion against Marna's complete acquiescence in the present scheme of things. But Marna slipped cheerfully into her gown.

"I shall keep my cloak on while we go down the aisle," she declared. "Nobody notices what one has on when one is safely seated. Particularly," she added, with one of her old-time flashes, "if one's neck is not half bad. Now I'm ready to be fastened, mavourneen. Dear me, it *is* rather tight, isn't it? But never mind that. Get the hooks together somehow. I'll hold my breath. Now, see, with this scarf about me, I shan't look such a terrible dowd, shall I? Only my gloves are unmistakably shabby and not any too clean, either. George won't let me use gasoline, you know, and it takes both money and thought to get them to the cleaners. Do you remember the boxes of long white gloves I used to have in the days when *tante* Barsaloux was my fairy godmother? Gloves were an immaterial incident then. 'Nevermore, nevermore,' as our friend the raven remarked. Come, we'll go. I won't wear my old opera cloak in the street-car; that would be too absurd, especially now that the bullion on it has tarnished. That long black coat of mine is just the thing--equally appropriate for market, mass, or levee. Oh, George, dear, good-bye! Good-bye, you sweetheart. I hate to leave you, truly I do. And I do hope and pray the baby won't wake. If he does--"

"Come along, Marna," commanded Kate. "We mustn't miss that next car."

They barely were in their seats when the lights went up, and before them glittered the Auditorium, that vast and noble audience chamber identified with innumerable hours of artistic satisfaction. The receding arches of the ceiling glittered like incandescent nebulae; the pictured procession upon the proscenium arch spoke of the march of ideas--of the passionate onflow of man's dreams--of whatever he has held beautiful and good.

Kate yielded herself over to the deep and happy sense of completion which this vast chamber always gave her, and while she and Marna sat there, silent, friendly, receptive, she felt her cares and frets slipping from her, and guessed that the drag of Mama's innumerable petty responsibilities was disappearing, too. For here was the pride of life--the power of man expressed in architecture, and in the high entrancement of music. The rich folds of the great curtain satisfied her, the innumerable lights enchanted her, and the loveliness of the women in their fairest gowns and their jewels added one more element to that indescribable thing, compacted of so many elements,--all artificial, all curiously and brightly related,--which the civilized world calls opera, and in which man rejoices with an inconsistent and more or less indefensible joy.

The lights dimmed; the curtain parted; the heights above Nagasaki were revealed. Below lay the city in purple haze; beyond dreamed the harbor where the battleships, the merchantmen and the little fishing-boats rode. The impossible, absurd, exquisite music-play of "Madame Butterfly" had begun.

Oh, the music that went whither it would, like wind or woman's hopes; that lifted like the song of a bird and sank like the whisper of waves. Vague as reverie, fitful as thought, yearning as frustrate love, it fluttered about them.

"The new music," whispered Marna.

"Like flame leaping and dying," responded Kate.

They did not realize the passage of time. They passed from chamber to chamber in that gleaming house of song.

"This was the best of all to me," breathed Marna, as Farrar's voice took up the first notes of that incomparable song of woven hopes and fears, "Some Day He'll Come." The wild cadences of the singer's voice, inarticulate, of universal appeal, like the cry of a lost child or the bleating of a lamb on a windy hill,--were they mere singing? Or were they singing at all? Yes, the new singing, where music and drama insistently meet.

The tale, heart-breaking for beauty and for pathos, neared its close. Oh, the little heart of flame expiring at its loveliest! Oh, the loyal feet that waited--eager to run on love's errands--till dawn brought the sight of faded flowers, the suddenly bleak apartment, the unpressed couch! Then the brave, swift flight of the spirit's wings to other altitudes, above pain and shame! And like love and sorrow, refined to a poignant essence, still the music brooded and cried and aspired.

What visions arose in Marna's brain, Kate wondered, quivering with vicarious anguish. Glancing down at her companion's small, close-clasped hands, she thought of their almost ceaseless toil in those commonplace rooms which she called home, and for the two in it--the ordinary man, the usual baby. And she might have had all this brightness, this celebrity, this splendid reward for high labor!

The curtain closed on the last act,--on the little dead Cio-Cio-San,--and the people stood on their feet to call Farrar, giving her unstintedly of their *bravas*. Kate and Marna stood with the others, but they were silent. There were large, glistening tears on Marna's cheeks, and Kate refrained from adding to her silent singing-bird's distress by one word of appreciation of the evening's pleasure; but as they moved down the thronged aisle together, she caught Marna's hand in her own, and felt her fingers close about it tenaciously.

Outside a bitter wind was blowing, and with such purpose that it had cleared the sky of the day's murk so that countless stars glittered with unwonted brilliancy from a purple-black heaven. Crowded before the entrance were the motors, pouring on in a steady stream, their lamps half dazzling the pedestrians as they struggled against the wind that roared between the high buildings.

Though Marna was to take the Madison Street car, they could not resist the temptation to turn upon the boulevard where the scene was even more exhilarating. The high standing lights that guarded the great drive offered a long and dazzling vista, and between them, sweeping steadily on, were the motor-cars. Laughing, talking, shivering, the people hastened along--the men of fashion stimulated and alert, their women splendid in furs and cloaks of velvet while they waited for their conveyances; by them tripped the music students, who had been incomparably happy in the highest balcony, and who now cringed before the penetrating cold; among them marched sedately the phalanx of middle-class people who permitted themselves an opera or two a year, and who walked sedately, carrying their musical feast with a certain sense of indigestion;--all moved along together, thronging the wide pavement. The restaurants were awaiting those who had the courage for further dissipation; the suburban trains had arranged their schedules to convenience the crowd; and the lights burned low in the hallways of mansions, or apartments, or neat outlying houses, awaiting the return of these adventurers into another world--the world of music. All would talk of Farrar. Not alone that night, nor that week, but always, as long as they lived, at intervals, when they were happy, when their thoughts were uplifted, they would talk of her. And it might have been Marna Cartan instead of Geraldine Farrar of whom they spoke!

"Marna of the far quest" might have made this "flight unhazarded"; might have been the core of all this fine excitement. But she had put herself out of it. She had sold herself for a price--the usual price. Kate would not go so far as to say that a birthright had been sold for a mess of pottage, but Ray McCrea's stock was far below par at that moment. Yet Ray, as she admitted, would not doom her to a life of monotony and heavy toil. With him she would have the free and useful, the amusing and excursive life of an American woman married to a man of wealth. No, her programme would not be a petty one--and yet--

"Do take a cab, Marna," she urged. "My treat! Please."

"No, no," said Marna in a strained voice. "I'll not do that. A five-cent ride in the car will take me almost to my door; and besides the cars are warm, which is an advantage."

It was understood tacitly that Kate was the protector, and the one who wouldn't mind being on the street alone. They had but a moment to wait for Marna's car, but in that moment Kate was thinking how terrible it would be for Marna, in her worn evening gown, to be crowded into that common conveyance and tormented with those futile regrets which must be her so numerous companions.

She was not surprised when Marna snatched her hand, crying:--

"Oh, Kate!"

"Yes, yes, I know," murmured Kate soothingly.

"No, you don't," retorted Marna. "How can you? It's--it's the milk."

There was a catch in her voice.

"The milk!" echoed Kate blankly. "What milk? I thought--"

"Oh, I know," Marna cried impatiently. "You thought I was worrying about that old opera, and that I wanted to be up there behind that screen stabbing myself. Well, of course, knowing the score so well, and having hoped once to do so much with it, the notes did rather try to jump out of my throat. But, goodness, what does all that matter? It's the baby's milk that I'm carrying on about. I don't believe I told George to warm it." Her voice ceased in a wail.

The car swung around the corner, and Kate half lifted Marna up the huge step, and saw her go reeling down the aisle as the cumbersome vehicle lurched forward. Then she turned her own steps toward the stairs of the elevated station.

"The milk!" she ejaculated with commingled tenderness and impatience. "Then that's why she didn't say anything about going behind the scenes. I thought it was because she couldn't endure the old surroundings and the pity of her associates of the opera-days. The milk! I wonder--"

What she wondered she did not precisely say; but more than one person on the crowded elevated train noticed that the handsome woman in black velvet (it really was velveteen, purchased at a bargain) had something on her mind.

CHAPTER XXV

Kate slept lightly that night. She had gone to bed with a sense of gentle happiness, which arose from the furtive conviction that she was going to surrender to Ray and to his point of view. He could take all the responsibility if he liked and she would follow the old instincts of woman and let the Causes of Righteousness with which she had allied herself contrive to get along without her. It was nothing, she told herself, but sheer egotism for her to suppose that she was necessary to their prosperity.

She half awoke many times, and each time she had a vague, sweet longing which refused to resolve itself into definite shape. But when the full morning came she knew it was Ray she wanted. She couldn't wait out the long week he had prescribed as a season of fasting and prayer before she gave her answer, and she was shamelessly glad when her superior, over there at the Settlement House, informed her that she would be required to go to a dance-hall at South Chicago that night--a terrible place, which might well have been called "The Girl Trap." This gave Kate a legitimate excuse to ask for Ray's company, because he had besought her not to go to such places at night without his escort.

"But ought I to be seeing you?" he asked over the telephone in answer to her request. "Wouldn't it be better for my cause if I stayed away?"

In spite of the fact that he laughed, she knew he was quite in earnest, and she wondered why he hadn't discerned her compliant mood from her intonations.

"But I had to mind you, hadn't I?" she sent back. "You said I mustn't go to such places without you."

From her tone she might have been the most betendriled feminine vine that ever wrapped a self-satisfied masculine oak.

"Oh, I'll come," he answered. "Of course I'll come. You knew you had only to give me the chance."

He was on time, impeccable, as always, in appearance. Kate was glad that he was as tall as she. She knew, down in her inner consciousness, that they made a fine appearance together, that they stepped off gallantly. It came to her that perhaps they were to be envied, and that they weren't--or at least that she wasn't--giving their good fortune its full valuation.

She told him about her dinner with the Fitzgeralds and about the opera, but she held back her discovery, so to speak, of the baby, and the episode of Marna's wistful tears when she heard the music, and her amazing *volte-face* at remembering the baby's feeding-time. She would have loved to spin out the story to him--she could have deepened the colors just enough to make it all very telling. But she wasn't willing to give away the reason for her changed mood. It was enough, after all, that he was aware of it, and that when he drew her hand within his arm he held it in a clasp that asserted his right to keep it.

They were happy to be in each other's company again. Kate had to admit it. For the moment it seemed to both of them that it didn't matter much where they went so long as they could go together. They rode out to South Chicago on the ill-smelling South Deering cars, crowded with men and women with foreign faces. One of the men trod on Kate's foot with his hobnailed shoe and gave an inarticulate grunt by way of apology.

"He's crushed it, hasn't he?" asked Ray anxiously, seeing the tears spring to her eyes. "What a brute!"

"Oh, it was an accident," Kate protested. "Any one might have done it."

"But anyone except that unspeakable Huniack would have done more than grunt!"

"I dare say he doesn't know English," Kate insisted. "He'll probably remember the incident longer and be sorrier about it than some who would have been able to make graceful apologies."

"Not he," declared Ray. "Don't you think it! Bless me, Kate, why you prefer these people to any others passes my comprehension. Can't you leave these people to work out their own salvation--which to my notion is the only way they ever can get it--and content yourself with your own kind and class?"

"Not variety enough," retorted Kate, feeling her tenderness evaporate and her tantalizing mood--her usual one when she was with Ray--come back. "Don't I know just what you, for example, are going to think and say about any given circumstances? Don't I know your enthusiasms and reactions as if I'd invented 'em?"

"Well, I know yours, too, but that's because I love you, not because you're like everybody else. I wish you were rather more like other women, Kate. I'd have an easier time."

"If we were married," said Kate, with that cheerful directness which showed how her sentimentality had taken flight, "you'd never give up till you'd made me precisely like Mrs. Brown, Mrs. Smith, and Mrs. Johnson. Men fall in love with women because they're different from other women, and then put in the first years of their married life trying to make them like everybody else. I've noticed, however, that when they've finished the job, they're so bored with the result that they go and look up another 'different' woman. Oh, I know!"

He couldn't say what he wished in reply because the car filled up just then with a party of young people bound for a dance in Russell Square. It always made Kate's heart glow to think of things like that--of what the city was trying to do for its people. These young people came from small, comfortable homes, quite capacious enough for happiness and self-respect, but not large enough for a dance. Very well; all that was needed was a simple request for the use of the field-house and they could have at their disposal a fine, airy hall, well-warmed and lighted, with an excellent floor, charming decorations, and a room where they might prepare their refreshments. All they had to pay for was the music. Proper chaperonage was required and the hall closed at midnight. Kate descanted on the beauties of the system till Ray yawned.

"Think how different it is at the dance-hall where we are going," she went on, not heeding his disinclination for the subject. "They'll keep it up till dawn and drink between every dance. There's not a party of the kind the whole winter through that doesn't see the steps of some young girl set toward destruction. Oh, I can't see why it isn't stopped! If women had the management of things, it would be, I can tell you. It would take about one day to do it."

"That's one of the reasons why the liquor men combine to kill suffrage," said Ray. "They know it will be a sorry day for them when the women get in. Positively, the women seem to think that's all there is to politics--some moral question; and the whole truth is they'd do a lot of damage to business with their slap-dash methods, as they'd learn to their cost. When they found their pin-money being cut down, they'd sing another tune, for they're the most reckless spenders in the world, American women are."

"They're the purchasing agents for the most extravagant nation in the world, if you like," Kate replied. "Men seem to think that shopping is a mere feminine diversion. They forget that it's what supports their business and supplies their homes. Not to speak of any place beyond our own town, think of the labor involved in buying food and clothing for the two million and a half human beings here in Chicago. It's no joke, I assure you."

"Joke!" echoed Ray. "A good deal of the shopping I've seen at my father's store seems to me to come under the head of vice. The look I've seen on some of those faces! It was ravaging greed, nothing less. Why, we had a sale the other day of cheap jewelry, salesmen's samples, and the women swarmed and snatched and glared like savages. I declare, when I saw them like that, so indecently eager for their trumpery ornaments, I said to myself that you'd only to scratch the civilized woman to get at the squaw any day."

Kate kept a leash on her tongue. She supposed it was inevitable that they should get back to the old quarrel. Deep down in Ray, she felt, was an unconquerable contempt for women. He made an exception of her because he loved her; because she drew him with the mysterious sex attraction. It was that, and not any sense of spiritual or intellectual approval of her, which made him set her apart as worthy of admiration and of his devoted service. If ever their lives were joined, she would be his treasure to be kept close in his personal casket,--with the key to the golden padlock in his pocket,--and he would all but say his prayers to her. But all that would not keep him from openly discountenancing her judgment before people. She could imagine him putting off a suggestion of hers with that patient married tone which husbands assume when they discover too much independent cerebration on the part of their wives.

"I couldn't stand that," she inwardly declared, as she let him think that he was assisting her from the car. "If any man ever used that patient tone to me, I'd murder him!"

She couldn't keep back her sardonic chuckle.

"What are you laughing at?" he asked irritatedly.

"At the mad world, master," she answered.

"Where is this dance-hall?" he demanded, as if he suspected her of concealing it.

The tone was precisely the "married" one she had been imagining, and she burst out with a laugh that made him stop and visibly wrap his dignity about him. Nothing was more evident than that he thought her silly. But as she paused, too, standing beneath the street-lamp, and he saw her with her nonchalant tilt of her head,--that handsome head poised on her strong, erect body,--her force and value were so impressed upon him that he had to retract. But she was provoking, no getting around that.

At that moment another sound than laughter cut the air--a terrible sound--the shriek of a tortured child. It rang out three times in quick succession, and Kate's blood curdled.

"Oh, oh," she gasped; "she's being beaten! Come, Ray."

"Mix up in some family mess and get slugged for my pains? Not I! But I'll call a policeman if you say."

"Oh, it might be too late! I'm a policeman, you know. Get the patrol wagon if you like. But I can't stand that--"

Once more that agonized scream! Kate flashed from him into the mesh of mean homes, standing three deep in each yard, flanking each other with only a narrow passage between, and was lost to him. He couldn't see where she had gone, but he knew that he must follow. He fell down a short flight of steps that led from the street to the lower level of the yard, and groped forward. He could hear people running, and when a large woman, draping her wrapper about her, floundered out of a basement door near him, he followed her. She seemed to know where to go. The squalid drama with the same actors evidently had been played before.

Mid-length of the building the woman turned up some stairs and came to a long hall which divided the front and rear stairs. At the end of it a light was burning, and Kate's voice was ringing out like that of an officer excoriating his delinquent troops.

"I'm glad you can't speak English," he heard her say, "for if you could I'd say things I'd be sorry for. I'd shrivel you up, you great brute. If you've got the devil in you, can't you take it out on some one else beside a little child? You're her father, are you? She has no mother, I suppose. Well, you 're under arrest, do you understand? Tell him, some of you who can talk English. He's to sit in that chair and never move from it till the patrol wagon comes. I shall care for the child myself, and she'll be placed where he can't treat her like that again. Poor little thing! Thank you, that's a good woman. Just hold her awhile and comfort her. I can see you've children of your own."

Ray found the courage at length to peer above the heads of the others in that miserable, crowded room. The dark faces of weary men and women, heavy with Old-World, inherited woe, showed in the gloom. The short, shaking man on the chair, dully contrite for his spasm of rage, was cringing before Kate, who stood there, amazingly tall among these low-statured beings. Never had she looked to Ray so like an eagle, so keen, so fierce, so fit for braving either sun or tenebrous cavern. She dominated them all; had them, who only partly understood what she said, at her command. She had thrown back her cloak, and the star of the Juvenile Court officer which she wore carried meaning to them. Though perhaps it had not needed that. Ray tried to think her theatrical, to be angry at her, but the chagrin of knowing that she had forgotten him, and was not caring about his opinion, scourged his criticisms back. She had lifted from the floor the stick with its leathern thong with which the man had castigated the tender body of his motherless child. She held it in her hand, looking at it with the angry aversion that she might have turned upon a venomous serpent. Then slowly, with unspeakable rebuke, she swung her gaze upon the wretch in the chair. For a moment she silently accused him. Then he dropped his head in his hands and sobbed. He seemed in his voiceless way to say that he, too, had been castigated by a million invisible thongs held in dead men's hands, and that his soul, like his child's body, was hideous with welts.

Kate turned to Ray.

"Is the patrol wagon on its way?" she inquired.

"I--I--didn't call it," he stammered.

"Please do," she said simply.

He went out of the room, silently raging, and was grateful that one of the men followed to show him the patrol box. He waited outside for the wagon to come, and when the officers brought out the shaking prisoner, he saw Kate with them carrying the child in her arms.

"I must go to the station," she said to Ray, in a matter-of-fact tone that put him far away from her. "So I'll say good-night. It wouldn't be pleasant for you to ride in the wagon, you know. I'll be quite all right. One of the officers will see me safe home. Anyway, I shall have to go to the dance-hall before the evening's over."

"Kate!" he protested.

"Oh, I know," she said to him apart softly while the others concerned themselves with assisting the blubbering Huniack into the wagon, "you think it isn't nice of me to be going around like this, saving babies from beatings and young girls from much worse. You think it isn't ladylike. But it's what the coming lady is either going to do or see done. It's a new idea, you understand, Ray. Quite different from the squaw idea, isn't it? Good-night!"

An officer stood at the door of the wagon waiting for her. He touched his hat and smiled at her in a comradely fashion, and she responded with as courteous a bow as she ever had made to Ray.

The wagon drove off.

"I've been given my answer," said Ray aloud. He wondered if he were more relieved or disappointed at the outcome. But really he could neither feel nor think reasonably. He went home in a tumult, dismayed at his own sufferings, and in no condition to realize that the old ideas and the new were at death grips in his consciousness.

CHAPTER XXVI

Karl Wander rode wearily up the hill on his black mare. Honora saw him coming and waved to him from the window. There was no one to put up his horse, and he drove her into the stables and fed her and spread her bed while Honora watched what he and she had laughingly termed "the outposts." For she believed she had need to be on guard, and she thanked heaven that all of the approaches to the house were in the open and that there was nothing nearer than the rather remote grove of piñon trees which could shelter any creeping enemy.

Wander came on at last to the house, making his way deliberately and scorning, it would seem, all chance of attack. But Honora's ears fairly reverberated with the pistol shot which did not come; the explosion which was now so long delayed. She ran to open the door for him and to drag him into the friendly kitchen, where, in the absence of any domestic help, she had spread their evening meal.

There was a look in his face which she had not seen there before--a look of quietude, of finality.

"Well?" she asked.

He flung his hat on a settle and sat down to loosen his leggings.

"They've gone," he said, "bag and baggage."

"The miners?"

"Yes, left this afternoon--confiscated some trains and made the crews haul them out of town. They shook their fists at the mines and the works as if they had been the haunt of the devil. I couldn't bring myself to skulk. I rode Nell right down to the station and sat there till the last carload pulled out with the men and women standing together on the platform to curse me."

"Karl! How could you? It's a marvel you weren't shot."

"Too easy a mark, I reckon."

"And Elena?"

"Lifted on board by two rival suitors. She didn't even look at me." He drew a long breath. "I was guiltless in that, Honora. You've stood by through everything, and you've made a cult of believing in me, and I want you to know that, so far as Elena was concerned, you were right to do it. I may have been a fool--but not consciously--not consciously."

"I know it. I believe you."

A silence fell between them while Honora set the hot supper on the table and put the tea to draw.

"It's very still," he said finally. "But the stillness here is nothing to what it is down where my village stood. I've made a frightful mess of things, Honora."

"No," she said, "you built up; another has torn down. You must get more workmen. There may be a year or two of depression, but you're going to win out, Karl."

"I've fought a good many fights first and last, Honora,--fights you know nothing about. Some of them have been with men, some with ideas, some of the worst ones with myself. It would be a long story and a strange one if I were to tell it all."

"I dare say it would."

"I suppose I must seem very strange to a civilized woman like you, or-- or your friend, Kate Barrington."

"You seem very like a brave man, Karl, and an interesting one."

"But I'm tired, Honora,--extraordinarily tired. I don't feel like fighting. Quiet and rest are what I'm longing for, and I'm to begin all over again, it appears. I've got to struggle up again almost from the bottom."

"Come to supper, Karl. Never mind all that. We have food and we have shelter. No doubt we shall sleep. Things like that deserve our gratitude. Accept these blessings. There are many who lack them."

Suddenly he threw up his arms with a despairing gesture.

"Oh, it isn't myself, Honora, that I'm grieving for! It's those hot-headed, misguided, wayward fellows of mine! They've left the homes I tried to help them win, they've followed a self-seeking, half-mad, wholly vicious agitator, and their lives, that I meant to have flow on so smoothly, will be troubled and wasted. I know so well what will happen! And then, their hate! It hangs over me like a cloud! I'm not supposed to be sensitive. I'm looked on as a swaggering, reckless, devil-may-care fellow with a pretty good heart and a mighty sure aim; but I tell you, cousin, among them, they've taken the life out of me."

"It's your dark hour, Karl. You're standing the worst of it right now. To-morrow things will look better."

"I couldn't ask a woman to come out here and stand amid this ruin with me, Honora. You know I couldn't. The only person who would be willing to share my present life with me would be some poor, devil-driven creature like Elena--come to think of it, even she wouldn't! She's off and away with a lover at each elbow!"

"Here!" said Honora imperatively. She held a plate toward him laden with steaming food.

He arose, took it, seated himself, and tried a mouthful, but he had to wash it down with water.

"I'm too tired," he said. "Really, Honora, you'll have to forgive me."

She got up then and lighted the lamp in his bedroom.

"Thank you," he said. "Rest is what I need. It was odd they didn't shoot, wasn't it? I thought every moment that they would."

"You surely didn't wish that they would, Karl?"

"No." He paused for a moment at the door. "No--only everything appeared to be so futile. My bad deeds never turned on me as my good ones have done. It makes everything seem incoherent. What--what would a woman like Miss Barrington make of all that--of harm coming from good?"

"I don't know," said Honora, rather sharply. "She hasn't written. I told her all the trouble we were in,--the danger and the distress,--but she hasn't written a word."

"Why should she?" demanded Wander. "It's none of her concern. I suppose she thinks a fool is best left with his folly. Good-night, cousin. You're a good woman if ever there was one. What should I have done without you?"

Honora smiled wanly. He seemed to have forgotten that it was she who would have fared poorly without him.

She closed up the house for the night, looking out in the bright moonlight to see that all was quiet. For many days and nights she had been continually on the outlook for lurking figures, but now she was inclined to believe that she had overestimated the animosity of the strikers. After all, try as they might, they could bring no accusations against the man who, hurt to the soul by their misunderstanding of him, was now laying his tired head upon his pillow.

All was very still. The moonlight touched to silver the snow upon the mountains; the sound of the leaping river was like a distant flute; the wind was rising with long, wavelike sounds. Honora lingered in the doorway, looking and listening. Her heart was big with pity--pity for that disheartened man whose buoyancy and self-love had been so deeply wounded, pity for those wandering, angry, aimless men and women who might have rested secure in his guardianship; pity for all the hot, misguided hearts of men and women. Pity, too, for the man with the most impetuous heart of them all, who wandered in some foreign land with a woman whose beauty had been his lure and his undoing. Yes, she had been given grace in those days, when she seemed to stand face to face with death, to pity even David and Mary!

She walked with a slow firm step up to her room, holding her head high. She had learned trust as well as compassion. She trusted Karl and the issue of his sorrow. She even trusted the issue of her own sorrow, which, a short time before, had seemed so shameful. She threw wide her great windows, and the wind and the moonlight filled her chamber.

Two days later Karl Wander and Honora Fulham rode together to the village, now dismantled and desolate.

"I remember," said Karl, "what a boyish pride I took in the little town at first, Honora, to have built it, and had it called after me and all. Such silly fools as men are, trying to perpetuate themselves by such childish methods."

"Perpetuation is an instinct with us," said Honora calmly, "Immortality is our greatest hope. I'm so thankful I have my children, Karl. They seem to carry one's personality on, you know, no matter how different they actually may be from one's self."

"Oh, yes," said Karl, with a short sigh, "you're right there. You've a beautiful brace of babies, Honora. I believe I'll have to ask you to appoint me their guardian. I must have some share in them. It will give me a fresh reason for going on."

"Are you a trifle short of reasons for going on, Karl?" Honora asked gently, averting her look so that she might not seem to be watching him.

"Yes, I am," he admitted frankly. "Although, now that the worst of my chagrin is over at having failed so completely in the pet scheme of my life, I can feel my fighting blood getting up again. I'm going to make a success of the town of Wander yet, my cousin, and those three mines that lie there so silently are going to hum in the old way. You'll see a string of men pouring in and out of those gates yet, take my word for it. But as for me, I proceed henceforth on a humbler policy."

"Humbler? Isn't it humble to be kind, Karl? That's what you were first and last--kind. You were forever thinking of the good of your people."

"It was outrageously insolent of me to do it, my cousin. Who am I that I should try to run another man's affairs? How should I know what is best for him--isn't he the one to be the judge of that? patronage, patronage, that's what they can't stand--that's what natural overmen like myself with amiable dispositions try to impose on those we think inferior to ourselves. We can't seem to comprehend that the way to make them grow is to leave them alone."

"Don't be bitter, Karl."

"I'm not bitter, Honora. I'm rebuked. I'm literal. I'm instructed. I have brought you down here to talk the situation over with me. I can get men in plenty to advise me, but I want to know what you think about a number of things. Moreover, I want you to tell me what you imagine Miss Barrington would think about them."

"Why don't you write and ask her?" asked Honora. She herself was hurt at not having heard from Kate.

"I gave her notice that I wasn't going to write any more," said Karl sharply. "I couldn't have her counting on me when I wasn't sure that I was a man to be counted on."

"Oh," cried Honora, enlightened. "That's the trouble, is it? But still, I should think she'd write to me. I told her of all you and I were going through together--" she broke off suddenly. Her words presented to her for the first time some hint of the idea she might have conveyed to Kate. She smiled upon her cousin beautifully, while he stared at her, puzzled at her unexpected radiance.

"Kate loves him," she decided, looking at the man beside her with fresh appreciation of his power. She was the more conscious of it that she saw him now in his hour of defeat and perceived his hope and ingenuity, his courage and determination gathering together slowly but steadily for a fresh effort.

"Dear old Kate," she mused. "Karl rebuffed her in his misery, and I misled her. If she hadn't cared she'd have written anyway. As it is--"

But Karl was talking.

"Now there's the matter of the company store," he was saying. "What would Miss Barrington think about the ethical objections to that?"

Honora turned her attention to the matter in hand, and when, late that afternoon, the two rode their jaded horses home, a new campaign had been planned. Within a week Wander left for Denver. Honora heard nothing from him for a fortnight. Then a wire came. He was returning to Wander with five hundred men.

"They're hoboes--pick-ups," he told Honora that night as the two sat together at supper. "Long-stake and short-stake men--down-and-outs--vagrants--drunkards, God knows what. I advertised for them. 'Previous character not called into question,' was what I said. 'Must open up my mines. Come and work as long as you feel like it.' I haven't promised them anything and they haven't promised me anything, except that I give them wages for work. A few of them have women with them, but not more than one in twenty. I don't know what kind of a mess the town of Wander will be now, but at any rate, it's sticking to its old programme of 'open shop.' Any one who wants to take these fellows away from me is quite welcome to do it. No affection shall exist between them and me. There are no obligations on either side. But they seem a hearty, good-natured lot, and they said they liked my grit."

Something that was wild and reckless in all of the Wanders flashed in Honora's usually quiet eyes.

"A band of brigands," she laughed. "Really, Karl, I think you'll make a good chief for them. There's one thing certain, they'll never let you patronize them."

"I shan't try," declared Karl. "They needn't look to me for benefits of any sort. I want miners."

Honora chuckled pleasantly and looked at her cousin from the corner of her eye. She had her own ideas about his ability to maintain such detachment.

He amused her a little later by telling her how he had formed a town government and he described the men he had appointed to office.

"They take it seriously, too," he declared. "We have a ragamuffin government and regulations that would commend themselves to the most judicious. 'Pon my soul, Honora, though it's only play, I swear some of these fellows begin to take on little affectations of self-respect. We're going to have a council meeting to-morrow. You ought to come down."

That gave Honora a cue. She was wanting something more to do than to look after the house, now that servants had again been secured. It occurred to her that it might be a good idea to call on the women down at Wander. She was under no error as to their character. Broken-down followers of weak men's fortunes,--some with the wedding ring and some without,-- they nevertheless were there, flesh and blood, and possibly heart and soul. Not the ideal but the actual commended itself to her these days. Kate had taught her that lesson. So, quite simply, she went among them.

"Call on me when you want anything," she said to them. "I'm a woman who has seen trouble, and I'd like to be of use to any of you if trouble should come your way. Anyhow, trouble or no trouble, let us be friends."

In her simple dress, with her quiet, sad face and her deep eyes, she convinced them of sincerity as few women could have done. They bade her enter their doors and sit in their sloven homes amid the broken things the Italians had left behind them.

"Why not start a furniture shop?" asked Honora. "We could find some men here who could make plain furniture. I'll see Mr. Wander about it."

That was a simple enough plan, and she had no trouble in carrying it out. She got the women to cooperate with her in other ways. Among them they cleaned up the town, set out some gardens, and began spending their men's money for necessaries.

"Do watch out," warned Karl; "you'll get to be a Lady Bountiful--"

"And you a benevolent magnate--"

"Damned if I will! Well, play with your hobo brides if you like, Honora, but don't look for gratitude or rectitude or any beatitude."

"Not I," declared Honora. "I'm only amusing myself."

They kept insisting to each other that they had no higher intention. They were hilarious over their failures and they persisted in taking even their successes humorously. At first the "short-stake men" drifted away, but presently they began to drift back again. They liked it at Wander,- -liked being mildly and tolerantly controlled by men of their own sort,-- men with some vested authority, however, and a reawakened perception of responsibility. Wander was their town--the hoboes' own city. It was one of the few places where something was expected of the hobo. Well, a hobo was a man, wasn't he? The point was provable. A number of Karl Wander's vagrants chose to prove that they were not reprobates. Those who had been "down and out" by their own will, or lack of it, as well as those whom misfortune had dogged, began to see in this wild village, in the heart of these rich and terrific mountains, that wonderful thing, "another chance."

"Would Miss Barrington approve of us now?" Karl would sometimes ask Honora.

"Why should she?" Honora would retort. "We're not in earnest. We're only fighting bankruptcy and ennui."

"That's it," declared Karl. "By the way, I must scrape up some more capital somewhere, Honora. I've borrowed everything I could lay my hands on in Denver. Now I've written to some Chicago capitalists about my affairs and they show a disposition to help me out. They'll meet in Denver next week. Perhaps I shall bring them here. I've told them frankly what my position was. You see, if I can swing things for six months more, the tide will turn. Do you think my interesting rabble will stick to me?"

"Don't count on them," said Honora. "Don't count on anybody or anything. But if you like to take your chance, do it. It's no more of a gamble than anything else a Colorado man is likely to invest in."

"You don't think much of us Colorado men, do you, my cousin?"

"I don't think you are quite civilized," she said. Then a twinge of memory twisted her face. "But I don't care for civilized men. I like glorious barbarians like you, Karl."

"Men who are shot at from behind bushes, eh? If I ever have to hide in a cave, Honora, will you go with me?"

"Yes, and load the guns."

He flashed her a curious look; one which she could not quite interpret. Was he thinking that he would like her to keep beside him? For a second, with a thrill of something like fear, this occurred to her. Then by some mysterious process she read his mind, and she read it aright. He was really thinking how stirring a thing life would seem if he could hear words like that from the lips of Kate Barrington.

CHAPTER XXVII

It had been a busy day for Honora. She had been superintending the house-cleaning and taking rather an aggressive part in it herself. She rejoiced that her strength had come back to her, and she felt a keen satisfaction in putting it forth in service of the man who had taken her into community of interest with him when, as he had once put it, she was bankrupted of all that had made her think herself rich.

Moreover, she loved the roomy, bare house, with its uncurtained windows facing the mountains, and revealing the spectacles of the day and night. Because of them she had learned to make the most of her sleepless hours. The slow, majestic procession in the heavens, the hours of tumult when the moon struggled through the troubled sky, the dawns with their swift, wide-spreading clarity, were the finest diversions she ever had known.

She remembered how, in the old days, she and David had patronized the unspeakably puerile musical comedies under the impression that they "rested" them. Now, she was able to imagine nothing more fatiguing.

They had an early supper, for Karl was leaving for a day or two in Denver and had to be driven ten miles to the station. He was unusually silent, and Honora was well pleased that he should be so, for, though she had kept herself so busily occupied all the day, she had not been able to rid herself of the feeling that a storm of memories was waiting to burst upon her. The feeling had grown as the hours of the day went on, and she at once dreaded and longed for the solitude she should have when Karl was gone. She was relieved to find that the little girls were weary and quite ready for their beds. She watched Karl drive away, standing at the door for a few moments till she heard his clear voice calling a last good-bye as the station wagon swept around the piñon grove; then she locked the house and went to her own room. A fire had been laid for her, and she touched a match to the kindling, lighted her lamp, and took up some sewing. But she found herself too weary to sew, and, moreover, this assailant of recollection was upon her again.

She had once seen the Northern lights when the many-hued glory seemed to be poured from vast, invisible pitchers, till it spread over the floor of heaven and spilled earthward. Her memories had come upon her like that.

Then she faced the fact she had been trying all day not to recognize.

It was David's birthday!

She admitted it now, and even had the courage to go back over the ways they had celebrated the day in former years; at first she held to the old idea that these recollections made her suffer, but presently she perceived that it was not so. Had her help come from the hills, as Karl had told her it would?

She sat so still that she could hear the ashes falling in the fireplace--so still that the ticking of her watch on the dressing-table teased her ears. She seemed to be listening for something--for something beautiful and solemn. And by and by the thing she had been waiting for came.

It swept into the house as if all the doors and windows had been thrown wide to receive it. It was as invisible as the wind, as scentless as a star, as complete as birth or death. It was peace--or forgiveness--or, in a white way, perhaps it was love.

Suddenly she sprang to her feet.

"David!" she cried. "David! Oh, I *believe I understand!*"

She went to her desk, and, as if she were compelled, began to write. Afterward she found she had written this:--

> "DEAR DAVID:--
>
> "It is your birthday, and I, who am so used to sending you a present, cannot be deterred now. Oh, David, my husband, you who fathered my children, you, who, in spite of all, belong to me, let me tell you how I have at last come, out of the storm of angers and torments of the past year, into a sheltered room where you seem to sit waiting to hear me say, 'I forgive you.'
>
> "That is my present to you--my forgiveness. Take it from me with lifted hands as if it were a sacrament; feed on it, for it is holy bread. Now we shall both be at peace, shall we not? You will forgive me, too, *for all I did not do.*
>
> "We are willful children, all of us, and night over-takes us before we have half learned our lessons.
>
> "Oh, David--"

She broke off suddenly. Something cold seemed to envelop her--cold as a crevasse and black as death. She gave a strangled cry, wrenched the collar from her throat, fighting in vain against the mounting waves that overwhelmed her.

Long afterward, she shuddered up out of her unconsciousness. The fire had burned itself out; the lamp was sputtering for lack of oil. Somewhere in the distance a coyote called. She was dripping with cold sweat, and had hardly strength to find the thing that would warm her and to get off her clothes and creep into bed.

At first she was afraid to put out the light. It seemed as if, should she do so, the very form and substance of Terror would come and grip her. But after a time, slowly, wave upon wave, the sea of Peace rolled over her--submerging her. She reached out then and extinguished the light and let herself sink down, down, through the obliterating waters of sleep--waters as deep, as cold, as protecting as the sea.

"Into the Eternal Arms," she breathed, not knowing why.

But when she awakened the next morning in response to the punctual gong, she remembered that she had said that.

"Into the Eternal Arms."

She came down to breakfast with the face of one who has eaten of the sacred bread of the spirit. The next two days passed vaguely. A gray veil appeared to hang between her and the realities, and she had the effect of merely going through the motions of life. The children caused her no trouble. They were, indeed, the most normal of children, and Mrs. Hays, their old-time nurse, had reduced their days to an agreeable system. Honora derived that peculiar delight from them which a mother may have when she is not obliged to be the bodily servitor and constant attendant of her children. She was able to feel the poetry of their childhood, seeing them as she did at fortunate and picturesque moments; and though their lives were literally braided into her own,--were the golden threads in her otherwise dun fabric of existence,--she was thankful that she did not have the task of caring for them. It would have been torture to have been tied to their small needs all day and every day. She liked far better the heavier work she did about the house, her long walks, her rides to town, and, when Karl was away, her supervision of the ranch. Above all, there was her work at the village. She could return from that to the children for refreshment and for spiritual illumination. In the purity of their eyes, in the liquid sweetness of their voices, in their adorable grace and caprice, there was a healing force beyond her power to compute.

During these days, however, her pleasure in them was dim, though sweet. She had been through a mystic experience which left a profound influence upon her, and she was too much under the spell of it even to make an effort to shake it off. She slept lightly and woke often, to peer into the velvet blackness of the night and to listen to the deep silence. She was as one who stands apart, the viewer of some tremendous but uncomprehended event.

The third day she sent the horses for Karl, and as twilight neared, he came driving home. She heard his approach and threw open the door for him. He saw her with a halo of light about her, curiously enlarged and glorified, and came slowly and heavily toward her, holding out both hands. At first she thought he was ill, but as his hands grasped hers, she saw that he was not bringing a personal sorrow to her but a brotherly compassion. And then she knew that something had happened to David. She read his mind so far, almost as if it had been a printed page, and she might have read further, perhaps, if she had waited, but she cried out:--

"What is it? You've news of David?"

"Yes," he said. "Come in."

"You've seen the papers?" he asked when they were within the house. She shook her head.

"I haven't sent over for the mail since you left, Karl. I seemed to like the silence."

"There's silence enough in all patience!" he cried. "Sixteen hundred voices have ceased."

"I don't understand."

"The Cyclops has gone down--a new ship, the largest on the sea."

"Why, that seems impossible."

"Not when there are icebergs floating off the banks and when the bergs carry submerged knives of ice. One of them gored the ship. It was fatal."

"How terrible!" For a second's space she had forgotten the possible application to her. Then the knowledge came rushing back upon her.

She put her hands over her heart with the gesture of one wounded.

"David?" she gasped.

Karl nodded.

"He was on it--with Mary. They were coming back to America. He had been given the Norden prize, as you know,--the prize you earned for him. I think he was to take a position in some Eastern university. He and Mary had gone to their room, the paper says, when the shock came. They ran out together, half-dressed, and Mary asked a steward if there was anything the matter. 'Yes, madam,' he said quietly, just like that, 'I believe we are sinking.' You'll read all about it there in those papers. Mary was interviewed. Well, they lowered the boats. There were enough for about a third of the passengers. They had made every provision for luxury, but not nearly enough for safety. The men helped the women into the boats and sent them away. Then they sat down together, folded their arms, and died like gentlemen, with the good musicians heartening them with their music to the last. The captain went down with his ship, of course. All of the officers did that. Almost all of the men did it, too. It was very gallant in its terrible way, and David was among the most gallant. The papers mention him particularly. He worked till the last helping the others off, and then he sat down and waited for the end."

Honora turned on her cousin a face in which all the candles of her soul were lit.

"Oh, Karl, how wonderful! How beautiful!"

He said nothing for amazement.

"In that half-hour," she went on, speaking with such swiftness that he could hardly follow her, "all his thoughts streamed off across the miles of sea and land to me! I felt the warmth of them all about me. It was myself he was thinking of. He came back to me, his wife! I was alone, waiting for something, I couldn't tell what. Then I remembered it was his birthday, and that I should be sending him a gift. So I sent him my forgiveness. I wrote a letter, but for some reason I have not sent it. It is here, the letter!" She drew it from her bosom. "See, the date and hour is upon it. Read it."

Karl arose and held the letter in a shaking hand. He made a calculation.

"The moments correspond," he said. "You are right; his spirit sought yours."

"And then the--the drowning, Karl. I felt it all, but I could not understand. I died and was dead for a long time, but I came up again, to live. Only since then life has been very curious. I have felt like a ghost that missed its grave.

I've been walking around, pretending to live, but really half hearing and half seeing, and waiting for you to come back and explain."

"I have explained," said Karl with infinite gentleness. "Mary is saved. She was taken up with others by the Urbania, and friends are caring for her in New York. She gave a very lucid interview; a feeling one, too. She lives, but the man she ruined went down, for her sake."

"No," said Honora, "he went down for my sake. He went down for the sake of his ideals, and his ideals were mine. Oh, how beautiful that I have forgiven him--and how wonderful that he knew it, and that I--" She spoke as one to whom a great happiness had come. Then she wavered, reached out groping hands, and fell forward in Karl's arms.

For days she lay in her bed. She had no desire to arise. She seemed to dread interruption to her passionate drama of emotion, in which sorrow and joy were combined in indeterminate parts. From her window she could see the snow-capped peaks of the Williston range, rising with immortal and changeful beauty into the purple heavens. As she watched them with incurious eyes, marking them in the first light of the day, when their iridescence made them seem as impalpable as a dream of heaven; eyeing them in the noon-height, when their sides were the hue of ruddy granite; watching them at sunset when they faded from swimming gold to rose, from rose to purple, they seemed less like mountains than like those fair and fatal bergs of the Northern Atlantic. She had read of them, though she had not seen them. She knew how they sloughed from the inexhaustible ice-cap of Greenland's bleak continent and marched, stately as an army, down the mighty plain of the ocean. Fair beyond word were they, with jeweled crevasses and mother-of-pearl changefulness, indomitable, treacherous, menacing. Honora, closing weary eyes, still saw them sailing, sailing, white as angels, radiant as dawn, changing, changing, lovely and cold as death.

Mind and gaze were fixed upon their enchantment. She would not think of certain other things--of that incredible catastrophe, that rent ship, crashing to its doom, of that vast company tossed upon the sea, of those cries in the dark. No, she shut her eyes and her ears to those things! They seemed to be the servitors at the doors of madness, and she let them crook their fingers at her in vain. Now and then, when she was not on guard, they swarmed upon her, whispering stories of black struggle, of heart-breaking separation of mother and child, of husband and wife. Sometimes they told her how Mary--so luxurious, so smiling, so avid of warmth and food and kisses--had shivered in that bleak wind, as she sat coatless, torn from David's sheltering embrace. They had given her elfish reminders of how soft, how pink, how perfumed was that woman's tender flesh. Then as she looked the blue eyes glazed with agony, the supple body grew rigid with cold, and down, down, through miles of water, sank the man they both had loved.

No, no, it was better to watch the bergs, those glistering, fair, white ships of death! Yes, there from the window she seemed to see them! How the sun glorified them! Was the sun setting, then? Had there been another day?

"To-morrow and to-morrow and to-morrow--"

Darkness was falling. But even in the darkness she saw the ice-ships slipping down from that great frozen waste, along the glacial rivers, past the bleak *lisière*, into the bitter sea, and on down, down to meet that other ship--that ship bearing its mighty burden of living men--and to break it in unequal combat.

Oh, could she never sleep! Would those white ships never reach port!

Did she hear Karl say he had telegraphed for Kate Barrington? But what did it matter? Neither Kate nor Karl, strong and kind as they were, could stem the tide that bore those ships along the never-quiet seas.

CHAPTER XXVIII

So Kate was coming!

He had cravenly rebuffed her, and she had borne the rebuff in silence. Yet now that he needed her, she was coming. Ah, that was what women meant to men. They were created for the comforting of them. He always had known it, but he had impiously doubted them--doubted Her. Because fortune had turned from him, he had turned from Her--from Kate Barrington. He had imagined that she wanted more than he could give; whereas, evidently, all she ever had wanted was to be needed. He had called. She had answered. It had been as swift as telegraphy could make it. And now he was driving to the station to meet her.

Life, it appeared, was just as simple as that. A man, lost in the darkness, could cry for a star to guide him, and it would come. It would shine miraculously out of the heavens, and his path would be made plain. It seemed absurd that the horses should be jogging along at their usual pace over the familiar road. Why had they not grown shining wings? Why was the old station wagon not transformed, by the mere glory of its errand, into a crystal coach? But, no, the horses went no faster because they were going on this world-changing errand. The resuscitated village, with the American litter heaped on the Italian dirt, looked none the less slovenly because She was coming into it in a few minutes. The clock kept its round; the sun showed its usual inclination toward the west. But notwithstanding this torpidity, She was coming, and that day stood apart from all other days.

That it was Honora's desperate need which she was answering, in no way lessened the value of her response to him. His need and Honora's were indissoluble now; it was he who had called, and it was not to Honora alone that she was coming with healing in her hands.

He saw her as she leaped from the train,--tall, alert, green-clad,--and he ran forward, sweeping his Stetson from his head. Their hands met--clung.

"You!" he said under his breath.

She laughed into his eyes.

"No, *you*!" she retorted.

He took her bags and they walked side by side, looking at each other as if their eyes required the sight.

"How is she?" asked Kate.

"Very bad."

"What is it?"

"The doorway to madness."

"You've had a specialist?"

"Yes. He wanted to take her to a sanatorium. I begged him to wait--to let you try. How could I let her go out from my door to be cast in with the lost?"

"I suppose it was David's death that caused it."

"Oh, yes. What else could it be?"

"Then she loved him--to the end."

"And after it, I am sure."

He led the way to the station wagon and helped her in; then brought her luggage on his own shoulder.

"Oh," she cried in distress. "Do you have to be your own stevedore? I don't like to have you doing that for me."

"Out here we wait on ourselves," he replied when he had tumbled the trunk into the wagon. He seated himself beside her as if he were doing an accustomed thing, and she, too, felt as if she had been there beside him many times before.

As they entered the village, he said:--

"You must note my rowdy town. Never was there such a place--such organized success built on so much individual failure. From boss to water-boy we were failures all; so we understood each other. We haven't sworn brotherhood, but we're pulling together. Some of us had known no law, and most of us had a prejudice against it, but now we're making our own laws and we rather enjoy the process. We've made the town and the mines our own cause, so what is the use of playing the traitor? Some of us are short-stake men habitually and constitutionally. Very well, say we, let us look at the facts. Since there are short-stake men in the world, why not make allowances for them? Use their limited powers of endurance and concentration, then let 'em off to rest up. If there are enough short-stake men around, some one will always be working. We find it works well."

"Have you many women in your midst?"

"At first we had very few. Just some bedraggled wives and a few less responsible ladies with magenta feathers in their hats. At least, two of them had, and the magenta feather came to be a badge. But they've disappeared--the feathers, not the ladies. Honora had a hand in it. I think she pulled off one marriage. She seemed to think there were arguments in favor of the wedding ceremony. But, mind you, she didn't want any of the poor women to go because they were bad. We are sinners all here. Stay and take a chance, that's our motto. It isn't often you can get a good woman like Honora to hang up a sign like that."

"Honora couldn't have done it once," said Kate. "But think of all she's learned."

"Learned? Yes. And I, too. I've been learning my lessons, too,--they were long and hard and I sulked at some of them, but I'm more tractable new."

"I had my own hard conning," Kate said softly. "You never could have done what I did, Mr. Wander. You couldn't have been cruel to an old father."

"Honora has made all that clear to me," said Karl with compassion. "When we are fighting for liberty we forget the sufferings of the enemy."

There was a little pause. Then Karl spoke.

"But I forgot to begin at the beginning in telling you about my made-over mining town. Yet you seemed to know about it."

"Oh, I read about it in the papers. Your experiment is famous. All of the people I am associated with, the welfare workers and sociologists, are immensely interested in it. That's one of the problems now--how to use the hobo, how to get him back into an understanding of regulated communities."

"Put him in charge," laughed Karl. "The answer's easy. Treat him like a fellow-man. Don't annoy him by an exhibition of your useless virtues."

"I never thought of that," said Kate.

They turned their backs on the straggling town and faced the peaks. Presently they skirted the Williston River which thundered among boulders and raged on toward the low-lying valley. From above, the roar of the pines came to them, reverberant and melancholy.

"What sounds! What sounds!" cried Kate.

"The mountains breathing," answered Wander.

He drove well, and he knew the road. It was a dangerous road, which, ever ascending, skirted sharp declivities and rounded buttressed rocks. Kate, prairie-reared, could not "escape the inevitable thrill," but she showed, and perhaps felt, no fear. She let the matter rest with him--this man with great shoulders and firm hands, who knew the primitive art of "waiting on himself." Their brief speech sufficed them for a time, and now they sat silent, well content. The old, tormenting question as to his relations with Honora did not intrude itself. It was swept out of sight like flotsam in the plenteous stream of present content.

They swung upon a purple mesa, and in the distance Kate saw a light which she felt was shining from the window of his home.

"It's just as I thought it would be," she said.

"Perhaps you are just the way it thought you would be," he replied. "Perhaps the soul of a place waits and watches for the right person, just as we human beings wander about searching for the right spot."

"*I'm* suited," affirmed Kate. "I hope the mesa is."

"I know it well and I can answer for it."

The road continued to mount; they entered the piñon grove and rode in aromatic dusk for a while, and when they emerged they were at the doorway.

He lifted her down and held her with a gesture as if he had something to say.

"It's about my letter," he ventured. "You knew very well it wasn't that I didn't want you to write. But my life was getting tangled--I wasn't willing to involve you in any way in the débris. I couldn't be sure that letters sent me would always reach my hands. Worst of all, I accused myself of unworthiness. I do so still."

"I'm not one who worries much about worthiness or unworthiness," she said. "Each of us is worthy and unworthy. But I thought--"

"What?"

"I was confused. Honora said I was to congratulate you--and her. I didn't know--"

He stared incredulously.

"You didn't know--" He broke off, too, then laughed shortly. "I wish you had known," he added. "I would like to think that you never could misunderstand."

She felt herself rebuked. He opened the door for her and she stepped for the first time across the threshold of his house.

Half an hour later, Wander, sitting in his study at the end of the upper hall, saw his guest hastening toward Honora's room. She wore a plain brown house dress and looked uniformed and ready for service. She did not speak to him, but hastened down the corridor and let herself into that solemn chamber where Honora Fulham lay with wide-staring eyes gazing mountain ward. That Honora was in some cold, still, and appalling place it took Kate but a moment to apprehend. She could hardly keep from springing to her as if to snatch her from impending doom, but she forced all panic from her manner.

"Kate's come," she said, leaning down and kissing those chilly lips with a passion of pity and reassurance. "She's come to stay, sister Honora, and to drive everything bad away from you. Give her a kiss if you are glad."

Did she feel an answering salute? She could not be sure. She moved aside and watched. Those fixed, vision-seeing eyes were upon the snow-capped peaks purpling in the decline of the day.

"What is it you see, sister?" she asked. "Is there something out there that troubles you?"

Honora lifted a tragic hand and pointed to those darkening snows.

"See how the bergs keep floating!" she whispered. "They float slowly, but they are on their way. By and by they will meet the ship. Then everything will be crushed or frozen. I try to make them stay still, but they won't do it, and I'm so tired--oh, I'm so terribly tired, Kate."

Kate's heart leaped. She had, at any rate, recognized her.

"They really are still, Honora," she cried. "Truly they are. I am looking at them, and I can see that they are still. They are not bergs at all, but only your good mountains, and by and by all of that ice and snow will melt and flowers will be growing there."

She pulled down the high-rolled shades at the windows with a decisive gesture.

"But I must have them up," cried Honora, beginning to sob. "I have to keep watching them."

"It's time to have in the lamps," declared Kate; and went to the door to ask for them.

"And tea, too, please, Mrs. Hays," she called; "quite hot."

"We've been keeping her very still," warned Wander, rejoicing in Kate's cheerful voice, yet dreading the effect of it on his cousin.

"It's been too still where her soul has been dwelling," Kate replied in a whisper. "Can't you see she's on those bitter seas watching for the ice to crush David's ship? It's not yet madness, only a profound dream--a recurring hallucination. We must break it up--oh, we must!"

She carried in the lamps when they came, placing them where their glow would not trouble those burning eyes; and when Mrs. Hays brought the tea and toast, whispering, "She'll take nothing," Kate lifted her friend in her determined arms, and, having made her comfortable, placed the tray before her.

"For old sake's sake, Honora," she said. "Come, let us play we are girls again, back at Foster, drinking our tea!"

Mechanically, Honora lifted the cup and sipped it. When Kate broke pieces of the toast and set them before her, she ate them.

"You are telling me nothing about the babies," Kate reproached her finally. "Mayn't we have them in for a moment?"

"I don't think they ought to come here," said Honora faintly. "It doesn't seem as if they ought to be brought to such a place as this."

But Kate commanded their presence, and, having softly fondled them, dropped them on Honora's bed and let them crawl about there. They swarmed up to their mother and hung upon her, patting her cheeks, and investigating the use of eyelids and of ropes of hair. But when they could not provoke her to play, they began to whimper.

"Honora," said Kate sharply, "you must laugh at them at once! They mustn't go away without a kiss."

So Honora dragged herself from those green waters beyond the fatal Banks, half across the continent to the little children at her side, and held them for a moment--the two of them at once--in her embrace.

"But I'm so tired, Kate," she said wearily.

"Rest, then," said Kate. "Rest. But it wouldn't have been right to rest without saying good-night to the kiddies, would it? A mother has to think of that, hasn't she? They need you so dreadfully, you see."

She slipped the extra pillows from beneath the heavy head, and stood a moment by the bedside in silence as if she would impress the fact of her protection upon that stricken heart and brain.

"It is safe, here, Honora," she said softly. "Love and care are all about you. No harm shall come near you. Do you believe that?"

Honora looked at her from beneath heavy lids, then slowly let her eyes close. Kate walked to the window and waited. At first Honora's body was convulsed with nervous spasms, but little by little they ceased. Honora slept. Kate threw wide the windows, extinguished the light, and crept from the room, not ill-satisfied with her first conflict with the dread enemy.

Karl was waiting for her in the corridor when she came from Honora's room, and he caught both of her hands in his.

"You're cold with horror!" he said. "What a thing that is to see!"

"But it isn't going to last," protested Kate with a quivering accent. "We can't have it last."

"Come into the light," he urged. "Supper is waiting."

He led her down the stairs and into the simple dining-room. The table was laid for two before a leaping blaze. There was no other light save that of two great candles in sticks of wrought bronze. The room was bare but beautiful--so seemly were its proportions, so fitted to its use its quiet furnishings.

He placed her chair where she could feel the glow and see, through the wide window, a crescent moon mounting delicately into the clear sky. There was game and salad, custard and coffee--a charming feast. Mrs. Hays came and went quietly serving them. Karl said little. He was content with the essential richness of the moment. It was as if Destiny had distilled this hour for him, giving it to him to quaff. He was grave, but he did not resent her sorrowfulness. Sorrow, he observed, might have as sweet a flavor as joy. It did not matter by what name the present hour was called. It was there--he rested in it as in a state of being which had been appointed--a goal toward which he had been journeying.

"What's to be done?" he asked.

"I've been thinking," said Kate, "that we had better move her from that room. Is there none from which no mountains are visible? She ought not to have the continual reminder of those icebergs."

"Why didn't I think of that?" he cried with vexation. "That shows how stupid a man can be. Certainly we have such a room as you wish. It looks over the barnyard. It's cheerful but noisy. You can hear the burros and the chickens and pigs and calves and babies all day long."

"It's precisely what she needs. Her thoughts are the things to fear, and I know of no way to break those up except by crowding others in. Is the room pleasant--gay?"

"No--hardly clean, I should say. But we can work on it like fiends."

"Let's do it, then,--put in chintz, pictures, flowers, books, a jar of goldfish, a cage of finches,--anything that will make her forget that terrible white procession of bergs."

"You think it isn't too late? You think we can save her?"

"I won't admit anything else," declared Kate.

The wind began to rise. It came rushing from far heights and moaned around the house. The silence yielded to this mournful sound, yet kept its essential quality.

"It's a wild place," said Kate; "wilder than any place I have been in before. But it seems secure. I find it hard to believe that you have been in danger here."

"I am in danger now," said Karl. "Much worse danger than I was in when the poor excited dagoes were threatening me."

"What is your danger?" asked Kate.

She was incapable of coquetry after that experience in Honora's room; nor did the noble solitude of the place permit the thought of an excursion into the realms of any sort of dalliance. Moreover, though Karl's words might have led her to think of him as ready to play with a sentimental situation, the essential loftiness of his gaze forbade her to entertain the thought.

"I am in danger," he said gravely, "of experiencing a happiness so great that I shall never again be satisfied with life under less perfect conditions. Can you imagine how the fresh air seems to a man just released from prison? Well, life has a tang like that for me now. I tell you, I have been a discouraged man. It looked to me as if all of the things I had been fighting for throughout my manhood were going to ruin. I saw my theories shattered, my fortune disappearing, my reputation, as the successful manipulator of other men's money, being lost. I've been looked upon as a lucky man and a reliable one out here in Colorado. They swear by you or at you out in this part of the country, and I've been accustomed to having them count on me. I even had some political expectations, and was justified in them, I imagine. I had an idea I might go to the state legislature and then take a jump to Washington. Well, it was a soap-bubble dream, of course. I lost out. This tatterdemalion crew of mine is all there is left of my cohorts. I suppose I'm looked on now as a wild experimenter."

"Would it seem that way to men?" asked Kate, surprised. "To take what lies at hand and make use of it--to win with a broken sword--that strikes me as magnificent."

She forgot to put a guard on herself for a moment and let her admiration, her deep confidence in him, shine from her eyes. She saw him whiten, saw a look of almost terrible happiness in his eyes, and withdrew her gaze. She could hear him breathing deeply, but he said nothing. There fell upon them a profound and wonderful silence which held when they had arisen and were sitting before his hearth. They were alone with elemental things--night, silence, wind, and fire. They had the essentials, roof and food, clothing and companionship. Back and forth between them flashed the mystic currents of understanding. A happiness such as neither had known suffused them.

When they said "good-night," each made the discovery that the simple word has occult and beautiful meanings.

CHAPTER XXIX

At the end of a week Honora showed a decided change for the better. The horror had gone out of her face; she ate without persuasion; she slept briefly but often. The conclusion of a fortnight saw her still sad, but beyond immediate danger of melancholy. She began to assume some slight responsibility toward the children, and she loved to have them playing about her, although she soon wearied of them.

Kate had decided not to go back to Chicago until her return from California. She was to speak to the Federation of Women's Clubs which met at Los Angeles, and she proposed taking Honora with her. Honora was not averse if Kate and Karl thought it best for her. The babies were to remain safe at home.

"I wouldn't dare experiment with babies," said Kate. "At least, not with other people's."

"You surely wouldn't experiment with your own, ma'am!" cried the privileged Mrs. Hays.

"Oh, I might," Kate insisted. "If I had babies of my own, I'd like them to be hard, brown little savages--the sort you could put on donkey-back or camel-back and take anywhere."

Mrs. Hays shook her head at the idea of camels. It hardly sounded Christian, and certainly it in no way met her notion of the need of infants.

"Mrs. Browning writes about taking her baby to a mountain-top not far from the stars," Kate went on. "They rode donkey-back, I believe. Personally, however, I should prefer the camel. For one thing, you could get more babies on his back."

Mrs. Hays threw a glance at her mistress as if to say: "Is it proper for a young woman to talk like this?"

The young woman in question said many things which, according to the always discreet and sensible Mrs. Hays, were hardly to be commended.

There was, for example, the evening she had stood in the westward end of the veranda and called:--

"Archangels! Come quick and see them!"

The summons was so stirring that they all ran,-- even Honora, who was just beginning to move about the house,--but Wander reached Kate's side first.

"She's right, Honora," he announced. "It is archangels--a whole party of them. Come, see!"

But it had been nothing save a sunset rather brighter than usual, with wing-like radiations.

"Pshaw!" said Mrs. Hays confidentially to the cook.

"Shouldn't you think they'd burn up with all that flaming crimson on them?" Kate cried. "And, oh, their golden hair! Or does that belong to the Damosel? Probably she is leaning over the bar of heaven at this minute."

In Mrs. Hays's estimation, the one good thing about all such talk was that Mrs. Fulham seemed to like it. Sometimes she smiled; and she hung upon the arm of her friend and looked at her as if wondering how one could be so young and strong and gay. Mr. Wander, too, seemed never tired of listening; and the way that letters trailed after this young woman showed her that a number--quite an astonishingly large number--of persons were pleased to whet their ideas on her. Clarinda Hays decided that she would like to try it herself; so one morning when she sat on the veranda watching the slumbers of the little girls in their hammocks, and Miss Barrington sat near at hand fashioning a blouse for Honora's journey, she ventured:--

"You're a suffragette, ain't you, Miss?"

"Why, yes," admitted Kate. "I suppose I am. I believe in suffrage for women, at any rate."

"Well, what do you make of all them carryings-on over there in England, ma'am? You don't approve of acid-throwing and window-breaking and cutting men's faces with knives, do you?" She looked at Kate with an almost poignant anxiety, her face twitching a little with her excitement. "A decent woman couldn't put her stamp on that kind o' thing."

"But the puzzling part of it all is, Mrs. Hays, that it appears to be decent women who are doing it. Moreover, it's not an impulse with them but a plan. That rather sets one thinking, doesn't it? You see, it's a sort of revolution. Revolutions have got us almost everything we have that is really worth while in the way of personal liberty; but I don't suppose any of them seemed very 'decent' to the non-combatants who were looking on.

Then, too, you have to realize that women are very much handicapped in conducting a fight."

"What have they got to fight against, I should like to know?" demanded Mrs. Hays, dropping her sewing and grasping the arms of her chair in her indignation.

"Well," said Kate, "I fancy we American women haven't much idea of all that the Englishwomen are called upon to resent. I do know, though, that an English husband of whatever station thinks that he is the commander, and that he feels at liberty to address his wife as few American husbands would think of doing. It's quite allowed them to beat their wives if they are so minded. I hope that not many of them are minded to do anything of the kind, but I feel very sure that women are 'kept in their place' over there. So, as they've been hectored themselves, they've taken up hectoring tactics in retaliation. They demand a share in the government and the lawmaking. They want to have a say about the schools and the courts of justice. If men were fighting for some new form of liberty, we should think them heroic. Why should we think women silly for doing the same thing?"

"It won't get them anywhere," affirmed Clarinda Hays. "It won't do for them what the old way of behaving did for them, Miss. Now, who, I should like to know, does a young fellow, dying off in foreign parts, turn his thoughts to in his last moments? Why, to his good mother or his nice sweetheart! You don't suppose that men are going to turn their dying thoughts to any such screaming, kicking harridans as them suffragettes over there in England, do you?"

Kate heard a chuckle beyond the door--the disrespectful chuckle, as she took it, of the master of the house. It armed her for the fray.

"I don't think the militant women are doing these things to induce men to feel tenderly toward them, Mrs. Hays. I don't believe they care just now whether the men feel tenderly toward them or not. Women have been low-voiced and sweet and docile for a good many centuries, but it hasn't gained them the right to claim their own children, or to stand up beside men and share their higher responsibilities and privileges. I don't like the manner of warfare, myself. While I could die at the stake if it would do any good, I couldn't break windows and throw acid. For one thing, it doesn't seem to me quite logical, as the damage is inflicted on the property of persons who have nothing to do with the case. But, of course, I can't be sure that, after the fight is won, future generations will not honor the women who forgot their personal preferences and who made the fight in the only way they could."

"You're such a grand talker, Miss, that it's hard running opposite to you, but I was brought up to think that a woman ought to be as near an angel as she could be. I never answered my husband back, no matter what he said to me, and I moved here and there to suit him. I was always waiting for him at home, and when he got there I stood ready to do for him in any way I could. We was happy together, Miss, and when he was dying he said that I had been a good wife. Them words repaid me, Miss, as having my own way never could."

Clarinda Hays had grown fervid. There were tears in her patient eyes, and her face was frankly broken with emotion.

Kate permitted a little silence to fall. Then she said gently:--

"I can see it is very sweet to you--that memory--very sweet and sacred. I don't wonder you treasure it."

She let the subject lie there and arose presently and, in passing, laid her firm brown hand on Mrs. Hays's work-worn one.

Wander was in the sitting-room and as she entered it he motioned her to get her hat and sweater. She did so silently and accepted from him the alpenstock he held out to her.

"Is it right to leave Honora?" he asked when they were beyond hearing. "I had little or nothing to do down in town, and it occurred to me that we might slip away for once and go adventuring."

"Oh, Honora's particularly well this morning. She's been reading a little, and after she has rested she is going to try to sew. Not that she can do much, but it means that she's taking an interest again."

"Ah, that does me good! What a nightmare it's been! We seem to have had one nightmare after another, Honora and I."

They turned their steps up the trail that mounted westward.

"It follows this foothill for a way," said Wander, striding ahead, since they could not walk side by side. "Then it takes that level up there and strikes the mountain. It goes on over the pass."

"And where does it end? Why was it made?"

"I'm not quite sure where it ends. But it was made because men love to climb."

She gave a throaty laugh, crying, "I might have known!" for answer, and he led on, stopping to assist her when the way was broken or unusually steep, and she, less accustomed but throbbing with the joy of it, followed.

They reached an irregular "bench" of the mountain, and rested there on a great boulder. Below them lay the ranch amid its little hills, dust-of-gold in hue.

"I have dreamed countless times of trailing this path with you," he said.

"Then you have exhausted the best of the experience already. What equals a dream? Doesn't it exceed all possible fact?"

"I think you know very well," he answered, "that this is more to me than any dream."

An eagle lifted from a tree near at hand and sailed away with confidence, the master of the air.

"I don't wonder men die trying to imitate him," breathed Kate, wrapt in the splendor of his flight. "They are the little brothers of Icarus."

"I always hope," replied Wander, "when I hear of an aviator who has been killed, that he has had at least one perfect flight, when he soared as high as he wished and saw and felt all that a man in his circumstances could. Since he has had to pay so great a price, I want him to have had full value."

"It's a fine thing to be willing to pay the price," mused Kate. "If you can face whatever-gods-there-be and say, 'I've had my adventure. What's due?' you're pretty well done with fears and flurries."

"Wise one!" laughed Wander. "What do you know about paying?"

"You think I don't know!" she cried. Then she flushed and drew back. "The last folly of the braggart is to boast of misfortune," she said. "But, really, I have paid, if missing some precious things that might have been mine is a payment for pride and wilfullness."

"I hope you haven't missed very much, then,--not anything that you'll be regretting in the years to come."

"Oh, regret is never going to be a specialty of mine," declared Kate. "To-morrow's the chance! I shall never be able to do much with yesterday, no matter how wise I become."

"Right you are!" said Wander sharply. "The only thing is that you don't know quite the full bearing of your remark--and I do."

She laughed sympathetically.

"Truth is truth," she said.

"Yes." He hung over the obvious aphorism boyishly. "Yes, truth is truth, no matter who utters it."

"Thanks, kind sir."

"Oh, I was thinking of the excellent Clarinda Hays. I listened to your conversation this morning and it seemed to me that she was giving you about all the truth you could find bins for. I couldn't help but take it in, it was so complacently offered. But Clarinda was getting her 'sacred feelings' mixed up with the truth. However, I suppose there is an essential truth about sacred feelings even when they're founded on an error. I surmised that you were holding back vastly more than you were saying. Now that we 're pretty well toward a mountain-top, with nobody listening, you might tell me what you *were* thinking."

Kate smiled slowly. She looked at the man beside her as if appraising him.

"I'm terribly afraid," she said at length, "that you are soul-kin to Clarinda. You'll walk in a mist of sacred feelings, too, and truth will play hide and seek with you all over the place."

"Nonsense!" he cried. "Why can't I hear what you have to say? You stand on platforms and tell it to hundreds. Why should you grudge it to me?"

She swept her hand toward the landscape around them.

"It has to do with change," she said. "And with evolution. Look at this scarred mountain-side, how confused and senseless the upheavals seem which have given it its grandeur! Nor is it static yet. It is continually wearing down. Erosion is diminishing it, that river is denuding it. Eternal change is the only law."

"I understand," said Wander, his eyes glowing.

"In the world of thought it is the same."

"Verily."

"But I speak for women--and I am afraid that you'll not understand."

"I should like to be given a chance to try," he answered.

"Clarinda," she said, after a moment's pause, "like the larger part of the world, is looking at a mirage. She sees these shining pictures on the hot sand of the world and she says: 'These are the real things. I will fix my gaze on them. What does the hot sand and the trackless waste matter so long as I have these beautiful mirages to look at?' When you say that mirages are insubstantial, evanishing, mere tricks of air and eye, the Clarindas retort, 'But if you take away our mirages, where are we to turn? What will you give us in the place of them?' She thinks, for example, if a dying soldier calls on his mother or his sweetheart that they must be good women. This is not the case. He calls on them because confronts the great loneliness of death. He is quite as likely to call on a wicked woman if she is the one whose name comes to his flickering sense. But even supposing that one had to be sacrificial, subservient, and to possess all the other Clarinda virtues in order to have a dying man call on one, still, would that burst of delirious wistfulness compensate one for years of servitude?"

She let the statement hang in the air for a moment, while Wander's color deepened yet more. He was being wounded in the place of his dreams and the pang was sharp.

"If some one, dying, called you 'Faithful slave,'" resumed Kate, "would that make you proud? Would it not rather be a humiliation? Now, 'good wife' might be synonymous with 'faithful slave.' That's what I'd have to ascertain before I could be complimented as Clarinda was complimented by those words. I'd have to have my own approval. No one else could comfort me with a 'well done' unless my own conscience echoed the words. 'Good wife,' indeed!"

"What would reconcile you to such commendations?" asked Wander with a reproach that was almost personal.

"The possession of those privileges and mediums by which liberty is sustained."

"For example?"

"My own independent powers of thought; my own religion, politics, taste, and direction of self-development--above all, my own money. By that I mean money for which I did not have to ask and which never was given to me as an indulgence. Then I should want definite work commensurate with my powers; and the right to a voice in all matters affecting my life or the life of my family."

"That is what you would take. But what would you give?"

"I would not 'take' these things any more than my husband would 'take' them. Nor could he bestow them upon me, for they are mine by inherent right."

"Could he give you nothing, then?"

"Love. Yet it may not be correct to say that he could give that. He would not love me because he chose to do so, but because he could not help doing so. At least, that is my idea of love. He would love me as I was, with all my faults and follies, and I should love him the same way. I should be as proud of his personality as I would be defensive of my own. I should not ask him to be like me; I should only ask him to be truly himself and to let me be truly myself. If our personalities diverged, perhaps they would go around the circle and meet on the other side."

"Do you think, my dear woman, that you would be able to recognize each other after such a long journey?"

"There would be distinguishing marks," laughed Kate; "birthmarks of the soul. But I neglected to say that it would not satisfy me merely to be given a portion of the earnings of the family--that portion which I would require to conduct the household and which I might claim as my share of the result of labor. I should also wish, when there was a surplus, to be given half of it that I might make my own experiments."

"A full partnership!"

"That's the idea, precisely: a full partnership. There is an assumption that marriages are that now, but it is not so, as all frank persons must concede."

"*I* concede it, at any rate."

"Now, you must understand that we women are asking these things because we are acquiring new ideas of duty. A duty is like a command; it must be obeyed. It has been laid upon us to demand rights and privileges equal to those enjoyed by men, and we wish them to be extended to us not because we are young or beautiful or winning or chaste, but because we are members of a common humanity with men and are entitled to the same inheritance. We want our status established, so that when we make a marriage alliance we can do it for love and no other reason--not for a home, or support, or children or protection. Marriage should be a privilege and a reward--not a necessity. It should be so that if we spinsters want a home, we can earn one; if we desire children, we can take to ourselves some of the motherless ones; and we should be able to entrust society with our protection. By society I mean, of course, the structure which civilized people have fashioned for themselves, the portals of which are personal rights and the law."

"But what will all the lovers do? If everything is adjusted to such a nicety, what will they be able to sacrifice for each other?"

"Lovers," smiled Kate, "will always be able to make their own paradise, and a jewelled sacrifice will be the keystone of each window in their house of love. But there are only a few lovers in the world compared with those who have come down through the realm of little morning clouds and are bearing the heat and burden of the day."

"How do you know all of these things, Wise Woman? Have you had so much experience?"

"We each have all the accumulated experience of the centuries. We don't have to keep to the limits of our own little individual lives."

"I often have dreamed of bringing you up on this trail," said Wander whimsically, "but never for the purpose of hearing you make your declaration of independence."

"Why not?" demanded Kate. "In what better place could I make it?"

Beside the clamorous waterfall was a huge boulder squared almost as if the hand of a mason had shaped it. Kate stepped on it, before Wander could prevent her, and stood laughing back at him, the wind blowing her garments about her and lifting strands of her loosened hair.

"I declare my freedom!" she cried with grandiose mockery. "Freedom to think my own thoughts, preach my own creeds, do my own work, and make the sacrifices of my own choosing. I declare that I will have no master and no mistress, no slave and no neophyte, but that I will strive to preserve my own personality and to help all of my brothers and sisters, the world over, to preserve theirs. I declare that I will let no superstition or prejudice set limits to my good will, my influence, or my ambition!"

"You are standing on a precipice," he warned.

"It's glorious!"

"But it may be fatal."

"But I have the head for it," she retorted. "I shall not fall!"

"Others may who try to emulate you."

"That's Fear--the most subtle of foes!"

"Oh, come back," he pleaded seriously, "I can't bear to see you standing there!"

"Very well," she said, giving him her hand with a gay gesture of capitulation. "But didn't you say that men liked to climb? Well, women do, too."

They were conscious of being late for dinner and they turned their faces toward home.

"How ridiculous," remarked Wander, "that we should think ourselves obliged to return for dinner!"

"On the contrary," said Kate, "I think it bears witness to both our health and our sanity. I've got over being afraid that I shall be injured by the commonplace. When I open your door and smell the roast or the turnips or whatever food has been provided, I shall like it just as well as if it were flowers."

Wander helped her down a jagged descent and laughed up in her face.

"What a materialist!" he cried. "And I thought you were interested only in the ideal."

"Things aren't ideal because they have been labeled so," declared Kate. "When people tell you they are clinging to old ideals, it's well to find out if they aren't napping in some musty old room beneath the cobwebs. I'm a materialist, very likely, but that's only incidental to my realism. I like to be allowed to realize the truth about things, and you know yourself that you men--who really are the sentimental sex--have tried as hard as you could not to let us."

"You speak as if we had deliberately fooled you."

"You haven't fooled us any more than we have fooled ourselves." They had reached the lower level now, and could walk side by side. "You've kept us supplemental, and we've thought we were noble when we played the supplemental part. But it doesn't look so to us any longer. We want to be ourselves and to justify ourselves. There's a good deal of complaint about women not having enough to do--about the factories and shops taking their work away from them and leaving them idle and inexpressive. Well, in a way, that's true, and I'm a strong advocate of new vocations, so that women can have their own purses and all that. But I know in my heart all this is incidental. What we really need is a definite set of principles; if we can acquire an inner stability, we shall do very well whether our hands are perpetually occupied or not. But just at present we poor women are sitting in the ruins of our collapsed faiths, and we haven't decided what sort of architecture to use in erecting the new one."

"There doesn't seem to be much peace left in the world," mused Wander. "Do you women think you will have peace when you get this new faith?"

"Oh, dear me," retorted Kate, "what would you have us do with peace? You can get that in any garlanded sepulcher. Peace is like perfection, it isn't desirable. We should perish of it. As long as there is life there is struggle and change. But when we have our inner faith, when we can see what the thing is for which we are to strive, then we shall cease to be so spasmodic in our efforts. We'll not be doing such grotesque things. We'll come into new dignity."

"What you're trying to say," said Wander, "is that it is ourselves who are to be our best achievement. It's what we make of ourselves that matters."

"Oh, that's it! That's it!" cried Kate, beating her gloved hands together like a child. "You're getting it! You're getting it! It's what we make of ourselves that matters, and we must all have the right to find ourselves--to keep exploring till we find our highest selves. There mustn't be such a waste of ability and power and hope as there has been. We must all have our share in the essentials--our own relation to reality."

"I see," he said, pausing at the door, and looking into her face as if he would spell out her incommunicable self. "That's what you mean by universal liberty."

"That's what I mean."

"And the man you marry must let you pick your own way, make your own blunders, grow by your own experience."

"Yes."

Honora opened the door and looked at them. She was weak and she leaned against the casing for her support, but her face was tender and calm, and she was regnant over her own mind.

"What is the matter with you two?" she asked. "Aren't you coming in to dinner? Haven't you any appetites?"

Kate threw her arms about her.

"Oh, Honora," she cried. "How lovely you look! Appetites? We're famished."

CHAPTER XXX

Another week went by, and though it went swiftly, still at the end of the time it seemed long, as very happy and significant times do. Honora was still weak, but as every comfort had been provided for her journey, it seemed more than probable that she would be benefited in the long run by the change, however exhausting it might be temporarily.

"It's the morning of the last day," said Wander at breakfast. "Honora is to treat herself as if she were the finest and most highly decorated bohemian glass, and save herself up for her journey. All preparations, I am told, are completed. Very well, then. Do you and I ride to-day, Miss Barrington?"

"'Here we ride,'" quoted Kate. Then she flushed, remembering the reference.

Did Karl recognize it--or know it? She could not tell. He could, at will, show a superb inscrutability.

Whether he knew Browning's poem or not, Kate found to her irritation that she did. Lines she thought she had forgotten, trooped--galloped--back into her brain. The thud of them fell like rhythmic hoofs upon the road.

"Then we began to ride. My soul
Smoothed itself out, a long-cramped scroll
Freshening and fluttering in the wind.
Past hopes already lay behind.
What need to strive with a life awry?
Had I said that, had I done this,
So might I gain, so might I miss."

She wove her braids about her head to the measure; buckled her boots and buttoned her habit; and then, veiled and gauntleted she went down the stairs, still keeping time to the inaudible tune:--

"So might I gain, so might I miss."

The mare Wander held for her was one which she had ridden several times before and with which she was already on terms of good feeling. That subtle, quick understanding which goes from horse to rider, when all is well in their relations, and when both are eager to face the wind, passed now from Lady Bel to Kate. She let the creature nose her for a moment, then accepted Wander's hand and mounted. The fine animal quivered delicately, shook herself, pawed the dust with a motion as graceful as any lady could have made, threw a pleasant, sociable look over her shoulder, and at Kate's vivacious lift of the rein was off. Wander was mounted magnificently on Nell, a mare of heavier build, a black animal, which made a good contrast to Lady Bel's shining roan coat.

The animals were too fresh and impatient to permit much conversation between their riders. They were answering to the call of the road as much as were the humans who rode them. Kate tried to think of the scenes which were flashing by, or of the village,--Wander's "rowdy" village, teeming with its human stories; but, after all, it was Browning's lines which had their way with her. They trumpeted themselves in her ear, changing a word here and there, impishly, to suit her case.

> "We rode; it seemed my spirit flew,
> Saw other regions, cities new,
> As the world rushed by on either side.
> I thought, All labor, yet no less
> Bear up beneath their unsuccess.
> Look at the end of work, contrast
> The petty Done, the Undone vast,
> This present of theirs with the hopeful past!
> I hoped he would love me. Here we ride."

They were to the north of the village, heading for a cañon. The road was good, the day not too warm, and the passionate mountain springtime was bursting into flower and leaf. Presently walls of rock began to rise about them. They were of innumerable, indefinable rock colors--grayish-yellows, dull olives, old rose, elusive purples, and browns as rich as prairie soil. Coiling like a cobra, the Little Williston raced singing through the midst of the chasm, sun-mottled and bright as the trout that hid in its cold shallows. Was all the world singing? Were the invisible stars of heaven rhyming with one another? Had a lost rhythm been recaptured, and did she hear the pulsations of a deep Earth-harmony--or was it, after all, only the insistent beat of the poet's line?

> "What if we still ride on, we two,
> With life forever old, yet new,

Changed not in kind but in degree,
The instant made eternity,--
And Heaven just prove that I and he
Ride, ride together, forever ride?"

What Wander said, when he spoke, was, "Walk," and the remark was made to his horse. Lady Bel slackened, too. They were in the midst of great beauty--complex, almost chaotic, beauty, such as the Rocky Mountains often display.

Wander drew his horse nearer to Kate's, and as a turning of the road shut them in a solitary paradise where alders and willows fringed the way with fresh-born green, he laid his hand on her saddle.

"Kate," he said, "can you make up your mind to stay here with me?"

Kate drew in her breath sharply. Then she laughed.

"Am I to understand that you are introducing or continuing a topic?" she asked.

He laughed, too. They were as willing to play with the subject as children are to play with flowers.

"I am continuing it," he affirmed.

"Really?"

"And you know it."

"Do I?"

"From the first moment that I laid eyes on you, all the time that I was writing to Honora and really was trying to snare your interest, and after she came here,--even when I absurdly commanded you not to write to me,--and now, every moment since you set foot in my wild country, what have I done but say: 'Kate, will you stay with me?'"

"And will I?" mused Kate. "What do you offer?"

She once had asked the same question of McCrea.

"A faulty man's unchanging love."

"What makes you think it will not change--especially since you are a faulty man?"

"I think it will not change because I am so faulty that I must have something perfect to which to cling."

"Nonsense! A Clarinda dream! There's nothing perfect about me! The whole truth is that you don't know whether you'll change or not!"

"Well, say that I change! Say that I pass from shimmering moonlight to common sunlight love! Say that we walk a heavy road and carry burdens and that our throats are so parched we forget to turn our eyes toward each other. Still we shall be side by side, and in the end the dust of us shall mingle in one earth. As for our spirits--if they have triumphed together, where is the logic in supposing that they will know separation?"

"You will give me love," said Kate, "changing, faulty, human love! I ask no better--in the way of love. I can match you in faultiness and in changefulness and in hope. But now what else can you give me--what work--what chance to justify myself, what exercise for my powers? You have your work laid out for you. Where is mine?"

Wander stared at her a moment with a bewildered expression. Then he leaped from his horse and caught Kate's bridle.

"Where is your work, woman?" he thundered. "Are you teasing me still or are you in earnest? Your work is in your home! With all your wisdom, don't you know that yet? It is in your home, bearing and rearing your sons and your daughters, and adding to my sum of joy and your own. It is in learning secrets of happiness which only experience can teach. Listen to me: If my back ached and my face dripped sweat because I was toiling for you and your children, I would count it a privilege. It would be the crown of my life. Justify yourself? How can you justify yourself except by being of the Earth, learning of her; her obedient and happy child? Justify yourself? Kate Barrington, you'll have to justify yourself to me."

"How dare you?" asked Kate under her breath. "Who has given you a right to take me to task?"

"Our love," he said, and looked her unflinchingly in the eye. "My love for you and your love for me. I demand the truth of you,--the deepest truth of your deepest soul,--because we are mates and can never escape each other as long as we live, though half the earth divides us and all our years. Wherever we go, our thoughts will turn toward each other. When we meet, though we have striven to hate each other, yet our hands will long to clasp. We may be at war, but we will love it better than peace with others. I tell you, I march to the tune of your piping; you keep step to my drum-beats. What is the use of theorizing? I speak of a fact."

"I am going to turn my horse," she said. "Will you please stand aside?"

He dropped her bridle.

"Is that all you have to say?"

She looked at him haughtily for a moment and whirled her horse. Then she drew the mare up.

"Karl!" she called.

No answer.

"I say--Karl!"

He came to her.

"I am not angry. I know quite well what you mean. You were speaking of the fundamentals."

"I was."

"But how about me? Am I to have no importance save in my relation to you?"

"You cannot have your greatest importance save in your relation to me."

She looked at him long. Her eyes underwent a dozen changes. They taunted him, tempted him, comforted him, bade him hope, bade him fear.

"We must ride home," she said at length.

"And my question? I asked you if you were willing to stay here with me?"

"The question," she said with a dry little smile, "is laid very respectfully on the knees of the gods."

He turned from her and swung into his saddle. They pounded home in silence. The lines of "The Last Ride" were besetting her still.

> "Who knows what's fit for us? Had fate
> Proposed bliss here should sublimate
> My being; had I signed the bond--
> Still one must lead some life beyond,--
> Have a bliss to die with, dim-descried.
> This foot once planted on the goal,
> This glory-garland round my soul,
> Could I descry such? Try and test?"

She gave him no chance to help her dismount, but leaping to the ground, turned the good mare's head stableward, and ran to her room. He did not see her till dinner-time. Honora was at the table, and occupied their care and thought.

Afterward there was the ten-mile ride to the station, but Kate sat beside Honora. There was a full moon--and the world ached for lovers. But if any touched lips, Karl Wander and Kate Barrington knew nothing of it. At the station they shook hands.

"Are you coming back?" asked Wander. "Will you bring Honora back home?"

In the moonlight Kate turned a sudden smile on him.

"Of course I'm coming back," she said. "I always put a period to my sentences."

"Good!" he said. "But that's a very different matter from writing a 'Finis' to your book."

"I shall conclude on an interrupted sentence," laughed Kate, "and I'll let some one else write 'Finis.'"

The great train labored in, paused for no more than a moment, and was off again. It left Wander's world well denuded. The sense of aching loneliness was like an agony. She had evaded him. She belonged to him, and he had somehow let her go! What had he said, or failed to say? What had she desired that he had not given? He tried to assure himself that he had been guiltless, but as he passed his sleeping village and glimpsed the ever-increasing dumps before his mines, he knew in his heart that he had been asking her to play his game. Of course, on the other hand--

But what was the use of running around in a squirrel cage! She was gone. He was alone.

CHAPTER XXXI

The Federation of Women's Clubs!

Two thousand women gathered in the name of--what?

Why, of culture, of literature, of sisterhood, of benevolence, of music, art, town beautification, the abolition of child-labor, the abolition of sweat-shops, the extension of peace and opportunity.

And run how? By politics, sharp and keen, far-seeing and combative.

The results? The coöperation of forceful women, the encouragement of timid ones; the development of certain forms of talent, and the destruction of some old-time virtues.

The balance? On the side of good, incontestably.

"Yes, it's on the side of good," said Honora, who was, after all, like a nun (save that her laboratory had been her cell, and a man's fame her passion), and who therefore brought to this vast, highly energized, capable, various gathering a judgment unprejudiced, unworldly, and clear. As she saw these women of many types, from all of the States, united in great causes, united, too, in the cultivation of things not easy of definition, she felt that, in spite of drawbacks, it must be good. She listened to their papers, heard their earnest propaganda. A distinguished Jewess from New York told of the work among the immigrants and the methods by which they were created into intelligent citizens; a beautiful Kentuckian spoke of the work among the white mountaineers; a very venerable gentlewoman from Chicago, exquisitely frail, talked on behalf of the children in factories; a crisp, curt, efficient woman from Oregon advocated the dissemination of books among the "lumber-jacks." They were ingenious in their pursuit of benevolences, and their annual reports were the impersonal records of personal labors. They had started libraries, made little parks, inaugurated playgrounds, instituted exchanges for the sale of women's wares, secured women internes in hospitals, paid for truant officers, founded children's protective associations, installed branches of the Associated Charities, encouraged night schools, circulated art exhibits and traveling libraries;

they had placed pictures in the public schools, founded kindergartens--the list seemed inexhaustible.

"Oh, decidedly," Kate granted Honora, "the thing seems to be good."

Moreover, there was good being done of a less assertive but equally commendable nature. The lines of section grew vague when the social Georgian sat side by side with the genial woman from Michigan. Mrs. Johnson of Minnesota and Mrs. Cabot of Massachusetts, Mrs. Hardin of Kentucky and Mrs. Garcia of California, found no essential differences in each other. Ladies, the world over, have a similarity of tastes. So, as they lunched, dined, and drove together they established relationships more intimate than their convention hall could have fostered. If they had dissensions, these were counterbalanced by the exchange of amenities. If their points of view diverged in lesser matters, they converged in great ones.

And then the women of few opportunities--the farmers' wives representing their earnest clubs; the village women, wistful and rather shy; the emergent, onlooking company of few excursions, few indulgences--what of the Federation for them? At first, perhaps, they feared it; but cautiously, like unskilled swimmers, they took their experimental strokes. They found themselves secure; heard themselves applauded. They acquired boldness, and presently were exhilarated by the consciousness of their own power. If the great Federation could be cruel, it could be kind, too. One thing it had stood for from the first, and by that thing it still abided--the undeviating, disinterested determination to help women develop themselves. So the faltering voice was listened to, and the report of the eager, kind-eyed woman from the little-back-water-of-the-world was heard with interest. The Federation knew the value of this woman who said what she meant, and did what she promised. They sent her home to her town to be an inspiration. She was a little torch, carrying light.

Day succeeded day. From early morning till late at night the great convention read its papers, ate its luncheons, held its committee meetings--talked, aspired, lobbied, schemed, prayed, sang, rejoiced! Culture was splendidly on its way--progress was the watchword! It was wonderful and amusing and superb.

The Feminine mind, much in action, shooting back and forth like a shuttle, was weaving a curious and admirable fabric. There might be some trouble in discerning the design, but it was there, and if it was not arrestingly original, at least it was interesting. In places it was even beautiful. Now and then it gave suggestions of the grotesque. It was shot through with the silver of talent, the gold of genius. And with all of its defects it was splendid because the warp thereof was purpose and the woof enthusiasm.

Kate's day came. The great theater was packed--not a vacant seat remained. For it was mid-afternoon, the sun was shining, and the day was the last one of the convention.

The president presided with easy authority. It became her--that seat. Her keen eyes expressed themselves as being satisfied; her handsome head was carried proudly. Her voice, of medium pitch, had an accent of gracious command. She presented to the eye a pleasing, nay, an artistic, picture, and the very gown she wore was a symbol of efficiency--sign to the initiate.

Kate's heart was fluttering, her mouth dry. She greeted her chairwoman somewhat tremulously, and then faced her audience.

For a moment she faltered. Then a face came before her--Karl's face. She did not so much wish to succeed for him as in despite of him. He had said she would reach her greatest importance through her relationship to him. At that moment she thrilled to the belief that, independently of him, she was still important.

The great assemblage had ears for her. The idea of an extension of motherhood, an organized, scientific supervision of children, made an appeal such as nothing else could. For, after all, persistently--almost irritatingly, at times--this great federation, which was supposed to concern itself with many fine abstractions, swung back to that concrete and essentially womanly idea of the care of children. Women who had brought to it high messages of art and education had known what it was to be exasperated into speechlessness by what they were pleased to denominate the maternal obsession.

Kate swung them back to it now, by means of impersonal rather than personal arguments. She did not idealize paternity. She was bitterly well aware by this time that parents were no better than other folk, and that only a small proportion of those to whom the blessing came were qualified or willing to bear its responsibilities. She touched on eugenics--its advantages and its limitations; she referred to the inadequacy of present laws and protective measures. Then she went on to describe what a Bureau of Children might be.

"The business of this bureau," she said, "will be the removal of handicaps.

"Is the child blind, deaf, lame, tubercular, or possessed of any sorry inheritance? The Bureau of Children will devise some method of easing its way; some plan to save it from further degeneration. Is the child talented, and in need of special training? Has it genius, and should it, for the glory of the commonwealth and the enrichment of life, be given the right of way? Then the Bureau of Children will see to it that such provision is made. It will not be the idea merely to aid the deficient and protect the vicious. Nor shall its highest aspiration be to serve the average child, born of average parents. It would delight to reward successful and devoted parents by giving especial opportunity to their carefully trained and highly developed children. As the Bureau of Agriculture labors to propagate the best species of trees, fruit, and flowers, so we would labor to propagate the best examples of humanity--the finest, most sturdily reared, best intelligenced boys and girls.

"We would endeavor to prevent illness and loss of life among babies and children. Our circulars would be distributed in all languages among all of our citizens. We would employ specialists to direct the feeding, clothing, and general rearing of the children of all conditions. We would advocate the protection of children until they reached the age of sixteen; and would endeavor to assist in the supervision of these children until they were of legal age. My idea would be to have all young people under twenty-one remain in a sense the wards of schools. If they have had, at any early age, to leave school and take the burdens of bread-winning upon their young shoulders and their untried hearts, then I would advise an extension of school authority. The schools should be provided with assistant superintendents whose business it would be to help these young bread-winners find positions in keeping with their tastes and abilities, thus aiding them in the most practical and beneficent way, to hold their places in this struggling, modern world.

"It is an economic measure of the loftiest type. It will provide against the waste of bodies and souls; it is a device for the conservation and the scientific development of human beings. It is part and parcel of the new, practical religion--a new prayer.

"'Prayer,' says the old hymn, 'is the soul's sincere desire.'

"Many of us have lost our belief in the old forms of prayer. We are beginning to realize that, to a great extent, the answer to prayer lies in our own hands. Our answers come when we use the powers that have been bestowed upon us. More and more each year, those who employ their intellects for constructive purposes are turning their energies toward the betterment of the world. They have a new conception of 'the world to come.' It means to them our good brown Mother Earth, warm and fecund and laden with fruits for the consumption of her children as it may be under happier conditions. They wish to increase the happiness of those children, to elevate them physically and mentally, and to give their spirits, too often imprisoned and degraded by hard circumstance, a chance to grow.

"When you let the sunlight in to a stunted tree, with what exultant gratitude it lifts itself toward the sun! How its branches greet the wind and sing in them, how its little leaves come dancing out to make a shelter for man and the birds and the furred brothers of the forest! But this, wonderful and beautiful as it is, is but a small thing compared with the way in which the soul of a stunted child--stunted by evil or by sunless environment--leaps and grows and sings when the great spiritual elements of love and liberty are permitted to reach it.

"You have talked of the conservation of forests; and you speak of a great need--an imperative cause. I talk of the conservation of children--which is a greater need and a holier right.

"Mammalia are numerous in this world; real mothers are rare. Can we lift the mammalia up into the high estate of motherhood? I believe so. Can we grow superlative children, as we grow superlative fruits and animals? Oh, a thousand times, yes. I beg for your support of this new idea. Let the spirit of inspiration enter into your reflections concerning it. Let that concentration of purpose which you have learned in your clubs and federations be your aid here.

"Most of you whom I see before me are no longer engaged actively in the tasks of motherhood. The children have gone out from your homes into homes of their own. You are left denuded and hungry for the old sweet vocation. Your hands are too idle; your abilities lie unutilized. But here is a task at hand. I do not say that you are to use this extension to your motherhood for children alone, or merely in connection with this proposed Bureau. I urge you, indeed, to employ it in all conceivable ways. Be the mothers of men and women as well as of little children--the mothers of communities--the mothers of the state. And as a focus to these energies and disinterested activities, let us pray Washington to give us the Bureau of Children."

She turned from her responsive audience to the chairwoman, who handed her a yellow envelope.

"A telegram, Miss Barrington. Should I have given it to you before? I disliked interrupting."

Kate tore it open.

It was from the President of the United States. It ran:--

"I have the honor to inform you that the Bureau of Children will become a feature of our government within a year. It is the desire of those most interested, myself included, that you should accept the superintendence of it. I hope this will reach you on the day of your address before the Federation of Women's Clubs. Accept my congratulations."

It was signed by the chief executive. Kate passed the message to the chairwoman.

"May I read it?" the gratified president questioned. Kate nodded. The gavel fell, and the vibrant, tremulous voice of the president was heard reading the significant message. The women listened for a moment with something like incredulity--for they were more used to delays and frustrations than to coöperation; then the house filled with the curious muffled sounds of gloved hands in applause. Presently a voice shrilled out in inarticulate acclaim. Kate could not catch its meaning, but two thousand women, robed like flowers, swayed to their feet. Their handkerchiefs fluttered. The lovely Californian blossoms were snatched from their belts and their bosoms and flung upon the platform with enthusiastic, uncertain aim.

CHAPTER XXXII

Afterward Kate took Honora down to the sea. They found a little house that fairly bathed its feet in the surf, and here they passed the days very quietly, at least to outward seeming. The Pacific thundered in upon them; they could hear the winds, calling and calling with an immemorial invitation; they knew of the little jewelled islands that lay out in the seas and of the lands of eld on the far, far shore; and they dreamed strange dreams.

Sitting in the twilight, watching the light reluctantly leave the sea, they spoke of many things. They spoke most of all of women, and it sometimes seemed, as they sat there,--one at the doorway of the House of Life and one in a shaded inner chamber,--as if the rune of women came to them from their far sisters: from those in their harems, from others in the blare of commercial, Occidental life; from those in chambers of pain; from those freighted with the poignant burdens which women bear in their bodies and in their souls.

As the darkness deepened, they grew unashamed and then reticences fell from them. The eternally flowing sea, the ever-recurrent night gave them courage, though they were women, to speak the truth.

"When I found how deeply I loved David," said Honora, "and that I could serve him, too, by marrying him, I would no more have put the idea of marriage with him out of my mind than I would have cast away a hope of heaven if I had seen that shining before me. I would no more have turned from it than I would have turned from food, if I had been starving; or water after I had been thirsting in the desert. Why, Kate, to marry him was inevitable! The bird doesn't think when it sings or the bud when it flowers. It does what it was created to do. I married David the same way."

"I understand," said Kate.

They sat on their little low, sand-swept balcony, facing the sea. The rising tide filled the world with its soft and indescribable cadence. The stars came out into the sky according to their rank--the greatest first, and after them the less, and the less no more lacking in beauty than the great. All was as it should be--all was ordered--all was fit and wonderful.

"So," went on Honora, after a silence which the sea filled in with its low harmonies, "if you loved Karl--"

"Wait!" said Kate. So Honora waited. Another silence fell. Then Kate spoke brokenly.

"If to feel when I am with him that I have reached my home; if to suffer a strangeness even with myself, and to feel less familiar with myself than with him, is to love, then I love him, Honora. If to want to work with him, and to feel there could be no exultation like overcoming difficulties with him, is love, then truly I love him. If just to see him, at a distance, enriches the world and makes the stream of time turn from lead to gold is anything in the nature of love, then I am his lover. If to long to house with him, to go by the same name that he does, to wear him, so to speak, carved on my brow, is to love, then I do."

"Then I foresee that you will be one of the happiest women in the world."

"No! No; you mustn't say that. Aren't there other things than love, Honora,--better things than selfish delight?"

"My dear, you have no call to distress yourself about the occult meanings of that word 'selfish.' Unselfish people--or those who mean to be so--contrive, when they refuse to follow the instincts of their hearts, to cause more suffering even than the out-and-out selfish ones."

"But I have an opportunity to serve thousands--maybe hundreds of thousands of human beings. I can set in motion a movement which may have a more lasting effect upon my country than any victory ever gained by it on a field of battle; and perhaps in time the example set by this land will be followed by others. Dare I face that mystic, inner ME and say: 'I choose my man, I give him all my life, and I resign my birthright of labor. For this personal joy I refuse to be the Sister of the World; I let the dream perish; I hinder a great work'? Oh, Honora, I want him, I want him! But am I for that reason to be false to my destiny?"

"You want celebrity!" said Honora with sudden bitterness. "You want to go to Washington, to have your name numbered among the leading ones of the nation; you are not willing to spend your days in the solitude of Williston Ranch as wife to its master."

"I will not say that you are speaking falsely, but I think you know you are setting out only a little part of the truth. Admit it, Honora."

Honora sighed heavily.

"Oh, yes," she said at length, "I do admit it. You must forgive me, Kate. It seems so easy for you two to be happy that I can't help feeling it blasphemous for you to be anything else. If it were an ordinary marriage or an ordinary separation, I shouldn't feel so agonized over it. But you and Karl--such mates--the only free spirits I know! How you would love! It would be epic. And I should rejoice that you were living in that savage world instead of in a city. You two would need room--like great beautiful buildings. Who would wish to see you in the jumble of a city? With you to aid him, Karl may become a distinguished man. Your lives would go on together, widening, widening--"

"Oh!" interrupted Kate with a sharp ejaculation; "we'll not talk of it any more, Honora. You must not think because I cannot marry him that he will always be unhappy. In time he will find another woman--"

"Kate! Will you find another man?"

"You know I shall not! After Wander? Any man would be an anticlimax to me after him."

"Can you suspect him of a passion or a fealty less than your own? If you refuse to marry him, I believe you will frustrate a great purpose of Nature. Why, Kate, it will be a crime against Love. The thought as I feel it means more--oh, infinitely more--than I can make the words convey to you; but you must think them over, Kate,--I beg you to think them over!"

In the darkness, Kate heard Honora stealing away to her room.

So she was alone, and the hour had come for her decision.

"'Bitter, alas,'" she quoted to the rising trouble of the sea, "'the sorrow of lonely women.'" The distillation of that strange duplex soul, Fiona Macleod, was as a drop of poisoned truth upon her parched tongue.

"We who love are those who suffer;
We who suffer most are those who most do love."

She went down upon the sands. The tongues of the sea came up and lapped her feet. The winds of the sea enfolded her in an embrace. For the first time in her life, freely, without restraint, bravely, as sometime she might face God, she confronted the idea of Love. And a secret, wonderful knowledge came to her--the knowledge of lovely spiritual ecstasies, the realization of rich human delights. Sorrow and cruel loss might be on their way, but Joy was hers now. She feigned that Karl was waiting for her a little way on in the warm darkness--on, around that scimitar-shaped bend of the beach. She chose to believe that he was running to meet her, his eyes aflame, his great arms outstretched; she thrilled to the rain of his kisses; she thought those stars might hear the voice with which he shouted, "Kate!"

Then, calmer, yet as if she had run a race, panting, palpitant, she seated herself on the sands. She let her imagination roam through the years. She saw the road of life they would take together; how they would stand on peaks of lofty desire, in sunlight; how, unfaltering, they would pace tenebrous valleys. Always they would be together. Their laughter would chime and their tears would fall in unison. Where one failed, the other would redeem; where one doubted, the other would hope. They would bear their children to be the vehicle of their ideals--these fresh new creatures, born of their love, would be trained to achieve what they, their parents, had somehow missed.

Then her bolder thought died. She, who had forced herself so relentlessly to face the world as a woman faces it, with the knowledge and the courage of maturity, felt her wisdom slip from her. She was a girl, very lonely, facing a task too large for her, needing the comfort of her lover's word. She stretched herself upon the sand, face downward, weeping, because she was afraid of life--because she was wishful for the joy of woman and dared not take it.

"Have you decided?" asked Honora in the morning.

"I think so," answered Kate.

Honora scrutinized the face of her friend.

"Accept," she said, "my profound commiseration." Her tone seemed to imply that she included contempt.

After this, there was a change in Honora's attitude toward her. Kate felt herself more alone than she ever had been in her life. It was as if she had been cast out into a desert--a sandy plain smitten with the relentless Sun of Life, and in it was no house of refuge, no comfortable tree, no waters of healing. No, nor any other soul. Alone she walked there, and the only figures she saw were those of the mirage. It gave her a sort of relief to turn her face eastward and to feel that she must traverse the actual desert, and come at the end to literal combat.

CHAPTER XXXIII

Two dragons, shedding fire, had paused midway of the desert. One was the Overland Express racing from Los Angeles to Kansas City; its fellow was headed for the west. Both had halted for fuel and water and the refreshment of the passengers. The dusk was gathering over the illimitable sandy plain, and the sun, setting behind wind-blown buttes, wore a sinister glow. By its fantastic light the men and women from the trains paced back and forth on the wide platform, or visited the luxurious eating-house, where palms and dripping waters, roses and inviting food bade them forget that they were on the desert.

Kate and Honora had dined and were walking back and forth in the deep amber light.

"Such a world to live in," cried Kate admiringly, pressing Honora's arm to her side. "Do you know, of all the places that I might have imagined as desirable for residence, I believe I like our old earth the best!"

She was in an inconsequential mood, and Honora indulged her with smiling silence.

"I couldn't have thought of a finer desert than this if I had tried," she went on gayly. "And this wicked saffron glow is precisely the color to throw on it. What a mistake it would have been if some supernal electrician had dropped a green or a blue spot-light on the scene! Now, just hear that fountain dripping and that ground-wind whispering! Who wouldn't live in the arid lands? It's all as it should be. So are you, too, aren't you, Honora? You've forgiven me, too, I know you have; and you're getting stronger every day, and making ready for happiness, aren't you?"

She leaned forward to look in her companion's face.

"Oh, yes, Kate," said Honora. "It really is as it should be with me. I'm looking forward, now, to what is to come. To begin with, there are the children shining like little stars at the end of my journey; and there's the necessity of working for them. I'm glad of that--I'm glad I have to work for them. Perhaps I shall be offered a place at the University of Wisconsin. I think I should be if I gave any indication that I had such a desire. The president and I are old friends. Oh, yes, indeed, I'm very thankful that I'm able to look forward again with something like expectancy--"

The words died on her lips. She was arrested as if an angry god had halted her. Kate, startled, looked up. Before them, marble-faced and hideously abashed,--yet beautiful with an insistent beauty,--stood Mary Morrison, like Honora, static with pain.

It seemed as if it must be a part of that fantastic, dream-like scene. So many visions were born of the desert that this, not unreasonably, might be one. But, no, these two women who had played their parts in an appalling drama, were moving, involuntarily, as it seemed, nearer to each other. For a second Kate thought of dragging Honora away, till it came to her by some swift message of the spirit that Honora did not wish to avoid this encounter. Perhaps it seemed to her like a fulfillment--the last strain of a wild and dissonant symphony. It was the part of greater kindness to drop her arm and stand apart.

"Shall we speak, Mary," said Honora at length. "Or shall we pass on in silence?"

"It isn't for me to say," wavered the other. "Any way, it's too late for words to matter."

"Yes," agreed Honora. "Quite too late."

They continued to stare at each other--so like, yet so unlike. It was Honora's face which was ravaged, though Mary had sinned the sin. True, pallor and pain were visible in Mary's face, even in the disguising light of that strange hour and place, but back of it Kate perceived her indestructible frivolity. She surmised how rapidly the scenes of Mary's drama would succeed each other; how remorse would yield to regret, regret to diminishing grief, grief to hope, hope to fresh adventures with life. Here in all verity was "the eternal feminine," fugitive, provocative, unspiritualized, and shrinking the one quality, fecundity, which could have justified it.

But Honora was speaking, and her low tones, charged with a mortal grief, were audible above the tramping of many feet, the throbbing of the engines, and the talking and the laughter.

"If you had stayed to die with him," she was saying, "I could have forgiven you everything, because I should have known then that you loved him as he hungered to be loved."

"He wouldn't let me," Mary wailed. "Honestly, Honora--"

"Wouldn't let you!" The scorn whipped Mary's face scarlet.

"Nobody wants to die, Honora!" pleaded the other. "You wouldn't yourself, when it came to it."

A child might have spoken so. The puerility of the words caused Honora to check her speech. She looked with a merciless scrutiny at that face in which the dimples would come and go even at such a moment as this. The long lashes curled on the cheeks with unconscious coquetry; the eyes, that had looked on horrors, held an intrinsic brilliance. The Earth itself, with its perpetual renewals, was not more essentially expectant than this woman.

Honora's amazement at her cousin's hedonism gave way to contempt for it.

"Oh," she groaned, "to have had the power to destroy a great man and to have no knowledge of what you've done! To have lived through all that you have, and to have got no soul, after all!"

She had stepped back as if to measure the luscious opulence of Mary's form with an eye of passionate depreciation.

"Stop her, Miss Barrington," cried Mary, seizing Kate's arm. "There's no use in all this, and people will overhear. Can't you take her away?"

She might have gazed at the Medusa's head as she gazed at Honora's.

"Come," said Kate to Honora. "As Miss Morrison says, there's no use in all this."

"If David and I did wrong, it was quite as much Honora's fault as mine, really it was," urged "Blue-eyed Mary," her childish voice choking.

Kate shook her hand off and looked at her from a height.

"Don't dare to discuss that," she warned. "Don't dare!"

She threw her arm around Honora.

"Do come," she pleaded. "All this will make you worse again."

"I don't wish you ill," continued Honora, seeming not to hear and still addressing herself to Mary. "I know you will live on in luxury somehow or other, and that good men will fetch and carry for you. You exude an essence which they can no more resist than a bee can honey. I don't blame you. That's what you were born for. But don't think that makes a woman of you. You never can be a woman! Women have souls; they suffer; they love and work and forget themselves; they know how to go down to the gates of death. You don't know how to do any of those things, now, do you?"

She had grown terrible, and her questions had the effect of being spoken by some daemonic thing within her--something that made of her mouth a medium as the priestesses did of the mouths of the ancient oracles.

"Miss Barrington," shuddered Mary, "I'm trying to hold on to myself, but I don't think I can do it much longer. Something is hammering at my throat. I feel as if I were being strangled--" she was choking in the grasp of hysteria.

Kate drew Honora away with a determined violence.

"She'll be screaming horribly in a minute," she said. "You don't want to hear that, do you?"

Honora gave one last look at the miserable girl.

"Of course, you know," she said, throwing into her words an intensity which burned like acid, "that he did not die for you, Mary. He died to save his soul alive. He died to find himself--and me. Just that much I have to have you know."

At that Kate forced her to go into the Pullman, and seated her by the window where the rising wind, bringing its tale of eternal solitude, eternal barrenness, could fan her cheek. A gentleman who had been pacing the platform alone approached Mary and seemed to offer her assistance with anxious solicitude. She drooped upon his arm, and as she passed beneath the window the odor of her perfumes stole to Honora's nostrils.

"How dare she walk beneath my window?" Honora demanded of Kate. "Isn't she afraid I may kill her?"

"No, I don't think she is, Honora. Why should she suspect anything ignoble of you?"

Silence fell. A dull golden star blossomed in the West.

"All aboard! All aboard!" called the conductors. The people began straggling toward their trains, laughing their farewells.

"Hope I'll meet you again sometime!"

"East or West, home's the best."

"You're sure you're not going on my train?"

"Me for God's country! You'll find nothing but fleas and flubdub on the Coast."

"You'll be back again next year, just the same. Everybody comes back."

"All aboard! All aboard!"

"God willing," said Honora, "I shall never see her again."

Suddenly she ceased to be primitive and became a civilized woman with a trained conscience and artificial solicitude.

"How do you suppose she's going to live, Kate? She had no money. Will David have made any arrangement for her? Oughtn't I to see to that?"

"You are neither to kill nor pension her," said Kate angrily. "Keep still, Honora."

The fiery worms became active, and threshed their way across the fast-chilling and silent plain. On the eastbound one two women sat in heavy reverie. On the westbound one a group of solicitous ladies and gentlemen gathered about a golden-haired daughter of California offering her sal volatile, claret, brandy-and-water. She chose the claret and sipped it tremblingly. Its deep hue answered the glow in the great ruby in her ring. By a chance her eye caught it and she turned the jewel toward her palm.

"A superb stone," commented one of the kindly group. "You purchased it abroad?" The inquiry was meant to distract her thoughts. It did not quite succeed. She put the wine from her and covered her face with her hands, for suddenly she was assailed by a memory of the burning kisses with which that gem had been placed upon her finger by lips now many fathoms beneath the surface of the sun-warmed world.

CHAPTER XXXIV

Kate and Honora left the train at the station of Wander, and the man for whom it was named was there to meet them. If it was summer with the world, it was summer with him, too. Some new plenitude had come to him since Kate had seen him last. His full manhood seemed to be realized. A fine seriousness invested him--a seriousness which included, the observer felt sure, all imaginable fit forms of joy. Clothed in gray, save for the inevitable sombrero, clean-shaven, bright-eyed, capable, renewed with hope, he took both women with a protecting gesture into his embrace. The three rejoiced together in that honest demonstration which seems permissible in the West, where social forms and fears have not much foothold.

They talked as happily of little things as if great ones were not occupying their minds. To listen, one would have thought that only "little joys" and small vexations had come their way. It would be by looking into their faces that one could see the marks of passion--the passion of sorrow, of love, of sacrifice.

As they came out of the piñon grove, Honora discovered her babies. They were in white, fresh as lilies, or, perhaps, as little angels, well beloved of heavenly mothers; and they came running from the house, their golden hair shining like aureoles about their eager faces. Their sandaled feet hardly touched the ground, and, indeed, could they have been weighed at that moment, it surely had been found that they had become almost imponderable because of the ethereal lightness of their spirits. Their arms were outstretched; their eyes burning like the eyes of seraphs.

"Stop!" cried Honora to Karl in a choking voice. He drew up his restless, home-bound horses, and she leaped to the ground. As she ran toward her little ones on swift feet, the two who watched her were convinced that she had regained her old-time vigor, and had acquired an eloquence of personality which never before had been hers. She gathered her treasures in her arms and walked with them to the house.

Kate had not many minutes to wait in the living-room before Wander joined her. It was a long room, with triplicate, lofty windows facing the mountains which wheeled in majestic semicircle from north to west. At this hour the purple shadows were gathering on them, and great peace and beauty lay over the world.

There was but one door to this room and Wander closed it.

"I may as well know my fate now," he said. "I've waited for this from the moment I saw you last. Are you going to be my wife, Kate?"

He stood facing her, breathing rather heavily, his face commanded to a tense repose.

"My answer is 'no,'" cried Kate, holding out her hands to him. "I love you as my life, and my answer is 'no.'"

He took the hands she had extended.

"Kiss me!" He gathered her into his arms, and upon her welcoming lips he laid his own in such a kiss as a man places upon but one woman's lips.

"Now, what is your answer?" he breathed after a time. "Tell me your answer now, you much-loved woman--tell it, beloved."

She kissed his brow and his eyes; he felt her tears upon his cheeks.

"You know all that I have thought and felt," she said; "you know--for I have written--what my life may be. Do you ask me to let it go and to live here in this solitude with you?"

"Yes, by heaven," he said, his eyes blazing, "I ask it."

Some influence had gone out from them which seemed to create a palpitant atmosphere of delight in which they stood. It was as if the spiritual essence of them, mingling, had formed the perfect fluid of the soul, in which it was a privilege to live and breathe and dream.

"I am so blessed in you," whispered Karl, "so completed by you, that I cannot let you go, even though you go on to great usefulness and great goodness. I tell you, your place is here in my home. It is safe here. I have seen you standing on a precipice, Kate, up there in the mountain. I warned you of its danger; you told me of its glory. But I repeat my warning now, for I see you venturing on to that precipice of loneliness and fame on which none but sad and lonely women stand."

"Oh, I know what you say is true, Karl. I mean to do my work with all the power there is in me, and I shall be rejoicing in that and in Life--it's in me to be glad merely that I'm living. But deep within my heart I shall, as you say, be both lonely and sad. If there's any comfort in that for you--"

"No, there's no comfort at all for me in that, Kate. Stay with me, stay with me! Be my wife. Why, it's your destiny."

Kate crossed the room as if she would move beyond that aura which vibrated about him and in which she could not stand without a too dangerous delight. She was very pale, but she carried her head high still-- almost defiantly.

"I mean to be the mother to many, many children, Karl," she said in a voice which thrilled with sorrow and pride and a strange joy. "To thousands and thousands of children. But for the Idea I represent and the work I mean to do they would be trampled in the dust of the world. Can't you see that I am called to this as men are called to honorable services for their country? This is a woman's form of patriotism. It's a higher one than the soldier's, I think. It's come my way to be the banner-carrier, and I'm glad of it. I take my chance and my honor just as you would take your chance and your honor. But I could resign the glory, Karl, for your love, and count it worth while."

"Kate--"

"But the thing to which I am faithful is my opportunity for great service. Come with me, Karl, my dear. Think how we could work together in Washington--think what such a brain and heart as yours would mean to a new cause. We'd lose ourselves--and find ourselves--laboring for one of the kindest, lovingest ideas the hard old world has yet devised. Will you come and help me, Karl, man?"

He moved toward her, his hands outspread with a protesting gesture.

"You know that all my work is here, Kate. This is my home, these mines are mine, the town is mine. It is not only my own money which is invested, but the money of other men--friends who have trusted me and whose prosperity depends upon me."

"Oh, but, Karl, aren't there ways of arranging such things? You say I am dear to you--transfer your interests and come with me--Karl!" Her voice was a pleader's, yet it kept its pride.

"Kate! How can I? Do you want me to be a supplement to you--a hanger-on? Don't you see that you would make me ridiculous?"

"Would I?" said Kate. "Does it seem that way to you? Then you haven't learned to respect me, after all."

"I worship you," he cried.

Kate smiled sadly.

"I know," she said, "but worship passes--"

"No--" he flung out, starting toward her.

But she held him back with a gesture.

"You have stolen my word," she said with an accent of finality. "'No'" is the word you force me to speak. I am going on to Washington in the morning, Karl.

They heard the children running down the hall and pounding on the door with their soft fists. When Kate opened to them, they clambered up her skirts. She lifted them in her arms, and Karl saw their sunny heads nestling against her dark one. As she left the room, moving unseeingly, she heard the hard-wrung groan that came from his lips.

A moment later, as she mounted the stairs, she saw him striding up the trail which they, together, had ascended once when the sun of their hope was still high.

She did not meet him again that day. She and Honora ate their meals in silence, Honora dark with disapproval, Kate clinging to her spar of spiritual integrity.

If that "no" thundered in Karl's ears the night through while he kept the company of his ancient comforters the mountains, no less did it beat shatteringly in the ears of the woman who had spoken it.

"No," to the deep and mystic human joys; "no" to the most holy privilege of women; "no" to light laughter and a dancing heart; "no" to the lowly, satisfying labor of a home. For her the steep path, alone; for her the precipice. From it she might behold the sunrise and all the glory of the world, but no exalted sense of duty or of victory could blind her to its solitude and to its danger.

Yet now, if ever, women must be true to the cause of liberty. They had been, through all the ages, willing martyrs to the general good. Now it was laid upon them to assume the responsibilities of a new crusade, to undertake a fresh martyrdom, and this time it was for themselves. Leagued against them was half--quite half--of their sex. Vanity and prettiness, dalliance and dependence were their characteristics. With a shrug of half-bared shoulders they dismissed all those who, painfully, nobly, gravely, were fighting to restore woman's connection with reality--to put her back, somehow, into the procession; to make, by new methods, the "coming lady" as essential to the commonwealth as was the old-time châtelaine before commercialism filched her vocations and left her the most cultivated and useless of parasites.

Oh, it was no little thing for which she was fighting! Kate tried to console herself with that. If she passionately desired to create an organization which should exercise parental powers over orphaned or poorly guarded children, still more did she wish to set an example of efficiency for women, illustrating to them with how firm a step woman might tread the higher altitudes of public life, making an achievement, not a compromise, of labor.

Moreover, no other woman in the country had at present had an opportunity that equaled her own. Look at it how she would, throb as she might with a woman's immemorial nostalgia for a true man's love, she could not escape the relentless logic of the situation. It was not the hour for her to choose her own pleasure. She must march to battle leaving love behind, as the heroic had done since love and combat were known to the world.

CHAPTER XXXV

Morning came. She was called early that she might take the train for the East, and arising from her sleepless bed she summoned her courage imperatively. She determined that, however much she might suffer from the reproaches of her inner self,--that mystic and hidden self which so often refuses to abide by the decisions of the brain and the conscience,--she would not betray her falterings. So she was able to go down to the breakfast-room with an alert step and a sufficiently gallant carriage of the head.

Honora was there, as pale as Kate herself, and she did not scruple to turn upon her departing guest a glance both regretful and forbidding. Kate looked across the breakfast-table at her gloomy aspect.

"Honora," she said with some exasperation, "you've walked *your* path, and it wasn't the usual one, now, was it? But I stood fast for your right to be unusual, didn't I? Then, when the whole scheme of things went to pieces and you were suffering, I didn't lay your misfortune to the singularity of your life. I knew that thousands and thousands of women, who had done the usual thing and chosen the beaten way, had suffered just as much as you. I tried to give you a hand up--blunderingly, I suppose, but I did the best I could. Of course, I'm a beast for reminding you of it. But what I want to know is, why you should be looking at me with the eyes of a stony-hearted critic because I'm taking the hardest road for myself. You don't suppose I'd do it without sufficient reason, do you? Standing at the parting of the ways is a serious matter, however interesting it may be at the moment."

Honora's face flushed and her eyes filled.

"Oh," she cried, "I can't bear to see you putting happiness behind you. What's the use? Don't you realize that men and women are little more than motes in the sunshine, here for an hour and to-morrow--nothing! I'm pretty well through with those theories that people call principles and convictions. Why not be obedient to Nature? She's the great teacher. Doesn't she tell you to take love and joy when they come your way?"

"We've threshed all that out, haven't we?" asked Kate impatiently. "Why go over the ground again? But I must say, if a woman of your intelligence--and my friend at that--can't see why I'm taking an uphill road, alone, instead of walking in a pleasant valley with the best of companions, then I can hardly expect any one else to sympathize with me. However, what does it matter? I said I was going alone so why should I complain?"

Her glance fell on the fireplace before which she and Karl had sat the night when he first welcomed her beneath his roof. She remembered the wild silence of the hour, the sense she had had of the invisible presence of the mountains, and how Karl's love had streamed about her like shafts of light.

"I've seen nothing of Karl," said Honora abruptly. "He went up the trail yesterday morning, and hasn't been back to the house since."

"He didn't come home last night? He didn't sleep in his bed?"

"No, I tell you. He's had the Door of Life slammed in his face, and I suppose he's pretty badly humiliated. Karl isn't cut out to be a beggar hanging about the gates, is he? Pence and crumbs wouldn't interest him. I wonder if you have any idea how a man like that can suffer? Do you imagine he is another Ray McCrea?"

"Pour my coffee, please, Honora," said Kate.

Honora took the hint and said no more, while Kate hastily ate her breakfast. When she had finished she said as she left the table:--

"I'd be glad if you'll tell the stable-man that I'll not take the morning train. I'm sorry to change my mind, but it's unavoidable."

The smart traveling-suit she had purchased in Los Angeles was her equipment that morning. To this she added her hat and traveling-veil.

"If you're going up the mountain," said the maladroit Honora, "better not wear those things. They'll be ruined."

"Oh, things!" cried Kate angrily. She stopped at the doorway. "That wasn't decent of you, Honora. I *am* going up the mountain--but what right had you to suppose it?"

The whole household knew it a moment later--the maids, the men at the stables and the corral. They knew it, but they thought more of her. She went so proudly, so openly. The judgment they might have passed upon lesser folk, they set aside where Wander and his resistant sweetheart were concerned. They did not know the theater, these Western men and women, but they recognized drama when they saw it. Their deep love of romance was satisfied by these lovers, so strong, so compelling, who moved like demigods in their unconcern for the opinions of others.

Kate climbed the trail which she and Wander had taken together on the day when she had mockingly proclaimed her declaration of independence.

She smiled bitterly now to think of the futility of it. Independence? For whom did such a thing exist? Karl Wander was drawing her to him as that mountain of lode in the Yellowstone drew the lightnings of heaven.

In time she came to the bench beside the torrent where she and Wander had rested that other, unforgettable day. She paused there now for a long time, for the path was steep and the altitude great. The day had turned gray and a cold wind was arising--crying wind, that wailed among the tumbled boulders and drove before it clouds of somber hue.

After a time she went on, and as she mounted, encountering ever a steeper and more difficult way, she tore the leather of her shoes, rent the skirt of her traveling-frock, and ruined her gloves with soil and rock.

"If I have to go back as I came, alone," she reflected, "all in tatters like this, to find that he is at the mines or the village, attending to his work, I shall cut a fine figure, shan't I? The very gods will laugh at me."

She flamed scarlet at the thought, but she did not turn back.

Presently she came to a place where the path forked. A very narrow, appallingly deep gorge split the mountain at this point, each path skirting a side of this crevasse.

"I choose the right path," said Kate aloud.

Her heart and lungs were again rebelling at the altitude and the exertion, and she was forced to lie flat for a long time. She lay with her face to the sky watching the roll of the murky clouds. Above her towered the crest of the mountain, below her stretched the abyss. It was a place where one might draw apart from all the world and contemplate the little thing that men call Life. Neither ecstasy nor despair came to her, though some such excesses might have been expected of one whose troubled mind contemplated such magnificence, such terrific beauty. Instead, she seemed to face the great soul of Truth--to arrive at a conclusion of perfect sanity, of fine reasonableness.

Conventions, pettiness, foolish pride, waywardness, secret egotism, fell away from her. The customs of society, with what was valuable in them and what was inadequate, assumed their true proportions. It was as if her House of Life had been swept of fallacy by the besom of the mountain wind. A feeling of strength, courage, and clarity took possession of her. There was an expectation, too,--nay, the conviction,--that an event was at hand fraught for her with vast significance.

The trail, almost perpendicular now, led up a mighty rock. She pulled herself up, and emerging upon the crown of the mountain, beheld the proud peaks of the Rockies, bare or snow-capped, dripping with purple and gray mists, sweeping majestically into the distance. Such solemnity, such dark and passionate beauty, she never yet had seen, though she was by this time no stranger to the Rockies, and she had looked upon the wonders of the Sierras. She envisaged as much of this sublimity as eye and brain might hold; then, at a noise, glanced at that tortuous trail--yet more difficult than the one she had taken--which skirted the other side of the continuing crevasse.

On it stood Karl Wander, not as she had seen him last, impatient, racked with mental pain, and torn with pride and eager love. He was haggard, but he had arrived at peace. He was master over himself and no longer the creature of futile torments. To such a man a woman might well capitulate if capitulation was her intent. With such a chieftain might one well treat if one had a mind to maintain the suzerainty of one's soul.

The wind assailed Kate violently, and she caught at a spur of rock and clung, while her traveling-veil, escaped from bounds, flung out like a "home-going" pennant of a ship.

"A flag of truce, Kate?" thundered Wander's voice.

"Will you receive it?" cried Kate.

Now that she had sought and found him, she would not surrender without one glad glory of the hour.

"Name your conditions, beloved enemy."

"How can we talk like this?"

"We're not talking. We're shouting."

"Is there no way across?"

"Only for eagles."

"What did you mean by staying up here? I was terrified. What if you had been dying alone--"

"I came up to think things out."

"Have you?"

"Yes."

"Well?"

"Kate, we must be married."

"Yes," laughed Kate. "I know it."

"But--"

"Yes," called Kate, "that's it. But--"

"But you shall do your work: I shall do mine."

"I know," said Kate. "That's what I meant to say to you. There's more than one way of being happy and good."

"Go your way, Kate. Go to your great undertaking. Go as my wife. I stay with my task. It may carry me farther and bring me more honor than we yet know. I shall go to you when I can: you must come to me--when you will. What more exhilarating? A few years will bring changes. I hear they may send me to Washington, after all. But they'll not need to send me. Lead where you will, I will follow--on condition!"

"The condition?"

She stood laughing at him, shining at him, free and proud as the "victory" of a sculptor's dream.

"That you follow my leadership in turn. We'll have a Republic of Souls, Kate, with equal opportunity--none less, none greater--with high expediency for the watchword."

"Yes. Oh, Karl, I came to say all this!"

"Then some day we'll settle down beneath one roof--we'll have a hearthstone."

"Yes," cried Kate again, this time with an accent that drowned forever the memory of her "no."

"Turn about, Kate; turn about and go down the trail. You'll have to do it alone, I'm afraid. I can't get over there to help."

"I don't need help," retorted Kate. "It's fine doing it alone."

"Follow your path, and I will follow mine. We can keep in sight almost all the way, I think, and, as you know, a little below this height, the paths converge."

Kate stood a moment longer, looking at him, measuring him.

"How splendid to be a man," she called. "But I'm glad I'm a woman," she supplemented hastily.

"Not half so glad as I, Kate, my mate,--not a thousandth part so glad as I."

She held out her arms to him. He gave a great laugh and plunged down the path. Kate swept her glance once more over the dark beauty of the mountain-tops--her splendid world, wrought with illimitable joy in achievement by the Maker of Worlds,--and turning, ran down the great rock that led to the trail.